THE WITCHES OF VARDØ

ANYA BERGMAN

MANILLA
PRESS

First published in the UK by Manilla Press
an imprint of Bonnier Books UK
4th Floor, Victoria House
Bloomsbury Square
London, WC1B 4DA
England
Owned by Bonnier Books
Sveavägen 56, Stockholm, Sweden

facebook.com/bonnierbooksuk/
twitter.com/bonnierbooksuk

Hardback – 978-1-78658-191-4
Trade paperback – 978-1-78658-192-1
Ebook – 978-1-78658-193-8
Audio – 978-1-78658-194-5

A CIP catalogue of this book is available from the British Library.

Cover and interior art designed by Andrew Davis
Typeset by IDSUK (Data Connection) Ltd
Printed and bound by Clays Ltd, Elcograf S.p.A

1 3 5 7 9 10 8 6 4 2

Manilla Press is an imprint of Bonnier Books UK
www.bonnierbooks.co.uk

THE
WITCHES
OF
VARDØ

Anya Bergman became interested in the witch trials of Vardø and the vivid folk tales of the north while living in Norway. Travelling to the Steilneset memorial, in which Louise Bourgeois and Peter Zumthor commemorated those persecuted as witches, she became fascinated by their stories. Now resident in Ireland, she is currently undertaking a PhD by Published Works at Edinburgh Napier University in Scotland, where she also lectures as well as tutoring for Jericho Writers. She is working on her next novel, which unites the fates of two very different women against the tumultuous backdrop of the French Revolution.

For all the witches' gets
And especially for Marianne

'There are more witches in Norway .... than there are in the rest of the world.'

– Jean Bodin, De la Démonomanie des Sorciers, 1580

'All the inhabitants of Norway are devout Christians, except for those residing close to the ocean in the far North. So steeped in the skill of sorcery and conjuring are these people that they claim to know what every individual in the world is busy doing.'

– Adam of Bremen (1044–1080)

DENMARK
AND SWEDEN
AS AT
1662

COPENHAGEN

Denmark/Norway

Swedish Empire

Denmark

Arctic Circle

FINNMAR
(SÁMI LANDS

VARANGER PENINS

Andersby *Andersbyvatnet*

VARANGERFJORD

Vadsøya

MURMAN
SEA

VARANGER STRAITS

VARDØ

Svartnes

Domen Mountain
ENTRANCE WAY TO HELL

Riberg

VARDØ

HARBOUR

CHURCH

STEGELSNES

VARDØHUS
FORTRESS

PART ONE

Spring
1662

Chapter 1

Anna

Third day of April in the year of our Good Lord 1662

The savage north held me captive. I was imprisoned in falling snow and blinded by glaring white light, empty of all shadows. I stood upon the ship's deck, and nothing was before me.

I could see no way forward.

Without shelter, the snow blanketed my cape. Impervious as alabaster, I was cold but not shivering, my knuckles blue and my heart hollowed out. The hours stretched on, but I was in no hurry to make landfall.

By the time I was caked in snow its falling had begun to falter. I shook my shoulders and snow tumbled from my cape as a few final spinning flakes descended. Bluish dusk emerged.

Finally, I could see our destination.

The harbour was barely that, with a small enclave of rudimentary dwellings encircling it. I was ordered to disembark and staggered down the gangway, my legs uncertain after so many weeks at sea. A biting wind urged me onto the bleak northern lands as if a man's hand were pushing me, yet again.

It was here Captain Gunderson said his adieus. I was sorry to leave him. We had enjoyed several theological discussions on my journey along the treacherous coast of Norway. He had kept me safe from peril and imposed a level of respect upon his crew. I feared Captain Gunderson would be the last civilised man I ever laid eyes upon in this ravening region.

Certainly, it seemed so when a brute of a man approached me. His beard was a wild tangle of red and laced with ice, his skin grimy with filth. He paused to spit upon the snow, yellow phlegm staining its pure white. I took a step back, repelled, but he grabbed hold of my shoulders. 'Why are you not in chains?' He shook me. The stench of his breath was foul, and I detected a Scottish accent.

'It was deemed unnecessary,' I told the odious man, unable to hide the haughty tone in my voice.

He huffed, twisting a big key at his belt. 'You would do well to remember what you are, Fru Rhodius – the king's prisoner.' He spat again to emphasise his power over me. I pushed back my retch and held my head high as he continued to speak. 'I am Bailiff Lockhert, and you are now under my keeping for the foreseeable future.'

The foreseeable future. The words burned like brands upon my skin.

How cruel you have been to give me no day for your pardon. I am left hanging on a thread, hoping you will change your mind while you have sent me far away. Why so very far?

'If you're any trouble at all,' Lockhert said, grimly, 'the chains will be on you.'

How insulting! As if I would behave in any manner contrary to that which you had ordered! I gave my new captor a withering look, but it made little impact as he pushed me towards a sleigh tethered to three reindeer.

There was a driver bundled up in reindeer skins and fur hat, the reins slack in his hands. Despite their branching antlers, the reindeer possessed a meek air. The one at the back, closest to me, turned its head with an almost human glance of sympathy. I was surprised by the lurch in my heart and wanted very much to stroke its head, but the rough Lockhert pushed me into the back of the sleigh.

Darkness was now gathering, and it truly was the coldest night of my life. I was thankful for the stack of furs and skins piled all around me.

It had been a long time since I had felt such deep chill in my bones as, for the past few years, a fire had always burned in my belly, keeping my extremities warm; some nights I would awaken in my bedchamber in Bergen, the heat within me overpowering, as if I were aflame. I would fling the bed coverings to the floor, much to Ambrosius's annoyance, even going so far as to unlatch the window, no matter the season, to take in gulping breaths of cool air, despite my husband complaining he was in discomfort. Not long after, he ceased to share my bedchamber. We had slept apart for several weeks even before I left for Copenhagen.

I thought of my husband now, back home safe in Bergen, taking his daily stroll around the garden, collecting my herbs and my plants. I twisted in my seat with frustration. He would surely get all the remedies wrong, like he always did. Ambrosius could not be trusted not to poison some poor soul without me by his side aiding him.

But it would be evening in Bergen at this hour, and Doctor Ambrosius Rhodius would be sitting by his fireside in the green velvet chair, with his spectacles on the end of his nose reading *my* books. *Peace at last*, he would think.

All I once possessed – a beautiful house, a husband of standing, the most abundant garden in the whole of Bergen, and the biggest library in Norway – was gone. Gone. Gone.

So determined was I not to shed a tear I bit my lip and tasted blood.

It was a full moon and silvery light pooled around me. The village behind the harbour was silent and dark, all souls within their tiny shacks. As I waited for the sleigh to begin to move, I could hear the sea lapping between the fishing boats. My eye caught movement, and I struggled to upright myself a little in the sleigh. There, lurking between the cottages, I thought I could see a tall man in a cloak, a hat upon his head.

Ah, it was the trickery of moonlight, for the shadowy figure disappeared. In its stead emerged a memory of you when we were young, with your long, dark, curly hair upon your shoulders, the smile in your eyes as you reached out your hands to mine. 'Let us dance, Anna,' you had said.

I was so cold now, shivering without control, clenching my gloved hands into fists and pushing them deep into my muff.

We took off at a brisk pace and the Arctic chill stung my cheeks. I pulled my fur hat down as far as I could, and the sealskins up over my face, leaving only my eyes exposed. I could still smell the cold sea upon them, and they possessed an unpleasant oiliness. The ocean was full of heathen wickedness in these northern regions.

Captain Gunderson had told me I would be transported by sleigh across the Varanger Peninsula. When we reached the village of Svartnes I would be taken by another boat across the narrow Varanger Straits to the place of my exile, the fortress of Vardøhus, on the tiny island of Vardø.

The thought caused me to take one of my gloved hands out of my muff, and press it to my chest, where I could feel the faint indent of the cross – my most treasured possession. But, of course, this you must know.

We plunged into the wilderness, bumping across the snowy tundra beneath the vast night sky filling with stars. I stared up at the luminous full moon, the last before the pastoral season. Ambrosius called it the martyr moon. I thought upon Christ and his sacrifice for mankind.

Was I your sacrifice? I confess, it would be a relief to be by the Good Lord's side than living, shaking with dread as each lurch of the sleigh brought me closer to your kingdom's doorway into Hell.

You told me never to write one more word to you, so sick you were of my constant petitions. But you forget that just as my duty as your subject is to you, yours as my king is divine service to me too. You thought you would silence me by ordering all my ink be took from me, but this will not be enough.

You will receive my missives from the north, of this I am determined.

We tumbled beneath the silvered northern sky for hours, my bones rattled and my joints sore. My eyelids were falling, lulled by an image in my head. I knelt before my king, dressed in my best blue silk gown, and your hand, bejewelled with gems, was resting upon my head. I could feel the gratitude from your palm crowning me.

I was wrenched from my reverie by the sound of the driver crying out. I could see the rumps of the reindeer out of formation, skittering about on the treacherous snow. Bailiff Lockhert roared to hold steady, but it was no use for the sleigh had lost control. It skidded across the ice and mounted a drift of snow so high I had to cling on to the wooden sides of the sleigh so as not to fall upon my head. I braced myself to turn full circle, terrified I would break my bones, but instead we thumped back down upon the packed snow and skidded to a halt.

My hat had fallen over my face, and I could hear the heavy thump of Lockhert's boots landing in the snow. I pushed my hat back and could see his hulking figure striding away while the driver was soothing the startled reindeer. Neither man had attended to my welfare. I dragged myself out of the overturned sleigh, looking to see where my precious medicine chest might have landed. It was a short distance away, its contents strewn upon the snow and lit up by the moon. As I stumbled over towards it, I saw the most astonishing sight. Standing the other side of my chest was a dark-skinned girl, not quite a woman, with black hair unbound, dressed in a cloak of feathers. Most astonishing, by her side was a big wild cat. I had never seen such a creature before. Its soft fur was spotted lightly, and it had an underbelly of purest white. It had big ears, tapered with long tufts of fur upon them. Its eyes were the colour of amber stone, and they gazed at me steadily, unafraid, unflinching.

In this encounter with the girl, the cat and me, the air was as if made of fine glass. My breath plumed in heavy puffs, but despite the cold the girl did not so much as shiver.

She put her hand upon the great cat's head, which continued to stare at me, but it was the girl who bared her teeth, not the animal.

My heart leapt with fright for I had never seen a human, let alone a young woman, make such an expression.

The strange girl shook her head, her snarl turning into a peal of laughter as if delighted to frighten me.

'Who are you?' I called out.

But she opened her arms, so her cape of feathers turned into two big wings, and then she disappeared into a copse of silvery birch, the big cat at her heels.

I hastily retrieved the contents of my medicine chest fearful the girl and the beast would return, but when I looked up again, chest clutched tight in my hands, I saw Lockhert running back from the woods, a bow and arrow over his shoulder.

'Did you get it?' the driver asked him, securing the harnesses of the jittery reindeer.

'No, it was too fast,' Lockhert replied. 'What's a lynx doing in these parts?'

The other man shrugged. Of course, it was a lynx. I had heard of these large cats of the northern regions. How magnificent a cloak of its soft lustrous fur would be!

'And the girl?' I asked, dusting snow off my cape. 'What of the girl?'

Lockhert turned and frowned at me. 'What are you raving about?'

'There was a young woman with the lynx,' I persisted. 'Did you not see her? She had long black hair and wore a cloak of feathers . . .' I trailed off, realising how unlikely this sounded.

'We are two hours' ride from the nearest village, so who do you think might be running around in the woods with a lynx?' Lockhert challenged me with a sneer to his voice.

'She was right there,' I insisted. 'And she threatened me—'

'Enough! I've been warned of your wagging tongue, but this is hysteria from an old hag.'

My body stiffened from the insults. I had never been called old before; indeed, when he was up close, I could see I had fewer years on my captor for the begrimed wrinkles were dug deep in Lockhert's face.

'How dare you—' But before I could finish, he placed his filthy hand upon my mouth.

'Shut it,' he said, spit landing on my forehead. 'Your transportation has caused us enough trouble.' With that, he took a chain from his belt and began to wind it around my wrists.

In all my weeks of captivity, even during the trial, I had not been treated with such indignity. I tried to struggle but he pushed his hand into my chest so hard it felt he might break my heart.

Though, my king, my heart was already broken.

With the sleigh righted, and the reindeer calmed, we set off again. Lockhert had chained me up so tight I could not move and was forced to lie on my back. I stared up at the immense silver of the martyr moon with fury coursing through every part of me.

I drank in the light of the moon and made an oath. I would not be a martyr, accepting, mute and humble, for it was against my very nature.

The image of the snarling girl rose before me. There had been a moment of recognition, strange and without reason. I was certain she had been real, but I could make no sense of it.

Chapter 2

Ingeborg

The change in Ingeborg's mother had come about long before Merchant Heinrich first called upon them.

Two and a half years before, in the winter of 1659, they had been like all the other fishermen's families on the Varanger Peninsula: eking out a living as the dwindling shoals of cod drifted further south, hunkering down through long dark months with crippling debts to the Bergen merchants for grain, grasping at the brief summer to harvest as much as they could from the parched Arctic soil. Life was hard in their village of Ekkerøy, tucked between two crescents of white sand and white cliffs. But they had been a close family, comforted by their bond. There had been lightness and laughter. A mother and a father, one son and two daughters.

But now there were only three of them.

Ingeborg had lived through sixteen summers, according to her mother. She was four years older than her sister Kirsten, though they were the same height. Ingeborg was small, but she was strong and light on her feet. It was only in Ingeborg's face you could see she was the eldest: the brown of her eyes solemn, the set of her mouth revealing she had heard and seen much already.

It seemed only a short time since she and her younger brother, Axell, had roamed the shoreline collecting secrets from the sea: tiny snail shells, fronds of glossy seaweed, ribbed driftwood, spiky sea urchins, pebbles as smooth as polished gems and fluffy duck feathers.

It had been one of those rare summers up north. Rain held itself at bay in downy clouds, and the midnight sun blessed their village. Axell and Ingeborg had traipsed across the marshy land, rich with grasses green, yellow and brown, clusters of white bog cotton and purple heathers. To their right lay the smooth, pale grey sea contained by the distant mauve mountains of land they had never been to. The clear night swarmed with gnats, and flocks of gulls would race to the cliffs, bombarding them with their shrill notes.

Her brother led her around the jutting edge of Skagodden, to the rock face teeming with seabirds. He was teaching her how to climb.

'Imagine you are a cat,' he instructed her.

She had seen herself as a small tabby cat. Her trepidation fell away, she tucked up the ends of her skirt into her bodice so that she could clamber as easily as a boy, and she climbed with ease upon the rocks.

'We are hunters, Ingeborg,' Axell said from the top of the cliff, leaning down and offering his hand to her. 'Our eyes always on the prey. Never look down.'

Many times, after Axell was gone, Ingeborg retraced his footsteps. The stones were never too sharp for her bare feet, nor was she afraid she would slip on the wet rocks and fall. Axell had said she could do anything if she wanted to, despite only being a girl, despite being poor.

The last time she and her brother had climbed the cliff they stole a seagull's eggs.

'Do you see the nest?' Axell pointed. 'This is our quarry.'

'It's very high,' she had murmured in doubt.

'But you can do it, Ingeborg. You are a better climber than I.' He spat on his hands and rubbed them together. 'We must be very quiet, because if the gull sees us, she will attack.' He winked at her. 'You don't want your eye pecked out by a seagull, do you?'

They had edged their way up the cliff face; no thought to the fact they were so high that if they fell, they would be smashed upon the rocks below.

Axell let her steal the first two eggs. They were big, the palest blue, and speckled brown as the freckles upon her brother's nose. Ingeborg slipped them into the little sack around her neck, adding to that day's hoard of seaweed polyps and shells.

It was Axell who alerted the gull to their presence as he reached forward for a third egg. He had to suddenly grab on to an outcrop of rock, spraying them with tiny stones and sticks.

Quickly he snatched the last egg, pushing it into his pocket as they slithered back down the cliff, under the furious attack of the mother seagull. Ingeborg put her head down as the gull's wings batted the side of her cheek, its demented screeching piercing her ears. She felt wicked to be taking its eggs, and yet she was excited to be a thief.

They landed on the sludgy beach, the gull still swooping down to attack them. They ran hand in hand across strata of rock, splattered white from bird shit, and into a tiny cave.

They squatted on the wet rock and grinned at each other. The gull had pecked her brother on the top of his head, and a trail of blood trickled through his tawny hair onto his pale face.

Ingeborg pulled one of the seagull's eggs out of her little bag, and held it in her palm, admiring its delicacy. 'Is the baby bird still inside the egg?' she asked Axell.

'Possibly, possibly not,' he said, grabbing it from her hand and tossing it in the air.

'Careful!'

Axell laughed, throwing his head back in glee.

Her brother had told her that he would not be a fisherman, like their father. That one day he would be a merchant like the dashing young Heinrich Brasche.

Now, he turned to her and said: 'I will sail east and return laden with spices, gemstones and silks. I will have a grand house in Bergen. In my house I will place a cabinet filled with shells, skulls, nuts and bones from the four corners of the New World.' Axell took her hands in his. 'We will leave Ekkerøy, sister, and we will never come back.'

The summer's night they had stolen the eggs, Ingeborg and Axell had run home to present their bounty to her mother.

'What a clever boy you are,' she had said, ruffling her son's hair as if he alone had collected them.

'Ingeborg climbed higher than I!' Axell told their mother. But she did not appear to hear as she gazed at the large eggs her son had placed in her hands.

'We shall feast on them,' she said.

Nothing had ever equalled how those gull's eggs tasted. Ingeborg's mother broke the eggs upon the griddle, and with a sliver of butter, a pinch of salt, she cooked them over the fire. They looked like melted gold. There was one each: for her and Axell, for her mother, her father, and Kirsten.

After the last egg had been eaten, Axell had given the eggs' casings to their little sister, Kirsten. She had lined their open halves around the stone ledges of the cooking fire.

But their mother had told Kirsten to smash them and throw them away.

'I want to keep them,' Kirsten had protested.

'No, Kirsten, break them up. Witches use the shells to sail in upon the sea,' their mother told them. 'They will raise storms and wreck boats.'

Kirsten had looked at their father with pleading eyes, for he always intervened when their mother was being too harsh.

'Do as your mother says, Kirsten,' their father said gruffly.

Kirsten had gathered up the shells, a scowl on her face, her red curls unruly as she stomped outside with them cradled in her two small hands.

It was the seventh day of October in 1659 that Axell first went fishing with their father.

Ingeborg's mother had protested strongly. 'He's too young,' she'd told their father. 'Not yet.'

But they all knew twelve was the age fisherboys went to sea. Even though they would be away for weeks.

Besides, Axell wanted to go with their father. 'Mother, I will be fine,' he assured her. 'I don't want to stay behind with the women.'

Axell had always been their mother's favourite. After they left to go fishing, her mother became even more irritable with Kirsten. Ingeborg managed to avoid the smacks through being adept at the household tasks, but her sister always managed to rub her mother up the wrong way. She didn't churn the butter right, or sweep properly, or why on earth was she singing silly songs to the lamb?

As the winter lengthened, and her mother stood on the cliffs waiting for sight of the fishermen returning, her mood darkened. The cold eastern blizzards swept in with a mounting sense of foreboding.

Ingeborg would never forget the day the fishermen returned; her father standing in the open doorway of their cottage, palms outstretched, telling her mother their son was lost.

'He was only twelve!' her mother had wailed. 'Iver, I told you he was too young! I begged you not to take him!'

It had been a terrible thing to see her mother thump her fists upon her husband's chest and for her father to break before Ingeborg's eyes. He had returned, a shadow, from the sea. A man wringing his hands with guilt and unable to speak to his own wife and daughters of how he had lost Axell. Not even Kirsten could bring a smile to his haggard face, even when she sat upon his lap and tucked her curly mop of red beneath his chin, her blue eyes brimming with questions. Where had the laughter gone?

With Axell, Ingeborg thought. All the way to the bottom of the ocean.

When her father didn't return from the fishing season in the spring of 1661, Ingeborg knew in her heart he may well have greeted the ocean to him, his grief too heavy a burden to bear. His mouth wide open, drinking in salty redemption. How could he go home again without his son? It was easier to let the sea take his guilt than face the destruction of his wife. He never wanted to come back.

When Ingeborg thought upon her father all alone in the middle of the wild northern seas, making the decision never to come home again, the sorrow of it bit deeply into her heart. But she was also angry with him. He had known how capable she was. He had abandoned Ingeborg to care for her mother and her sister.

It wasn't *fair.*

It had been one month since their father had not returned with the other fishermen. Their bellies empty, they had spent the blustery May day scavenging the wild beach. After many back-breaking hours, Ingeborg and her mother had returned home laden with piles of seaweed to boil for themselves and their lambs to eat.

When they opened the cottage door, there was Kirsten kneeling by the fire, polishing the gull's eggs. A small smile on her face. Looking the happiest she had been since losing her papa.

Their mother didn't move, but Ingeborg sensed the anger building in her body.

'Where did you get those?' her mother said, dropping her seaweed on the cottage floor.

Kirsten turned white as she looked up and saw them. 'I kept them,' Kirsten whispered. 'They're so pretty, Mamma.'

Her mother walked over to the shells and smashed them with her old reindeer skin boots. Kirsten flinched. Then she hauled Kirsten up by her collar and smacked her hard across the face.

'Mother!' Ingeborg called out in alarm.

But all her mother's pent-up loss was funnelled into fury at her youngest child. 'You killed your own brother!' she screamed at Kirsten. 'I told you to smash the eggshells and look what happened! The witches made a storm and he drowned. You killed Axell, and your father too!'

Tears and snot trailed down Kirsten's face. 'I'm sorry, Mamma, please—'

'You wicked girl!' her mother yelled at Kirsten.

Ingeborg tugged on her mother's arms to let Kirsten go. 'She didn't mean any harm! Mother, please!'

'Of course, she did, the little witch,' her mother shouted, turning on Ingeborg, her eyes burning with bitter grief.

'She's *your* daughter, Mother. Stop!'

Her mother stared at her as if seeing Ingeborg for the first time. She let go of Kirsten and then she buried her face in her hands before running out of the cottage.

Ingeborg took her little sister in her arms, but Kirsten was inconsolable. 'Is Mamma right, am I wicked?' she whispered to Ingeborg.

'Of course not,' Ingeborg reassured Kirsten, wiping her face with her sleeve. 'It's only she misses Axell and Father very much.'

'So do I,' Kirsten said, in a small voice.

'I know,' Ingeborg replied, stroking her hair.

Kirsten bent down and tried to collect the broken shells. But most of them had been crushed into powder.

'Axell gave them to me. He said keep them.' Kirsten sniffed, trying to find pieces of the delicate shell.

Ingeborg picked up the broom. 'We have to sweep them up before she comes back.'

But Kirsten continued to collect the fragments of eggshell, counting them upon her fingertips: 'One, two, three, four, five, six, seven, eight, nine...'

How many numbers did it take for Axell to drown? How long before the sea filled his belly, and dragged him down to sleep forever upon the murky bed?

How many counts for her father?

They had swept the cottage and boiled the seaweed for themselves and the lambs alike. But their mother didn't return for hours.

When she did, she was a little different.

Never again did Ingeborg see her sob for her son or husband; never again did she touch or speak a kind word to her little girl Kirsten. She would talk to Ingeborg as if she were her sister, not her daughter.

Her mother's coldness gnawed at Ingeborg. But none had loved a son as much as her mother had adored Axell. With her boy gone, a part of her drowned with him.

This was the change. Her mother had always been beautiful but the melt in her summer blue eyes hardened to ice, and the way she spoke was different. It was as if she cared not what happened to them anymore. Whether they had enough to eat or not. It was all up to Ingeborg now.

Where had her mother gone the night she'd smashed the eggshells? So many hours Ingeborg had lain awake, waiting for her to return, the long May daylight stretching on and on, the birds crying outside, the wind whispering, *Danger, danger.* Ingeborg's mind racing.

Whom might a young widow meet running across the bog all on her own?

Chapter 3

Anna

How low you have brought me, my king. You had me transported across the vast, snow-filled tundra upon a rough, splintered sleigh as if kindling for fire, my whole body aching with discomfort. You had me pushed into a tiny vessel and rowed across the Varanger Straits towards Vardø island, the icy droplets of water stinging my cheeks each time the oars were lifted, the night blacker than ink.

Upon the water, I could not see any one thing. The full moon was buried in thick clouds, but my senses were keen. The knowledge of the Devil's domain in our vicinity made me shiver even more than the bone-chilling cold. You had shown me a picture of the mountain named Domen in a French explorer's travelogue in your library all those years ago. Who would have thought I would be so close to it now? I have never forgotten the image of the Domen with its low hump, and yawning belly of caves tunnelling all the way to Hell.

I am at the furthest corner of your kingdom in a region you have never had the courage to survey, and yet you sent me here.

The brutal Bailiff Lockhert had put me in fetters as if I were a common thief. You know this to be far from my crime. Truly of all my forty-seven years upon this earth I have never encountered such a repellent man. The stench from his sealskins was as a cloud of stagnant ditch water salted by sea, and his breath was rancid fish, so that every time he spoke to me, I became queasy with nausea so I must raise my handkerchief to inhale the dying essence of lavender which I had sprinkled upon it, weeks before.

The scene of my last day in my own home was still fresh within my memory. There I was packing my medicine chest with my husband Ambrosius tutting behind me.

'Anna, can you not leave it be?' he had said to me. 'Why must you go all the way to Copenhagen to petition the king?'

I had taken up a small stack of crisp white handkerchiefs, edged with lace, and, locating the lavender oil, I had sprinkled it upon the linen as if holy water, as if I were ordaining my endeavours. I had felt so righteous, blazing I was with it.

'Why would the king listen to you this time, Anna?' Ambrosius asked me. 'He has told you to leave off.'

'How can I not speak to him, Ambrosius?' I had turned, frustrated by my husband's lack of passion. 'The corruption is rank in this city, and it is our duty to protect our king from the insidious dealings of Statholder Trolle and his men.'

'Please, Anna, let others speak up,' Ambrosius said. 'Our situation is precarious.'

My husband was afraid, which I found hard to tolerate. I had seen the letter sent to him from Statholder Trolle instructing him to silence me, or there would be consequences.

I am no fool, and I believed in the special nature of our bond.

'The king will listen to me for the good of the people,' I had insisted.

Unlike Ambrosius, I do not claim to be able to predict the future. Maybe he had seen my future though, for my husband's countenance was grave and his complexion waxen as if the blood of courage drained from him.

'It's not your place, as my wife, to undertake such a task,' Ambrosius tried to convince me.

'Then you should go, husband.' I had challenged him, but he had looked down at the black and white floor tiles of our bedchamber.

'I cannot,' he murmured. 'I have my responsibilities in Bergen.'

My husband Doctor Ambrosius Rhodius is an esteemed individual as you well know. He is an academic and theologian, physician and schoolmaster at Bergen Latin Skole. But did you know all his titles I had acquired for him through *my* industry, knowledge and skill?

Surely you must have surmised it was so, my king. And yet I was viewed a failure by all who knew Doctor Ambrosius Rhodius, because I was a wife with no offspring. And by then it was too late, for my month-lies were unreliable, the moon's cycle a mere taunt.

I did not wish to curl up and wither like I had seen my mother do, and other women of my age. I did not desire to become a wife invisible as a speck of dust upon her husband's shoulder that he would wish to flick away. As his stature grows with age, with importance, with accolades, the wife dwindles to live through her children, her grandchildren; she becomes but a ghost in her own home. Silently watching her husband's ill-concealed affairs and the consequences of his vain trysts.

The last time this had happened to me had been almost too much to bear. Ambrosius had not even bothered to explain the monies missing from housekeeping that he was sending to a strumpet.

So, I would not disappear with no trace upon this world; oh no, I must have my say. This urge was a compulsion within me beyond all reason, but I believed you understood me, of all.

My husband followed me down the stairs and into our library. I pulled out my treasured Bible, and Christian Pedersen's translation of the New Testament for when I grew weary of Latin.

You never visited my house in Bergen but if you had, you would have seen how splendid it was. Within were corridors of burnished wood, glass windows latticed with fine ironwork, rugs from the Orient, silver candlesticks, and fires burning in every room preparing a welcome for any unforeseen visitor. My larder was brimming with the best of fare: creamy cheeses and pots of rich jellies, tarts and pies, oozing slabs of honeycomb, bags of sugared almonds and baskets of brown eggs. Upon the middle shelf were rows of yellow lemons, my daily delight along with a sliver of sugar cone acquired from Dutch traders from the distant island of Barbados. Most days I would break, grind and sprinkle a tiny piece of the sugar upon one lemon's juicy innards. Such a bittersweet joy it was to suck upon the sugared lemon! Such simple delight!

Believe me, my king, you would have received a grand welcome within my home, for I would have had a feast prepared for you more sumptuous than any before in Bergen.

Our library was the biggest in the whole of Norway. We possessed four hundred and fifty books! The winter before I had counted them and recorded each title with my own hand in a large ledger upon my husband's bureau.

I had always felt safe in a library, as if the books were there to protect me, like a fortress of words, thoughts and learning.

Do you remember how you found me hiding among the stacks of books in the palace library? I, the physician's daughter, had crept away on one of my father's visits to your ailing father. I was searching for any medical treatises, hungry for knowledge as my father's apprentice.

I was so engrossed in my reading I didn't even hear your footfall until you were standing above me. I dropped my book in alarm, and the expression on your face was just as shocked. You were so surprised to find a girl in the library! How old were we then? I believe you were a young man with nineteen years of age and I an awkward girl of thirteen years. Do you remember the words that passed between us?

'Who might you be?' you had challenged me.

I knew who *you* were: Prince Frederick, second son of our king. At that time, you were not expected to succeed your father and thus were able to wander the palace without a cohort of courtiers and servants. I remember you wore a doublet the colour of midnight, edged with silver, and your dark hair was thick, with curly locks. You had black lashes, long for a man, but so perfect for a prince, and a gold ring in your ear. Indeed, you were the picture of how I imagined a prince should look.

'I asked you who you are,' you said firmly again, observing me. 'You're too well dressed to be a maidservant. Besides, they can't read Latin.' You nodded to the book I had gathered up again in my hands.

'Anna Thorsteinsdatter,' I said in a shy whisper. 'I am the physician's daughter.'

'Ah,' you said, rubbing your chin. 'And you can read?'

I nodded. 'My father taught me.'

You leant over and whisked the book out of my hands. I felt a flutter in my chest as I caught scent of you: woody, not the smell of a prince, but more that of a gardener.

You looked at the title of the book: *Anatomicae Institutiones Corporis Humani.*

'So, you are interested in the anatomical writings of the physician and theologian Caspar Bartholin the elder, eh, Anna, daughter of our doctor?'

I had nodded again, unable to find my tongue.

You might laugh to remember how I found it hard to speak up as a young girl. I am sure the irony is not lost on you, for what were the last words you said to me?

Ti stille. Be quiet. Hold Kæft. Shut your mouth. Shut up. Shut up.

'Your father is indeed an expert at blood-letting, but what sickens my father, the king, comes from beyond an imbalance of his humours.'

You put forward your theory to me with confidence all those years ago, in the palace library. Sunshine was slanting in between the stacks of books, dust motes spinning around us as flecks of gold, and it had felt as though I were in a dream.

Your conjecturing on what ailed your father made little sense to me, for my father had told me often what ailed the body came from imbalances of the four humours: sanguine, melancholic, choleric and phlegmatic. The remedy of all ailments depended upon the diagnosis of the humours, and those remedies were bloodletting, vomiting or enemas. My father had also shared his interest in botanics with me, and the benefits of their usage for less serious ailments.

The greatest blessing of my childhood was the fact that my father, Thorstein Johansson king's physician, had no son to whom to pass on his knowledge.

But then, if I had had a brother, I would be a different woman now, maybe. Certainly, I would not be in fetters and a prisoner of the north, and most certainly not exiled by the one man I trusted even more than my own husband.

But let us return to the happy memory of our first meeting. There I was, a girl curled up among the books with fingers dusty from the shelves, hair slipping out of her white coif – you might have noted it was as black as yours – and blue eyes that I had been told by my disappointed mother were the shade of a duck egg and too pale for a girl.

Shy, and intimidated by your presence as a prince of Denmark, my curiosity was the stronger. 'What ails the king?' I ventured.

'He has been cursed.'

You did not need to explain further, for I had been told plenty of stories by my mother of the witches of the northern kingdoms.

'How do you know?' I whispered, desperate for more details.

'Because my father told me,' you declared, as if I were a simpleton. 'The great witch of Vardø has brought a curse down upon him,' you told me. 'I am here to search for all I can find on the dark ways of witches. I am looking for a volume called *Daemonologie* by the Scottish king, James. Have you seen it? We must break the curse.'

'And how can you break a curse?' I asked you.

'Through prayer, devotion to our Lord,' you replied, standing tall, hands clasped behind your back, the silver of your doublet's braid shimmering in the afternoon light. 'The most holy of people can always overcome the Devil.'

I had looked into your eyes and seen your conviction, and something else. Furthermore, no boy had looked directly at me ever before, though I suppose as a prince this was your right. I did not drop my gaze, for it felt as if I had no choice but to remain intent on you, as my chest tightened in my bodice and my cheeks bloomed.

'Are you a good girl, Anna?' you asked me, a slight smile playing upon your lips.

I was unable to find the words for a response and thus merely nodded as you handed me back the book.

'Be sure you are, Anna,' you said, continuing to smile. 'Be sure the Devil stays well away.'

Later that evening, as I sat with my parents at our supper of herring and bread, I questioned my father as to the king's malaise.

He did not answer at once, waiting for our serving girl to be gone from the chamber before he spoke. 'The king's symptoms vary on a daily basis.' My father sighed. 'One day it might be sickness of the stomach, another the bowels; on another day a powerful pain in his chest, or his head aches so he can barely see.'

'Do you believe he will recover?'

My mother frowned at me, for she did not approve of my keen interest in medicine; she didn't tell me to be silent, however, for she knew well the bond between my father and I was as between a father and son. I was his apprentice. That is, until Ambrosius came along.

'Well, daughter, there are some illnesses which cannot solely be cured through our administrations as physicians.'

How I had loved my father naming me as a physician, as if I were equal to him. I felt myself glowing from his attention and estimation, though again my mother frowned, shaking her head.

I had overheard her whispers at night, admonishing her husband.

'You are giving Anna notions, Thorstein. You must stop it.'

'What harm?' he responded. 'I am proud my daughter has intellect.'

'You are wrong, husband, it will do her much harm,' my mother had warned.

My fearful mother, who is now long buried in the heavy Danish earth, was quite right.

But I wish to return to my happy memory of the evening at supper with my parents when I was a girl of thirteen, which I hold to me like a small candle, a tiny light warming me, as I was dragged up the hill by the bailiff and his man from Vardø harbour to the fortress gleaming ghastly white in this, the darkest night of my life.

'What illnesses would they be, Father?' I had asked him.

'Delusion of the minds. Sickness that twists reason in the heads of men.'

My mother had given a sharp gasp. 'It is treason to say such thing about our king, Thorstein. Be careful – the servants might hear.'

I had been feeling bold in my own home with my loving parents – for that they were: not once in my whole childhood did either of them lay a hand upon me.

'I have heard talk of a witch's curse,' I had whispered, not wanting to reveal my meeting with you, the prince. 'Is such a thing true, Father?'

My father looked at me and I remember his thoughtful gaze, his eyes the softest grey, the same shade as rabbit fur.

'Well,' he said, tugging his neat beard. 'If you believe you have been cursed, you may as well be.'

His answer confused me.

'But is it possible the great witch of Vardø cursed our King Christian?'

'This is what our king believes,' my father had said, still refusing to commit to an answer.

*

21

All knew of Liren Sand, the great witch of Vardø in our king's country of Norway, named after the seabird from the northern regions and sending her dark magic across the kingdom of Denmark. The mere mention of her made grown men quake in trepidation, as if she could reach into their very hearts, all the leagues from north to south, and pull them out, to feed upon their stolen thoughts and secret wishes.

What would my parents think now to see me upon the very island that was her domain? I am grateful at least neither of them could ever know, for both went into the ground during the Great Plague over ten years ago.

Was it out of revenge for your father's demise, my prince, that you put an end to Liren Sand? Years later, when I lived in Bergen, I read of her capture by your loyal governor of Finnmark, and her trial in Vardø, in the broadsheets fluttering upon the cobbled streets. Words – with images for the illiterate – of the gory details of her many crimes and her fraternisation with the Devil. Liren Sand had apparently conjured weather magic and drowned Bergen merchants as they travailed the Varanger sea. It was Liren Sand who had blighted all of us in the kingdom of Denmark with the plague, and thus she had murdered many innocent souls. Liren Sand deserved to be cast into the pit of Hell; and you made her burn, in retaliation.

I still possess in a drawer in my library back in Bergen, the broadsheet with the image of the witch Liren Sand tied to the ladder as it was lowered into the flames. It took courage to act as you did against the forces of darkness – dare I say, more courage than your father had possessed, for Liren Sand was never able to cast her spells of sickness upon you.

I asked you once, years after our first meeting, what Liren Sand, the great witch of Vardø, had held against your father.

'His divinity!' you declared. 'Liren Sand wishes for terror and chaos. She wants to destroy the monarchy.'

Terror and chaos the plague did most certainly bring.

'I will put an end to her,' you said, and yes, my prince, some years later you did just that.

You had told me there would be more witches; that mothers gave their daughters over to the Devil. I could not forget these words, for I found the idea of it most shocking, that a mother could sacrifice her child to the Dark Lord.

How deep your betrayal wounds me, for now you have sent me to the place we both feared the most, oh my king. You have sent me to a region teeming with wild heathens and dark witchcraft.

As the rusted gates of Vardøhus fortress opened before me, I became overwhelmed with panic as my heart beat furiously in my chest, and I thought I might faint. I struggled against my captors, gasping for breath.

'No, this is undeserved, I am an innocent woman!' I pleaded with Bailiff Lockhert.

But the man snapped at me: 'Desist your wailing or I will have to bridle you, like the old nag you are!'

I fell on my knees in front of the desolate castle, black crows wheeling above as they jeered at me. I never wanted to get up again.

Chapter 4

Ingeborg

Hunger. The dull ache in Ingeborg's belly all the long winter of 1661. The summer past, they had managed. She had scooped up mussels and ample seaweed along Ekkerøy's white crescent-moon beach, Kirsten shuffling by her side, helping her. On her own, Ingeborg climbed the cliffs and collected more seagulls' eggs. Or she had gone inland. Laid snares and caught ptarmigan, and sometimes even a hare. Her mother did not praise her, merely took the small corpses from her hands, some still warm, and went to skin or pluck them. She would feed her girls, yes. Keep them alive; but that was all.

As the short summer of 1661 was snatched away, by the first cold rains of autumn, Ingeborg and Kirsten had searched for the last berries and mushrooms of the year. When the first snows had fallen, Ingeborg dug for moss to boil into jelly and roots for soup before the earth became too frozen. They had been forced to exchange all their lambs but one for the debt of grain owed to Merchant Brasche, because their father had not returned with fish to pay for it.

Ingeborg believed starvation was coming, for they had no dried fish stored, no cow nor goat for milk, and just the one little lamb, which Kirsten doted on.

Hunger. The hole inside her, gnawing away like a rat on her insides, the aching pain of it. Her lips dry, and licking them only for them to be dry again. Drinking melted snow to fill their bellies, and falling asleep, only to wake up in intense pain. She had given all she could to Kirsten, but her little sister often cried herself to sleep asking for more to eat. Her mother became thin, drifting as a red-haired ghost, wandering the moors, looking for her lost son.

Their neighbours had helped in little ways, but all were struggling. Their fishing yields had been dropping every year, and yet the price of grain was rising. The fishermen were forced to sell to the Bergen merchants what was needed to nourish their families, and still it was not enough to keep them in grain for *flatbrød*, or for their animals.

The choice was to starve, or go further into debt to Merchant Brasche, who held domain over the village of Ekkerøy.

His dwelling was placed in the best situation, of course, on a small rise of drier land, next to the kirk. Ingeborg and her family lived in a cluster of five turf cottages on the edge of the village. All of the doorways opened onto a common square of muck with a well in the middle, and a view of the sea. They lived so close to their neighbours, they could hear the coughs and moans of every household.

Days had gone by with the weight of hunger so heavy upon her that Ingeborg couldn't walk out to hunt. Soon it would be summer again, she kept telling her little sister, whimpering by her side. Kirsten, so waiflike, the colour of her hair – as red as their mother's – the most vibrant aspect of her: the rest fading, like the winter snows. There would be bounty to be had when the sun thawed the snow, Ingeborg promised her sobbing sister. She would trap lots of creatures. The patches of heathery ground would be black with blueberries, hazy pink-gold with cloudberries, and they would have apron pockets full of blue mussels from the sea. Abundance was on its way.

Word had spread of their predicament. On the morning of April's full Easter moon in 1662, her mother's cousin, Solve Nilsdatter, arrived upon their threshold. No longer impeded by the harsh winds and blizzards of previous months, she and her boys had skied over two hours from her village of Andersby to bring them some sustenance. On her back she carried provisions, while her youngest son was strapped to her front beneath the heavy reindeer skins. She greeted them with a wide smile, although it was hard for her to conceal the shock on her face as she took in the sight of Ingeborg's mother looking so gaunt.

Solve stepped inside without invite, her eldest boy tugging at her skirts, her cheeks rosy, as she set down her youngest before sliding the sack from off her shoulders. She placed her offerings upon the table:

sheaves of *flatbrød*, dried fish for broth, birds' eggs, cream and milk in sealskin sacks.

'Now, Zigri,' she said to their mother, after Ingeborg and Kirsten had drunk their beakers of milk, chewing on the dried fish, lips salty. 'Come and have some of my milk, from the very best of cows. It is quite sweet.' She offered Ingeborg's mother a beaker brimming with frothing white milk, and, slowly, coaxed by her cousin, she drank.

Solve smiled with approval.

'Thank you, cousin,' Zigri whispered, hoarsely.

Solve tsked. 'It is nothing,' she said. 'You would have done as much for me.'

From the bottom of her sack, she presented them with a small pat of butter wrapped in sealskin. 'Now I have a treat for you. Freshly churned butter to mix with the fish, so you can make *klinning*,' she told them. 'Is it not your favourite, Ingeborg?'

Ingeborg's stomach growled with delight. The last time she'd eaten *klinning* had been before Axell's drowning.

'You are too kind,' Zigri said, staring at the butter as if it were pure gold.

'Well, we actually have an abundance of milk since my husband's niece has come to live with us,' Solve said. 'Our two cows are yielding perhaps more than four might, even though they are old.'

There was a moment of silence as Zigri raised her head to look at her cousin. 'Is this the girl Maren Olufsdatter?' Zigri asked, a wary edge to her voice.

'Indeed, it is,' Solve replied, in a defensive tone.

'Then we can't take this, Solve,' Zigri said, pushing away the pat of butter. 'Witches were responsible for the death of my boy. I can't—'

'Zigri, come now, have some sense! Your poor girls need to eat,' Solve replied. 'She may be a little . . . odd.' She licked her lips. 'But Maren is no witch.'

'Her mother was Liren Sand! Put to the stake for witchcraft, Solve!' Zigri's voice dropped to a low whisper. 'How can you have her in your home?'

'I have no choice in the matter,' Solve said, tartly. 'Strycke insists she must stay.' She shook her head and sighed. 'She has her strange ways, that much is true, but I have found her company an asset in my daily housekeeping. If I were to have my own daughter, it would be different. But boys want to be outside with their adventures. They have no interest in chores.'

Zigri's eyes gazed upon her cousin's two sons. The younger, Peder, still near a babe, positioned on his mother's lap chewing on a strand of dried fish, his cheeks ruddy as apple shine. The elder boy, Erik, five years old, was running around their small hut, chased by Kirsten, who had bounded up from the table with new vigour after her repast of fish and milk.

Ingeborg could see the pain tight in her mother's eyes with remembering Axell and wished to distract her mother from such thoughts. Besides, she was curious to know more about the girl Maren Olufsdatter.

'Does Maren ever talk about what her mother did?' Ingeborg asked Solve.

Maren Olufsdatter's mother, Marette Andersdatter, had been the great Liren Sand, leader of all witches on the island of Vardø. Her curses had rained down not merely on the kingdom of Norway, but Denmark too. She had sent plague and suffering, as if poisoned arrows, all the way to Copenhagen.

She had learnt this skill from the Sámi woman, Elli, who had also taught her healing crafts. Such power Maren's mother had possessed in one pair of hands, yet none knew if she were from the dark or the light, for it was said she might arrive upon your doorstep with her bag of roots and herbs to help heal your sick child or aid you through a dangerous birthing, and yet this fisherman's widow, who lived in a small cottage on the island of Vardø with her only daughter Maren, had been behind the giant wave that had swallowed up the boat of Jon Jonson, the Bergen merchant, drowning all men aboard. She had summoned the storm out of vengeance for her lost husband who owed the merchant money. The governor of Vardø had seen her afterwards, circling the sea as a great sea petrel, watching the men perish right before her.

Ingeborg wanted to hear more stories of the powers of Liren Sand, preferring these tales to the ones of the Devil and his temptations, which Reverend Jacobsen would tell them about every week in church.

'Well, yes, Ingeborg, the girl will not desist from talking about her mother's powers.' Solve huffed. 'It is why I prefer to leave her behind on my visits, because I don't approve of these notions about my husband's sister.'

Ingeborg leant forward, intrigued. 'What else does she tell you about Liren Sand?'

But Solve was distracted by little Peder tugging on one of the curls that had sprung lose from her coif. 'Ow, you naughty boy! Now let me go,' she said cajolingly to her son.

Ingeborg tickled the little boy beneath the chin so that he wriggled away, giggling.

Her mother got up from the table sharply, her stool making a scraping sound against the earth floor, her face lined with grief. 'We must get on with our chores, Ingeborg,' she said. 'Thank you, cousin. We will keep the butter.'

Ingeborg reached forward and grabbed the pat of butter, cradling it in her hands. She wanted to lick it, like a cat.

Two days after Solve's visit a storm swept in, as if to warn the village not to assume that spring had come yet. Winter wanted to hold on, hurling hail and sleet against their quaking huts. The sea churned and raved, and all were grateful none had set out to fish.

Their turf and wood cottage shuddered against the wind, while Kirsten clung to the lamb as if it were her babe. The storm went on, day after day. The food Solve had brought them ran out. Ingeborg needed to go hunting, but every time she tried to push open the door of their cottage, she was slammed against its side by the wailing winds. Desperate, she suggested they slaughter the lamb, but Kirsten began to cry loudly, her upset made worse by her hunger.

'No, the lamb is all we have.' Her mother shook her head wearily. 'Soon the storm will end, and you can hunt, Ingeborg.'

At last, on the tenth day, the wind dropped so suddenly the silence of the village felt unworldly.

Ingeborg lay huddled next to her sister, so hungry she could barely move. Her mother was sitting at the table, straight-backed, hands gripping its wooden ledge, hanging on as if it were a raft and she were shipwrecked.

'Ingeborg,' she whispered, her voice hoarse and dry. 'Go and call on our neighbours. See if any have a bit to share.'

'I will go and hunt, Mamma,' she replied, knowing full well their neighbours would be as desperate as they.

She pulled down Axell's old jerkin and buttoned it on. She slipped his blade into her belt and gathered up all she needed to make her traps: a length of rope, and a big round stone with a hole in its centre. Hunger had sapped her strength so much it felt like she had to drag every bone in her body to work, and it took a long time to prepare.

At last, just as Ingeborg was about to step out, there came a rap on their door.

Her mother looked at her, eyes listless. 'Maybe it is Solve come back with more,' she said.

But it was not her mother's cousin upon the threshold with a basket of goods upon her arm. There stood a gentleman. Merchant Brasche's son, Heinrich.

He was tall and wearing a black cloak under which Ingeborg could spy a fine green doublet. He took off his hat and bent his head to enter the cottage. He had an abundance of chestnut curls upon his head, and brown eyes the same colour.

Her mother started with fright and stood up from the table.

'Are you the wife of Iver Rasmussen?' His voice was so different from the dialect they were used to, and he repeated his question twice but still Ingeborg's mother said nothing.

Heinrich took a long look at her mother, and, for a moment, Ingeborg saw her through the eyes of the merchant's son. Her mother was thin, but there were still curves to her figure, and her skin was flawless, unpocked or scarred despite the harshness of their lives. But it was her hair which was her crowning glory. It fell over her shoulders, a waterfall of red flames. As if sensing the indecency of her bare head, Ingeborg's mother hastily picked up her coif and push her curls up into it.

Heinrich Brasche repeated his question again.

'I am the *widow* of fisherman Iver Rasmussen.' Ingeborg's mother managed to find her voice.

Heinrich Brasche flinched.

'I am sorry to hear of it.' Heinrich coughed. 'But I am afraid . . .' –
he stumbled over his words, and it astonished Ingeborg to realise this
wealthy nobleman appeared a little nervous of her mother – 'there is a
debt,' Heinrich said, staring down at their earth floor, before speaking in
almost a whisper. 'It must be paid, so my father says.'

Ingeborg felt her belly drop.

They had nothing. Only the one lamb, Kirsten's pet.

Ingeborg watched her mother take a slow step forward, spread her
arms wide. She did not beg. Ingeborg had seen other fishermen's widows
do such: on their knees, pleading for mercy so as not to be sent to the
poorhouse in Bergen, and certain death. Not to be exiled and cast out
of the village as debtors. To wander the tundra and lie down and die.
Beggars. Wastrels. Lost women and girls.

'What is it you would have from me, Master Heinrich? For there is
nothing left of value to give.'

The merchant's son shuffled from foot to foot, once lifting his face,
unable to take his eyes off her mother. 'I will do what I can for you, mistress,' he said, finally, placing his hand upon her mother's arm. 'I will talk
to my father.'

Ingeborg was not sure what surprised her the most: this untoward
action of Heinrich Brasche, or the fact her mother did not push his hand
from her arm. Merely looked straight back at him. Fearless.

This was the change in Ingeborg's mother. She no longer cared what any
soul thought of her. What did it matter now her boy was gone and her
husband lost?

But this change was more dangerous than her mother could ever
imagine, more than Ingeborg had an inkling of. The end of their family
began on the day after the storm when Heinrich Brasche walked into
their cottage and offered to help, his disquieting words ruffling the dead-
still lull of the spent-out wind.

Words that would place her mother, Ingeborg and Kirsten in the
greatest of perils.

Chapter 5

Anna

I was through the entrance of the fortress, stumbling upon high ridges of iced snow, watched by two soldiers who stood guard at the gates. Here at last, Lockhert unchained me, and I was free of my fetters. I looked at my new home, rubbing my sore wrists.

To the right was the castle reaching up into the black sky, its white-washed stone revealed as the gleaming moon slipped out from behind the night clouds. I was standing in a small courtyard. It had an old well at its centre, and a castle with a small tower surrounded by tumbledown buildings with sagging turf roofs.

It was hard to believe this shabby collection of dwellings was the governor's fortress – and your seat of power in the furthest reaches of your northern kingdom.

Keen to rest my weary body I made towards the castle; I longed to warm my cold bones by a fire, and to lie down upon a bed.

But Lockhert tugged me back as if I were a dog on a leash. 'Where are you off to, lady?'

I turned, confused. 'Is the governor not expecting me?'

Lockhert gave a cruel laugh. 'Have you not forgotten you are a prisoner?' he taunted me. 'You have no place in the governor's house.'

He threw the light of his torch away from the castle to reveal a long, low house with a rotten turf roof. It had once been white, this building, but was now clearly dingy behind the banks of snow. My heart sank as I noticed that no cheering plume twisted out of its smoke hole.

Lockhert instructed one of the soldiers to shovel away the snow before the door, then he bellowed, 'Helwig!' and cursed her name for being slow.

A coarse-looking girl emerged from the back of the castle, skidding across the ice in her haste to reach us and avoid the wrath of her master.

'This is your maid, Helwig,' Lockhert told me. 'She will see to you.'

I held my head high but felt the scrutiny of the serving maid as Lockhert pushed open the door of the longhouse. There appeared to be neither key nor lock which pleased me, though this was a fleeting emotion as I took a tentative step forward.

No light shone within the longhouse. I peered inside and was greeted by frigid air that was thick with a stench that made me suspect the building had been used for animal storage. I looked desperately for a chink of light in the absolute dark, for the idea of residing in a windowless chamber made my heart flutter with panic, but the night made it impossible to see.

My whole body was in rebellion, and I found I was unable to take another step forward. I turned to my captor in the doorway, attempting to command my full height; even so, though I am a tall woman, Lockhert still towered over me.

'I can't stay here,' I protested. 'It's filthy, and there's no fire lit.'

The guard stopped shovelling snow and the girl Helwig stood quite still, her eyes open wide in shock. Clearly none had seen a prisoner speak back in such a way before but, as you know, I am no common prisoner.

Lockhert took me by the shoulders, spinning me around suddenly so that the breath was fairly whipped out of me. He pointed with his huge hand to a small turf hovel on the other side of the courtyard. It had no windows, just a barricaded door, and even from afar it reeked of horror and desperation.

'If you wish, I can put you in yonder witches' hole, Fru Rhodius,' Lockhert said. 'The Devil has been busy with his horde, and we are on the search for his mistresses. Maybe you are the first we have found?'

I looked at him aghast, even as anger rose within me at his audacity. I was no more a witch than he, and those very words were upon my lips.

But just as I was about to speak, Helwig tugged my sleeve. 'Come, lady, I will have the fire going quickly.'

I shrugged her filthy hand off me. What disease might I catch off this dingy girl?

'Very well,' I said to Lockhert, as if it were I who had made the decision, not wishing to show him a fragment of my distress. For I had known enough men like him to know he would take merriment in it.

I turned on my heel, instructing the guard to be careful conveying my chest of medicines into my new home. Trying my best not to show my utter desolation, I entered the abhorrent abode.

I sat by the tiny fire in my decrepit home, pressing my lavender kerchief to my nose, watching Helwig feeding the flames with tiny lumps of peat. As the fire grew, warmth returned to my stiff limbs and my courage came back to me.

I began to understand why it was that you exiled me to this isolated and savage island.

'Of course, my king,' I whispered to myself, thinking upon Lockhert's remarks on witches in the north and remembering the girl I had seen running into the woods on our journey.

Entrusted as our king, Frederick, divine ruler of us lesser mortals, you stood up to the nobles who would challenge your absolute rulership, and you did not shy away from battle with the Swedes to regain your dominions, and yet, my king, I suspect that, despite the grand show of burning Liren Sand, you are as afraid of the dark arts of women as your father.

Have you sent me to Vardø because you must have here a woman most loyal to the crown to enact your will; a woman even more devoted than your own wife; a woman with intelligence, grit and tenacity?

I am such a woman, am I not? And I will never waver from the task at hand.

Lockhert had said the Devil was afoot and so was his cohort – the sisters and the daughters of the great witch, Liren Sand, who had cursed your own father to his end. These witches had sent the plague to every edge of our northern kingdoms, ravaging Copenhagen, Christiania and Bergen, and still threatening to destroy you too.

Would they bring a plague like the last one, which had taken so much from me?

These vile creatures have to be purged once and for all. Yes, yes, now I understand your intent because my exile was a ruse, a pretence, was it not?

I am not a prisoner but a soldier under your command.

I will rid you of the witches, I promised you, as I huddled by the fire. *And you will return to me my liberty.* As I stared into the flames, I saw myself within your embrace again, my king, your heart beating against mine and a kiss upon my forehead.

'All is forgiven,' you would say to me, cupping my chin within your hands.

And I would forgive you too, my king.

Chapter 6

Ingeborg

Golden pats of butter, bowls of creamy cheese and pitchers of frothing milk from Heinrich Brasche's cows. Slabs of sweet *lefse* laced with sugar and cinnamon made by Widow Krog, who cooked for him. Slippery herring griddled in a knob of butter. Wind-dried cod from the fishing racks, stacks of it, added to every broth. Fresh fish! Caught upon the Brasches' own boat. A sturdier vessel than any owned in the whole village. One that had sailed the merchant and his son all the way south to the big city of Bergen, where Heinrich had traded with merchants from all over the world. Now he brought items he had procured in past trips to Bergen as gifts for Ingeborg's mother: a little pot of crystalised salt like snowflakes, or a yellow spice he told her mother came from the far East – Zigri had put it in their broth one day. It had turned the insides of their mouths to fire, and Kirsten had run outside to scoop up snow and swallow it down, which had made Ingeborg and her mother laugh.

It made Ingeborg think of Axell and his promises of becoming a merchant too. If only it had been her brother bringing them gifts from the Orient.

But it had been so long since Ingeborg had seen her mother even smile, let alone laugh. The sound of it so light, as if the years were falling away from her each time the merchant's son called. Such smiles were dangerous, but still Ingeborg was glad of Heinrich Brasche's gifts. She ate the hot spicy stew with enjoyment, understanding that if she took it slowly, spoon by spoon, she could discern how this exotic spice enhanced the broth of *klippfisk*.

Most precious of all was a bag of grain so her mother could bake *flatbrød*. Truly Ingeborg couldn't remember when their stores had been so full.

There were times her mother disappeared for hours, leaving Ingeborg to mash the fish bones for the lamb, collect water, and tend the cooking fire. When she reappeared, Ingeborg always detected a slight difference: her mother humming as she worked beside her, less chiding, less woeful. One time she returned with a blue ribbon braided in her red hair. Her mother didn't take it out for days. Ingeborg would catch her slipping fingers up and down its length as she gazed beyond their turf hut, up the hill to Heinrich Brasche's house.

What impossible dreams was she conjuring in her imagination?

The more gifts Heinrich Brasche bestowed upon them, the more distant her mother seemed to become. Not just from her and Kirsten, but from the whole community. Ingeborg caught sideways looks from the other women at the well whenever her mother went to collect water. She had heard Widow Krog muttering under her breath as she caught sight of Zigri's blue hair ribbon: 'Careful, girl.'

It wasn't until the rumours reached the village of Andersby and the ears of her cousin, Solve, that anyone challenged her mother. With the snows beginning to fade away Solve had trudged for four hours across the boggy land from Andersby to Ekkerøy, bringing a basket of dried fish and *flatbrød*, as well as the butter she told them was freshly churned by her husband's niece, Maren Olufsdatter. This time she was alone, her two little boys left with the niece, Maren, to mind back home.

Ingeborg made *klinning* with Solve's produce as she strained to listen to her talking with her mother.

'Be careful, cousin,' Solve whispered. 'He has a wife.'

Ingeborg licked the butter from her fingertips. Even Merchant Brasche's butter didn't taste as well as the butter churned by the mysterious Maren Olufsdatter. She looked at the little pot of light and fluffy cream. Licked her lips, slick with its sweetness.

'But he brings me food,' Ingeborg had heard her mother whisper back. 'Things I have never eaten before! How can I refuse his generosity?'

'That's not all he gives you, is it?'

The silence was long and tense between the two cousins.

'It is none of your minding, Solve Nilsdatter,' her mother said in a low voice.

'We are family,' Solve said. 'Thus, it is my matter too. How can you be so stupid? Do you want to make an enemy of his wife?'

'She knows nothing,' Zigri whispered. 'Besides, theirs was a marriage of convenience. She is so much older than he.'

'Even more reason not to make an enemy of her, Zigri,' Solve hissed. 'If you are lonely, there are plenty of fishermen without wives who would be glad to take care of you.'

'No,' Zigri snapped. 'I can never wed a fisherman again. Never!'

Ingeborg came over with the *klinning* piled on a platter.

'Go and get Kirsten,' her mother instructed her. 'She's outside with the lamb.'

Ingeborg reluctantly moved away from the two women towards the door of their cottage.

'Think of your daughters, of me and my family,' she heard Solve say to her mother. 'You risk us all.'

'What do you mean?' Her mother sounded confused.

'This behaviour is what Maren's mother was suspected of on the island of Vardø. The governor said she bewitched him. It was how the accusations of witchcraft started against her.'

Ingeborg paused on the threshold, the word *witchcraft* seizing her heart and squeezing it tight.

Her mother slammed her hand against the table. 'How can you say this to me when it was witches who took my boy away?'

Ingeborg turned to see Solve place a hand on her mother's sleeve. Her voice, when she spoke, was gentle. 'I know. But don't you see, cousin, they will say you bewitched him too.'

Her mother gave a short bark of a laugh. 'It is quite the other way around,' she said to Solve, but didn't continue on seeing Ingeborg still upon the threshold. 'I said to go and get your sister, Ingeborg.'

Ingeborg found Kirsten sitting on a mound of peat, her apron filthy as she tickled the belly of her little lamb, which though a female she had named Zacharias.

By the time they returned to the cottage, Solve was gathering up her skirts and scooping her basket onto her arm. The cousins' parting was not as warm as usual.

As Solve passed by, Ingeborg noticed the faded bloom of an old bruise upon her jaw almost as if it were a shadow. They were all used to Solve's bruises and bumps. Two summers ago, Solve had turned up with a black eye and Ingeborg had asked her mother how she got it. Zigri had frowned, shaking her head, saying Solve had been kicked by her cow while milking. Ingeborg knew every word was a lie.

When Strycke was away fishing, the cow never kicked Solve.

Kirsten exclaimed with glee as their mother put the platter of *klinning* Ingeborg had made on the table. They said a short prayer, and Kirsten tucked in, feeding titbits to her lamb which their mother ignored as she nibbled on a piece of *klinning*.

Ingeborg felt a tight stab of fear in her belly. Her hunger had made her foolish. She had not even considered the danger of Heinrich Brasche's gifts: her thoughts had been quieted by the nourishment of food, the pleasure it had brought; the fact Kirsten had a little bloom of colour in her cheeks and no longer cried herself to sleep with an aching, empty belly.

She had got lazy. Not bothered to hunt for their own food for weeks.

There was still light enough in the sky and the evenings were long, the sun dipping below the horizon to rise again early the next day.

Ingeborg rose from the table, crunching through her last piece of *klinning*. She gathered up her hunting things.

'Where are you going?' her mother asked her.

Ingeborg buttoned Axell's jerkin. 'I am going to lay some traps,' she said.

'But we have plenty of food,' her mother said. 'Heinrich Brasche brought us a hare.'

'Mother, you should give it back,' Ingeborg said to her.

Her mother's eyes widened but she said nothing in reply.

Ingeborg followed the coast. The Varanger sea surged with icy momentum onto the gentle sands of Ekkerøy. She longed for midsummer, and to run along its length barefoot. How she and Axell had used to.

Changing direction, she headed inland across the bog, its heavy earth pulling on her booted feet. With the snows thawing, the land had begun to fill with freezing water. Her progress was slow, and she had to be careful not to stray into marsh so mired she might never pull herself out.

Ingeborg picked her way across the moors to the sparse woodland between the bog and an inland fjord. She had a sense she was being watched or followed, but when she looked behind her all she could see was the wide sky leaching light, dark sleet clouds stacking above her.

It began to sleet just as she ducked in among the narrow birch trees, Axell's hat pulled down over her brow. The air was tight and cold on her cheeks, but at least the wind dropped in the sudden stillness of the winter woods. Her breath plumed in front of her as she studied the ground beneath her.

There was still snow where light and sleet had not reached to thaw it, and she crouched down, studying it for tracks. Again, she had the sense of being watched, the animal part of her prickling with sensation down her back. She stood up and turned in a slow circle, but she couldn't see any other soul.

A branch snapped above her, and Ingeborg jerked her head up to see a big crow sitting atop a tall, thin birch tree, its spindly branches swaying with the weight of the bird.

'Shoo,' she called to it, unnerved by its piercing stare.

But the crow didn't fly away.

Ingeborg hunched her shoulders, trying to ignore it as she searched for likely marks in the snow. Shadows began to creep in from the edges of the small wood, the birch trees stark in the gathering gloom.

At last, Ingeborg saw the distinctive imprint of hare tracks. She picked up a stick, quickly pointed its end with her knife, and pushed it into the snow and down into the hard earth with all her might. Tying a line around it, she attached the snare she'd made from fishing net, so sharp it had sliced her fingertips many times. Finally, she made her loop and, cutting a notch into a small, stunted trunk on the other side of the track, tied the snare to it.

She stood back. It was a good, open spot. A place a hare might pick up speed. Not notice her trap. She was hopeful that when she returned the next morning, she would be rewarded. Ingeborg set several more traps close to the hare tracks praying for at least one of them to offer up bounty the next day.

On her way back to the bog, she looked up to the tree where the crow had perched but it was gone. Even so, she felt its hard stare still behind her. She began to run, out into the open, the sleet falling brutal and icy upon her. The brief dark was falling, and she had no Axell now to keep her brave.

The next morning, the sky had stretched with light long before her awakening, Ingeborg was back walking through the thin birch woods, a sense of anticipation thumping tightly in her heart. If she had caught a hare, and could return with game for her mother, then she might turn away Heinrich Brasche's gifts of food. But as she wove through the trees, Ingeborg strove to ignore what she knew in her heart was the truth: Heinrich Brasche might visit with his pockets empty, and her mother would still slip out at night, her shadow flitting across the full-moon village up the hill towards the Brasche house.

It was so early, Ingeborg felt like the first creature awake. Her belly groaned; she had been so keen to check her traps she had not taken any food yet. But as she came upon the small rise of land where she had set the first snare, she saw that not only was it empty, but the sticks had been pulled out of the earth, and the snare itself was gone. She checked all the other traps she had set and every single one of them had been destroyed.

She stood with her hands on her hips in confusion, staring down at the place where she had put the first trap. No one in the village would do such a thing.

And again, suddenly, she had the feeling someone was watching her.

When she looked up, there was a girl standing in front of her. In her face she looked to be the same age as her, though she was a good deal taller. Her hair was the blackest Ingeborg had ever seen, thick and wild as sea bracken, her eyes the green of deep fjord ice, her skin the brown of brackish bog water. Although she had never met her, Ingeborg knew exactly who the girl must be: Maren Olufsdatter, Solve's strange niece. Since she had moved in with her uncle and aunt last winter, there had been whispers that Maren's real father had not been pale-faced fisherman, Oluf Mogensson, but a pirate from the Barbary Coast. Olaf's drowning two winters before had been cursed, for his witch wife had committed adultery. It had been the same storm Axell had drowned in; the one her mother blamed witches for too.

And Maren's mother had been their leader.

Ingeborg had heard many whispers about Maren that she was like her mother. A witch's get. And now this tall dark girl stood before her, a look in her eyes similar to the black crow's last night. Censoring and judgemental. But what had she to judge Ingeborg for?

As the girl stepped towards her, Ingeborg was stunned to see a small white hare behind her taking a big loping jump, before skidding off into the woods.

'I believe this must be yours.' Maren held up one of Ingeborg's snares. The silvery fishing net gleamed in the morning light.

'What do you think—'

Ingeborg was silenced by her own astonishment as Maren took a pair of shears from her apron pocket and snipped the snare into little pieces.

'Hey!' Ingeborg stormed towards her furiously. 'How *dare* you?'

Maren waved the shears, warning her to stay away as she snipped the last bit of the snare. It scattered like fine snow. 'Now, isn't that better?' Maren smiled sweetly at Ingeborg. 'I got here just in time.'

'I needed the hare to feed my family,' Ingeborg said, kicking the sticks from the trap. 'You've no right interfering and destroying my things.'

Maren cocked her head on one side. 'There's no need to get so upset,' she said, slipping the shears back in her apron pocket.

'Have you ever been so hungry you eat moss off stones?' Ingeborg threw at the girl, her voice cracking with emotion.

'Why, yes, indeed I have,' Maren said, a mocking hint to her voice. 'But if you hunt, you must do so with a thought for the consequences.'

'It's just a hare!'

But Maren appeared unbothered by Ingeborg's annoyance. Instead, she reached out a hand to her. 'Come with me,' she said. 'Let me show you what I mean.'

Chapter 7

Anna

I clung to my faith, but it was so hard. My new home – how can I call it such? – was the darkest place I had ever lived in, despite the lengthening hours of light in this northern domain; for within the dank walls of this miserable dwelling, the gloom is permanent. How my spirit plunges when shards of memory come to mind of my airy house in Bergen, and all the comfort I had benefited from, and taken for granted.

It didn't help to learn from the maid Helwig that the last inhabitant of my prison house – an exiled priest, from Rogaland – had died but one week before in the very bed I was to sleep upon.

Despite the inhospitable nature of my new home, the first evening I was so bone-tired from my travails I could have slept on the earth floor by the sputtering cooking fire, but Helwig bustled me into the grim bedchamber.

My bed looked ancient, with threadbare hangings and rank animal skins as coverings.

'Is this fresh bedding?' I asked Helwig, thinking of the old priest who had died upon it.

'Of course,' she said, affronted. 'Engelbert lost use of his bowels.' She huffed. 'I had to clean and replace it all.'

Looking at her dirty hands and greyish apron I was doubtful of her thoroughness. The odour in the bedchamber reminded me of the stink in some of the homes of the dying during the plague time. In the pool of light cast by her candle, I caught glimpse of a small window opening. I swept past her and pulled up the coverings, which appeared to be made of fish skins.

Helwig came over with her candle. 'There's a stick on the shelf you prop it on,' she said, not offering to assist me.

I gingerly propped the flap up with the stick as fresh air flooded into the chamber.

'It will become very cold, if you do not drop the flap,' Helwig warned, as her candle flame sputtered in the icy air streaming into the bedchamber.

But my spirit was lifted by the full-moon light flooding in. It was then I saw a large trunk placed in the corner of the bedchamber and gasped in shock and delight, unable to conceal my joy at its presence. 'Where did this come from?' I asked, pointing my shaking finger at it.

'It arrived by sleigh before the last storm,' Helwig said, her voice dropping to a whisper. 'I believe it is from the king!'

I knelt down by the large trunk and opened it up, all the while my hands shaking to see what you had sent me. Upon the top was a folded letter, the seal broken, with instructions to the governor of Finnmark that I was to receive all the items intact and at the bottom of which was your royal signature. I cast the letter aside on the cracked floorboards as Helwig looked in awe at all the finery packed within the chest. I am sure she had never seen such things in her entire life.

You had had the chest filled with crisp white linens: three coifs for my head; fresh petticoats, one with an ample pocket; three bobbin-laced collars; two nightgowns; and three high-necked chemises for under my satin gowns, of which there were two – one the colour of forget-me-nots to match my eyes, and one in black for formal occasions. There was more: a warm red *bøffelbay* bodice, a dark blue sash and an ornate stomacher decorated with black roses on gold, a new fur muff, a fur capelet, and a hat with an ostrich plume. For my feet, you had sent me a pair of *pantofles* in gold brocade for indoor wear, and a pair of shoes in dark blue with black silk roses; but more useful was a pair of wooden pattens.

Atop all of these items was a small hand mirror inlaid with mother of pearl, and a bottle of rosewater, along with a vial of rose oil, which I now picked up and inhaled deeply, banishing the stench in the rank bedchamber. It was then my eyes lit upon more treasure, for in one corner of the trunk was a wooden crate filled with lemons, and next to it, wrapped in paper, a delicate cone of sugar, still intact, despite the distance it must have travelled.

Each time I pushed my hands further into the trunk I found more: a flask of genever, a bag of sugared almonds, and two books to add to my battered Bible, and Pedersen's New Testament: a copy of King James's *Daemonologie*, and a new publication by Rasmus and Thomas Bartholin, the Danish physicians I so admired.

Your choices appeared conflicting for one was a theological discourse on daemonology but the second a scientific treatise: *De nivis usu medico observationes variae* – on the use of snow in various medical observations. Were these books your idea of a jest? I would have no shortage of snow in my new abode, and witches abounded.

The last item within the trunk was a cruel taunt, was it not? I picked up a scroll of parchment, thick creamy vellum awaiting my script upon it but, much as I hunted, I could find no ink and no quill, my king. In my heart I knew it was no accident these items were omitted.

I was in conflict over the meaning of the chest. Was its arrival a sign my pardon was coming soon, or were these gifts a final farewell? Or were you goading me with fine clothes I had no occasion to wear in the blasted place of my exile, and parchment I could not write upon? I feared it was so, for you have changed a great deal, as I discovered the last time I was with you. It is perhaps what happens when a prince becomes a king: he forsakes compassion in the place of authority; he no longer wishes to listen but must be above all souls.

All I had travelled with was the gown I had upon me, my mother's pearls sewed into the hem for safekeeping, and my medicine chest, for I never went anywhere without my herbs and tinctures. How glad I was I had brought it with me to Copenhagen, for of course I had no inkling that I would not be returning home to Bergen.

My joy at finding the trunk transformed to misery when a new thought came upon me: that you had sent me the trunk full of all I loved because of guilt, and that from this time forward you would endeavour to forget my very existence.

The stink of my new quarters hung around me, and I raised my rose oil again to inhale deeply before unlocking my medicine chest. Its contents always soothe me.

I pulled out a bundle of dried rosemary from my garden, bound with twine.

Helwig looked at my herbs suspiciously but said nothing.

'Bring the candle over,' I instructed her.

I lit the rosemary and blew it out slowly, letting the smoke billow into the foul bedchamber. She watched me as I wafted it around the room.

'I wouldn't let Lockhert see you doing that,' she said, shaking her head. 'He'll think it witchery.'

'Well, he is mistaken,' I said. 'I used these herbs many times when cleansing the homes of the plagued.'

Helwig looked even more worried at the word 'plague'. She placed the candle on a small table by the side of the bed. 'I shall be next door,' she said, before sidling away.

I waited for the governor to make his introductions but a whole week of days went by with no invitation from the castle. I was insulted by his ignorance, but the solitude wore on me too. My only companion was the common maid, Helwig, who I had to cajole to join me in daily prayers and was far from an equal companion for any conversation.

As the snow thawed the long hours of dark shrank, and daylight began in the middle of the night. The loss of the snow made the whole world appear greyer. Every morning I lifted the halibut flap to my tiny window, viewing the land wet and mucky underneath where the snow had lain. The whole vista of the grim settlement of Vardø was awash with rain, grey and relentless. The dim daylight began so early I was not yet awake, but the tone stayed the same dull for all my waking hours. I found myself missing the pure white of snow and the clear sky filled with stars, as it had been the night I arrived.

I was used to rain, living for so many years in Bergen. In the city, I had enjoyed the sight of the wet cobbles in the silvery rain-filled light when nestled in my home, by the fire, listening to the patter of the rain upon our roof. All this had made my house more of a comfort. But here, in the north, the rain was of a violent type and there was no beauty in it for me to find.

I could have sunk into melancholy and given up all hope as the old priest perished in my bed may have done, but this was not my way. You know this – I am as tenacious as a mountain goat – and so I busied myself placing order upon each day.

I began each morning on my knees praying, for I am a good suppliant. Most of my life I have asked God Almighty to hear my prayers, but as I gripped my fingers tight, pressing their tips into the knuckles of each hand, questions wandered into my mind, tempting me from humility.

I wished to ask you what it was like to be a king such as you, Frederick: an absolute monarch by divine sanction. Does the Good Lord hear every one of your prayers?

And yet, the last day we were together, I could not see your divinity, for your mouth was drawn in a hard line, and your eyes were dark and cruel. I think upon how you could have looked at me in such a way and your image haunts me as I pray, so I must squeeze my eyes tight and chant the psalms loudly to banish it.

After prayers I read from the Bible to Helwig, for I read well aloud and enjoyed the task of educating the girl.

The maid was enthralled by the plague of locusts in the Book of Exodus, and she had a taste for the God with little mercy in the Old Testament, but it was in reading upon our Good Lord's son, Jesus Christ, that I found most comfort. Forty days and forty nights he wandered in the desert, but my exile, I fear, will be longer.

As the church bell rang twelve peals, we would eat potage, and drink our ale. Afterwards, I would eat a slice of lemon sprinkled with sugar.

The first time I ate my lemon slice, Helwig stared at me in wonder.

'What is that?' she asked.

'A lemon.'

'And is that sugar?' she whispered in awe. Her mouth was watering as she licked her lips.

'It is a refined taste,' I explained, turning my back on her.

I did not give her a slice nor any sugar, because they are as precious to me as the pearls I have sewn into the hem of my dress.

After prayers and Bible reading, I read the books you sent me.

I had already read King James's *Daemonologie*. I knew that it was written before I was born, and I cannot say I agreed with all of his practices. His assertation a witch should be tortured to gain the truth from her I believed to be a contrary theory, and a witch-hunting tool that was not a lawful way to behave in our times.

After my reading, I opened up my medicine chest and examined its contents. Usually this would make me sigh very deeply, for how am I to replenish its stocks in this barren place?

Some days I joined Helwig in the washhouse to watch her work, scrubbing with birch lye, and I would breathe in the steam, absorbing the warmth from the heated water and sprinkling lavender from my medicine chest upon my own linens.

Every afternoon I walked in a circle around the fortress yard, whether the rain fell or not. I put on my cape and trudged in the mud in my new pattens. When I compared this place to your palace, and its vast grounds, I feel this bleak enclave of your power in its most northerly domain could hardly be called a fortress. I counted my steps, from my prison longhouse to the washhouse and the soldiers' turf hut, past the gatehouse where once or twice I saw the Bailiff Lockhert lurking, and past the governor's house. The castle windows were made of glass, but all dark apart from faint light gleaming from one or two. Now and again, I would see a guard at the gates but there were so few of them – only six soldiers to fight the battle against evil in the north.

The last building to pass before I completed my circle was the witches' hole. Its shadow fell long, or I imagined it so in the falling rain, and its dark, windowless contours made my mouth go dry and my heart tighten. It wasn't fear, but a sense of anticipation that made me feel so.

The witches' hole is empty now, but I know that soon it won't be.

Chapter 8

Ingeborg

Ingeborg followed Maren as she led her through the trees and beyond, across the wild tundra; further from her home village, than she had ever been before.

'Where are we going?' she asked, as she fell in step beside Maren.

'I want to show you something.'

The snow was almost thawed and the earth softening into heavy clumps which stuck to Ingeborg's boots. At last, they came to a stop, and Maren held up her hand, placing a finger to her lips to tell Ingeborg to be quiet. She crept forward, and Ingeborg crouched down behind her.

Under a ledge of rock in front of them, there was a white hare upon a nest lined with moss. Its long ears were straining back, and the nose was twitching, but it didn't run away.

'This is the hare you wished to eat,' Maren whispered to Ingeborg. 'But she is pregnant.'

Ingeborg shrugged. But a part of her was a little glad she had not killed the hare.

'In about twenty days, she will give birth to as many as eight baby hares,' Maren said to Ingeborg, turning to her. 'Did you know baby hares are born with their eyes open?'

Ingeborg shook her head. She looked at the white hare, and it stared right back at her. Why wasn't it frightened?

'When Mamma Hare goes off to feed, I will keep an eye on them,' Maren said, taking hold of Ingeborg's hand and guiding her backwards. 'Let's leave her in peace, will we?' she whispered to Ingeborg.

Everything was surprising about Maren. Her gentle care for the wild animal, and the fact she was holding Ingeborg's hand. Now, as they turned to walk back across the tundra, she stopped and rubbed Ingeborg's hands with her own.

'Your skin is freezing,' she said. 'But your eyes are warm.' Maren smiled. 'They're softest brown, just like the hare's eyes.'

Ingeborg snatched her hands away. She didn't like being called soft.

'I have to go back,' she said, in a cross voice. 'With empty hands and no dinner.'

'Not at all,' Maren said. 'I will give you some butter and milk. We have plenty.'

Ingeborg didn't want to accept anything from Maren, but then it was the girl's fault she had no game for their dinner.

'Are you Ingeborg Iversdatter? My aunt is a cousin of your mother,' Maren asked, taking such big strides Ingeborg had to trot to keep up. 'I thought at first you were a boy because you are dressed like one, but then you're too pretty.'

Ingeborg felt herself blush. The way Maren spoke was so untoward. It must be because of who she was.

The daughter of a witch. It reminded Ingeborg of how witches had killed her brother.

'I don't want any food from you—' Ingeborg began.

Maren turned to look at her, hands on her hips. 'Why ever not?'

'My mother says your mother was a witch.'

'Well, that is true,' Maren replied to Ingeborg's shock.

'She says she drowned my brother Axell.'

'But now that is a lie! She would never hurt any of the fishermen. Why, her own husband drowned!' Maren said, vehemently. 'My mother would never have harmed one of us. She was only trying to defend us from the merchants and how they use us.'

Ingeborg bit her lip, not daring to look Maren in the eye. 'So, what did your mother do?'

'The governor of Finnmark was scared of her because she was friends with the Sámi,' Maren said, reaching out and placing her warm hand upon Ingeborg's cold hand again.

'Reverend Jacobsen says the Sámi sing to the Devil,' Ingeborg said. 'They're heathens.'

'He only says so because of ignorance and fear,' Maren countered. 'The Sámi understand the ways of this northern land in a way we never can. They thrive when we starve.' As she spoke, Maren's eyes were brimming with all the colours of the Arctic oceans: green and grey, even flecks of icy blue. 'My mother and the Sámi woman, Elli, were friends, but they were not evil.'

Her gaze was altogether unsettling, but Ingeborg believed her. She could not reason why, but there was something about Maren that drew her to her. Made her stomach flutter, and her mouth go dry.

When Ingeborg got home, their cottage was empty. But she heard her mother's voice next door in Widow Krog's cottage, along with others, as they mended the fishing nets for the men. Husbands were not long back from the winter fishing season, and boats and nets needed to be repaired in preparation for the autumn, when they would depart once more to chase the big cod south.

Ingeborg fed the smouldering ashes of their cooking fire before preparing gruel, adding a little of the milk Maren had given her. She put it aside to eat later and got up, dusting down her skirts and picking up the bucket.

Outside the afternoon had drifted into shadows. As she lowered her pail into the well, Ingeborg looked up to see the tall figure of Heinrich Brasche making his way down the path from his fine house. Beside him was her little sister, Kirsten, carrying Zacharias the lamb in her arms. Heinrich had his hand on her head. If it wasn't for the difference in their attire – Heinrich in his fine green waistcoat and big black hat, and Kirsten in an old wool dress of Ingeborg's – they might have been father and daughter.

Ingeborg yanked up her pail. She needed to get her mother before the other women saw, but it was too late. They were all coming out of Widow Krog's cottage bearing the newly mended fishing net.

As soon as Ingeborg's mother caught sight of Heinrich Brasche, she reacted by tucking her hair into her coif and smoothing down her skirt.

Ingeborg lifted her heavy bucket, lugging it back to their cottage to arrive at the same time as the merchant's son.

'Good afternoon, Fru Sigvaldsdatter, I found this little one up on the bog,' Heinrich said to their mother, patting Kirsten's head.

The other women disappeared inside their cottages. None remained outside, for no woman wanted to be seen talking with the merchant's son or asked about their husband's debts. But Ingeborg felt their eyes peering through the cracks in the turf walls. Watching like hawks. Their busy thoughts a swarm of flies.

'What were you doing all the way up on the marshes, Kirsten?' her mother chided. 'The land is dangerous up there.'

Ingeborg knew full well if Heinrich hadn't been standing before her mother, she would have given her youngest daughter a slap.

'I lost Zacharias,' Kirsten admitted, waiting for more anger from their mother. But she was distracted by Heinrich Brasche.

'May I come into your dwelling for a few minutes, Fru Sigvaldsdatter?'

'Oh,' Ingeborg's mother said, her cheeks turning pink.

'It's about your late husband's debt,' Heinrich Brasche clarified with confidence.

'Yes, of course,' their mother answered, the pink spreading down her neck. 'Girls, wait outside.'

Ingeborg put her bucket down. Staring at the door closing of their cottage, she waited.

Widow Krog came out of her own cottage and hobbled towards her. 'What's your mother thinking of?' she hissed at Ingeborg. 'I can hear *everything*. She's playing with fire.'

'What can she do? He's the merchant's son,' Ingeborg said, defensively.

'I wish he was my new papa,' Kirsten spoke up.

'Shush,' Ingeborg said. 'He's married. Has his own children.'

'Indeed,' Widow Krog said, shaking her head sorrowfully. 'Your mother is risking us all. Wait until winter comes. I have seen this before.'

'What do you mean?' Ingeborg asked, though part of her didn't want to hear what the old woman had to say.

'Marette Andersdatter, the woman known as Liren Sand, bewitched the governor of Finnmark and tempted him to sin. Her immorality was a bell ringing for the Devil to come. And he did.'

Her mother's laughter could be heard from inside the cottage now. But it was forced, not natural.

Widow Krog shook her head. 'And may the Good Lord protect us all if the Devil awakens again, bringing storms, starvation, and disease upon us all.' She crossed herself.

'Tell Zigri to mind she doesn't end up accused of witchcraft, the same as Marette Andersdatter!' Widow Krog warned before shuffling back to her cottage, leaning on her stick.

Witchcraft. The word choked Ingeborg with terror. She squeezed her eyes shut, frozen as she stood by her full bucket of well water. She could still hear her mother's laughter. It echoed around the silent yard. High-pitched, like the call of a seagull. Surely Heinrich Brasche's wife could hear it back in their house on the hill? Surely it could be heard across the Varanger Straits to the governor in his fortress, and further still to the Hill of Domen and inside its caves?

The Dark Lord would hear her mother's laugh. Waiting with patience in the deep black, red eyes glinting with expectation.

PART TWO

Spring/Autumn
1662

The Blue Ribbon

Once a beggar girl was walking through a forest with her beggar mother. They had very little food and were wandering between villages searching for alms. But none would help them.

As they walked among the trees, they came upon a blue ribbon lying on the forest floor. The girl wanted to pick up the blue ribbon and tie it in her hair, but her mother told her it was of no value to them. How could a blue ribbon fill their hungry bellies? So, the girl left it but as they kept walking, she felt the tug of the blue ribbon. The desire to braid it in her hair made her forget how hungry she was.

Out of the forest, they climbed a snowy mountain. They had only climbed over one ridge when her mother grew very tired, declaring they would huddle under a nearby canopy of rock and rest. The girl asked if she could go and get some firewood back in the forest. She ran all the way down the hill, into the trees and found the blue ribbon still lying upon the forest floor. Knowing her mother would be cross if she found out she'd gone back to get it, she picked it up and tied it around her waist under her bodice. As soon as she had done so she felt an incredible strength overcome her. She bounded back up the hill with a stack of firewood on her back as if a giant elk herself.

When she reached her mother, she saw some lights in the distance, above them. 'Mother let's go towards the lights. It must be a village and maybe they will give us food and shelter out of this cold wind.'

'Very well,' said her mother but when she stood up, she nearly fell over again because she was so tired. So, her daughter picked her up and carried her on her shoulders. Her mother was surprised her daughter had such strength as she was a lot shorter than she. But the girl galloped up the hill as if her legs were like the giant elk's.

As they grew closer to the lights her mother became worried. 'This is not a normal village. This is a troll's house,' she said in a panic. 'We must turn away because the troll will want to steal you and hide you in the belly of the mountain.'

'Don't be afraid, Mother,' the girl said. 'Maybe he is a kindly troll.'

'There is no such thing,' her mother said, but despite her protests, the girl kept galloping towards the troll's house and the mother could not get down.

Suddenly they were surrounded by a circle of giant wolves. Her mother was very afraid, but the girl sang a song about tying a blue ribbon around the forest pine tree and coming home. The song pleased the wolves and they lay down for her as if puppies. They licked her hands, and she rubbed their bellies as they panted in delight.

The girl's mother was very shocked at her daughter's new powers. But she said nothing because she did not want to imagine where they might have come from.

Once she had put her mother down, the girl knocked on the door of the house. A big troll answered the door. A grumpier, uglier, and bigger troll you could not imagine. And he was not happy to see them.

The mother was terrified by the look of him and fainted, but the girl was not afraid because she had the blue ribbon tied around her waist, and her family of big wolves to protect her.

'We need food and shelter,' she said to the troll.

He was very angry at the girl's audacity. 'I will eat you up and your mother and all those big wolves too,' he shouted, brandishing a big club. But when he threw his club at the girl, she was able to bound in the air as high as a hare. His club landed within the circle of wolves and one of them picked it up in its mouth and brought it to the girl.

'My turn,' she said.

The troll laughed at her because he didn't think she could pick up such a big club as she was so small, but the blue ribbon gave her unseen strength. The girl picked up his club and whacked him on the head. She hit him so hard he was seeing stars and in confusion; he looked down at her mother and thought she was quite a beautiful woman.

'Come in, come in,' he said, all meek now. 'And eat your supper with me.'

The girl with the blue ribbon carried her mother into the troll's house.

When the mother awakened, still trembling and afraid, the troll served them *flatbrød* and butter, salty herrings, and jugs of creamy milk.

The girl with the blue ribbon taught the troll how to read all the books he had stolen from kings and princes. She gave him some manners and taught him how to be kind to the big wolves who lolled around outside his house. And the troll did all this because he had fallen in love with the girl's mother.

Eventually the troll asked the girl's mother if she would share his bed with him.

The girl's mother was very afraid because she believed he would eat her up in the bed, like all trolls do.

The girl with the blue ribbon took her mother's hands in hers.

'I believe this troll is not as wicked as they say. See how kindly he is being to us: sharing his food and shelter when no other would do so in the whole of this kingdom?'

'But he is a troll and it's in his nature to want to kill us,' her mother replied.

'Only because we have been told so,' the girl said. 'Do not judge him.'

So, the mother shared the bed with the troll because in truth she liked the colour of his eyes. They reminded her of green leaves on a warm spring day.

In the bed, the troll asked the woman if she would allow him to kiss her. She was very surprised to be asked this, for truly no man had ever asked her permission before, not even the father of her girl.

When the troll kissed the girl's mother, in her eyes he turned into the most gallant king in the whole wide world.

'See, daughter!' she declared at breakfast the next day. 'The troll has turned into a king. An evil witch must have cast a spell on him and now he is back to his former self.'

But, of course, the daughter could see the troll was still a troll and indeed the troll knew he was still a troll, but neither of them told the girl's mother she was wrong because she was so happy. And, indeed, the daughter's mother made the troll feel like a king.

The three of them lived happily in the troll's house for many years, though the girl's mother insisted it was a castle and she was its queen.

One day the girl told her mother and her new father she must leave. The blue ribbon was tugging on her heart, and she knew she must go and find her destiny. But before she left, she knew she must show her parents the source of her strength. So, she untied the blue ribbon from around her waist and braided it in her hair.

'Ah, the blue ribbon!' her mother declared. 'So, you did go back and get it?'

'Sometimes the smallest of things possess the most magic,' her daughter said, wisely.

The girl kissed her mother goodbye and the troll father goodbye and off she went. But she did not go alone for the wolves loved her and they followed her through the woods. And would follow her always to the ends of the earth.

Chapter 9

Anna

The persistent rainfall ceased and rather than trudging every afternoon in a circle with bent head, I was able to look up. The first clear day a crow circled above, cawing loudly, as if in protest to be within the fortress walls; but the idiot bird could fly away to the freedom I was denied. I wished to knock it down with stones, dash it to the fortress cobbles, for why was this vulgar bird allowed to make so much noise while I must bow my head in shame and hold my tongue?

Fie, Anna, command yourself with dignity. It is but a bird.

As my eyes dropped from the sky, I noticed a narrow staircase up the side of the fortress walls. The sight lifted my spirits for there was somewhere new to explore. I crossed the courtyard and climbed up the stairs, that were so slick with rain and damp moss I had to rest my hand against the wet wall to ensure I did not fall.

The top of the staircase led to the battlements, which comprised a walk around the circumference of the whole castle, with small look-out posts at each corner. There were no soldiers atop the fortress this cold May morning, for why would there be? What enemy army would consider attacking our bleak outpost at the end of the civilised world?

I let my gaze drop to my immediate surroundings and looked down at the whitewashed fortress walls rising vertiginously from the top of this muddy hill. We were so very high up above the tiny settlement of Vardø that the view stretched across the foaming Varanger Straits to the looming Domen Mountain, which we had passed in the boat, the night of my arrival.

My head began to spin, and I placed my hand atop the battlement wall to steady myself. Even if I could somehow fashion a rope, and tie it to one of the battlements, the sheer drop to the ground was terrifying. I chastised myself for these thoughts of escape, because I was the king's prisoner and it was my duty not to shirk the fate allotted me; for beyond my misery, my loyalty to you was the stronger. Moreover, even if I were to climb over the battlements and drop to the other side, I knew not one soul on this desperate island to help me.

Beyond the fortress, the hill sloped down towards the tiny village. Partway down I spied a small kirk. It had no spire or tower, but I could see its shape was a cross from above and imagine the tiny nave within. It was the only other stone building on the island apart from the castle within the fortress, and I hoped I might be allowed to visit it for prayer soon.

In the last few years, I have found my sight has changed and, at times, I borrowed Ambrosius's spectacles to read more clearly – much to his annoyance, of course. As I looked out from the top of the fortress now, I discovered this change in my vision allowed me to see a greater distance. I was able to discern the islanders' homes clustered around the harbour. They were mostly empty, for it was not long after noon, and a time I assumed all the fishermen were still out at this time of year. I could see one of the village women, and someone who I assumed to be her daughter, sweeping together, clearing muck from their little cottage threshold, working in unison. It made my heart ache to watch the two of them and I tore my eyes away and looked in the other direction.

There was a jagged finger of land pointing out into the sea, the sight of which made me shiver. I knew instinctively that this lonesome windswept premonitory was most likely the island's execution site. I looked beyond it, across the narrow strait of choppy sea between the island and the mainland on the other side.

Heavy clouds were gathering anew with rain falling in sweeping lines upon the Varanger Peninsula on their way to Vardø island. Grey curtains concealed and then revealed Domen, the Devil's domain.

'The witches go and meet the Devil on Domen,' Helwig had told me in whispers, the first night, after I had put my rosemary out. 'The governor is determined to be rid of all witches in the north.' She shook her head. 'Be careful, lady.'

I gave her a haughty laugh. What an ignorant creature she was to even imagine that I, Fru Anna Rhodius, daughter of a king's physician and the king's prisoner, could ever be suspected of witchcraft.

I looked beyond the contours of the Domen Mountain to the vast emptiness of the north. It was even more barren and wild than you could ever imagine. Where did our world end and Hell begin?

I placed a hand on my belly, feeling the heat rise within me, my heart a little panicked. Sensing a shadow by my side I turned in fright to see a man dressed in black with a starched white ruff around his neck.

I knew immediately who he was, for the battle scar gave him away. I had been told Regional Governor Christopher Orning had been one of your most loyal and brave commanders of your armies in the recent victorious war against the Swedish. Even before his time in your armies, he had fought for your father and survived at least a decade of the thirty years of war between the kingdoms of Denmark and Sweden.

As I looked at him under the leaden skies, Governor Orning stood with the height and strength of a young soldier, but his face was cracked with life and death. The scar was the most prominent feature, marking a white line from the tip of his eyebrow all down his left cheek to the tip of his chin.

'Fru Rhodius, what are you doing up here?' His voice was surprisingly soft, but he was looking at me with displeasure.

His lack of formality or introduction was insulting, and I am sure he intended it thus.

'I shall return to my house,' I said, declining to give him any explanation, for I was prisoner enough, was I not, within these fortress walls? None had me chained up.

'Your prison house,' Governor Orning clarified. 'You would do well to remember your status, Fru Rhodius, as a king's prisoner under my jurisdiction, and not wander as you please.'

'I was not under the impression I am denied a daily walk for my good health—'

'Silence, woman!' the governor snapped. 'Did I ask for your opinion?'

I bit my tongue, although I could feel rage boiling up inside. The rain swept in from the peninsula, cold and stinging, and I pulled the hood of my cape over my head.

'Down you must go, Fru Rhodius,' he said, giving me a rough push towards the steps.

I fairly stumbled down them but managed to regain my balance at the bottom. The governor was so close behind me he stepped on the back of my pattens, as if with the intention of tripping me so I might break my neck, and all the while speaking into my back, as if to himself.

'I was told you might be a problem,' he said. 'I have been warned of your reputation as a haranguer. Statholder Trolle wrote to me and advised me I might be best to put a scold's bridle upon you, for even your husband was unable to silence you.'

At the mention of Statholder Trolle I felt my body bristle and wanted badly to retort. Tucked up my sleeves were so many clever things that I could say to this governor, but I willed my mouth to stay closed. My situation was bad enough and the idea of having one of those hideous bridles affixed to my face – metal shoved into my mouth, to clamp the tongue down – was truly abhorrent. I had seen them on the faces of common women who had displeased their husbands, named scolds by the authorities in Copenhagen and Bergen. These scolds were usually older women who said too much, as if they could not help but speak truth without a care for the consequences.

I had been as they in my need to speak freely, and confident of it, because I believed my privilege protected me, but it seemed in Vardø it did not.

'Forgive me, Governor,' I said, in as meek a voice as I could muster, though I was taut with indignation.

The sky split then, and the rain fell hard as I scurried towards my long-house, nearly slipping and falling in the muck, feeling the most ignoble I ever had in my entire life.

As I clattered up to the doorway, I turned to see the governor still standing in the courtyard, arms crossed, but he was no longer looking at me. He was peering up into the rain, and, as I followed his gaze, I saw the crow circling again, buffeted this way and that by the wind.

I thought it an odd sight indeed: the regional governor of Finnmark watching the crow as if it were something so much more significant than a black bird, and the crow wheeling above, not winging away from the rain and such scrutiny.

Chapter 10

Ingeborg

The Eve of St Hans. Ingeborg used to adore this one radiant day in the whole year. All the fishing families from the local villages gathered around a big fire on the smooth crescent of Ekkerøy beach. Ale would flow from pewter jugs. There would be the treat of fresh seal meat roasted on sticks, and bowls of *rømmekolle*, thick and creamy, made by those women who possessed cows. If the Reverend Jacobsen's back were turned, the children would skip upon the soft sand in their bare feet, playing games.

The preparations for this event would begin a few weeks before. Husbands fished early and close to home in June; afternoons were spent collecting turf from the bog and repairing village roofs. They worked late into the bright nights mending their boats in readiness for autumn, when they would leave for the winter fishing grounds, leaving aside old planks for the St Hans fire.

On the day of the high midnight sun, none were thinking of the dark months and their dangers. The air was filled with tiny, spinning motes of bog cotton from their gathering of peat. Ingeborg could smell the scent of the rich earth upon her skin from all the time spent on the marshes. As if rooting her to the land, reminding her: *This is where you belong.* The long stark winter might conceal the soft earth, but Ingeborg always carried its presence from midsummer. It was what she called her hope.

Before her father and Axell were gone, the five of them would be laden with offerings for St Hans' Eve: her mother would be carrying the best of all *rømmekolle*, and her father's seal would be the fattest of all. Axell would carry an army of herrings to add to the roastings. Kirsten's hair would be plaited with blåveis flowers Ingeborg and she had gathered from the bog. Dark blue petal stars peeking out of red curls.

But the year after Axell drowned, the magic of midsummer had waned. Their mother had refused to leave the cottage, and Kirsten had had to beg their father to bring them down to the beach and the celebrations. But all the colour was gone. Her father as if a ghost, and her brother's ghost among them. Ingeborg could not think of the year before and Axell spinning her along the beach, so that they had lost control and fallen tumbling into the shallows. Laughing so hard it had ached.

Last St Hans' Eve had been even worse with their father gone, and their mother still refusing to leave the cottage. She and Kirsten had tried to join in, but the pity from their neighbours had made Ingeborg miserable.

But this June night her mother was no longer hiding. Indeed, she had disappeared as she had so often done over the past few weeks. Ingeborg didn't want to think about what she was up to. All she knew was that she proudly wore the blue ribbon that Heinrich Brasche had given her, plaited in her red-gold tresses.

Her skirts may have been tattered, but her mother's hair was still her crowning glory.

Ingeborg had wanted to go off across the bogs on her own. But Kirsten was by her side, pleading to be taken down to the midsummer fire.

'Everyone will be there, Ingeborg,' Kirsten said plaintively, little Zacharias at her feet.

'We had best wait for Mamma,' she said.

'But all the food will be gone,' Kirsten wailed, clutching her tummy. 'I can smell it!'

Ingeborg felt sorry for her little sister, growing up when half the family was already gone.

'Very well,' she said. 'But leave Zacharias here. You don't want someone to put her to roast on the fire!'

Kirsten gave a horrified squeal, but her eyes shone with excitement. Ingeborg prayed her mother would return soon, for her absence would surely be noted.

*

It was a cloudless night, the midnight sun a deep, steaming red reflected upon the still sea. Ingeborg felt the fever of this eternal light burning inside her chest. It touched all of them in the village, inducing a manic energy just like the screeching kittiwakes as they dived towards the nesting cliffs.

The men were loud as they knocked back their ale, the women moving faster as they prepared the foods.

Stout Reverend Jacobsen walked among the villagers to ensure none partook of too much merriment, while Solve, her mother's cousin, drifted among the throng, pouring ale from her jug.

'Will you have some ale, Ingeborg?' she teased, as she passed by them.

Ingeborg shook her head, aware of the reverend glaring at them.

'Solve Nilsdatter, I've warned you before not to offer the children ale.'

'It is but a small cup, Reverend, and Ingeborg is near a grown woman,' Solve retorted, giving Ingeborg a wink.

She could see bruises upon Solve's face again. The glimmer in her eyes told Ingeborg her mother's cousin had already drunk a fair bit of ale herself. Ingeborg glanced over at Solve's husband, the fisherman Strycke Anderson. He was with the other men, but she could see him staring at his wife and her antics with displeasure.

Solve moved on and Ingeborg felt the urge to shadow her. But what could she do to help her, anyway? She had enough to worry about with her own mother absent and avoiding the questions of her neighbours.

The scent of roasted seal wafted around them, and Kirsten groaned. 'I'm so hungry, Inge,' her sister complained. 'When can we eat?'

Ingeborg felt a tug upon her sleeve. But it wasn't Kirsten. For there was Maren Olufsdatter.

She was even taller than Ingeborg remembered. She hadn't seen her since the day the girl had showed her the hare in the nest. Her skin looked burnished by the light of the fire, and flames glinted in her eyes, which had turned the darkest green.

'Good evening, Ingeborg and Kirsten Iversdatter,' she said, smiling at them.

'Who are you?' Kirsten asked.

'It's Solve's niece,' Ingeborg said. 'Maren Olufsdatter.'

It was the first time Solve had brought Maren to Ekkerøy, and some of the other women were glaring at her. She was, after all, the daughter of a renowned witch.

Maren appeared indifferent, turning to look at the fire, her nose crinkling at the scent of the roasting seal. 'Have you ever swum with the seals?' she asked Ingeborg.

'I can't swim.'

'I will teach you,' Maren said.

Ingeborg felt a hot seed of annoyance. Axell was supposed to have taught her to swim – and what good had it done for her brother?

'Have *you* swum with seals?' Kirsten asked Maren, a note of awe in her voice.

'Of course!' Maren replied. 'They took me to the bottom of the sea and there I met a *havsfrue*.'

'Was she very beautiful?' Kirsten asked, her eyes wide with fascination.

'Yes, indeed, and she sang to me.' Maren smiled, clasping her hands. 'But if we make her angry, she can bring terrible storms down upon us.'

'Is that where Daddy is? And Axell? At the bottom of the sea with a *havsfrue*?' Kirsten asked.

'Of course not, they're in Heaven with God Almighty. It's a story, Kirsten, that is all.' Ingeborg darted Maren a warning look.

'It is the truth,' Maren said, defiantly.

'What are you doing here, anyway?' Ingeborg bristled. 'Why did Solve not leave you back in Andersby to mind her boys?'

'Why, they came with us. My uncle brought us all in his boat.' Maren indicated little Peder now sitting on his father's shoulders, and Erik tugging on his breeches. 'It is not the boys I need to mind but their mother,' she said meaningfully, bringing a finger up to her face.

Ingeborg knew well what she meant but it was a thing to be ignored. She was shocked at Maren's openness, though a little part of her admired it. 'Kirsten, the meat is ready. Let's eat,' she said, reaching for her sister as she saw some of the men tearing strips off the roasted seal and skewering it with sticks.

'Are you coming?' Kirsten turned to Maren, but the tall girl shook her head.

'I don't eat seals,' she said. 'Because I can talk to them.'

Kirsten frowned, but Ingeborg pulled her away.

'What does she mean, Inge?' Kirsten asked her.

'It's nonsense,' Ingeborg told her sister. 'I don't think she is quite right in her mind.' But truthfully, Ingeborg was as intrigued as Kirsten by Maren's claim.

She felt the girl's gaze upon her as they made their way to the fire, and the idea of Maren Olufsdatter looking at her made her cheeks redden unbidden.

The two sisters ate every morsel of the roasted seal meat given to them. It was so fresh it still tasted of the sea, a flavour richer than any fish, flesh dense and dark as a reindeer's. Ingeborg licked her fingers, slick with seal oil. Her belly felt so full.

She was still perplexed by Maren Olufsdatter's claims. *How can you talk with a seal?* Seals existed for them to hunt. They would perish without their sustenance.

After they had eaten, Ingeborg and Kirsten sat upon the dunes, among the sea grass, watching all the other families. She had been asked by a few neighbours where her mother was.

Widow Krog had sighed and shaken her head when Ingeborg had lied that her mother was at home and Kirsten had shown her up by saying she wasn't.

The men were singing old folk songs, their voices heavy with the drink – once he had his large portion of seal meat, Reverend Jacobsen had disappeared home.

Solve had drained the last jug of ale and was trying to persuade some of the other women to dance with her, but they all shook their heads. She lifted the mucky hems of her skirt and staggered over towards Ingeborg.

'Girls, where's your mother?' Her words slurred. 'For surely, she will dance with me?'

'I will dance with you, Aunty,' Maren said.

Here Maren Olufsdatter was again, slinking up behind her. Hands on her hips. Encouraging her aunt to make a scene.

'But we need more than two to dance in a circle,' Solve declared, reaching out her hands to Kirsten.

Before Ingeborg could stop her, Kirsten had hopped up and was jumping up and down with glee.

'The thick clergyman has gone to his bed,' Maren said, offering her hand. 'There is none to care what we do now. When else can we be as free?'

Ingeborg tried not to look at Maren's face. The village called her 'strange looking', 'cast by a different colour', and 'foreigner'. But under the glow of the midnight sun, Ingeborg could not help but think she looked magnificent. She shrugged, but all the same she let Maren take her hand in hers.

The other girl's fingers curled around her own, and the warmth of their palms pressed together was surprisingly soothing.

On one side of Ingeborg was Kirsten, on the other Maren, and there in front of her the laughing face of Solve, pretty in her red *bøffelbay* skirt and lace collar, though her eyes were steeped in sadness.

There was no music, and as they danced the men stopped their singing. Ingeborg could feel their silent, censorious stares. Maren squeezed her hand and as Ingeborg turned to look at her, Maren's lips were moving, as if in silent prayer. But this was no homily. Ingeborg caught stray words upon the wind – *ring-a-ring* and *red curls* – entwined with the sound of the sea sweeping the shore.

As they slowly spun, all eyes upon them, Maren's voice grew bolder.

Ring-a-ring the girls
A pocket full of red curls
Hush-sha, push-ma.
We all fall down.

Ingeborg knew she should break up the dance. She knew it was wrong. But her body wouldn't let her. The rhyme was one she had never heard before, and yet it felt as if she knew the words before Maren uttered them.

Ring-a-ring the girls
A pocket full of red curls
To ashes! To ashes!
We all burn up.

Whose red curls? Solve's copper ringlets glittering beneath the midnight sun? Or her sister Kirsten's flaming locks, startling against her pale skin? But the image that flashed into Ingeborg's mind was of her mother's red hair, golden rivers of wantonness, tumbling over her shoulders.

Maren caught her eye with a dare in her expression, and Ingeborg wanted to sing with her with the taste of free spirit upon her lips. Sweet it would be, she was sure of it. How she wanted to sing along with Maren Olufsdatter.

> *Ring-a-ring the girls*
> *A pocket full of red curls*
> *Hush-sha, curse-ya.*
> *Now you fall down.*

Round and round the four of them spun, dancing to the jaunty rhythm of Maren's strange verse. Widow Krog stepped forward, her crooked walking stick held aloft. Ingeborg braced herself for its crack upon her back, and her admonition for them to stop their shameful spectacle. But the old woman didn't break their tiny ring. Far from it. She thumped her stick onto the heavy sand and then again. *Thump. Thump. Thump.* In time with Maren's verse.

The other women did not turn their backs on them, either. Was it the fever of Midsummer's Eve which led them astray? For one by one they stepped forward and joined their circle.

Barbra Olsdatter was first, pushing between Solve and Kirsten. Ingeborg let go of Kirsten's hand to allow Maritte Rasumusdatter in, who brought with her Karen Olsdatter, and then her sister Gundelle. After the mothers, sisters, cousins came the daughters. All the girls of their village. The ring of dancing women and girls grew and grew so that now Kirsten was right the other side of the circle. A wide smile had spread itself upon her sister's face, and her red curls bounced upon her shoulders. They danced in one waving spiral to the wind upon the sea, the birds calling in the sky, and the pounding of Widow Krog's walking stick. *Thump. Thump. Thump.* In time with the beating of their hearts.

How long did the women and girls dance for? Not long, but it felt like forever. The men in a hushed crowd, suddenly sober.

Which of those fishermen was so disturbed by the sight of his wife dancing that he had run from the beach to the reverend's house? Told him to come quick for the women were entranced.

'Stop this devilishness at once!' Reverend Jacobsen came tearing onto the sand, his black garments flapping as if the wings of a giant cormorant.

But it was as if the women's hands were interlocked with each other's. As if they couldn't stop even if they had wanted to. They were bewitched, but not by the Devil – no, by each other.

It was the husbands who broke the circle. Strycke wrenched Solve away, shaking her as if she were a bag of sticks. Ingeborg caught the heat on Maren's face as she stood between her uncle and his wife. The women scattered, some still with the light of abandon on their faces, but others confused, as if waking from a spell.

Reverend Jacobsen continued to berate them, picking on Widow Krog, who had stopped thumping her stick. She was gazing in bewilderment at the clergyman. 'I believed better of you, Dorette Krog,' Reverend Jacobsen was saying. 'I am not sure what Merchant Brasche will make of all this.'

Kirsten ran over to Ingeborg, tears glinting in her eyes. 'What did we do wrong, Inge?'

But before Ingeborg could reply, a woman's voice spoke up from behind them. 'Dancing is the invention of the Devil, child.'

Ingeborg wheeled around. Heinrich Brasche's wife stood there, looking at the scene on the beach in disgust. Pale wispy curls of hair strayed from beneath her white coif. Arms crossed, she was as tall and narrow as a stone pillar.

'I am shocked you allow such heathen practices in our village. What will my father-in-law Merchant Brasche say on it?' Fru Brasche turned to the Reverend Jacobsen.

'It's but one night in the year,' Reverend Jacobsen said, his forehead damp with sweat. 'And the fire and feasting were sanctioned by Merchant Brasche, as he believes it distracts them from their hardships.'

Fru Brasche did not look convinced, scowling when she saw Widow Krog. 'Well, here you are, Dorette,' she exclaimed. 'I have been waiting for my supper this long hour!'

Widow Krog lowered her head and scrambled up the dunes towards Fru Brasche. 'I am sorry, mistress,' she said, scuttering past Ingeborg and Kirsten. 'I will get to it.'

'Wait and return with me to my house,' Fru Brasche said. 'I have been looking for Heinrich.' She turned to the reverend, lowering her voice. 'Have you seen my husband? He can be a little familiar sometimes with the fisherfolk. Was he among the gathering?'

'No, indeed I have not seen Herr Brasche,' the reverend said, sounding shocked.

Widow Krog's eyes flickered involuntarily towards Ingeborg and Kirsten.

As quick as a hawk, Fru Brasche noticed the movement, casting a cold gaze their way. 'Who are these girls?' she asked the reverend.

'They are Widow Sigvaldsdatter's daughters,' he said.

Fru Brasche's expression turned even harder at the mention of their mother's name. 'I have heard of her; she owes us a great deal of money.' She eyed Ingeborg coldly before turning on her heel, Widow Krog scurrying behind her.

'Where is your mother, girls?' the reverend asked.

Ingeborg squeezed Kirsten's hand tight in warning. 'Home,' she lied. 'She finds Midsummer's Eve too sad since our father and brother's passing.'

'Indeed.' The reverend nodded, but with no glimmer of sympathy in his eyes. 'Go home, girls, and say your prayers. Ask for the Good Lord's forgiveness for taking part in your wicked dancing this evening.'

'Why did you lie to the priest?' Kirsten hissed to Ingeborg as they made their way up the dunes to the soft marshy grass. 'We don't know where Mamma is.'

'It's better no one knows, Kirsten.'

Upon the marsh they came across Maren Olufsdatter carrying Solve's youngest boy, Peder, on her hip, and dragging the other weary little soul, Erik, by the arm.

'Where's Solve?' Ingeborg asked.

'Fulfilling her wifely duties, in the sand dunes,' Maren spat out.

Ingeborg reddened, hoping Kirsten did not understand what Maren meant.

But Kirsten had other questions for Maren. 'Was your mamma a witch?' she piped up.

'Hush, Kirsten,' Ingeborg chided her, but Maren looked pleased to be asked such a question.

'Yes, of course. A very powerful witch. The governor himself was afraid of her.'

'Maren, you shouldn't talk about such things,' Ingeborg warned.

Maren shifted Peder onto her other hip, while little Erik looked ready to drop. Out of kindness to the little boy, Ingeborg picked him up.

'Why not?' Maren said. 'For I believe the only way to protect ourselves is to make them afraid of us.'

'Who are they?' Kirsten asked, wide eyed.

'The men in authority, little one,' she said, tousling Kirsten's red curls with her free hand. 'My mother was not like the other witches,' she said. 'Two familiars served her. One was a black crow and the other a great elk.'

'Have you ever seen the Devil?' Kirsten whispered, her voice hoarse with excitement.

Mischief danced in Maren's eyes. 'Of course, Kirsten Iversdatter. And so have you, for he can appear in many guises.'

Kirsten stopped walking and looked up at Maren in shock.

'The Devil can transform into all manner of creatures. He can be a big snapping hound, or a sly black cat, or even a little sparrow hopping across your cottage floor. Most times he comes as a man all in black. Disguised as a minister, but underneath his robe he is half beast, his hands as claws, with horns beneath his hat.'

Ingeborg felt her chest tighten and her mouth go dry. She had lived so many years dreading an encounter with the Devil. But Maren's words were nonsense, surely?

They passed Heinrich Brasche's house, aware of the flickering glow of candlelight within, imagining browbeaten Widow Krog serving the bad-tempered Fru Brasche as she waited upon her husband.

Why had they walked this way? Surely it was the longer route? And what was Maren doing with them? She should have waited for her aunt and uncle back at the beach.

Down the hill the three girls walked, the little boys asleep and heavy in their arms. Past the door of Heinrich Brasche's cowshed, which was a little ajar.

Ingeborg could hear a noise inside, apart from the rustling of the cows. Another sound. Panting, but not that of a dog. And then a woman's sigh, long and laden with release.

The three girls turned to look.

'Oh,' Maren breathed softly.

They walked back to their cottage wordlessly. Even Kirsten had no questions for Ingeborg. The sight of what Ingeborg had seen was stinging her eyes, making her want to scream. But she had to stay calm. Pretend they saw nothing at all.

'You had best sleep here,' she told Maren, pulling out skins for her, unable to meet her eyes. 'You can't carry both boys all the way back to Andersby.'

Maren put her hand upon her arm. 'Thank you, Ingeborg,' she said in a gentle voice, and Ingeborg was shamed to see the pity in her eyes.

They lay down but it was hard to sleep. The light streamed in through the cracks in the walls of their cottage and still her mother did not come home. Had she lost all reason? Or did she not care what might happen to her two daughters – worth so much less than one son?

Ingeborg watched Kirsten curl around Zacharias, two innocent lambs together, and the boys cosied in next to Maren. She could see the girl's chest rising and falling in slumber. She waited for her mother's return, but the birds kept on screeching the whole night long, and still, she didn't appear.

The dreadful image remained. Her mother with skirts up around her waist, backside naked, skin gleaming opalescent in the shadowy cowshed; Heinrich Brasche pushed up behind her, his green doublet discarded on the byre. His buttocks bare. Try as she might, Ingeborg couldn't push the picture away, but it began to take on a different form: Heinrich Brasche taller, dressed in black, horns sprouting from the top of his head, keeping hold of her mother's waist with claws not fingers.

When she fell asleep at last, Ingeborg could hear them panting in sinful fornication in her dreams.

Her sigh, and then his howl, like a wolf to the moon.

Chapter 11

Anna

It was well-nigh impossible to sleep during the summer weeks of eternal light. I pulled the window flap down permanently to retain the bedchamber gloom, but it was not the light that bothered me so much as the cacophony of seabirds screeching relentlessly on their way to the nesting cliffs.

The first night they came, I woke up in fright and ran into the other chamber to the pallet where Helwig slept.

'Wake up!' I shook her shoulders. 'Who's that screaming?'

'Mistress, it's just the birds,' she said, rubbing her eyes with grubby hands.

'But such a hellish noise, one I have never heard before.'

'They come back to nest for the summer,' Helwig explained. 'They're flying to the cliffs across the sea at the village of Ekkerøy.' She hauled herself off her pallet, clearly pleased that here was something she knew all about and I knew nothing of. 'Come and see.'

She opened our door – for it was never locked. All Lockhert needed to do was fasten the fortress gates and this was a prison for us all.

I followed Helwig out into the fortress courtyard. I had no idea what time it was, for it may have been the middle of the night since the sun never set in this month up north. The delicate northern sky looked as those in the tiny Netherlandish paintings inlaid within the panels of your winter room while its serenity was assaulted by white birds, thousands of them, flying in a horde over the fortress.

'They come from the east,' she said. 'Always to nest in Ekkerøy, along with the seagulls and peregrines. Their eggs are delicious.' She smiled, a toothy grin. 'If we are fortunate, the governor might allow us a few.'

The idea of eggs made my stomach groan. In my home in Bergen, we were often wont to eat quails' eggs, griddled with a little butter.

We returned to the grim prison longhouse and, granted, it was gloomy – always so gloomy – but the loudness of birds screeching meant I could not find sleep again. There was a panic in their sound that made my heart race with anticipation faster and faster, so I was afraid it might burst from me.

The next day the clamour of the birds continued. Helwig told me I must get used to it as the noise would persist the whole of our short summer.

I was not sure how much I could trust Helwig. A lady should be able to share all her secrets with her maid, but Helwig was also my gaoler, was she not? She watched me with a suspicious eye as I opened up my medicine chest and catalogued its contents. How I wished I could grow some herbs and plants, but I doubted this rock of an island had much to offer me by way of botanical resources.

Helwig asked me from time to time what each dried leaf, root, jar of powder or tincture might be used for. I told her comfrey root was good for so many ailments, especially bleedings; the mint leaves soften the stomach relieving excess wind, and if powdered eased childbirth pains; while my decoction of red roses was very good for headaches, and pains in the eyes, ears and gums.

She reached over and picked up my bottle of stinking arrach syrup. 'And what is this for?'

I was annoyed she had touched my precious concoction, so I told her to pull out the stopper and smell it. She immediately recoiled as if stung, and I bit my lip to supress an unladylike guffaw.

'It stinks,' she said. 'Like rotten fish. What is this foul stuff?'

'Just by smelling the syrup you have benefited your womb,' I informed Helwig. 'Truly there is no better syrup to be taken for a woman in childbirth. It cools the womb – it is over-heating of the womb which is the greatest cause of hard labour.'

She gave me a queer look.

'Stinking arrach is ruled by the planet Venus, under the sign of Scorpio,' I told Helwig. 'There is no better cure for afflictions of the womb or aid in childbirth.'

'Are you experienced in the art of birthing?'

I raised my head, my chest proud.

'I have brought over one hundred babies into this world,' I said. 'My husband and my father were physicians. I learnt much from them, but my midwifery was also passed on to me by my mother.'

'There is no midwife any more on Vardø'.

'What happened to her?'

'She was a witch,' Helwig said in a low voice. Although there was none around to hear us. 'We've not had a midwife for ten years. No woman wishes to be called such in these times.'

She didn't need to explain further, for many of the witches I had heard of had been midwives. But I was grounded in science and respectability and a different kind of midwife from these cunning country women.

'We have had to help each other,' Helwig said, shaking her head sorrowfully. 'Many of the island women have died birthing babies.'

'This is a shame,' I said, and I meant it. My purpose has always been to preserve the life of the innocent and I wish at least some of the island women have some simple level of my knowledge to assist them.

'And mistress, the governor's wife, is with child too,' she said. 'Have you seen her?'

'I have not been invited within the governor's house yet,' I said, tartly.

Near three months had passed and still I had not been introduced to the only other lady on the island of Vardø.

'Fru Orning isn't as hardy as an island woman,' Helwig said, carefully.

I didn't grace her comment with a reply, for what was the governor's wife to me, but a phantom denied my introduction?

'She is quite a tiny thing,' Helwig continued.

The image of the tall governor returned in my mind. Yesterday I had seen him, Lockhert and some of his men loaded with weaponry, depart on a big hunt.

Only three soldiers, including the young Captain Hans, were left guarding me, stationed in the gatehouse. I had walked by them earlier while taking a surreptitious look at the sturdy fortress gates – and the chains around them. As I circled once more around the fortress, my back prickled and I wheeled around, but there was not a soul in the yard. Steam plumed from the washhouse where Helwig was occupied in her work, so it could not have been she.

I spun slowly, looking up instinctively to the windows of the castle. Up high in one of the smallest windows I caught sight of a face hidden, apart from the eyes, by a big black fan. Maybe she had been watching me every day of my captivity, gloating at my weary, lonesome walks around the courtyard. I looked up at her, for why should I hide my head in shame?

Her eyes opened wide, and her eyebrows arched in surprise to have been caught out.

I curtsied, spreading my skirts wide, my head bowed. When I raised my eyes to her again, she was gone from the window.

I was a little insulted, because no lady should walk away from a curtsey.

With the help of poppy-oil-infused treacle, I was able to fall asleep in the endless bright of the June nights. But the noise of the shrieking birds inhabited my dreams, and I awoke with my heart racing, slick with sweat, while the skins I slept beneath were wet from my heat.

When I opened the halibut flap to let in some cool, clean air into my sticky chamber, it was impossible to tell what time it might be. The middle of the night and the morning looked the same, with no shade to take refuge in.

Oh, my king, how exposed I feel every waking moment.

The governor, Lockhert and his men returned with game from their hunt on the mainland. I watched them through a crack in my door as they marched into the castle courtyard. It did not seem to me they had much to show for their endeavours: a brace of hares, and a pile of ptarmigan – no catch worthy to be proud of.

Helwig later revealed the governor was in foul humour because they had tracked an elk for three days, dug a pit for it – which never failed to catch the beasts – and yet the elk had eluded them.

'The rumour is someone destroyed the trap in the woods,' she told me. 'The governor is saying it is witches.'

'How do you know all this?' I asked Helwig.

'Guri told me. She's the maid to the governor's wife,' Helwig said, crossing her arms, pleased with her tale. 'They chased the elk and sent it straight towards their pit. It should have fallen in, but it flew over it as if by magic!'

The governor did not allow any of the game to grace my table. The waft of roasting ptarmigan drifted across the courtyard and scoffed at me as I shovelled my greasy fish broth into my mouth. My belly ached and how I hungered for victuals that filled me – cheese, meat, and bread.

I alleviated my cravings by sucking on one of my sugared almonds, and then I took another slice of one of my lemons, sprinkling it with more sugar, and a sup of something else to help me sleep – but I could not. The infernal caterwauling of the birds was as if inside my head, and when I closed my eyes all I saw was the court in Copenhagen dancing, coloured gowns twirling around and around and all the gay memories of my past gibing at me.

I must have drifted off because I was rudely awakened by Helwig tugging on my sleeve. 'Mistress,' she said. 'Mistress, wake up.'

'How dare you lay your hands upon me—?' I began to say, but she talked over me in a panic.

'It's Fru Orning, the governor's wife,' she said. 'You must come. Guri told the governor you have the skills of a midwife.'

'How did she know?' I was furious.

'I told her,' Helwig said in a small voice. 'He has ordered that you must come and assist in the birth.'

I had no desire whatsoever to help the governor's wife in her birthing, but then Helwig said something else. 'Maybe he will be softer on you afterwards,' she said.

I clenched my teeth. 'Only if it goes well.'

As soon as I entered the birthing chamber, I could see it was too late, for the stench of blood hit me in a wave. The governor's wife lay upon a vast bed, tiny and washed up, as if flotsam. The skin upon her cheeks was pocked and ghastly white, but all around her lower regions was red, while her bedsheets were bathed in crimson.

Her maid, Guri, was distraught, cradling a tiny bundle in her arms, tears dripping down her face and not becoming her station.

'Give the baby to me,' I ordered her, and she handed me the precious shape.

Ah, my king, it was a perfect baby with skin so pale, dark curls of hair as if pasted upon its head, yet clearly not one breath had been taken in this life as its lips were tinged blue and it was silent.

Guri had cleaned the babe, and it was swaddled tight, only the moon of its tiny perfect face visible, eyes closed, never to have opened.

'It's too late,' I said. 'The babe is dead.'

'It came too soon,' Guri said, her face swollen from crying.

I placed the dead babe in the crib, not knowing where else to put the poor whelp down, for I needed rid of the sensation of the babe's still body against my breast.

Helwig was behind me muttering prayers as Guri placed a clammy hand on my arm.

I shook it off. How familiar these northern women were.

'Save my mistress,' she begged me, her eyes wide with dread.

'Does the governor know the babe is stillborn?' I asked the maid.

She shook her head slowly.

'Let's not tell him, then, not yet, for we need no disturbances.'

The governor's wife was frail and young, and I was not sure her life could be saved. She had lost so much blood, and still she was bleeding, but as any good physician I refused to retreat and opened up my medicine chest, closing my eyes and taking a deep breath before I began.

I took out my bottle of stinking arrach syrup and ladled a spoonful into the girl's mouth.

She curled her nose at the smell and taste, which was a good sign indeed.

'Bring me hot water boiled, plenty of salt and more linens,' I ordered Helwig, while Guri began to sob again.

'She won't stop bleeding, lady!' she cried.

'Cease your weeping,' I snapped at her. 'Do precisely as I say.'

Guri smeared her wet face with her sleeve and applied herself with dedication to the tasks I set her.

'Go and boil some wine and add a thimbleful of fennel seed to it,' I told her, handing her my bottle of fennel seeds. 'Bring it back as soon as you can.'

I took out my green hoarhound syrup and, raising the governor's wife up, encouraged her to take a spoonful. Her eyes fluttered and she moaned. I prayed this would be enough to expel the afterbirth.

'I need you to push again,' I whispered into her ear. 'To save your life, Fru Orning.'

The slight girl raised herself up on her elbows and looked at me. She had beautiful brown eyes, like a gentle doe, though her face was badly scarred from the pox.

'It's coming,' she whispered.

Thank the Good Lord, the afterbirth flooded out in one big gush of blood. In the meantime, Guri had returned with the fennel wine.

'Help your mistress drink it up,' I told her. 'It will ensure her womb is fully cleansed.'

Guri was shaking as she helped her mistress drink the wine. 'This is the work of witches,' she whispered.

I ignored her comment and busied myself staying the bleeding by making a poultice with some of my comfrey root. It looked to me as if the governor's wife was of melancholic humours, ruled by the moon, and in the sign of Cancer.

When she had recovered a little strength – for by now I did not doubt my ability to save her – I would prescribe a bath with my decoction of bay leaves and berries. The bay tree is of the Sun, in the sign of Leo, and thus has great defence against any witchcraft.

This is my battleground, my king. You send your men out to fight for our kingdom, with so many boys slain before they have more than a few chin hairs. But we women fight too, for our war is on the birthing bed. Your soldiers come into the world through their mothers' struggles, and we go into battle willingly because the rewards are great. But when they are not . . . well, I have known this pain, for it is buried deep within me. I may have lost the key to it, and it is indeed as well, for I never wish to open my suffering up again. Though each time I'm called as a midwife, the old wounds begin to open and a part of me wonders if this young girl would be better off in the next world. For if it were so, years of pregnancies – some miscarrying, some birthing – would be avoided and her suffering lessened.

I have seen so many young women die in the birthing chamber – more than the babes born; each girl giving their life for the new life.

But the governor's wife would not die, I was sure of it.

Helwig returned with the water and linens. She and Guri pulled away the bloody sheets, and slid fresh linens under the governor's wife, while I encouraged her to finish the wine warmed with fennel.

When I brought the cup to her mouth her eyelids fluttered, and she gave a soft moan.

'What is her Christian name?' I asked Guri.

'It's Elisa,' she said.

'Elisa,' I said, gently. 'Drink all of this.'

This girl looked no more than twenty years and yet her husband Governor Orning was the age of her father. It was distasteful to me, but a common enough occurrence in our times.

Now that she was more alert, Elisa's eyes were darting around the chamber. I knew what she was looking for, of course, but also knew that she must drink the brew. The bleeding could begin again if she did not, and already she was as white as the linens, looking as if she might crumble into nothing any moment.

'My baby,' she whispered, hoarsely.

I ignored her, slowly spooning the fennel wine into her protesting mouth. 'You must drink this,' I told her.

She pushed my hand away with more strength than I expected. 'The baby!' She turned to look at her maid. 'Guri, where's the baby?'

Guri began to cry again, unable to look at her mistress and turning away her head.

'No!' Elisa gasped, looking frightened. 'He will be so angry.'

'Fru Orning, you must drink this to get well,' I insisted, attempting to spoon more of my healing brew into her mouth.

'No,' she declared, shaking her head. 'Tell me what happened!'

The words were heavy in my mouth. 'I am sorry. I was called too late,' I said. 'The baby is with God in Heaven now.'

She stared at me, wild eyed. 'He will kill me!' she whispered in horror.

Before I could stop her, Guri picked up the swaddled bundle that I had placed, still as a cold stone, in the crib. We had forgotten all about the babe, so busy we had been trying to save its mother's life.

'What are you doing?' I hissed at Guri, but she was already offering the bundle to the governor's wife.

'She was a girl,' Guri told her mistress.

Elisa pushed the bundle away. 'Get it away from me! I can't look, I can't,' she said, in great distress.

Guri looked shocked and confused, clutching the dead baby to her.

'Can the babe not be saved?' Elisa said, turning to me. 'Fru Rhodius, please, I beg you!'

We had never met, but of course she knew who I was, for Fru Orning had been the face at the castle window watching me on my ambulation.

'I am sorry,' I said. 'The baby had passed over by the time I arrived.'

She bent her head down and her fair fine hair trailed onto her wet cheeks. I could not be sure who she was crying for: herself or the lost baby.

None spoke, and for the first time that night I could hear the birds outside, screaming and squalling as in lamentation.

'Does he know yet?' I heard the faint whisper of Fru Orning, from the bed.

The room went quite still, the menace of the governor already present.

'No, mistress,' Guri replied.

Fru Orning turned to me. Her scarred face was tinged yellow, but she had stopped bleeding.

'Fru Rhodius, will you tell him?' she said in a small voice. 'I can't face his rage.'

The maids looked frightened, but I was not afraid of the governor.

'I will, but you must drink the potion I made you,' I promised. 'It will bring you healing.'

The contrast between the great hall in the governor's house and my longhouse prison could not have been greater. Light flooded through high glass windows, filling the whole room with a golden glow. The wooden floors were clean-swept and polished, and the walls were covered in beautiful old tapestries of hunting scenes from the past – men high on their horses, throwing spears at a small brown bear, its eyes rolling in terror.

As I walked further into the hall, it felt to me as though it were pulsing with heat, but I couldn't take my cape off as my skirts and chemise were spattered with blood from the governor's wife. I cast my eyes down to my feet and saw the brocade slippers you gave me were smeared with muck from my hasty run across the dirty courtyard, despite my pattens.

As I walked the length of the chamber the governor rose from his chair by the fireplace and strode towards me, his expression grim.

He knows about his lost child, I thought; indeed, the news would have spread as soon as Helwig went to get the water and linens. Governor Orning was a man who would know every word his servants said. But why had he not climbed the stairs to his wife's bedchamber to console her?

'Is it true?' he asked me. 'Is my child perished?'

'I am afraid it is so, Governor,' I said, bowing my head.

'But you are a skilled midwife, Fru Rhodius. Why could you not save my son?'

'It was a girl,' I corrected, immediately wishing I had held my tongue upon this detail, as his face clouded.

'I was called too late, for by the time I arrived the baby had already been born.' I licked my lips. 'She never took breath. She is with baby Jesus and the Good Lord now.'

'Damn you, Fru Rhodius.' The governor slammed his hand upon the table so suddenly I started in fright.

'It is not my fault,' I said, hastily. 'I have seen this many times. The babe came too soon.'

'But why did the baby come too soon, Fru Rhodius?' He ranted at me. 'Why is my child taken from me? When I am a loyal servant of the king and God, why have I been blighted?'

'It is God's will, Governor.'

'But what is new here on our island of Vardø? Who has brought the Devil himself into my home, to curse me and my child?'

I refused to respond to his abhorrent implication.

'Your maid Helwig has told me you have a chest full of strange potions and herbs,' the governor continued.

That little snake. Helwig! 'Is this not witchery? Have you come into my home and cursed my family, woman? For I believe it is so!'

'I possess a physician's chest of herbs and tinctures which has saved your wife's life, Governor,' I defended myself, alarmed by the Governor's accusations.

He waved his hand away dismissively as if the life of his wife were of little value to him. I noted for the first time two large wolfhounds either side of him, their big tongues lolling out of their heavy jaws.

'I believe you a witch, Fru Rhodius, directing maleficium towards me.' He threw the words at me, and I recoiled.

'Governor, I am a devout servant of our Lord—' I began, panic flooding through my veins.

'It was witches who sabotaged our hunt, gave the elk the power to fly over the pit!' he declared. 'Truly, it was a lurid spectacle to witness!'

He took a threatening step towards me, and the wolfhounds growled as he moved closer. 'I believe you are in coven with other witches, in league with the Devil and I shall have you burned upon the stake for it!' he raged.

Terror swept through me at his threat.

'I am a goodly, devout woman, a loyal servant of our king,' I pleaded.

'But that is what all witches claim!'

For a moment, an image flickered in my head of the execution site I could see from the fortress walls and a fire blazing there, and I imagined Governor Orning might be thinking of it too, by the look in his eyes.

I had no time to dally if I were to save myself. 'I believe King Frederick has sent me to Vardø to help you, Governor,' I said in a rush.

The governor raised his eyebrows, curiosity calming his rage. 'Do you now, Fru Rhodius?'

'You speak the truth, Governor, for there are witches here in the north, but I am not one of them. The king wishes us to rid this region of them.'

'And what makes you presume you are chosen by the king in this task?' The governor said looking grim. 'Are you not an enemy of the king, a prisoner—'

'Never!' I declared passionately. 'I love my king and would pledge my life to him.'

Indeed, you know this! I have done all for you, my king!

The look in Governor Orning's eyes lifted, their slate lightening to cold grey.

'I can be of assistance to you.' I licked my lips nervously. 'Under the laws of our land you may arrest the suspected witches, but you will have to hear their confessions to gain your convictions. Witches, as you may know, are wily creatures, but the women will confide in me because I am another woman, and a prisoner, too. I will soften them to trust me and then they will reveal their darkest secrets.'

He looked thoughtful, his grey eyes lit by sparked flints. 'I have heard these witches cavort with the Devil on Domen when their husbands are gone fishing. They sneak up to the top of the mountain and they bare themselves naked to him.' He continued, stroking the head of one of his wolfhounds, his eyes fixed on me, a gleam of fervour in them. 'If that were not depraved enough, these mothers sacrifice their own daughters to the Devil. Young girls, virgins, are betrothed to the Dark Lord.'

'Such wickedness,' I whispered, my heart tight in my chest. 'What woman could do such a thing to her own daughter?'

'Fru Rhodius, I command you to assist me in the battle against the witches of Varanger!'

I nodded with as much dignity as I could muster, relief flooding me as well as shame. I had deflected his suspicion to others. I desired to know if he would reward me, but I decided it need not be said for I did not require his rewards.

I will purge the north of evil and when you, my king, have seen what I have done for you, surely I will go home?

It was only as I was walking out of his golden hall that the governor called out to me, an afterthought. 'Will Fru Orning live?'

'I believe she will,' I told him, turning.

'Get rid of the dead babe, Fru Rhodius,' he said. 'I do not wish to look at the cursed thing.'

He stood with his back against one of the windows. Light illuminated the white of his hair and the lines in his skin. I was struck by how very advanced his years were, while his wife was little more than a child.

Back upstairs, Fru Orning was suffering from terrible pains in her belly. To abate them, I dropped some poppy oil into the fennel wine.

'Take her away,' she whispered, as her eyelids closed.

I waited to hear her breath deepen, and then I instructed Helwig to pick up the babe.

'Please, no, Fru Rhodius,' she said, aghast.

'You must do as I say,' I insisted – my revenge upon Helwig for telling the governor I was a midwife and possessed herbal and healing remedies.

I picked up my medicine chest, and Helwig, carrying the stiff bundle, followed me out of the bedchamber and down the stairs of the castle. We passed not a soul and it could have been night, although it was impossible to tell for the light was relentless without.

We crossed the fortress courtyard. The governor had not told me where to bury the babe, but the ground was as hard as rock.

'Where should we bring it?' Helwig asked. 'Fru Rhodius, I want rid of it.'

'We need a means by which to dig a hole,' I told her, wishing there had been an opportunity to baptise the babe before it had perished. The poor lost soul surely belonged in a Christian burial ground. But I was learning that the governor's ways were cruel and strange.

I could think of no other person who might have a tool for our task than Bailiff Lockhert. I walked to the gatehouse and banged on the door. It was opened by the hulking figure of the man himself, who glowered down at me.

'The governor has requested we bury the babe lost to him and Fru Orning, but we have no means to dig—' I said in a rush.

'Give it to me.' The bailiff butted in, his countenance expressing no reaction. 'The Governor came and told me witches cursed his son.'

'But what will you do?' I heard myself ask, for I didn't like to pass over this lost soul to the gruesome bailiff.

'It was not baptised. Best 'tis burnt so the Devil can't possess its soul.'

Helwig gave a little hiccup of distress but handed the dead babe over all the same. Lockhert took hold as if it were a lump of turf, nothing more.

I pivoted towards the door in my clunky pattens, for I wished no more of the sorry matter.

'Are you to help us hunt the witches now, Fru Anna?' Lockhert called out to me as I walked away, a jeering note in his voice. 'You had better not let the governor down!'

I collapsed on my bed, lugging the cold skins over my worn-out bones, and kicking my muddied slippers off. I was still in my chemise stained with Fru Orning's blood, but I was too tired to remove it. Though when I tried to sleep I could not, for my heart was beating rapidly, and thoughts whirled in my mind.

I had made promises to the governor I was worried I could not keep.

Chapter 12

Ingeborg

Reverend Jacobsen preached with new fervour after the dancing on the Eve of St Hans. The fleeting summer faded, while the rain and wind swept in from the west, drenching their village in bleak grey light, washing across the bog, and whistling through the scrawny birch woods.

On rare days of dry, Ingeborg gathered the last flares of colour in the woods, under her feet a pale path of light as she wandered through the trees. She brought them into the dim cottage: the heathers upon the marsh, purple and green above the black earth; leaves of gold falling from the birch trees and spinning to the ground.

Ingeborg had given up hunting in the woods. Her snares were always tampered with. In their place, however, would always be a gift: a lidded dish full of blueberries, a small pot of creamy butter, bunches of herbs and root tubers, clusters of earthy mushrooms, or fronds of seaweed, roasted and salty. Her annoyance had turned to wonder how this girl, Maren Olufsdatter, could conjure such delicious nourishment from foraging in their bleak terrain.

On Sundays, all the village women wore what best they had. Wool skirts and bodices in faded dyes. Their linens cream or beige from wear, as were the kerchiefs around their shoulders, aprons, and coifs to cover their hair. Not one curl of hair allowed to stray. A challenge always for Kirsten, whose red mop refused to submit to the confinement.

All the fisherfolk were scrubbed clean with cold well water as they shuffled, stiff and uncomfortable, with ruddy faces, into the tiny kirk. Everyone crammed into the standing space. All their smells mixing, making Ingeborg feel queasy as Reverend Jacobsen's voice droned on.

The only way she could stop herself from running out of the stuffy kirk, was to let her mind drift. As though she could separate her thought from her body.

It was a nice feeling then, to float over the whole mass of the village and watch them. Her neighbours trying to hide their boredom and yawns. She would float over Merchant Brasche, and his son Heinrich, his wife and their children in the front pews of the church. Marvel at their straight backs, and their dignified concentration. Even the children sat upright and composed. But maybe it was easier to sit still in your own pew, with soft cushions to kneel upon. She lingered over them, taking in the finery of Fru Brasche's silk bodice embroidered in the deepest blue of the northern spring skies. How well it would look upon her mother. Fru Brasche was rapt, absorbing every word Reverend Jacobsen said, her mouth whispering prayers, while her husband Heinrich, with restless eyes, looked more like a horse about to bolt. Clouds of misery emanated from the couple.

Reverend Jacobsen preached, framed by his grand altarpiece with its carvings, little pillars and twisting vines. Behind him a large oil paint-ing of the same Brasche family – the old merchant and his wife, along with their two sons, one of them Heinrich, and two daughters. All of them dressed in austere black, with large white ruffs, their hands clasped in prayer. At the front of the painting were three swaddled babies, the infants that had not survived. These painted Brasches gazed back at the congregation in judgement.

Ingeborg floated back to her body, squashed in next to her mother and her sister. Now she listened to what the reverend was telling them, set to the sound of the waves crashing against the rocks outside the tiny kirk.

'The Devil may appear to you at first as a man,' he warned them, 'but if you look closely you will know it is the Evil One, for he may have claws for hands, or strange staring eyes like a cow. And always' – he raised his finger, pointing at the villagers – 'he will be dressed in black from head to toe.'

Was not Reverend Jacobsen himself dressed all in black? Apart from the stiff white ruff attached so tightly around his neck his flesh bulged over its edge, red and angry. But the rest of him was layer after layer of black. So much cloth, it was hard to make out the shape of his rotund body beneath.

'The Devil will make promises to you of wealth, but he does not have the power to give you these things. Do not believe it. He wishes to make you his servant. The Evil One directs you to wreak destruction and death upon your own husbands, brothers and sons.'

Ah, of course, Reverend Jacobsen was warning the women. For soon, their husbands would be leaving for the winter fishing grounds and gone for months. The dark weeks were the time of temptation.

The reverend took a step forward, sweeping his hand as if to bless the whole congregation. 'There are many devils,' he said in a dramatic hush. 'Each witch serves her own demon, whom she gives herself to.'

Ingeborg couldn't see Fru Brasche's face now, but she noticed the tilt of her head, imagined the fervent expression on her face. What the reverend meant was very bad women had sex with the Devil and then they became witches.

An unwelcome image surfaced in her mind. Her mother and Heinrich Brasche together in his cowshed on Midsummer's Eve. She glanced down at Kirsten fidgeting next to her. Was she remembering the same? But her little sister didn't appear to be listening to the reverend. Instead, she was twirling a loose thread of her apron around her little finger, tugging it so it might fray.

Ingeborg looked at her mother. She was so very beautiful – such a danger for a young widow. There was the slender line of her neck, with tiny tufts of gold hair visible at the nape of her coif. Her unblemished skin so soft upon her cheek, unlike the wrinkles of Fru Brasche.

Her mother was standing very still, and she was rapt too. But when Ingeborg followed her mother's gaze it was not directed at Reverend Jacobsen.

She was staring quite openly at the back of Heinrich Brasche's head.

There were the thick chestnut locks of the young gentleman; his straight back, unworn by hauling nets and gruelling labour. So tall, unweighted by the worries of feeding his family. Was he the Devil sitting among them even?

'To practise their dark magic, these foul women will call for their devil's apostle or their familiar,' Reverend Jacobsen continued.

Hadn't Maren Olufsdatter told Ingeborg and Kirsten her mother had two familiars – a black crow and a big elk? Ingeborg licked her lips. They were so dry and, more than anything, she wanted a drink of water. The kirk felt suffocating. What had Maren said? *The only way to protect ourselves is to make them afraid of us.*

They had claimed Maren's mother had sat atop a barrel floating on the ocean, arms raised, striking jagged white lightning into the wild sea, black hair as hissing snakes in the winter storm.

Was this how to make them afraid, with stories of witchcraft and weather magic?

Reverend Jacobsen had finished his sermon. They were all kneeling. The cold floor of the kirk, hard upon her knees and all the villagers huddled together. Someone farted, and Kirsten giggled next to her.

Ingeborg felt the urge to laugh too. She pressed her hands together and closed her eyes. Gave Kirsten a pinch to stop her giggles. They had been told laughter, and pleasure, belonged to the Devil.

'Protect my mother from the Evil One and his temptation of pleasure,' she whispered.

The Devil was dancing in her head. He had the same thick brown hair and hazelnut eyes as Heinrich Brasche. Kicking his legs in a little jig, hands on his hips and taking her mother's hand, her red-gold hair flying free like a flag of abandon. The Devil and her mother spinning and spinning. Dancing so wild not a soul could break them.

The last Sunday in August was golden with a soft breeze slipping in from the west. A rare flourishing of warmth before the cold east wind began to blow. The villagers streamed out of the church, gasping in the sweet air and light as if taking their first breaths of life.

When they got home, Ingeborg and Kirsten pulled off their confining coifs and shook out their hair.

'Let's collect the last of the blueberries,' Ingeborg suggested.

Kirsten clapped her hands in delight. 'Can I bring Zacharias?'

'No, silly billy, she'll get in the way.'

'She's a very good lambkins, better than a dog.'

'She might get snatched by a fox,' Ingeborg warned. 'You don't want to lose Zacharias, do you?'

'Don't encourage your sister in her affections for the lamb,' their mother said in a cold voice. 'Kirsten, you know well the lamb is our livestock. One day it will be slaughtered for its flesh.'

Kirsten's face clouded but she said nothing, knowing their mother would slap her for insolence if she responded.

'Mother, will you come with us to collect berries in the woods?' Ingeborg suggested, while Kirsten tugged on her skirt, hissing, 'No!'

Ingeborg wanted to keep her mother close by and away from the merchant's son.

But Zigri Sigvaldsdatter shook her head. She had already shaken out her blue ribbon and was twisting it in her hair. 'No, girls, I have other business to attend to,' she said.

'Mother, remember Reverend Jacobsen's words this morning,' Ingeborg warned in a low voice.

Her mother looked startled, her pale cheeks at once rosy. 'What are you implying, Ingeborg?'

There was a heavy, difficult silence. The words dried up in Ingeborg's throat. She wanted to shout at her mother. *Don't go dallying in Heinrich Brasche's cowshed because someone else will see you, just like we did!* But her mother's expression was resolute. She had tasted something she clearly craved more of, and Ingeborg knew all her warnings would only result in a slap across her own face.

She shook her head and shrugged her shoulders, picking up one of the baskets, and handing the other to Kirsten.

How Ingeborg treasured their scant woods. She had heard there was not one tree on the island of Vardø where the governor of Finnmark dwelled. How could those who lived there bear it? She adored her trees, thin and spindly as they were.

She and Kirsten ran among the birch and pine. Many leaves had already fallen, but of course the spruce was still thick, and she inhaled the clearing scent of pine. Let her fears about her mother and Heinrich Brasche fade.

As they approached the bushes of blueberries, they saw another figure with a basket on her arm, bending down and collecting the plump, dusky berries.

'Maren Olufsdatter!' Kirsten called out.

Maren spun around.

'Greetings, Iversdatter girls,' she welcomed them. 'The land is rich!'

Maren's flurries of crow-black hair fell all the way to her waist. She was as tall as Ingeborg's father had been, narrow-hipped, and long-legged as a colt.

Maren led them into an enclave within the woods, the ground carpeted with blueberry shrubs.

'My Sámi friend, Zare, showed me this place,' she said, licking the tips of her fingers already blue from berry juice. 'He's the son of the Sámi woman, Elli, who was arrested with my mother.'

'Did she die as your mother did?' Ingeborg asked.

'No, she escaped the fortress!' Maren exclaimed. 'Elli still lives.'

They ate and they picked, until their lips were mauve, and their bellies ached.

After a while, Kirsten sat down heavily in the undergrowth, clasping her tummy. 'I am sick,' she said, groaning.

'Chew on this and all will be well again.' Maren handed Kirsten a sprig of mint.

Maren plonked her brimming basket down and stretched out on the ground next to Kirsten. Her arms and legs were splayed in an unseemly manner and Ingeborg could see the dark skin of her legs under her bunched-up skirts. 'Let's rest for a little while,' she declared, and Kirsten, delighted to be escaping berry-collecting duties, lay down next to her.

'Kirsten, the ground could be damp. Get up at once,' Ingeborg protested.

'Oh, but it's not,' Maren said, sitting up. 'Take a rest, Ingeborg. You work so hard all the time.'

Ingeborg gingerly sat down. She expected the earth to be cold and hard, but it felt softer than their birch branch beds. Moreover, she could feel warmth within the ground, and it was comforting.

'Would you like to hear a story?' Maren said, producing some green leaves and knotwood stems out of her skirt pockets.

'Oh, yes,' Kirsten said, taking the succulent green stem Maren gave her and chewing on it as if she were a small woodland creature.

'Well, I shall begin then,' Maren said, looking pleased to have an audience. 'There was once a girl walking through the woods in the south of Norway where the hazel trees grow. She was cracking nuts she had gathered from one of these trees.' Maren looked at Ingeborg with her bewitching green eyes. Unbidden, Ingeborg felt her cheeks bloom red. She wondered had Maren ever seen or tasted a hazelnut? Did her father the pirate bring them to her? 'This girl – shall we say her name is Freyja, named after the goddess of love *and* war?'

'Hush,' Ingeborg admonished Maren. 'It's dangerous to speak of the old religion.'

'Who is to hear us?' Maren countered, as she selected the longest, juiciest knotwood stem and offered it to Ingeborg.

Unable to resist, Ingeborg began sucking the juice out of the stem while Maren continued to speak.

'Freyja found a worm inside one of the nuts, and was about to cast the nut aside, when she came upon the Devil. She knew he was the Devil because he had a big black hat upon his head, and claws for hands.'

Kirsten clasped her own hands, eyes shining with intrigue.

'"Is it true what everyone says about you?" Freyja asked the Devil. "That you can change to whatever size you wish? As big as a mountain and as tiny as a worm?"'

Maren dropped her voice. '"Of course, I can!" said the Devil, proudly.' She grinned at Kirsten before continuing. '"Well then," said Freyja. "I'd like to see you squeeze through the wormhole in my hazelnut." And she opened her palm to show it to the Devil, with the small brown nut with the tiny wormhole in its shell.

'The Devil laughed with amusement at her challenge. He took his hat off and placed it carefully by the roots of a tree. He clapped his hands three times and turned into a tiny worm on the girl's outstretched hand. Then he slunk into the hole in the nut.'

'Oh, how can the big Devil fit into the little hole?' Kirsten interrupted.

'He can be any size he wishes, like he said!' Maren replied.

Ingeborg shook her head. She should stop Maren filling her sister's head with such nonsense, but she hadn't seen Kirsten so happy in such a long time. Besides, there was a part of her that was enjoying the moment too: filling her head with the voices of the characters and watching Maren.

Maren was a poor fisher girl like the rest of them, and yet when she narrated her story Ingeborg could see the old Norse Goddess Freyja within her – in the dewy dark softness of her eyes, and the bite of her over lip. Love and War.

'Freyja picked up a twig and stuck it in the hole of the nut. Then she collected the Devil's grand hat and placed it upon her head.' Maren mimed placing an imaginary hat upon her head. '"Now," she thought, "I have the Devil in the palm of my hand." She felt quite clever as she carried on through the woods with the Devil's hat upon her.'

Kirsten rested her head in Ingeborg's lap, her red curls scattered upon her white apron. Ingeborg twirled her sister's hair around her fingers as if they were gold rings, all the while the two of them watching Maren.

'After a while, Freyja came out of the trees and went down the hill into the village. She thought, "I would like to teach this pompous Devil a lesson or two," so she went to the smithy who was working outside his forge.'

Maren jumped up and tipped an imaginary hat, pretending to be Freyja.

'"Please, Master Smithy," she asked him in her politest voice, "can you smash this nut for me?" and Freyja took the Devil's hazelnut out of her pocket.'

Maren put her hands on her hips, legs astride as she mimicked the blacksmith.

Kirsten gave a squeal of delight.

'"Why are you bothering me with such silliness?" the smithy said, looking far more fearsome than the Devil ever had. "Take that ridiculous hat off your head immediately."

'But Freyja refused to take the hat off, and she begged the smithy to try to crack the nut.

'He grabbed the nut, shaking his head at her stupidity, but much to his surprise, though he tried with all his might to crush the shell in his huge, strong fist, he could not crack the nut.'

Maren flopped down onto the ground next to Ingeborg and Kirsten. She leant over Ingeborg, and stroked Kirsten's hair.

Maren's scent is that of the forest, Ingeborg thought. *Pine, and woodsmoke.* As Ingeborg curled her fingers in Kirsten's hair, she touched Maren's hands. She looked up and Maren was smiling at her. Slowly, Ingeborg removed her hand from her sister's hair as she felt heat in her cheeks. Maren withdrew her hand too, still smiling at Ingeborg.

'So, the smithy picked up a small hammer saying, "How strange this is." He placed the nut on his anvil and brought down the hammer, but it did not crack.' Maren demonstrated an imaginary hammer slamming down upon an imaginary nut. 'He picked up a bigger hammer and brought it down upon the nut but still it would not crack.

'By now the smithy was getting quite cross. Why could he not get this little nut to crack? He picked up his biggest sledgehammer and brought it down with all his might. And the nut cracked open with such force the roof of his forge blew off.'

'How loud was it?' Kirsten asked Maren, agog.

'So loud the noise of the nut cracking open made the whole village run inside their cottages and batten down the hatches, thinking a big thunderstorm was rolling in!'

'Oh, they're so stupid!' Kirsten exclaimed, eyes bright.

'The blacksmith was quite stunned. "Well, that nut was so hard to crack, the Devil himself could have been inside," he declared, annoyed his roof had blown off.

'"Why, yes, he was," said Freyja, pulling her big Devil hat down lower upon her brow and skipping off out of the village and back into the woods. When she was alone again, she ate up all of the inside of the cracked nut. She took off his hat and left it by the trunk of the tree for him to find, but she never saw the Devil again.'

'But does that mean the Devil is inside Freyja now, if she ate the nut?' Kirsten piped up.

Maren shrugged. 'Well, that's how the story goes.'

'It's make-believe, Kirsten, a silly story,' Ingeborg interceded.

'There's always a grain of truth in every bedtime tale, Ingeborg,' Maren challenged her.

'Where did you hear such a ridiculous story, anyway?' Ingeborg got up, sweeping the remains of the knotwood leaves and stems from her skirts. She had eaten too much of Maren's fare and now she felt a little queasy and her jaw ached from chewing.

'My mother told it to me,' Maren said, looking up at her with solemn eyes.

'Your mother the witch?' Kirsten whispered in awe.

Maren nodded.

'Tell me another story your mother told you,' Kirsten asked.

'That's enough,' Ingeborg said firmly, taking hold of her sister's hand and dragging her up, though her heart was telling her, *Yes, more, more!* 'It's time to go.'

She felt Maren's eyes upon her back as she stalked back through the birch trees, tugging Kirsten behind her, basket banging against her legs. Maren and her story were pulling her back, for Ingeborg craved to hear more of clever girls who could outwit the Devil, but no good would come of letting their imaginations wander. None at all.

Ingeborg broke into a run, despite Kirsten's protestations at being dragged along. It was as if she were running into the wind, although not one branch stirred above her.

Chapter 13

Anna

The brief summer had blown away as if linens lost from Helwig's drying line. And then the rain came, washing in from the west – warm at first, but heavy, drenching the whole island. Little rivers ran down the castle roof and pooled in the courtyard. Soon we were ankle-deep in thick mud every time we travailed to the well, or the washhouse.

As for my dank prison longhouse, rain trickled through the sagging turf roof and down the walls within as if my whole interior were crying long slow trails of tears. Helwig was in a frenzy, stuffing lumps of peat into all the holes in the cracked walls to keep the rats out. To me it seemed a pointless exercise, for no sooner had one hole been found and plugged than she would spy another.

'Soon, they'll be coming,' she said, a panicked staccato to her voice.

I was not afraid of rats, though my association with them was a grim one. During the plague years, when I attended to the sick in Bergen, there were always rats lurking around the afflicted. I saw one rat bite the finger off a dying child's hand. The small boy, so lost in fever, didn't even cry out. Not long after, the poor lamb was one more innocent soul gone to the Good Lord.

So many angels' brows I had mopped and given solace to, some of these dying children all alone in the world, the plague having taken their parents before them.

When the wind on the island changed direction, blowing in from Russia, the rain chilled to small balls of hail hammering me every time I was called to speak with the governor. And after the hail came sleet, violent and penetrating.

How I miss long-ago golden Septembers in Copenhagen. I longed to stroll once more through your gardens, my king, pausing to admire the peacocks displaying their fans of colour. Ah, how the sunshine scattered all around me, light and shade, and there I see you, yet again. The sunlight upon your hands as you lifted them to my cheek, your face hidden in the shade of your hat, your eyes unreadable as the peacock's tail feathers lowered and his blue chest pulsated, calling for his mate.

As I lay in bed trying to sleep last night, against the howls of the eastern wind I fancied I heard the peacock's shrill scream again. I could see the shimmering blue length of his neck and narrow chest as his whole body became a wave of need. The penetrating tempo of his shriek, and its persistence, pierced my skull, awakening me.

But I was not in the tiny bedchamber of my longhouse prison, nor was I back home in my husband's house in Bergen. Years, decades had fallen away, and I was in my father's cabinet of curiosities in my childhood home in Copenhagen. This the most special of rooms filled with his collection of artefacts gathered during the whole of his life as a physician and a philosopher. It was of more value to him than anything in the whole world – including his wife and daughter, I suspect. I recalled the large table piled with my most recent finds in the middle of the black and white tiled floor. Shelves filled with discoveries lined the walls and above them hung a vast array of skeletons and stuffed creatures the like we have never seen in our lands. Giant turtle shells, little upright arctic birds, antlers, horns and the strangest of fish with razor fins, or big gaping mouths. Two big, latticed windows faced out onto our botanical garden, the sun spilling into the room in the morning illuminating the ancient dust spinning air. Ah I see myself now upon the window seat, feet tucked beneath my skirts, perusing shells and stones upon my palms and imagining the hot dry lands from where they came. Truly my father's legacy was a magnificent collection.

Well, now you have possession of it, my king, for my father's cabinet of curiosities was bequeathed to the State after he passed away and I wonder, will you take care of my father's life's work?

Hours I would spend as a girl within the cabinet of curiosities helping my father categorise and classify.

It is my script in Latin upon the boxes. I entreat you to trace your fingers upon the letters: *Lapides* for stones and fossils; *Conchilia Marina* for seashells, *Ceraunia* the thunderstones we believed fell to the earth in flashes of lightning.

My father shared his knowledge with me for in his eyes I was neither boy nor girl, but his heritage, and he considered it his right and duty to educate me. In my father's cabinet of curiosities there was science, but magic and mystery too.

Do you see the unicorn's horn? Take note of its twisted spiralling length – the most remarkable sight indeed, is it not?

You know, as my father told you, too, the unicorn is a mythical creature, and this twisting horn does not belong to a folktale unicorn. My father had found this horn attached to a skull, and, after careful research, concluded it came from a whale, the magnificent beasts that dwell here in the north. If you came to the hyperborean edge of your kingdom, you might catch me upon the fortress battlements, gazing at the icy waters, searching for the narwhales – creatures my father had longed to see living and breathing.

I will find one for you, and if you allow me ink, draw it for you upon the parchment you gave me.

If it pleases you, my king, all you need do is send me ink and quill.

In the chamber that was my father's cabinet of curiosities, I would gaze up to the ceiling at the stuffed baby polar bear, snarling already, and wonder at how huge it could have been, so immense – even the size of the whole chamber. This polar bear could have torn the room apart and devoured us whole. Sometimes when I looked up at the bear, I could see its dead eyes blinking at me to say, *If only, little Anna, you would set me free.*

When my father showed you the cabinet of curiosities I was there by his side. At the time I was fifteen years of age. Do you remember me, my king, awkward in my most recent incarnation as a young woman, and blushing in my sober black gown? It had been such an honour for a royal prince to deign to visit my father's cabinet of curiosities, but you had heard mention of it, and you desired to see his treasures. How delighted you were indeed, and I remember you intently examined each article, no matter how small or trivial it might seem. You were ignited by the same passion for the unknown just as my father, just as I. You turned over every stone, and perused every bone, you laughed at the tiny clockwork mouse and was intrigued by our automaton native from the Americas. But what drew your attention most of all was the one article I feared too – the troll's skull.

'Where did you come by this?' You turned to my father, flicking your long black curls from your shoulders.

How lustrous your hair was! I remember your finery to be as dazzling as the peacocks in your gardens. You wore a shimmering gold silk doublet, with ribbons on the sleeves and edged in red brocade; your collar was purest white lace, for you were a young, fashionable prince, twenty-one years of age, with no need of antiquated ruffs. Your stockings were an alarming shade of brightest scarlet that day, and I found myself unable to ignore the contours of your calves, and your slender ankles in your golden shoes with bows as ornate as the ribbons on your sleeves. What a sight you were, and how plain I was in my black dress, though my coif, kerchief and apron were purest white.

Your fingers touched the skull of the troll as you traced the empty eye sockets.

'It came to me on my travels to Amsterdam,' my father told you. 'But I believe it is from the far north of Norway.'

'Ah, of course.' You nodded. 'For is not this the region in which the trolls dwell? Could even this troll have been in the service of the Devil himself?'

'Are not *all* trolls in service to the Devil, my prince?' my father had replied.

You nodded, not taking your eyes from the giant skull.

You had understood my father's obsession with the natural world because you were a prince, and now a king, who wished to know all about his kingdom.

We, as people, categorised and classified, are just like the animals, so that when our flesh falls away as it surely does, and our souls are freed, our bones are all that is left. We share a faith rooted in the real world, you and I, my king, for we are for the people, are we not?

My husband Ambrosius was a different creature altogether, with his head in the stars, looking up and away from our world as he strove to find patterns and predictions in the movement of the planets. Though I am an astrological botanist, I am not like my husband, for I see the planets' properties in the material realm, upon the earth and in the plants which can heal us.

However, one fact made my husband and I the same, and this was that we were outsiders in the city of Bergen. Our enemy was Statholder Trolle, and he still is *your* enemy, my king! Consider his name: *Trolle*. How apt an appellation I cannot but help thinking – although Statholder Trolle of Bergen was a small, scrawny man and not remotely giant in stature. Ah, but his opinion of himself was immense indeed.

He protects those who would tear you down – the depraved, and the corrupt of Bergen. Dare I say, my king, that I do believe Statholder Trolle has knowledge of the Dark Lord?

I will find his collaborators here in the far north of Norway, and the coven of witches who would bring chaos and destruction upon your kingdom. With my every breath, I will protect you, my king, for then you will know how true my love for you has always been.

Beyond the meagre confines of my own heart, beyond my husband and a family, I am your servant always.

Let me tell you how the governor and I began our work together.

Ever since I had saved the life of his young wife, I was on occasion invited to dine at his table, an event which displeased Bailiff Lockhert, who was fond of no woman.

The governor had heard of the size of the library in my house in Bergen, and how educated I was. Thus, he wanted to discuss the writings of the great demonologists with me. Governor Orning was inordinately fond of James VI's *Daemonologie*, Kramer and Sprenger's *Malleus Maleficarum* and in particular Niels Hemmingsen's *Undervisning*. His theory was that witches had sex with the Devil – despite my observation that all three volumes were somewhat dated, in particular *Malleus Maleficarum*, having first been published near two hundred years before our time.

'There are other theologians worth considering in the modern age,' I told the governor. 'Not long before I arrived in Vardø, I came across the writings of the English theologian Thomas Ady. Are you familiar with his treatise concerning the nature of witches and witchcraft entitled *A Candle in the Dark*? It is written as advice to judges, and magistrates, such as yourself.'

I expanded no further, for it was a risk to mention Thomas Ady and his well-known scepticism of witchcraft. Are you familiar with his writings, my king? What think you upon his argument that the bloody Civil War in England was God's punishment for their brutal witch trials? For he claims there is no place in the Bible where our ways of proving witchcraft is cited. I hunted through my own Bible after reading his treatise and began to perceive how it is possible the name 'witch' could be conceived as popish, just as he claims.

Thomas Ady and his strong words did throw me somewhat in confusion, and a part of me repelled his notion that witches are merely deluded melancholics. For the Devil is real, is he not, and for all time we have known witches to be his servants. And we know the Dark Lord's temptations well, you and I.

'Ah, but I prefer my own authorities upon the matter of witchcraft,' the governor countered. 'For are not Luther's proclamations upon witches the ones we need stand by the most, as he was most clear upon the matter of witches.' The governor paused for effect, casting me a sober look before quoting from Martin Luther himself: '"There is no compassion to be had for these women; I would burn all of them myself, according to the law."'

'These witches are like rats.' Lockhert spoke up, clearly bored by our scholarly debate. 'Where there is one, there are others, and they accumulate quickly.'

'How can we tell who the witches are?' the governor asked me intently.

I had placed my linen napkin carefully on his fine dining table, my appetite sated by fresh fish, *gullbrød*, and sweet red wine. I pushed all thoughts of Thomas Ady's reasoning from my mind.

If all went well, I was confident the governor would acknowledge the aid I had given him, and then – oh, and then – your pardon would arrive as if a blessing from the very heavens.

'It is not as complicated as you might believe,' I told the governor. 'For a witch reveals her true nature in her behaviour.'

The governor's wife looked up from the plate of food she had barely touched and peered at me curiously.

'Take the case of Maren Spliid,' I said to Orning. 'The witch from Ribe in Denmark. She had the sharpest tongue in the whole of Denmark, and she could not cease from cursing her neighbours and blaspheming against the Good Lord.'

'If this be the case, Fru Rhodius, one might name you a witch!' Bailiff Lockhert guffawed loudly.

'I have never uttered a curse in my entire life,' I said in a cold voice.

'Lockhert, desist from mocking Fru Rhodius, she is a guest at our table.' The governor glared at his bailiff.

Lockhert gave me a sour look while the malicious gleam in his eyes goaded me.

I was repeating all I had read upon the nature of witches and saying it to the governor as if I believed in it, my pardon hanging before my eyes like sweet, ripening fruit.

'There are other ways, too, of knowing a woman is a witch by her character,' I continued. 'For example, if a woman is with child and out of wedlock.'

'Ah, so a big mouth and loose morals.' Bailiff Lockhert spoke up again. 'Most women on the Varanger Peninsula could be described as such.'

'Then they must be witches,' Governor Orning said, looking pleased.

'There are easier ways to prove a witch,' Lockhert said, his Scottish accent strangling the Danish words. 'We had simple ways back home. But they were effective.'

Helwig had told me this was why Governor Orning had looked to Scotland for his bailiff, with your approval – to aid him in his hunt for witches.

Everyone knew there were more witches in Scotland than any other land in Christendom. King James VI of Scotland and I of England had married the Danish princess, Anne, and the union of the two countries had brought about a great attack upon them by witches. The long-dead King James had spent decades purging Scotland but, according to Lockhert, they were still rampant from the cities to the wild Highlands.

'The water test is a good way to tell a witch or pricking for the mark of the Devil upon their skin,' Lockhert told the governor. 'And then, we have tools of interrogation such as the pinniwinks which have never failed me—'

'It is important that we act properly,' the governor interrupted him while I wondered what these Scottish pinniwinks might be. 'All women accused will be offered a trial and opportunity to prove their innocence. A courtesy the Devil in his evil deeds doesn't offer us.'

'But when do we begin?' Lockhert boomed. 'When can I go and hunt these vile bitches?'

The governor tugged on his beard and looked thoughtful. 'I think it best we wait until the fishermen have left for the winter fishing grounds,' he said. 'It is during midwinter when the Dark Lord calls his witches to him. But we will not suffer it!' He banged his hand upon the table suddenly and his wife looked up, startled. 'It was witches who took my son from me, and I *will* have my revenge.'

Fru Orning's eyes widened as she stared at her husband.

'If it were not for you, Fru Rhodius, my sweet Elisa would have perished too,' Governor Orning said, placing his hand upon his wife's, who flinched ever so slightly.

I gave a dignified nod and took note to store the governor's debt as if tucking it up my sleeve, relieved he had forgotten his theory that I had brought a curse with me.

'There is one detail I am particularly keen for you to investigate, Fru Anna,' the governor said as he rose from the table, his tiny wife picking herself up though her food was untouched. 'It is the most heinous crime of all. I have read in some pamphlets recounting the scourge of witches in central Germany, that these foul creatures baptise their own daughters over to the Dark Lord in a binding covenant.'

The governor's wife looked at him with wide-eyed horror at the notion.

Governor Orning gave me a piercing look. 'We must purge our region not just of the witch mothers, but of their daughters too. I expect your help in this in particular, Fru Anna.'

I watched the governor and his child bride depart for their bedchamber. Fru Orning was still quaking as they left, and I pushed away the unwelcome image of how the governor might act in private with the girl. It appeared to me she was more afraid of her own husband than any witch.

As soon as the governor had left, Lockhert stood and kicked the leg of my chair. 'Don't forget you are my prisoner too, Fru Rhodius,' he said, in a nasty voice. 'Back to your longhouse before I decide to chain you up in the governor's cellar.'

Although my heart was thumping erratically in my chest, I forced a look of composure on my face, and rose with dignity. I returned across the mucky courtyard, doing my best to protect the slippers you gave me and to step with care in my pattens, back to my bleak and freezing longhouse.

Helwig had fallen asleep on her pallet and the cooking fire was almost out. I threw some more turf upon it and huddled over it to draw some heat into my bones. I thought upon the words the governor had spoken about mothers sacrificing their daughters to the Devil and it made my chest squeeze tight with dread.

The governor's abhorrent theory of mothers giving their daughters over to the Devil was not one I agreed with and his keenness on it worried me. For, my king, are not all children innocent in the eyes of the Good Lord? But I had detected the fervour in the governor's countenance, and I knew well the look of a man on a mission. He would not be easily persuaded otherwise, and what could I do, in any case, for in his eyes I was now an instrument of his will.

I prayed the witches he hunted had no daughters.

In my bedchamber, it took many hours to fall asleep. When I did, I returned to the cabinet of curiosities in my dreams. This time I was picking up a jar of one of the misshapen foetuses in my father's collection. It was an oddity, a rare, unborn, unopened tangle of tiny limbs that God had not blessed with living breath. And yet it was ours.

Chapter 14

Ingeborg

The day the fishermen sailed, rains had cleared away early snow. The last autumn heathers flared red and amber, upon the marshes. Soon more snow would come, and all colours disappear; the two extremes of winter settling in for the dreaded dark weeks of black sky and white land.

Not one fisherwoman of Ekkerøy was glad to see her husband go. Even if he were sometime a brute or liked his liquor too much, it was better to be within his protection than without. All knew this was the season of witching, when they could be cursed or, worse still, pulled into league with the Devil.

'Now my aunt's scolds will become all the sharper,' Maren told Ingeborg, as they watched the fishing boats disappearing around the headland, old sails stitched up a thousand times flapping valiantly in the south-westerlies. 'She is more afraid of the Devil than her man. Though truly if it were I, it would be the other way around. My uncle is not a kind husband.'

Ingeborg glanced at Maren in concern. What was there to be more afraid of than the Devil? No mortal man came close. Even the fists of Solve's husband.

A sudden gust of chill blew across the sea. Ingeborg shivered as it penetrated her shawl. She crossed herself and began to say a prayer for the safe passage of the fishermen.

'It is for us you should pray,' Maren commented. 'For now, our men-folk are gone, the governor and his men will come to hunt for their witches.' She pulled back the tangle of black hair streaking across her face. 'Listen to me, Ingeborg.' She reached out and touched her sleeve.

Ingeborg looked down at the skin of Maren's fingers. Dark as the velvet snout of an arctic fox. 'The only way to protect yourself is to show you have power. Make them afraid of you.'

There were those words again. Ingeborg shook her hand off, annoyed at Maren's ridiculous suggestion. Surely it was better to make less noise, become smaller, disappear? This was the only way to survive.

'How could the governor of Vardø ever be afraid of the likes of me!' she declared.

'I can show you,' Maren whispered, her gaze at once furtive.

Ingeborg shook her head in refusal and stomped back to the village. It was talk such as Maren's that would put them in danger, not help them.

Ingeborg hoped with all her heart that Maren was wrong about the witch hunt, as the whispers about her mother in the village were rife.

The week before, at divine service, Fru Brasche had stopped on her way out of the kirk and stared right at her mother. Heinrich Brasche had turned the colour of lingonberries, his cheeks blooming red, and he had pushed his wife forwards, but not before she had spat on the ground in front of Ingeborg's mother.

Fru Brasche knew. *Oh, dear Lord.* Ingeborg had crossed herself. *She knew!* Who had told her?

There had been a hushed, horrified silence as everyone stared down at the glob of spit before Ingeborg's mother, who had said nothing at all, merely lifted her head high and stepped over it. Walking light-footed back down the hill to their cottage.

Was this what love could do to a woman? Make her dumb witted? If so, Ingeborg never wanted to fall in love. Her mother had become a reckless fool.

As Maren had predicted, five days after the fishermen had departed, a boat from Vardø appeared on the horizon. Upon it was the hulking figure of Bailiff Lockhert, red hair flaming in the wet wind, shaggy beard laced with ice drops, searching for his quarry.

Most of the women were out on the bog, collecting the last of their turf, but as soon as the boat was sighted stacks were dropped on the marsh land and they all ran back through the village, barrelling into their cottages. As if the flimsy walls of turf could keep the ogre out.

Ingeborg's mother ordered her to mash the fish bones for Heinrich Brasche's cows, while Kirsten squirreled away in the corner with Zacharias.

'Stay busy, Ingeborg.'

Her voice was calm, but Ingeborg could see fear flickering in her eyes. *Too late, Mother!* she wanted to yell at her. *It's too late now.*

Together she and her mother battered away at the boiled bones in the big cauldron, while Lockhert and his men stomped through the village to Merchant Brasche's house. Deadly silence fell upon all the cottages like a thick fog. Ingeborg imagined all their neighbours holding their breath, remembering the witch hunt that had ended in Maren's mother's persecution.

The silence was shattered by the thumping of men through their cluster of cottages, Lockhert banging open doors and roaring at the women within.

Ingeborg's hands were shaking with fear while Kirsten clung on tightly to Zacharias.

'We've had no dealings with the Devil, girls. Why would the bailiff come here?'

But her mother's words did not appease her. Ingeborg felt a sickness in the pit of her belly, terror sliding down her spine icy with premonition.

Sure enough, the door of their cottage was suddenly pushed open, and Lockhert came barging in, two soldiers at his side.

Her mother sprang back in fright, knocking over the cauldron of fish bones. Thick sludgy fish entrails sprayed the cooking fire and hut all around them.

Lockhert ignored the disarray, as his eyes had one point of focus. Ingeborg's mother. He took a menacing step towards her. 'I am here to arrest you, Zigri Sigvaldsdatter,' he growled.

Her mother backed away, her body pressed against the cracked walls of the turf hut. Kirsten curled around Zacharias, her eyes squeezed shut. But Ingeborg couldn't move. The boiling broth of fish bones was seeping into the earth floor, its odour churning her stomach, her bare toes squishing in its vile swamp.

'Under the orders of the most honourable Governor of Vardø, I am instructed to bring you, Zigri Sigvaldsdatter, to Vardø fortress for questioning regarding accusations of witchcraft.'

'Who has accused me?' her mother protested, panic flashing in her eyes.

'We have a witness who saw you in coven with the Devil.'

'I am a God-fearing widow – ask Reverend Jacobsen, for I'm in kirk, every week. I have made no pacts with the Devil.'

'It is Fru Brasche who has seen you with the Devil, mistress. Are you saying the Merchant Brasche's daughter-in-law speaks false? She, a devout Christian lady? And what are you?' He swept his arms around their tiny hovel.

It silenced her mother, but Ingeborg had to speak up. 'Fru Brasche denounces my mother out of spite,' she protested.

The bailiff ignored her, ordering his soldiers to arrest her mother. There was nowhere for her mother to run as she clung to the cracked walls. They prised her away as she shrieked that it was untrue. Dragged her across the cottage.

In desperation, Ingeborg stepped in front of Bailiff Lockhert. 'Believe me, my mother is not a witch.'

Lockhert raised his eyebrows, noticing her at last, smiling thinly at her audacity. Swiftly, he slapped her down, and she smacked hard to the earthen floor, narrowly missing the mess of fish bones.

'Leave her be,' her mother screeched.

'Silence, you bitch!' Lockhert snarled.

Ingeborg was up again in a flash, and she was angry. Felt it burn inside of her. It would do her mother no good if she were to let fly but she wanted to smash the bailiff's face in with her mashing stick. She gripped it tightly, feeling an animal need to destroy him.

'Ingeborg, no! Hold back!'

Her mother's pleas stopped her. Ingeborg let the stick slip from her grasp and fall to the floor.

Ingeborg and Kirsten crept behind Lockhert and his men as they marched their shivering mother to Merchant Brasche's house. Her mother didn't call out or protest her innocence, for she knew well enough it would result in pain and suffering.

None stirred in the little hamlet. All the other women and children were still hiding. Though Ingeborg felt their eyes upon them, peering out of cracks and holes in their walls.

They walked from their little enclave, past the crescent beach, and to the rise of drier richer land, where Merchant Brasche's big wooden house was situated. The great man himself came out to stand upon his front steps, arms crossed across his broad chest, to survey the arrested witch.

Lockhert pushed their mother down outside steps into Merchant Brasche's cellar, the sound of the heavy bolts seeming to ring across the hushed village.

Afterwards, Bailiff Lockhert followed the merchant into his house, the latter giving him an approving slap on the back.

Ingeborg pressed her hands against the cellar door. 'Mother?' she whispered. 'Mother?'

'Girls, all will be well.' Ingeborg heard her mother's shaky voice.

Out in the gathering dusk, the stout figure of Reverend Jacobsen scurried towards them, his black robes trailing in the mud.

'Reverend Jacobsen is here,' Ingeborg told her mother. 'I will ask him to speak for you.'

Ingeborg staggered to her feet, pulling Kirsten up beside her. They ran back up the steps to the priest as it began to rain heavily.

'Reverend, please help my mother,' Ingeborg beseeched him. 'They've imprisoned her in Merchant Brasche's cellar on charges of witchcraft.'

The reverend surveyed her with cold eyes. 'I know this, child,' he said. 'I am on my way to question her.'

'Can she come home afterward?' Kirsten asked him.

He looked at her little sister, and his expression softened. 'No, there is a case made against her,' he told them, as rain slid off his fat nose. 'She will be taken to Vardø tomorrow morning to stand trial.'

His words dug into Ingeborg like a knife in her chest. None who went on trial in Vardø ever returned.

'Will you not speak for my mother, Reverend?' Ingeborg begged.

'She has been named as a witch, and must answer for it to the governor himself,' the Reverend said bluntly. He produced a large linen handkerchief from his pocket and wiped his dripping nose. 'Go home and pray for her soul. That is all you can do for her now.'

How could she go home and pray? Her mother a few paces away behind the cellar walls. After the priest had gone inside, Ingeborg crept around the sides of the merchant's house. She could hear men talking inside. Laughter even. Merry with their ale and their victuals while her mother was trapped beneath them in terror.

Kirsten crawled next to her, pulling back muck from the cellar walls. 'Inge, there's a hole, here!'

Together they pulled away at the rotten wood, splinters piercing their fingertips, but what did they care? The anger Ingeborg had felt towards her mother's wantonness fell away. Despite it all, she was her mother, and Ingeborg needed her. She couldn't lose another loved one, not again. Besides her mother was no witch.

'Mother,' Ingeborg called out. 'We're coming!'

Their mother was on the other side, pulling at the wood as well. But the rotten part was slight, and no matter how hard they tugged, the biggest they could make the hole was the size of their mother's hand.

She reached through with her cold, shaking fingers and Ingeborg clasped them. 'Ingeborg, you must go to Heinrich now, and ask for his help,' her mother said.

'But it's his wife who accuses you.'

'Even so, I believe he will save me.'

There was confidence in her mother's voice as she withdrew her hand.

Ingeborg couldn't see what she was doing, but then her mother reached out again. Clasped between her fingers was the blue ribbon.

'Give him the ribbon,' she said.

The air was thick with the scent of turf smoke, twisting white plumes in the black sky, as Ingeborg and Kirsten crept past Merchant Brasche's door and trudged back along the heathery track, moss encrusted with fresh ice, to his son's house.

Kirsten was shivering, and she must have been so hungry. Yet she didn't complain.

'Why don't you go home and dry off?' Ingeborg suggested to her little sister.

'No,' Kirsten said fiercely, two spots of colour flaming on her pale cheeks. 'I want to help you, Ingeborg.'

The Brasches' door was opened by Widow Krog. 'God bless us, what are you doing here, Ingeborg Iversdatter?' Widow Krog whispered, her face pale and drawn.

'I need to talk to Heinrich Brasche,' Ingeborg said, her voice trembling despite her determination.

'Oh, no,' Widow Krog said, her eyes dropping to the blue ribbon clutched in Ingeborg's hand. 'Don't come in here, girl.'

'Please, Fru Krog, our mother has been arrested on charges of witchcraft.'

Widow Krog's faced blanched. 'I warned her. How many times did I tell her it would be the end of her?'

'But she's innocent of witchcraft,' Ingeborg said, holding the ribbon to Widow Krog. 'Please, he is the only chance she has!'

Widow Krog looked very troubled indeed, her eyes wavering between Ingeborg and Kirsten. 'Of course, your mother isn't a witch, Ingeborg Iversdatter,' Widow Krog said, opening the door a little wider so that Ingeborg and Kirsten could slip through. 'Come inside if you must.'

Husband and wife were seated either side of their fire. It was no meagre cooking fire but a proper hearth with a mantel and a real chimney. Upon the mantel were three silver Sámi bowls, and by the fire, a large copper bucket filled with turf alongside hanging poker, and tongs, with the fire bellows lying upon an alcove shelf. Beside the couple, a big table was covered in a tapestry cloth richly patterned with leaves, flowers and fruit. What a pretty picture it was – the husband smoking his pipe while his wife was busy at her embroidery.

Both looked up in surprise as Ingeborg made her entrance.

'Who are these bedraggled fishermen's girls, Heinrich?' Fru Brasche's voice was immediately hostile. 'Look how their dirty feet are leaving muck on our clean floors.'

Fru Brasche called for Widow Krog, but the older woman had melted away. Hiding in the kitchen no doubt, praying she would not be blamed for the Iversdatter girls' intrusion.

Ingeborg turned to address the merchant's son. 'Sir, our mother has been arrested by Bailiff Lockhert and accused of witchcraft,' Ingeborg told him, her voice savage with emotion. 'She's imprisoned in your father's cellar.'

Heinrich stood up in alarm, his pipe clattering to the floor. Ingeborg felt the cold eyes of his wife upon her.

'None told me of this,' he said, looking greatly disturbed.

'Of course, you knew, Heinrich,' Fru Brasche said. 'Your father spoke of it only yesterday. He is committed to helping the governor rid our village of witchcraft.'

'My mother is innocent,' Ingeborg declared, eyes fixed upon the troubled face of Heinrich Brasche.

'But she was seen with the Devil, girl.' Fru Brasche spoke up again, in an icy voice.

Ingeborg could hold back no longer, turning on Fru Brasche as she saw the glint of triumph in her eyes. 'It was *you* who accused her.'

'What is the meaning of this, wife?' Heinrich asked Fru Brasche. 'Why would you accuse Zigri Sigvaldsdatter of witchcraft?'

'As I told the girl,' his wife replied, patting her skirts with her hands and trying to look composed, though Ingeborg could see them shaking, 'I saw her with the Devil in our cowshed. It was quite clear to me. They were fornicating.'

Kirsten gave a small gasp, and Ingeborg grabbed her hand, squeezing it tight to keep her silent. She kept her eyes on Heinrich Brasche, his face a confliction of emotion, a deep shade of red shame stretching from out of his collar up his neck.

Ingeborg pulled her mother's blue ribbon from her pocket and dangled it before the merchant's son. The sight of it had a great effect on the young man. He brought a hand to his chest and began to gasp like a stranded fish.

'You must tell your father, and the governor of Vardø, that my mother is innocent, and your wife was mistaken,' Ingeborg insisted, sounding braver than she felt.

114

'How dare you accost my husband with such demands?' Fru Brasche retorted, looking furious. Two rows of pearls were wound tightly around her neck, and she was wearing a sumptuous green silk bodice. Yet for all Fru Brasche's finery, Ingeborg's mother far outstripped her in beauty. 'Get away with you!' she said, pointing to the doorway.

But Ingeborg was not giving up. 'You know my mother is no witch, you know it,' she pleaded to Heinrich, her voice rising in frustration.

He had gone very pale now, his red flush gone. His hazel eyes had darkened to black.

'You must help her.'

How could this man of power and wealth not act for her mother?

'I have no influence with Governor Orning in Vardø.' Heinrich finally spoke.

'But your father does,' Ingeborg protested.

'My father will not listen to me,' Heinrich said, in a bitter voice. 'He believes near every fisherman's wife in Ekkerøy is a witch.'

'Get rid of these girls, Heinrich,' his wife said, staring at the blue ribbon. 'What do you care about their witch mother?'

'Leave me be, wife,' Heinrich snapped, grabbing the ribbon from Ingeborg and curling it into his fist.

Fru Brasche's face lit up with fury, yet she said no more. Her damage had been done after all. Picking up her embroidery, she stared at Ingeborg and Kirsten with loathing.

Heinrich opened up his palm and gazed down at the blue ribbon. 'I am sorry, child, but you must go.'

'But why did you give her the ribbon?' Ingeborg persisted, tugging on Heinrich Brasche's sleeve in her desperation.

Heinrich pushed her hand off, not meeting her gaze, and Ingeborg felt the heat of Fru Brasche's wrath, but she didn't care anymore. She was angry with Heinrich.

'My mother gave you so much!' Ingeborg reached up and pulled the blue ribbon from out of Heinrich's open palm. It belonged to her mother, and she would have it back.

'The insolence of you, girl! Should she not be locked up too?' Fru Brasche's voice was dagger-edged.

Heinrich turned on his wife. 'Lisebet, silence, I beg you!'

She looked at him, the hate gone from her eyes. All that remained was naked hurt.

'I will try to speak for your mother.' Heinrich turned to Ingeborg again. 'But it could make things worse for her.' He sighed long and deep. 'I will go to my father. See what can be done.'

He called for Widow Krog to bring his hat and cloak.

'Go home,' he said to Ingeborg. 'Pray for your mother. I will do my best for her.'

Fru Brasche glared at Ingeborg and Kirsten from beside the fire. Her embroidery had slipped to the floor, and her eyes gleamed with tears.

'Go home, Ingeborg,' Heinrich ordered Ingeborg and Kirsten again.

Black clouds swirled above them, and the wind howled. Ingeborg and Kirsten followed Heinrich Brasche.

Heinrich's long black cape flapped around him like two big wings as he strode across the bog to his father's house. They watched him go inside.

The sisters huddled down by the cellar and whispered to their mother. 'He is here now. Your Heinrich has come. He will save you, Mamma.' But there was no sound from within. Was she in there still? Or had they put her somewhere else? Or worse, had she been beaten so hard she lay half-dead upon the cellar floor?

Ingeborg and Kirsten waited deep into the dark night. Until the rain stopped, the clouds cleared, and they could see the first crescent of the new moon. Ingeborg imagined the moment Heinrich would bring her mother out of his father's house, the two of them walking down the steps as if a prince with his princess. But hours passed, and still he did not come out.

Kirsten trembled with cold and hunger. Ingeborg knew to stay out longer risked sickness for her little sister. They stumbled back to their cottage. It would soon be morning. They would return then.

But once her sister was wrapped up in skins, the lamb Zacharias beside her, Ingeborg went back to Merchant Brasche's house. Crawling and scratching at the cellar walls like a cat looking for rats. There had to be a way in. She knocked upon the wall by the hole. Whispered 'Mother!'

Behind her, she suddenly heard a savage barking. It was Merchant Brasche's big black dog snarling at her, its eyes red and rolling, saliva drooling from its fanged mouth.

Ingeborg drew in a deep breath of fear and rage, and then . . . hissed at the dog. The sound that came out of her mouth surprised her. It was feral, wild, not human in its making. She felt her whole spine arching, her skin itching. The dog slathered before her, growling. She hissed again, and then she ran.

The dog leapt at her, bit her upon the hand, and she gave out a yelp, but she kept running. Faster than she had ever run before. The dog chased her and yet she was faster than the big black beast.

She fled down the hill and into the village, her whole body sleek with speed. She slipped into their cottage and slammed the door behind her so hard surely every neighbour would wake. But not a soul stirred. All she could hear was the hound sniffing outside their house.

Ingeborg hugged her sides, leaning hard against the door. There was no lock, and the beast could easily push it open. It kept on sniffing and snuffling – she could feel its hot breath so close to her. At last, it tired, and she heard it trotting away.

Ingeborg sat by the dying embers of the cooking fire, warming the wet, puckered skin of her feet. Blood dripped steadily from the wound on her hand. Her mother would make her clean and bind it, but she was too tired. She drew her hand to her face and sucked on her own blood. It was not a deep wound. The dog had merely grazed her skin with its sharp teeth. But how had she managed to run so fast?

Ingeborg licked the blood off her skin, kept licking until her hand gleamed white and soft in the firelight.

It was only then that she saw Kirsten was still awake. Huddled up next to the sleeping lamb and staring at her with wide eyes. 'I saw Mother with the Devil, Ingeborg,' she whispered. 'Just like Fru Brasche said.'

'No, Kirsten, my love, that's not what you saw, I promise you.'

'What will happen to Mother?' her sister whispered in a fearful voice.

'She will be saved,' Ingeborg said, not knowing why she said it with such conviction.

'But how?' Kirsten asked.

Ingeborg drew her mother's blue ribbon from her pocket. 'Remember the story of the blue ribbon which Axell used to tell us?'

Kirsten nodded.

'It gave the girl special powers. And this is what Mother's blue ribbon is for her.'

'But we have the ribbon, Ingeborg. Not Mother.'

'Then we must give it back to her.'

Ingeborg slid into the bed beside her sister and pulled the reindeer skins over her shoulders. She was cold and so tired, but every time she closed her eyes, she saw the red rolling eyes of Merchant Brasche's big dog. The Devil could come in the form of a black hound – she had heard it enough times from the lips of Reverend Jacobsen.

Her hand was throbbing although it no longer bled. Had she been marked?

She shivered as she pressed her shaking hands to her chest and squeezed her cold toes, rubbing the soles of her feet together.

'If we give Mamma the blue ribbon, will she run away like the girl in the story?' Kirsten whispered. 'Will she run away with the wolves?'

They had been raised to fear wolves, but now Ingeborg wished her mother were among those beasts rather than the men who ruled.

As soon as the grey dawn seeped in through the cracks of their cottage Ingeborg woke Kirsten.

In clean aprons and white coifs, they knelt in prayer outside Merchant Brasche's house while the rain pelted them, drenching the thin linen upon their heads, penetrating their woollen jackets. They were shivering with the cold but still Ingeborg didn't leave off. It was all she could do now: work on the pity of the men in power, even as they were ignored by the village women as they hurried past on their way to the well. How she wished her mother's cousin Solve were there, and even Maren Olufsdatter, for she was certain they would get down on their knees with them. But word had most likely not reached them yet in the village of Andersby.

When at last Ingeborg saw her mother again, it was clear that shock at her arrest had given way to pure terror. Her body was convulsing in fear as Bailiff Lockhert and his men led her out of Merchant Brasche's house. Her wrists were bound so tightly Ingeborg could see red welts rising on her pale skin. Her coif had been pulled off her head, and her red-gold hair fell loose. Ingeborg could see the bloom of fresh bruises upon her arms, and a cut on her lip, the sight of which pierced her.

Behind her, Ingeborg caught sight of Heinrich, held back by his father and his serving man.

'I beg you, Father!' Ingeborg could hear Heinrich's desperate voice. 'Lisebet is mistaken. It was not the Devil she saw with Zigri.'

But Fru Brasche was nowhere to be seen to admit her lie.

Heinrich's father glared at him. 'You've been bewitched, can you not see it, son?'

'Father, she's innocent! I beg you!'

In one swift movement, the old merchant pulled out a knife and held it to his son's throat. 'If you don't stop your caterwauling I will suspect you are in league too,' he said. 'And no longer *my* son. I will dispossess you of all, Heinrich!' he hissed, indicating to his hefty serving man to push Heinrich back inside his house. The door slammed behind them.

Bailiff Lockhert and his men began dragging their mother in the direction of the harbour, as if pulling a reluctant mare.

Kirsten broke into a run behind them. Ingeborg chased after her. 'Mamma!' Kirsten called. 'Mamma, here's your blue ribbon.'

Kirsten clasped at her mother's hand, pushing the now tattered blue ribbon into it. But though her mother took the ribbon, she said nothing to her youngest daughter.

'Oh, Heinrich,' her mother moaned, looking at Ingeborg.

But the merchant's son did not re-appear from his father's house.

Not one door twitched as Bailiff Lockhert dragged Zigri through the village of Ekkerøy.

They arrived at the harbour, where Bailiff Lockhert's boat was ready for departure. The soldiers flung her mother in. She stumbled and fell to her knees, sobbing; tears cascading down her cheeks at the understanding that Heinrich Brasche had been unable to save her from Vardøhus.

It hurt Ingeborg's whole body to watch. She must get to her mother. 'She's innocent, I tell you!' Ingeborg called out, shoving through the soldiers.

The bailiff saw her and let out an exasperated bellow. Clasping her by the collar, he lifted Ingeborg so that her feet were dangling in the air. 'You whelp! If you don't desist, I will put you in the witches' hole of Vardø along with your witch mother.'

She writhed, useless, a fish on a hook.

'Please let her go, Bailiff, she's but a girl,' her mother begged.

Lockhert dropped her and Ingeborg landed on bent knees with a thump, pain jarring through her whole body.

Her mother sat huddled and bound upon the deck, her eyes full of terror. 'Ingeborg, get help,' she whispered. 'Swear it!'

'I do,' Ingeborg whispered.

Her mother raised her bound hands in supplication, the ribbon dangling between them, the begging blue of her eyes tearing into Ingeborg.

She had sworn to help her. But *how*?

The bailiff's men cast off, white sails billowing as the boat rocked upon the grey nothingness of the sea, the rafts of winter ducks their only witnesses as the boat disappeared around the edges of the cliffs.

Ingeborg kept watch long after the last flutter of sails, and the last sight of their mother's hair flying loose like a tiny banner of gold. She imagined her shivering mother curled up in the bottom of the foul bailiff's boat, taken across the Murman sea to the island of Vardø and the governor's fortress.

How could she ever bring her back home?

PART THREE

Winter
1662

The Three Mothers

In a time beyond our imagining, there were once three mothers who lived at the bottom of Yggdrasil, the great tree of life, in the kingdom of Aesir, by the sacred spring of fate. It was their task to nurture the great tree with the pure waters of the sacred spring, to preserve its life with the white clay from the spring and collect drops from the spring to sprinkle upon the grass as dew. The three mothers' names were Urth, Verthandi and Skuld, and it was they who wove the destinies of all.

For the three mothers, all were treated the same because none – not even Odin, the father of all gods and men – had domain over them. All were subject to their fate. The mothers, or the Norns as they were otherwise known, were maybe sisters, maybe not, but one could not exist without the other. It was the work of the mothers to attend the birth of every new-born baby and weave the story of their lives. It was not a duty they took lightly, and as each soul was born the mothers poured care and consideration into creating the pattern of each life.

Urth was known as the Past, or Fate. She possessed long, free-flowing hair that changed colour with the seasons between shades of gold and brown: in the winter, it was the dark brown of bog water, but in the summer, it became the colour of a field of barley. Her skin also changed with the season, as did her eyes: honey and hazel in the summer, cream and burnt embers in the winter. Urth was full of laughter and light, offering so many different stories of a person's existence as she sang existence into the pattern of people's fate. Each note she uttered turned to a thread, each colour illuminating a pathway for the soul.

Verthandi was known as the Present or Being. She had curling hair which was a thousand shades of red. Verthandi was the smallest of the three mothers – as neat and tiny as one of the elf-dwarves – but she possessed the most power. It was she who wove the secret to joy in a soul's life. But her essence was the hardest thread to find. She did not sing or speak but breathed life softly in and out of people's hearts; she was as the sound of the sea upon the shore on a calm summer's day, or the soft sway of the wind in the branches.

Skuld was known as the Future, or Necessity. Her hair was the blackest black ever seen, with a lightning bolt of pure white shot through it. Skuld was the most troublesome of the mothers. Sometimes she did not want to be a mother at all and would rebel against her sisters.

'What's the point of all our hard work weaving the fates of each new-born soul when our own futures are forever uncertain?' she would complain, waving her unwritten scroll in her hand.

But at other times, when the other two mothers had soothed her with fruits and wine, Skuld would pick up her scroll and write and write and write. She never spoke the stories of the new-born soul's fate but accounted for their life in ink upon parchment.

None of us can pass by the three mothers when we come into life. Whether we are gods, goddesses, humans, elves, dwarves, trolls or frost giants. To the three mothers we are all the same. Some of us will have golden fates, and some of us will struggle to leave the shadows, but we are all mothered, whether we like it or not, whether by blood or heart.

The three mothers considered it their most important duty to protect women in childbirth. They drew healing from the great tree of life, and plucked fruits from its boughs, which they would burn on a fire at its roots. These burnt fruits they would administer to women in their labours so that what was within may pass out.

The three mothers wove into every single new-born soul heaven and earth, with purple threads of faith from Urth, green threads of love from Verthandi, and orange threads of hope from Skuld.

These were their gifts to all who opened their hearts to receiving the wisdom of the mothers, that we possess destiny, but we can pull upon the threads we wish.

The greatest gift of all was the gemstone Verthandi buried within the hidden third eye of all who breathe upon this earth. Even one-eyed Odin possesses it.

It is there, in the space between our eyes, on our brow.

Close your eyes and seek it out. Can you see it shining? It is a gemstone, the purest and richest of all, set into the cloth of your life by the Three Mothers.

It is your truth.

Chapter 15

Anna

The evening the first Varanger witch arrived in the fortress at Vardøhus, I had spent the whole day in pain and discomfort with a heavy bleed. The arrival of my menses at this time was unexpected, for I had not been cursed with a bleed since before my trial last winter. It was my maid Helwig to blame, for it is common knowledge that women who dwell within the same abode bleed together. Every month my serving women and I in Bergen would cramp under the full moon, and I dare say for some women who had not been goodly, it was always a blessed bloody relief.

For years, the sight of my monthly streak of red had cut down my hope once more, for my time for motherhood had faded, and I had been unable to provide my husband one living heir.

For a man, nay for a king, you possessed a keen interest in the workings of women's bodies, for I remember you asking me how it felt to bleed each month, the before and the after.

'Always it is different,' I told you. 'And for every woman too. I am fortunate not to suffer from the cramps or heavy flow.'

But these past few years, my body's rhythm has changed for I pass through months without a bleed, and then a sudden onslaught, the flow unstoppable, and heavy, with cramps doubling me up. I have tried different remedies, but they would give only the merest of ease. The violence within my own body felt as if a rebellion was upon me.

Sometime, at night, a heat would come upon me so fierce my skin was aflame, with my heart's desire only clinging on, for when my menses stopped for good then so did my hope.

As a prisoner, what small promise I might have held for another baby was gone for good.

And so, upon this wet, chill October day the witch was to arrive, Helwig collected our bloody rags to boil with birch lye in the washhouse, her body hunched in pain, her face wan.

'Wait,' I instructed her, feeling an unexpected compassion for the girl, while clutching my own hand to my throbbing belly. 'I will give you something to ease the pain.'

I opened up my medicine chest, lifted the top lid, and pulled out the small piece of comfrey root. Taking a sharp knife from the same place, I shaved off a little piece of root.

'Place a pot of water on the fire,' I told Helwig.

She put down the washing and did as I said, watching suspiciously as I put the comfrey root in the water and brought it to the boil. I could smell the ditchy scent of the soft, damp beds in my botanical garden in Bergen and the memory made my heart ache, matching the cramps in my belly.

I let the decoction cool, and then offered a cup of it to Helwig, who had been waiting to leave the cottage with her basket of bloody rags all the while.

'What is it?' she asked, eyes narrowed.

'The root of the comfrey plant,' I said. 'We used it to ease the bleeding of Fru Orning, remember?'

She looked appeased and grabbed the cup, gulping it down. 'It tastes strange,' she said, belching and wiping her mouth.

I curled my nose in distaste at her vulgarity, regretting sharing my precious comfrey root with the uncouth girl.

'It will make your cramps go away,' I told her, drinking my own cup.

Helwig huffed as if unbelieving, yet when she returned a few hours later with our clean rags, she had colour in her cheeks and even hummed contentedly as she prepared our dinner.

For my part, the comfrey root had eased my bleeding and I had been able to continue scratching out my writing in secret while Helwig's eyes were not upon me.

Our fish broth ready for consumption, I was about to sit at the table for Helwig to serve me when there was the sound of men's voices, and boots upon the hard ground outside. It was so rare to hear any happenings in our quiet fortress, empty of all prisoners apart from me, that my instinct was to rise from the table. Equally curious, Helwig followed me over to the small window on the courtyard side of our longhouse prison. I lifted up the flap and peered outside.

The short hours of daylight had drifted into shades of sapphire seeping into black, and the full moon had risen, brimming with silvering light, casting it upon the courtyard. There I could see figures lit up by the light from torches: the troll-like silhouette of huge Bailiff Lockhert, and several of the guardsmen, but the figure that drew my attention was that of a woman chained, hair hung loose, obscuring her face. From the soft contours of her breasts and hips I surmised she was a young enough woman but while the men appeared solid, she was quivering and shaking uncontrollably.

'Put her in the witches' hole,' Lockhert instructed.

She offered no resistance as Lockhert's men dragged her across the courtyard.

'Who is she?' Helwig whispered to me, her fishy breath making me recoil.

'Step back from the window,' I ordered her, bringing my lavender-scented handkerchief to my nose.

'But who is the woman?' Helwig repeated, her face already telling me she knew well enough.

'I would imagine she is a woman accused of witchcraft since they are putting her in the witches' hole.'

I returned to the table and my now cold dinner. I stared down at the congealing globs of fat and fish – more bones than flesh – as one stray carrot bobbed up and down. I had no desire to finish my repast and my chest heaved, pressing against the confines of my bodice, my lips dry with anticipation and dread.

Soon, I would have to play my part.

Chapter 16

Ingeborg

The Murman sea glittered, a vast grey expanse, the distant mountains clad all in white against the darkening sky. Ingeborg's thoughts were with her mother. Did she have enough to eat, a fire to warm herself by in the darkening frigid weeks of November?

She imagined her trim figure once again: golden hair concealed beneath a white cap, waving to her from a boat drifting to shore. Heinrich Brasche beside her. Her saviour. Yet the more she stared out to sea, the more the dream of it derided her.

Those rafts of winter ducks seemed so content and unafraid, a family of hundreds. She wished she were one of those ducks – floating and free upon the icy eddies of the fjord.

At night, when Ingeborg closed her eyes, there was her mother still. In long-gone times, before her fever over Heinrich Brasche, before Axell and her father were lost. Times when she was little, before Kirsten was born, and her mother had been kind to her. Ingeborg could conjure the scent of that long-ago era: sage from her mother's cooking and seagrass from their gathering by the sea. Feel the velvet of her mother's skin, the strength in her hands as she cupped them around her own.

She wanted this mother back so much. It hurt like a deep ache in her belly. The kind from eating too many sharp lingonberries.

A few days after her mother had been taken, Ingeborg had returned to Heinrich Brasche's house so early in the morning it was still dark; the time when only servants would be awake. She had seen how desperate Heinrich had been to help her mother. Surely he could be persuaded to go to speak with the governor on her behalf?

But what little hope she had of his intervention faded at the news Widow Krog delivered to her: 'I am sorry to tell you that Heinrich Brasche has gone away, Ingeborg,' Widow Krog whispered to her; the door opened a crack.

'Where has he gone?' she demanded.

'He is away on business for his father in Bergen.'

'Bergen!' Ingeborg gasped in horror. The merchant's home city was leagues way. A journey that would take several weeks. 'But he promised to help my mother,' she said, her voice cracking with despair.

Widow Krog reached out. Touched her hand with her own cold one. Thrust a bundle of sweet *lefse* into her palm. 'I am sorry, child,' she said. 'Your mother is no witch, but she humiliated Fru Brasche.' Widow Krog sighed. 'This will not be forgiven, I fear.'

As Widow Krog spoke, Ingeborg heard the sharp call of Fru Brasche herself. With all her heart she wanted to push the door open and confront her. But what could she say to dissuade her? And before Ingeborg could act, Widow Krog had hurriedly shut the door in her face.

She had run back to her cottage, fury filling her. Faster and faster, the wind tearing at her cheeks.

Heinrich Brasche had lied. He had run away and abandoned her mother. He was a coward, like her father had been.

As the snows began to fall in earnest, she and Kirsten shut up their little cottage. With Zacharias stumbling along in the gathering snow behind them, Ingeborg and Kirsten put on their skis.

Kirsten insisted they could not leave Zacharias behind. The lamb had got so big and was heavy, but her sister would not consider it. After-all, Zacharias was the only thing of value they possessed so Ingeborg strapped the bleating lamb to a small sleigh she pulled alongside her with the rest of their paltry provisions packed in sealskin bags.

They pushed off across the fresh snow. Over the vast white they slid, and through the scraggy birch woods. Along the edge of the Varanger Peninsula, the Murman sea stilling into the glassy Varangerfjord while the livid midday sky pressed down upon them.

When they arrived at Solve's house in the village of Andersby, her mother's cousin was not pleased to see them.

'It's a terrible business about Zigri,' Solve said, not even inviting them across the threshold. 'But you shouldn't have come here, girls.'

'We've nowhere else to go,' Ingeborg said, hurt by the reaction of her mother's cousin.

'Ask Reverend Jacobsen to have you fostered,' Solve suggested.

'What other family would have us?'

'They might take Kirsten. She's still so small.'

'No, no,' Kirsten said, in panic. 'Don't leave me, Ingeborg.'

'Calm yourself, Kirsten. Of course, I won't,' Ingeborg said, taking her sister's hand. She looked up at Solve. 'Please, we need shelter,' Ingeborg begged her. 'I have brought food with us and our lamb for milking when she grows. We'll work hard for our board, I promise!'

'Ingeborg, I can't be associated with you,' Solve said, her hand on the head of Peder, who was gripping tightly onto her skirts. 'We already have Maren here, and I have my boys to consider.'

As she spoke, Maren and Erik came out of the cowshed carrying two full pails of creamy milk.

'She did it again, Mamma!' Erik cried out with a delighted look upon his face. 'Look how much milk Maren got the cow to make!'

Solve went puce. 'Quiet, child.'

As soon as Maren laid eyes on Ingeborg and Kirsten, her face broke into a wide smile.

'At last, you have come,' she said. 'I've been waiting for you.'

'They're not staying, niece, We can't take them in,' her aunt said.

Maren spun around. 'But we have plenty, enough for all of us!'

'That is not why,' Solve said, licking her lips nervously. 'It's too dangerous for us to fraternise with Zigri's daughters.'

Maren put her hands on her hips and looked at her aunt as if she were a poor fool. 'It's too late to be worrying about all of that now!' she said. 'Your husband put you in danger the day he took *me* in. My mother was condemned a witch too!'

Solve fidgeted. 'I had no choice in the matter, and that is all past and done with.'

'It is never done with, Aunt,' Maren said in a cool voice. 'We need to come together, show our strength.'

Solve gave a brittle laugh. 'What strength, you wretched girl!'

But Maren ignored her and turned to Ingeborg and Kirsten. 'Come inside, sisters.'

Ingeborg detected a softening in Solve's expression. She would not turn away her cousin's children.

'I suppose you are just girls, and what would the governor's men want with you?'

Reflections from the hidden winter sun shimmered low over Varanger-fjord. Steam like smoke rising off the shoreline where ice met the sea, a brew from Hell. Devil's breath. Ingeborg sat on its icy edge as the fleeting light disappeared. The sky was a sigh of blue, the snow blushed pink. This was where the ice burned, where the air was thin and brittle.

Was there any place as powerful as this? She could feel it as her fingertips pricked as if with pins, and in her itching skin. How she wished to harness this power and breathe fire. How she wished to melt away the leagues of ice and snow between her and her mother.

Maren found Ingeborg by Varangerfjord. Her skis thrown off. Still star-ing at the vapour above the ice, wondering if it was thick enough to take her weight. If it had been summer, the air would have been filled with the screeching Arctic terns on their way to the resting ledges back in their village of Ekkerøy, but in the shadowy tones of the November day the air was silent, with only a wintry moon present in the sky. All that could be heard was the lone call of a sea petrel swooping in the stark air, and the creak of snow upon the thin fjord-side trees.

Ingeborg stared at the fjord as tears hot on her ice-cold cheeks streamed down her face. She was angry with Heinrich Brasche, and with her mother for falling in love with him. She was angry with her father for never coming back from sea, and with Axell for drowning. She was angry for who she was: a poor girl, the daughter of a dead fisherman. Who would listen to her? How could she ever save her mother? She didn't even know the way to Vardø.

'Don't cry,' Maren said, placing her hand on Ingeborg's arm. 'Turn your sorrow outwards and let it strengthen your resolve to help your mother.'

'But my mother is doomed,' Ingeborg said trying to stop her tears, though they just kept coming. 'Branded a witch.'

'And so was mine! But remember Merchant Brasche, the governor, and even Bailiff Lockhert are afraid of witches.' Maren gripped Ingeborg's shoulders. 'And their fear gives us power!'

Ingeborg brushed her cheeks with her sleeve. Maren was wrong. Not a soul was afraid of her. She was not even an adult woman. Just a girl struggling to emerge into the world with the whole of it set against her.

'They're *not* afraid of us!' she spat at Maren, turning her frustration on her. 'They keep us down. Make us afraid of *them*.'

'And yet still they would put all us women to the stake if they rightly could,' Maren said in a cold voice, her sea-green eyes lit up by hidden lights. 'It does us no good to let them dominate us,' Maren continued. 'But these men are not invincible. They believe in the Devil. They believe he can destroy them, and that witches are his agents.'

'But how can this help my mother?' Ingeborg wailed. 'She's locked up in the governor's fortress all the way across the Murman sea—'

'There are ways we can help her,' Maren whispered, as she looked around her. But there was no other soul out by Varangerfjord. The last remnants of light sank into the early dusk. The moon shimmered above them, reflected slabs of floating ice, casting silvery light upon Maren's dark cheeks. 'Who do you think the witches are, Ingeborg?'

'I don't know,' she faltered, 'but not my mother—'

'The witches are the outcasts,' Maren said. 'Those who are different. Spat at. Defiled and abused. Together we lift ourselves up, we give each other strength.'

'What are you saying?' Ingeborg said, in a faint whisper.

'The governor, Merchant Brasche and Bailiff Lockhert – why, King Frederick himself, tar us with the same black brush of witchcraft. They are intent upon the destruction of all witches of the north. But why? Why bother with poor fishermen's wives and widows? Because, as I said, they are frightened of the power we possess in harmony with nature, with the animals and the phases of the moon. They are frightened of women together. All our wisdom eludes them.'

'I have no power, Maren. No one will listen to me!'

'*Make* them listen to you, Ingeborg,' Maren declared. 'Become mistress of the unknown, for this is the only way you can protect yourself and Kirsten.'

'But how?'

Maren chewed her lip, giving her a thoughtful look. 'I have a secret, one you must never tell my aunt, Solve,' she said. 'Do you promise?'

Ingeborg nodded. 'I promise,' she said, for the expression on Maren's face gave her a little hope.

'I will bring you to someone who can help us.'

'Who?' There were no other influential men in their neighbourhood. The Brasches were in complete control.

'Put your skis back on, and follow me,' Maren said. 'We are going to the Sámi.'

Ingeborg hesitated, but she had spent too many fruitless hours praying to the Good Lord. It was time to ask for the Devil's help if indeed Reverend Jacobsen was right, and the Sámi were his disciples.

Chapter 17

Anna

The week after the witch arrived at the fortress, I was called to dine with Governor Orning and his wife. The warmth of their chambers almost knocked me backwards after my own freezing hovel: as a fire blazed in the hearth, its radiance seemed to seep into every aspect of the room, including myself. The colours of the hunting tapestries on the walls appeared even more vibrant, and the rugs on the wooden floors danced with patterns.

As I approached the table, I could smell the luxury of their repast. Before me was a pile of freshly baked crisp *flatbrød*, along with another platter of herrings gridled in butter, and a big bowl of steaming *rømmekolle* laced with cinnamon.

I took a small portion, though I wished to gobble the whole feast down. Governor Orning filled a glass with wine, and I took a discreet delicious sip. Ah, to drink out of such fine glass! The liquid called to me of summers in the south, dark cherries and forest blackberries, and spices so sweet after all my weeks of bitter ale.

'Our work begins in earnest, Fru Rhodius,' Governor Orning announced, looking solemn as a man should who is about to go to war with witches.

'Yes indeed, Governor Orning,' I responded, sipping the wine again.

'The first witch, by the name of Zigri Sigvaldsdatter from the village of Ekkerøy, has been imprisoned in the witches' hole awaiting our interrogation.'

'Of what maleficium is she accused?' I asked.

The governor leant his elbows upon the dining table, interlacing his fingers and propping his chin upon them, frowning all the while with the import of his words. 'A merchant, Brasche, informs me Zigri Sigvalds-datter was one of the witches responsible for weather magic that wrecked his ship last winter as it headed south with a full cargo of *klippfisk*. Not only did all the crew perish but the loss in riksdaler was considerable.' Governor Orning lowered his voice to a conspiratorial whisper, although the only ones present were myself and his good wife Fru Orning, whom as ever picked at her food in a nervous manner. 'Moreover, this Sigvalds-datter woman was seen fornicating with the Devil.'

I felt a jolt of despair, though I was careful not to show it. I listened carefully with my hands meekly folded upon my lap, my eyes fixed on the alluring victuals. The governor had caught the first of his prey and yet all I could think about was the cinnamon cream of *rømmekolle* in my watering mouth.

'If it were not for Merchant Brasche and his ships we would have no trading routes to Bergen,' Governor Orning said. 'Our settlement would be quite impoverished without his resources. But he has told me that the peninsula is so rife with witches his family is afraid.' Governor Orning paused and leant back in his seat, picking up his glass of wine and sip-ping from it before continuing. 'The fishermen keep complaining about their debts of grain, but it is they who get themselves into such debt by not catching enough fish to pay back Merchant Brasche. And their wives are lured by the Devil.' Governor Orning dabbed his mouth with his nap-kin before placing it neatly folded by his platter. 'Merchant Brasche has hinted of his wish to return to live in Bergen. But, Fru Rhodius, we can't have that at all. He must be assured Varanger Peninsula is rid of these fisherwomen witches once and for all.'

'Who accuses the woman Zigri Sigvaldsdatter?' I asked. *Gather all the evidence, Anna. Make your case invincible.*

'Why, the merchant himself, for he saw the witches as birds taking flight and casting their weather magic.' He paused, leaning forward. 'But it is the wife of his son, Heinrich, who witnessed Zigri Sigvaldsdatter cavorting with the Devil in their cowshed.'

'Are they both willing to testify?'

'But of course. In fact, the merchant testified before in the trial of the witch Marette Andersdatter. And as for Fru Brasche, she's a goodly woman,' the governor said. 'However, it would please me greatly if we could persuade Zigri to confess and repent her sins. According to our laws, we need the witch to confess to ascertain a conviction.'

The governor scrutinised me, and I found myself meekly dropping my gaze, wishing I might take one more slice of *flatbrød*.

'This is why I wish you to speak with Zigri Sigvaldsdatter, and use your gentle, persuasive means as a woman to gain a confession, and moreover, denouncements of the other witches involved in the heinous misdeed of weather magic.'

Governor Orning snapped his fingers, and Guri began to remove the plates before I had a chance to snatch the desired *flatbrød*. I noted that Fru Orning had once again touched none of her repast, and just by looking at her scarred face, the skin seemingly stretched over bone, I could see she was in need of a good tonic.

The governor stood, and I rose too. 'Come with me, Fru Rhodius,' he said.

I followed the tall governor out of the warmth of his living chamber, his two wolfhounds at his heels, and I trotting behind them. We passed down a corridor and then into a high-ceilinged, vast chamber. The air within was so cold vapour plumed from our mouths, and I drew my shawl more tightly about my shoulders, wishing I was wearing the fur capelet you had given me.

There was a huge tapestry along one wall, lit up by the moonlight shimmering in from a row of high windows, and I was able to discern it was yet another hunting scene; this time a group of hunters rounding on one lone wolf, its body twisting as they pierced it with spears. Beneath the windows was a grand chair, like a throne, with an elk's antlers hanging above it, and beside this was a huge chest.

It was without doubt an impressive room and yet walking its length, I felt a pressing upon my chest and a sense of confinement greater than that within my prison longhouse.

The governor swept his hand around the great hall. 'This, my dear lady, is our trial chamber,' he said. 'Close your eyes now and imagine it full, because in time it will be.'

'For the trial of Zigri Sigvaldsdatter?'

'For the trial of *all* the witches of Varanger, because she's not the only one,' he said, sitting in the grand chair and placing his hands upon the carved arm rests. 'Have you heard of Liren Sand?'

'No, Governor,' I lied, not wanting to reveal any knowledge of Vardø witches.

'She was the leader of the witches, and I am pleased to say she was caught, and burned at the stake two years ago,' the governor said, his voice a low growl. 'But her accomplice was a Sámi woman named Elli and she escaped. I have been searching for her since.' He got up from the chair and stood before me with his arms behind his back. 'I have heard she is known to some of the women of Ekkerøy.'

I mulled over what he had told me as the governor knelt down at the big chest and opened it, pulling out an iron key. The governor's crusade against the witches had begun long before my arrival.

Standing up again, the governor wheeled around and walked towards me.

'See how I trust you, Fru Rhodius, more even than our blessed king does,' he said, waving the key before me. 'But I need you, and you need me.' He gave me a little half-smile, though his eyes had a merciless cast within them. 'Together we can do great things for our kingdom, can we not?'

'Yes, Governor Orning,' I whispered. But I didn't trust him, even though he was dangling the chance to be free again right in front of me.

He took a step forward and I could feel his breath upon my cheek. For a moment I wondered what his intent might be because he placed one hand upon my waist and his eyes investigated mine. His were hard, brutal eyes that had fought many battles and were immune to suffering.

I didn't flinch, for I knew he must not detect one chink of weakness within me.

With the key in his free hand, he swung it before my eyes. 'This, madam, is one of the keys to the witches' hole,' he said. 'I endow you with the authority to come and go into the witches' hole as often as you please.' He moved his hand from my waist up the side of my body until it came to my chest. He pulled back my kerchief to reveal the cream of my bosoms, heaving in my bodice with unease. The corners of Governor Orning's thin lips curled into an unpleasant smile as he slipped the cold key between my breasts before patting them. 'I believe it will be safe there, will it not, Fru Rhodius? You are a chaste woman.'

I felt myself blushing crimson, much to my own annoyance.

'I do not give you this key lightly. It is your task to speak with Zigri Sigvaldsdatter and get her to confess to her crime. Find out if Sámi Elli is behind the witchcraft. Get her to denounce all the other women who are witches on the Varanger Peninsula.'

'Yes, Governor,' I responded obediently, for what else could I say?

'If you are unable to persuade Zigri Sigvaldsdatter to freely confess, you must inform her of the consequences.' The governor stamped his foot upon the wooden floor so suddenly it made me start. 'Do you know what lies in my cellar, underneath this vast chamber, Fru Rhodius?' He stamped his foot again, a cruel snarl upon his face. 'It is Bailiff Lockhert's domain,' he said. 'With all his instruments of persuasion, including his beloved pinniwinks and the rack.'

'Your honour, I-I believe it's against Danish law to torture a suspected witch until she confesses.' The Good Lord only knows what possessed me to speak up, stammering as I did so.

'These are extraordinary times, Fru Rhodius, and require extraordinary measures. We are in a reign of terror, and we must do whatever is needed to protect our king and country.'

I did not want to think upon Lockhert's torture chamber and prayed Zigri Sigvaldsdatter would be pliable, but then a thought occurred to me. 'Is the witch a married woman, with children?'

Governor Orning sat down on his big judge chair, legs splayed, the scar down the side of his face as white and blanched as the elk antlers above him.

'She is a widow, Fru Rhodius – it would seem a young merry widow, with two daughters.'

'Your honour, may I suggest the bailiff undertakes a journey to her village to question her daughters?'

The governor folded his hands upon his lap.

'How clever you are, Fru Rhodius,' he said. 'But I will go myself with my good wife. She has a gentle touch and can talk to them. Indeed, the daughters' words may be just what we need.'

My heart sank, for it had been my intention to send Lockhert away so the woman would not be tormented by him. I did not want to be party to any torture.

However, if I were to tell the accused witch the governor was bound for her home village to question her offspring, might she more readily give up the truth? There was not much Governor Orning could do to children, for even he would not break such laws. But I could bring Zigri Sigvaldsdatter back to our Good Lord and lead her meekly to her end.

I could save her soul.

For I have never broken any of your laws in the entirety of my life, despite being your prisoner.

Remember, my king, I broke *no* laws.

Chapter 18

Ingeborg

They sped past Andersbyvatnet, going a way Ingeborg had never been before, across marsh thick with snow. Ingeborg's wooden skis sliced through the untouched snow, the grey sky slowly seeping to indigo, turning the snow blue, their skin blue. All around them became deep, daring blue.

Maren kept on skiing and led them further inland. The sky filled with stars as the snow gleamed, brilliant under the full moon. Eventually, she slowed so Ingeborg could join her at her side.

Ingeborg was panting, her skin damp with sweat beneath her skins despite the intense cold, and yet Maren looked as if she had hardly exerted herself. Instead, she was gazing into the distance. Without looking at Ingeborg, she said, 'The moon lights a pathway for us.'

'How far are we going?' Ingeborg asked, a little nervously. 'What if a blizzard comes in from the east?' They were too far away from Andersby to find shelter.

Maren sniffed the air. 'No storm!' she said, with confidence.

The sky appeared vast before them, the tundra rolling away in small, snowy hillocks. They staggered their skis in the thick snow, now going steadily up hill. By the time they topped a small crest of land, both girls were puffing plumes of steam into the frigid air.

'Here we are!' Maren pointed.

A cluster of wizened birch trees twisted out of the snow, but it was beyond the trees where Maren pointed. On the edges of an inland lake was a ring of four Sámi *lávvu* – taut circles of reindeer skins with poles thrusting out of their smoke holes.

Her father had often visited the Sámi to trade for reindeer meat and skins, but this was Ingeborg's first sight of a Sámi settlement. She felt a small thrum in her chest, but she wasn't frightened. Not like she had been when Lockhert had taken her mother.

A twig snapped behind them, and Ingeborg turned around to see a Sámi boy standing with his back against the wizened birch trees, staring at her with unblinking eyes. He was possibly a little older than she and had on a striking blue hat with four corners, braided with red, yellow and white trim. Her father had always called the hats the Sámi men wore 'four winds' hats for the star-shape they made. How colourful the hat appeared to Ingeborg, compared to the black high-crowned hat that Heinrich Brasche wore.

'Zare!' Maren called out.

The boy's face broke into a smile, though his eyes were still scrutinising Ingeborg. She felt a flush spread upon her cheeks despite the intense cold.

Maren began to speak in Sámi, much to Ingeborg's surprise. 'Do you speak Sámi?' Maren turned to Ingeborg, and she shook her head.

'Let us speak in Norwegian then,' she said to Zare. 'This is my friend, Ingeborg Iversdatter,' she added.

The Sámi her father had traded with had been shadowy figures from her childhood. Her father had brought fish, and sometimes grain, and in return they had received reindeer meat, skins and boots made from reindeer skins. The Sámi had been different from them, and Ingeborg had never thought much upon the Sámi folk, but now she took in the small circle of *lávvu*, and the families moving between them; the scent of food cooking, and the hum of voices. It felt peaceful, and so different from the tension in their village, overlooked as they were by the merchant's house.

'Come with me to check on the reindeer,' Zare said to them.

They turned their skis in the direction Zare went and passed through the *siida*. Just one of the Sámi women glanced their way. It was clear Maren was no stranger to them.

The reindeer were up on the plateau and in the thin birch woods in the winter grazing grounds. They took off their skis and balanced them against a tree, while Zare handed them both clumps of moss. There was already a Sámi boy up with the reindeer, minding them and keeping a look out for predators.

Maren waved at him before going up close to the reindeer. They gathered around her, antlers knocking together, and pushed their muzzles into her hands. 'One at a time, my loves,' Maren said, as she stroked their heads.

Ingeborg proffered a palm full of moss, and one of Maren's reindeer trotted over to her. Its hairy lips tickled her palm.

Zare joined her, placing his hand on the reindeer's head.

'They're so gentle,' Ingeborg said.

'I do not know why God blessed them with antlers, for to my mind the reindeers possess not one drop of fight in them,' Maren declared.

'The bull has plenty of fight in him, Maren,' Zare told her, before giving her a keen look. 'We have not seen you in many days. What brings you here?'

Maren paused from her feeding. She looked at Ingeborg first, with an expression in her eyes as if to say *Trust me* before turning to Zare.

'We need to ask for your mother's help,' she said. 'Ingeborg's mother has been arrested for witchcraft and taken to Vardøhus for trial. You know well what that means.'

Zare was very still for a moment, as if he held his breath. 'Yes,' he said, in a low voice. 'That I do.'

'Will you bring us to your mother?' Maren asked. 'She can help us.'

Zare's eyes turned to Ingeborg. 'I am sorry about your mother,' he said. 'But I have to protect my own.'

'Elli owes me,' Maren demanded. 'She escaped, and my mother did not.' Zare stiffened. 'Surely it is her choice if she decides to help or not?' Maren continued.

Zare fed a reindeer the last of his moss. 'Very well,' he said, his tone reluctant. 'I will bring you to her.'

They skied down from the winter grazing grounds and back into the *siida*, sliding off their skis and following Zare as he made for the middle *lávvu* in the circle.

Pulling back the reindeer skin entrance flap, he indicated for them to step inside.

Smoke from a central fire spun up towards the opening. Light from the snow outside reflected within the *lávvu*.

Ingeborg crouched down next to Maren beside a pile of peat and a scruffy black and white dog, which sniffed their feet. Ingeborg could smell sorrel leaves, and imagined their slightly sour taste, made sweet with milk and sugar, upon her tongue.

A very small woman was stirring a pot over the fire. She was even shorter than Ingeborg. The Sámi woman looked up and nodded at Zare. The tiny movement was enough invitation, and Maren shuffled forward to sit upon some reindeer skins, Ingeborg following her. The skins were soft and springy from their bedding of birch on the guest side of the fire.

Zare went to the other side of the fire and sat down. The woman poured three cups of warmed and herbed reindeer milk, and Zare passed one to Maren and one to Ingeborg before taking one himself.

They sat in silence, cradling their birch cups of brew before taking the first delicious sips.

At last, the woman spoke in Norwegian. 'How can I help you, Maren Olufsdatter?'

This must be Elli. At first glance, Ingeborg had thought her old, but she could see now she was not much older than her mother, her skin lined by her life spent outdoors but her eyes the same piercing blue as her son's. And as Elli cupped her drink of reindeer milk and drank, Ingeborg could see some of her fingers were stunted and broken.

'Will you send some spells against Governor Orning and his men?' Maren asked Elli.

'Why would you wish me to do such a thing?' Elli asked.

'Because they have my mother in the witches' hole,' Ingeborg spoke up, unable to hold back any longer.

Elli gave a sigh. It was long, and sad, and made Ingeborg's hope drop like a stone.

'Spells will do no good for your mother,' she said to her gently.

'But can you not shoot a *gand*?' Maren asked. 'After all, you sell them to the merchants, so they can send them against enemies in the south.'

Ingeborg shivered. Axell had once told her that Sámi sorcerers were able to send these *gands*, magic spells, great distances: 'They shoot their curses like arrows, their tips as deadly as the real thing,' he had said, mimicking the spell casting with his own imaginary bow and arrow.

Elli barked a short laugh. 'Oh, Maren!' she said. 'They're not real curses. We sell them to the imbecile merchants for the money.'

Maren looked crestfallen.

'I am sorry, girls,' Elli said. 'I can't send any spells to help your mother.'

'But my mother said you both cast spells—'

'Your mother was a dear friend,' Elli said, her voice heavy with sadness. 'It is thanks to her I am sitting before you now. But we didn't practise witchcraft together.'

The fire crackled and a spark shot out onto the reindeer skins, which Zare stamped out.

Maren was frowning at Elli, displeased by this revelation. Ingeborg followed her gaze.

The Sámi woman was staring into the flames, shadows and light flickering across her face, deep in thought. 'There is one way you might be able to save your mother.' Elli turned to Ingeborg. 'But it's dangerous.'

Maren's eyes brightened. 'Tell us how, Elli, we beg you.'

'There's a tunnel,' she said. 'Your mother and I found a big pit in the witches' hole unseen by the guards, so we dug and dug with our bare hands while Zare and his father dug outside the fortress walls. It took weeks, but at last the two halves met, and we had made a tunnel. This was how we escaped.'

'My mother escaped?' Maren said now, in a small voice.

'Yes, yes, she did. I am sorry I've never told you this,' Elli said, her eyes on the fire. 'We got out of the tunnel, but the soldiers saw us running away towards the boat Zare's father had hidden in the bay.'

Maren's expression was fierce as she listened intently to Elli.

'She slipped on the rocks. They caught her.'

'Oh, no!' Maren gripped her cup of reindeer milk with shaking hands as its contents slopped over onto her lap.

'She was going to get you at your uncle's house, and then come and live with us,' Elli said softly. 'She belonged with the Sámi.'

None of them spoke. Ingeborg was thinking of Maren's mother. The desperate chase across the slippery rocks and falling. Knowing she was all alone as her Sámi friends sailed away.

'Why did you never tell me this before?' Maren asked Elli, in a hurt voice.

'I thought to know would make it even harder for you,' Elli said, looking at Maren with compassion.

Maren put down her cup, brushing the speckles of spilt reindeer milk from her lap. 'I am glad you told me now,' she said, her voice strong again. 'If my mother was able to escape, so can yours, Ingeborg.'

'If we find the tunnel,' Ingeborg said, not daring to believe there was a chance she might be able to help her mother. 'Will you tell us how to get there? Where it is?'

'Zare will show you,' Elli said.

'No!' Zare protested, turning to his mother. 'What if they come looking for you again? I need to protect you.'

'I am indebted to Maren's mother, Zare, and we should help Maren's friend,' Elli said to her son.

Zare looked furious. 'Mother, the people from Ekkerøy would never return the same debt to us!' he declared. 'The governor's men will come here and take you away.'

'I promise you, my son, I will never be locked up again,' Elli said, her voice suddenly fierce. 'Think of this poor girl's plight.'

Elli raised her hand and opened her palm towards Ingeborg. Zare stared at Ingeborg, and she couldn't pull her gaze away. His eyes were the strangest, wildest blue she had ever encountered. As icy as the frozen fjord and just as deep.

'We understand you want to protect your mother, Zare,' Maren spoke up. 'But remember how we felt when our mothers were imprisoned? Now Elli is safe, although I have lost my mother. But we could still save Ingeborg's mother.'

'I beg you,' Ingeborg whispered. She could see the edge of Zare's fury softening, the ice in his eyes melting. She felt herself blushing at the directness of his look, but she did not drop her gaze.

The fire crackled as the wind tugged on the edges of the *lávvu*. Ingeborg shivered, although it was warm in their small circle. But she knew how cold and dark it was outside, and her mother was so far away, imprisoned in the darkest, coldest place of all.

'I beg you,' she repeated, clutching on to the tiny hope this Sámi boy could give her.

'Very well,' he said, shaking his head and looking far from compliant. 'We'll leave in a few hours.'

Ingeborg's chest fluttered with panic. 'But I need to go back and tell my sister we're going—'

'There's no time for that, Ingeborg!' Maren declared. 'We have to get to Vardø as soon as we can. Kirsten is safe with Aunt Solve and the boys.'

Ingeborg felt wretched. 'She'll think I ran away without her.'

'But she will know in the end you went to save your mother,' Maren told her. 'Kirsten will be so happy when you return with her!'

Ingeborg felt a prick of doubt. Shook it away. Of course, Kirsten loved their mother, just as much as she. When Ingeborg brought her home again, their mother would be as she had been long ago, just as she had dreamed.

'You must rest for now,' Elli said, offering her a reindeer skin. 'Close your eyes and gather your strength, for you will need it.'

Curled in the corner of the Sámi *lávvu* beside Maren, Ingeborg thought she would never feel sufficiently at ease to sleep. But though they were in a moveable home, a mere tent made of reindeer skins and sticks, it felt sturdier than their turf-roofed cottage in Ekkerøy. The warm, woody interior and the low moan of the wind outside lulled her into fitful dreams.

She saw her mother attired in Fru Brasche's sumptuous green silk gown, red hair falling free, and the blue ribbon wound within it. In Ingeborg's dream, she was mistaken: her mother had not been imprisoned in the fortress on the island of Vardø; indeed, no, she had been rescued by Heinrich Brasche and was living a life of liberty in the city of Bergen.

'Mother, why have you forsaken me and Kirsten? Why do you forget us?' she beseeched her mother. But it was she, Ingeborg, who was the ghost and her mother looked right through her.

There she was, Zigri Sigvaldsdatter with her Heinrich, sitting at the head of a great feast, with towers of sugar cones and platters of ripe fruits the like of which Ingeborg had only seen on the tapestry coverings in

Heinrich Brasche's parlour in Ekkerøy. The couple were red cheeked and bonny, gorging on the sweet fruit, juices dripping from their chins. More and more they ate, their appetites insatiable. They feasted with guests from another realm, creatures from the dark netherworld: foxes in red jackets; goats wearing jerkins; oafish trolls grizzly as bears; wolves with tall hats; and centaurs, half-man and half-horse, their bare chests thick with curling hair.

A liveried black cat was banging a drum to announce the greatest guest of all. Ingeborg wanted to look away, not see who he was, but it felt as though two hands were either side of her head, holding it in place, and she could not close her eyes.

He made a grand entrance, as only the Prince of Darkness should, sweeping into the great hall of Heinrich Brasche's Bergen home in a big black cape.

The cat kept banging the drum. *I. AM. HERE. FOR. YOU.*

The Devil looked at her. His eyes were like only one other's she had ever seen before.

She jolted in shock. 'Maren!' she cried out.

'I am here!'

Ingeborg was being shaken, falling out of the diabolical dream.

'Wake up, Ingeborg.' Maren's voice.

Ingeborg opened her eyes to look into Maren's sea-bright irises – seaweed green, sundown gold, fish-scaled silver – colours beyond human, just like the Devil's own eyes in her dream. She shivered with dread. This was a terrible mistake. What if she was endangering her mother further by associating with the daughter of a witch, and the Sámi?

But who else could she turn to?

The drum was still beating. No longer in her dream, nor her head. She realised the sound was coming from the Sámi settlement outside. 'Why are they playing a drum?' she whispered in a hoarse voice to Maren.

'It is the *noaidi*, the Sámi shaman,' Maren replied, looking excited. 'Come on, let's go and see.' She tugged on Ingeborg's limp hand.

The relentless thrumming of the drum was echoing across the *vidda*. They were at the centre of its beat, and there was another sound too. Voices calling, strange and ethereal.

'The *noaidi* is *rune*ing and *yoik*ing with his magic drum.' Maren's eyes were bright with intrigue. 'Let's go closer so we can hear the better.'

'No,' Ingeborg protested in alarm. 'This is sorcery! The Devil makes these sounds.'

'And so, what if he does?' Maren challenged her, as she scrambled out of the *lávvu* into the stark night. 'I'm not afraid of the Dark Lord.' She lifted the flap with one hand, and beckoned Ingeborg to follow.

Ingeborg obeyed, bitten now by an urge within her she couldn't quell.

Outside the air was brimming with the strange sounds. Were they even human? She hesitated.

'Maren, we should go back within.' She pulled on the other girl's sleeve, regretting that she had let curiosity get better of her.

Maren pulled away from her touch and made towards the sound of the drumming. This girl's lack of fear was foolish, not brave. Did Maren not know she was meddling in a world that could swallow them up? Never allow them back to their own people?

As the drumming grew louder, and the wailing continued Ingeborg sensed it coming from a *lávvu* in the centre of the *siida*. Now one voice emerged as if the song of a wolf.

They were so close to the tent that Ingeborg imagined the gathering of the Sámi within. The drumming had seized her heart. It beat in time to it. Reverend Jacobsen had told them the playing of the Sámi *runebomme* awakened demons. Was she now answering the call of the Evil One?

Maren plunged on through the snow to place her hands upon the taut reindeer skin of the tent. Would she dare go inside? Surely it would offend the Sámi greatly if they interrupted their rituals? But Maren didn't go within the *lávvu*, instead kneeling in the dry chill of the snow.

As Ingeborg joined her, she could see she was peering through a crack in the folds of the reindeer skin against one of the support sticks. Maren leant back for Ingeborg to peek in. She pressed her face to the stiff reindeer skin and peered into the tent.

Inside the *lávvu*, the *noaidi* was playing his *runebomme*. He was not dressed in black like the Devil but was a figure of colour, with his ornate embroidered jacket in red and blue. He had a pointed beard, and the skin of his face looked as leathery as dried reindeer meat. He beat his drum with a little hammer, as copper rings bounced upon it. There were symbols dancing over the drum's taut skin – Ingeborg could make out the sun in the centre of it, and little men with reindeer. The *noaidi* was playing his drum but looked beyond it. The expression in his eyes was distant, and it seemed to Ingeborg as if his soul had gone on a journey, such as the witches when they flew with the Devil.

Was he casting *gands*? But Elli had said their *gands* were merely trick spells they sold to superstitious Bergen merchants intent on revenge.

So, what did those pictures on the drum mean? Ingeborg longed to take it into her own hands and read the stories upon it, understand the symbols.

'The drum is a gift from the Dark Lord,' Maren whispered to her as she squeezed in beside her to look through the crack in the tent. There were others in the *lávvu* besides the *noaidi* – men and women from the *siida*. They were all repeating the sounds the *noaidi* made, the men in higher voices, and the women in lower ones. There was Elli, sitting close to the shaman, by the smoking fire, her eyes locked upon the movements of the *noaidi* as he continued to drum.

Then, quite suddenly, he stopped. Placing his drum down, he gathered ashes from the fire and threw them over himself. Then he sat back down and drank from a cup as the others continued to chant the wild, unbound song.

To Ingeborg's surprise, the *noaidi* lay down and closed his eyes, while Elli got up and came to sit by him. Her voice was now the dominant one as she sang the twisting, uncontained notes.

'The shaman is looking for wisdom in another world,' Maren whispered. 'Elli must bring him back, otherwise he will die.'

Ingeborg was astounded by the power Elli exuded as she called to the *noaidi*. But she pulled back suddenly, feeling wicked for looking into a private world she should not be privy too.

Maren's eyes were glinting in the moonlight, and she looked pleased, as if what they had seen was a good thing. But it was far from it. Ingeborg was sure Reverend Jacobsen would declare their souls in mortal danger. But, more than her fear, Ingeborg felt their intrusion. This ceremony did not belong to the likes of her, nor Maren. They had no place spying on the Sámi and their *noaidi*.

She pulled on Maren's arm. 'We should go.'

Maren sat back on her haunches. 'I wonder if the ceremony is for us, Ingeborg,' she mused, ignoring her. 'I wonder if the *noaidi* is looking into our futures. I wonder what animal spirit guides him? I think the reindeer bull – he is the most powerful of all!'

Ingeborg snorted in derision. Why would a *noaidi* undertake such a ritual for her and Maren? But the sound of the drum was still in her body, like the waves of the ocean pounding upon Ekkerøy beach. She found herself leaning in and peering through the little crack in the tent again.

Elli was still sitting guard over the fallen shaman and singing the jagged song as before. Hazy behind the smoke, Ingeborg caught sight of the burning blue eyes of Zare, and his fierce concentration.

She pulled back. What if he had seen her?

'Zare is in there,' she whispered to Maren.

'Of course,' Maren said. 'It is his father who is the *noaidi*, and one day he will be one too.'

'Oh,' Ingeborg said in astonishment.

'Zare is very loyal to his people,' Maren said, a glint of something in her eye. Was it challenge? 'They will always come first to him, before finding a wife or children.'

'Is that not the case with most men?' Ingeborg replied hotly, feeling her cheeks bloom, to her annoyance. 'Duty comes before love.'

Maren shrugged. 'The marital whys and wherefores of men are not something that bothers me.'

'But, one day, you shall be wed, Maren,' Ingeborg said. 'As shall I.'

'I do not believe I will,' Maren said, firmly. 'For they can never give me what I want.'

'Do you not wish for children?' Ingeborg asked in surprise.

'Do you, Ingeborg Iversdatter?' Maren held her gaze. 'In your heart, *do you?*'

Ingeborg felt flustered by Maren's question. She had never thought upon whether she did or did not want to have her own family one day. It didn't seem to be a happening of choice for any of the fisherwives of Ekkerøy. But there in the Sámi *siida*, the life laid down for her in her home village felt as if it had peeled away like old bark from a birch tree, curling and silvered whispers of what might have been.

She shivered, her breath as vapour in the moonlight. While they had been talking, the singing had stopped. Silence spread thick around them. The tent was full of bodies, and yet not a hush could be heard from within.

A twig snapped behind them, and Ingeborg whirled around to see Zare staring down at them, hands on his hips. How had he slipped out of the tent? Immediately her cheeks heated, and she scrambled to her feet.

'The drumming was so loud it woke us up!' Maren declared in their defence, before he had even spoken to them. 'We wanted to see.'

Zare cocked his head on one side. 'And are you satisfied, Maren Olufsdatter?'

Maren gave a big sigh before linking her arm with Ingeborg. 'No, we are not, are we, Ingeborg? Because we would like to know what your father was doing. Did Elli get him back?'

'My father is well,' Zare said.

'Where did he go? What did he see?' Maren pushed.

Zare shook his head, but he was looking at Ingeborg, not Maren. Ingeborg was unsure if he was angered by their presence or indifferent. But when he spoke, the tone of his voice was mocking: 'Back to your slumbering, Norwegian girls,' he said. 'You need to rest, because we must cover a great distance to Vardø on our plucky – even foolish – venture.'

Ingeborg felt herself bristling with indignation. Did he think the life of her mother a jesting matter?

'It is far from foolish!' Maren retorted on Ingeborg's behalf. 'We are merely refusing to submit to the will of the governor. There are more of *us* than them, Zare, if your people were to resist. I do not understand why we let them beat us down!'

'Well, they do have muskets, Maren,' Zare protested, his tone still mocking.

'But we have magic,' Maren countered, squeezing Ingeborg's arm.

Zare sighed, as if Maren was a child with too much imagination. 'Off to sleep with you.' Zare shooed them away. 'If my mother returns to find you both out in the cold, she will be most unhappy.'

Ingeborg woke to the sensation of hot wet licks upon her hand; the one that Merchant Brasche's black hound had bitten. She opened her eyes to see one of the Sámi dogs devotedly licking her damaged hand. Only now she noticed the skin had raised red with infection and it itched. There was little light in the *lávvu*, but she could hear the sound of the fire crackling and the scent of smouldering turf mixed with that of meaty broth bubbling in the kettle above the fire.

She sat up, still allowing the dog to lick her hand. The touch of its tongue upon her irritated skin was soothing. As her eyes adjusted to the gloomy interior, she noticed Maren was no longer sleeping by her side; indeed, the *lávvu* was empty apart from Elli, who was crouching by the fire, removing the thin sheaves of dried fish from a stone slab to stack upon another stone behind her. She then stirred the kettle above the fire. The scent of meaty stew wafted anew towards Ingeborg, making her mouth water. Elli added some more reindeer meat to the bubbling pot before raising her eyes to Ingeborg.

'Where is Maren?' Ingeborg asked.

'She is with Zare and his father. They are gathering provisions for your journey.' Elli's eyes dropped to look at Ingeborg's injured hand. 'What ails your hand?' she asked.

'Merchant Brasche's dog bit it.'

'It is a brute of a dog, like its master,' Elli said, leaving aside her pot of stew and moving towards Ingeborg. 'Away with you.' She gently patted the dog away, then she picked up Ingeborg's hand.

Ingeborg found herself staring at Elli's twisted thumb and broken fingers. She wondered how she managed to do any of her chores with such disfigurements.

'I will heat milk with sorrel leaves in it,' she said. 'It is not a deep cut, and the sorrel will help it heal. You are small but strong, are you not, Ingeborg Iversdatter?'

Ingeborg nodded, a little awed by the Sámi woman, unable to take her eyes away from her gnarled hands.

'What is it you wish to ask me, girl?' Elli said.

'Your hands,' Ingeborg whispered. 'What happened to your hands?'

Ingeborg immediately regretted her question, for there was no answer forthcoming. When she looked up, Elli's expression was clouded, and her lips had narrowed into a tight line. 'It is better for you if you do not know,' she replied. 'Especially because of where you are going.' Elli wrapped her shawl tight about her.

'Did it happen there – on Vardø?'

Rather than answering Ingeborg's question, Elli lifted her twisted hands to her face and gazed upon them. 'My dear friend, Marette Andersdatter, was denied a proper burial and she may never find her way to the *sáivu*.'

'Who are the *sáivu*?' Ingeborg asked in a whisper.

'They are the *huldrefolk*, our ancestors in the next world. They live among us though we can't see them, but they have their own herds of reindeer. They never go hungry or suffer as do we. And where they live, the governor can never touch them.'

Ingeborg wondered if this was where her father and Axell now resided, although Reverend Jacobsen's description of Heaven was high above and far away. A realm a girl such as she could only hope to get to.

'My battered hands are my remembering for Maren's mother, for I never forget. They ache, they pain me often. When Maren asked for my help yesterday, they throbbed until I complied.' Elli paused, licked her lips, and pulled Ingeborg in with a fierce glare. 'I know my son, Zare, is as wily as a wolf, and he can slip any snare, but Maren . . .' She paused. 'Don't let her be caught, Ingeborg Iversdatter, because the governor's feelings for her mother run deep. He loved Marette Andersdatter, and then he hated her. How this man hated a woman so. He will not suffer her only daughter to live, even though she is not yet fully a woman.'

Chapter 19

Anna

The key, nestled between my breasts, was cold, hard metal upon my warm skin. But I liked to feel it. To possess a key that unlocked a door! It was just one, granted, and to a place none would wish to reside, but still, the trust the governor had placed in me by putting the key upon my person, and the task he had given to me, made me swell with pride. I was worthy of being a keyholder to the witches' hole.

As soon as I was returned to my prison longhouse, I fished the key out from between my breasts and slipped it into the pocket beneath my petticoats. I walked around the chamber feeling its pleasing knock against my thigh. Every now and again, I stopped, pulled the key out and admired it upon my palm.

When Helwig saw me taking out the key, she looked quite put out. This pleased me, as she would constantly remind me that she was my gaoler, and not my maid.

'Who gave you this key?' she asked me.

'The governor himself.'

'Where is it for?' she asked. 'It doesn't look big enough for the castle gates.'

'The witches' hole.' I slid the key back into my pocket. 'The governor has instructed me to come and go as I please. I am to interrogate the accused witch.'

Helwig's expression fell further into dismay. 'Fru Rhodius, this is a matter you might not wish to be involved in.'

I was annoyed at her presumptive manner and put my back to her. But no matter what, I could see her downcast expression and hear her words of warning. She had taken the joy out of my small triumph, and

I was furious with her. 'Do you see how filthy the floor of this house is?' I snapped at her. 'I would remind you to perform your duties and keep your thoughts to yourself.'

I collected my Bible, doused my handkerchief with more lavender water, and prepared to question the accused witch.

All the while Helwig was shaking her head at me, as she swept the floor with little enthusiasm.

I had not expected it to be so dark, but of course there was no window in the witches' hole. The smallest and darkest of all cells in the fortress was, in fact, more a hut than a hole. From the outside I had seen a tiny opening beneath the sagging turf roof, but this belonged to the ammunition store, which was above the witches' hole separated by a ceiling of rotting beams. The soldier by my side, Captain Hans, held a blazing torch for me, and it flickered in the draughts coming from all directions. The light the torch cast revealed a bleak, coffin-shaped space, much the same size as my pantry back in Bergen. There were no items of domestic comfort within it: no candles, not a stool, nor a fire, not even a smoke hole. I had stepped into a black box, an icy, rough-floored chamber filled with the stench of rotting fish, unwashed bodies and defecation.

I took out my handkerchief and pressed it against my nose. 'Where is the witch?' I whispered to Captain Hans, for though I could smell her I could not see her.

He lifted the torch before him, and in the far corner of this tiny hovel I saw a curled-up figure, the white of a face lifted up, devoid of distinctive features in the dark.

'Pass me the torch,' I requested Captain Hans as my eyes began to adjust. 'Wait outside.'

'Should I not stay by your side?' he said. 'She's a witch.'

'I will be perfectly fine,' I assured the young man.

He held his gaze away from the accused woman, clearly fearful of bewitchment, but I was a woman too, and I firmly believed she could not cast this spell upon me.

As I approached the accused witch, Zigri Sigvaldsdatter, I discerned big eyes in the moon face, which emerged as huge discs of sorrow. It was hard to make out her shape and form as she was huddled under a pile of reindeer skins. I was pleased to see that these skins had been provided for her, although it was only a small act of kindness since I imagined the governor did not wish her to perish from the cold in the witches' hole before she could confess all she knew about the witches of the north.

'My name is Fru Anna Rhodius,' I informed Zigri. 'The governor has sent me to care for you.'

'Care for me?' she asked in a cracked voice.

'Yes,' I said, softly. 'Are you hungry? Thirsty?'

Witches must be tamed, my king, for it doesn't work to push hard against them.

'I am,' she whispered shakily.

'I will make arrangements for victuals to be brought,' I said, turning towards the door again, my beautiful key all the while in its secret pocket banging against my thigh.

'Don't leave me here,' she cried out, 'in the dark!'

'I will return with sustenance,' I assured her. 'Have faith.'

As Zigri Sigvaldsdatter gulped down the ale and gobbled up the *flatbrød* with a slab of brown cheese, I had the opportunity to examine her. She was a striking beauty, which did not seem possible for one from such common circumstances. Her lustrous hair rolled in waves down each side of her dirty face, and a straggle of blue ribbon hung twisted around one of her tresses. I was relieved to see she was relatively free of bruising apart from where her wrists had been cuffed.

'Tell me, my dear.' I spoke gently as I crouched down beside her. 'Why are you here?'

She swallowed down the last of her ale and I could see it gave her some vigour. 'It's a misunderstanding,' she said. 'I have been slandered, and falsely accused.'

'Who accuses you?'

'Fru Brasche,' Zigri said, her voice laced with hatred. 'She is a shrew!'

'But on what grounds does she accuse you?'

Zigri Sigvaldsdatter pulled forward the lock of hair twisted with the blue ribbon and began to rub its length. 'It is a delicate matter,' she said, looking at me furtively. 'She claims she saw me in the cowshed with the Devil but that is not the case.' She sighed deeply. 'I was in the cowshed with her husband. This is why she attacks me!'

'Fornicating with a married man is a terrible sin,' I said.

I had to say these words to her, although as you know I do not believe it so when true love occurs among the special few. Why, then this love unlaces all moral strictures.

Zigri Sigvaldsdatter bowed her head. 'I know, Fru Rhodius,' she said in a meek voice. 'But it doesn't make me a witch.'

I paused, then licked my lips, remembering the governor's instructions that I was to extract a confession, not sympathise with the accused.

'Fru Brasche swears on the Holy Bible she saw you with the Devil, Zigri Sigvaldsdatter, and that her husband was with his father at the time.'

'But what does Heinrich say? Where is he?' She stopped rubbing the ribbon and reached forward, grabbing my arm with her grubby hands. 'Where is Heinrich? He promised me no harm would come to me.'

With her proximity to me the stench of her unwashed body became even stronger; and there was another smell beneath it – the scent of terror: vomit and urine. I pressed my handkerchief to my face again and inhaled deeply upon its lavender scent.

'Where is Heinrich?' she repeated.

I lowered my handkerchief to speak. 'He is not in Vardøhus, Zigri Sigvaldsdatter. That is all I can tell you.'

She clutched her belly beneath the piles of skins, and her eyes widened in disbelief.

'But he promised me,' she said, in a hoarse whisper.

'I will enquire for you,' I said, rising from my crouched position. My legs were aching, and I was feeling overcome from the smell in the place. I dabbed my face with my scented handkerchief again. 'In the meantime, Zigri, you must think back. Was it truly Heinrich Brasche in the cowshed, for his father, Merchant Brasche, claims he was elsewhere? Could the Devil have tricked you?'

'No, no.' She shook her head. 'No, it was Heinrich, and he loves me!'

Ah, my king, was she not a very simple woman indeed? For you know well that a man's love is not enough to protect a fallen woman. Passion shrivels in the face of duty, no matter however grand a one it may be. Heinrich Brasche would not come to her aid for the wanton wretch had been seduced by the dream of a grand life to which she did not belong.

Weighing on my mind was the need to question her about the claims made by Merchant Brasche about the weather magic she and other witches had performed to wreck his ship, but I could face the broken creature no longer.

Clutching the key, I held the torch out in front of me and stumbled back to the entrance of the witches' hole.

'Please,' she begged. 'Please find out where Heinrich is. He will speak for me.'

Her pleas were still ringing in my head as I walked briskly back to my longhouse. The ache that laced those pleas echoed inside my body, the deep longing she possessed for her lover.

My king, I felt her abandonment as keenly as my own.

Chapter 20

Ingeborg

They skied through the sparse forest, Zare leading the way as the two girls followed, the silence of their solitude unchallenged apart from the creaking of scraggy branches laden with snow, and the swishing of their skis.

They emerged upon yet another frozen lake. The thick dark clouds of night had dropped away, and although the moon still burned silver above, the sky was lifting to a deep spirit blue. Ingeborg spied a wolverine running across the lake. It did not see them for they moved as part of nature themselves.

What they were doing was pure madness: two girls and one Sámi boy on a quest to save an imprisoned witch in Vardø fortress. But Ingeborg had lost all reason. She needed to get to Vardø before it was too late.

They skied for two days, most times in the dark; brief dusky respites folding back into winter darkness. Ingeborg was exhausted from the exertion of it; Maren and Zare never tired but allowed her some rest.

The Sámi boy would seek out a place to build a fire. Then he and Ingeborg would go in search of wood or dig up some peat protected from damp beneath the snow-covered moss to feed it. Meanwhile, Maren would disappear and return with the sweet nutty roots of alpine bistort, young tender leaf stalks of angelica, among other plants she had foraged.

'Why don't we snare a hare?' Zare asked Maren.

'We have no need of its flesh,' she said.

'You are a strange one,' Zare said, producing some dried reindeer meat from his pocket and offering some to Ingeborg.

Ingeborg liked gathering fuel for the fire with Zare. They worked in silence most times, but his presence was a comfort.

As they sat huddled around the fire, sharing the same skins to keep warm and alive in the frozen wilds, the three of them would go over the plan together. Ingeborg had so many questions, so many what ifs. But she was afraid to utter them. It was impossible to consider their failure.

On the second night, swathes of swirling, iridescent lights appeared – shimmering curtains of violet and green dancing across the night sky. Maren rose from beside the fire, lifting her head and her arms to the luminescence as if receiving a gift the colours were bestowing upon her.

'Lower your head,' Zare hissed at her. 'You must always show humility to *Guovssahas*, the lights of the north.'

Ingeborg's father had told her how the Sámi revered the northern lights, whereas in the Christian world their sight was something to be dreaded, a prophecy from Hell itself, and of dark magic brewing.

They were beyond all the grey colours of her everyday world.

Maren spun to face them, her eyes gleaming. 'My mother is up there, dancing in the lights. She told me I would always find her there.'

Zare shook his head and poked the fire with a stick.

'Her magic still pumps through my body, Ingeborg,' she said, sitting down. 'She will protect us.'

'Your talk of magic will send you to the stake,' Zare warned.

A wolf howled, joined by the rest of its pack. Ingeborg looked nervously into the dark woods.

'They will stay away from the fire,' Zare reassured her.

'These wolves will not bother us,' Maren added confidently.

But Ingeborg was too afraid to sleep in case the fire went out. She lay down like the others but kept her eyes open, listening to the howling wolves and wondering if they were coming closer.

'I will watch the fire,' Zare called across to her. 'You need to sleep, Ingeborg.'

She looked into his eyes blue as the flames of their fire, and they made her feel safe. Slowly she closed her own.

It was the third morning of their journey. The moon lit a silver path upon the thick snow as twists of hazy green and violet light pranced above them. The northern lights had glimmered for all the hours of her anxious rest and now she was at the foot of Domen, the Devil's kingdom. With sealskin sleeves upon them to give them more grip, they dug their skis into the snowy sides of the hill and began to pace their way upwards. It was not a steep mountain, but it was broad, and the snow thick. Ingeborg kept sinking in up to her knees.

She and Maren had tucked their skirts up under the waistband and the tail of the reed staffs of their bodices. Beneath, they wore old breeches once belonging to Maren's uncle which Ingeborg had been wearing since she had moved in with Maren's aunt. They were huge on Ingeborg, and hindered her further, becoming saggy, wet and heavy on her legs. She was envious of Zare in his belted Sámi *gákti* and reindeer skin *gálssohat* leggings as he climbed upward with ease.

They reached the summit. Through the swirling mist wide white land spread in three directions – north, south and west – as far as they could see. There were no wolves following them, nor ahead. To the east was the edge of the mountain. The ethereal lights of the northern skies had faded away and darkness transformed to a brief spell of azure tinged as golden pink as cloudberries high above the mist. Ingeborg staggered over to the edge of the cliff. Below was the Murman sea, hissing upon the shores of the mountain. If she peered over to her right, she could see the curve of the mountain and a dark opening to one of the caves.

'Imagine,' Maren said in a low voice, 'beneath our feet are a labyrinth of caves they say leads to the one entranceway to Hell!'

Ingeborg didn't want to imagine it at all. But Maren's words had amused Zare. He laughed at her. 'Christian superstitions!'

'What is Domen to you, Zare?' Maren challenged him.

'It is a hill. Merely this.'

'Don't you believe in magic? What kind of Sámi are you, anyway?'

'There is magic, Maren, but not the way you say it is.'

'You're wrong!' she declared, pushing off on her skis again and flying as if the wind itself across the top of the mountain. A small dark figure in the vast emptiness gliding upon the Domen's empty back.

'We should catch up with her,' Ingeborg said, anxious for Maren being so alone.

'She will be fine,' Zare said. 'Maren has spent enough time alone in the wilderness to fend for herself.' He pointed to the edge of the cliff. 'Do you wish to see our destination?'

The mist had begun to lift from the top of the mountain, and she could discern shadows of land out to sea.

Vardø. The winged island. A lump of rock with a ragged coastline and a treeless hump of hill. Not one tree grew upon the savage-looking island. She could see the tiny harbour, with a cluster of cottages around it, the kirk, and the silhouette of the white fortress.

She stared at that fortress. Inside was her mother.

Zare gazed at Vardøhus, and then he raised his eyes to the sky. 'A storm is coming. We should cross before it arrives.'

Ingeborg didn't know how he could tell this, because it felt so still there on the mountain. All she could hear was the distant rocking of the water, and the gulls crying. She was about to continue after Maren when Zare placed a hand on her arm in warning.

'Move very slowly,' he whispered.

Her skin crawled with alarm, her spine prickling. She looked into his eyes to read more in his words. His gaze was reassuring as if to say, *Do not worry, I will protect you*, but she could also see his alarm beneath it.

As they both pivoted very slowly away from the cliff, Ingeborg saw what Zare had spotted.

A big lynx, prowling towards them.

Chapter 21

Anna

You sought me out. Remember, my king? It was who you came to me first.

It was the fifth day of October 1634, and the night of *Det Store Bilager* – the grandest wedding Copenhagen had ever seen and the matrimonial day of your brother, the prince elect, Christian, to Magdalene Sybille of Saxony. Your brother and his young wife were bathed in the full glory and splendour of Danish royalty. The preparations went on for weeks though, most likely, you had no idea of the labour involved, but my father was kept busy attending to kitchen maids who had scalded themselves, and servants who had fallen off ladders as they hung garlands in the king's garden. The weather was still mild enough to let guests wander in the grounds enjoying the last languid sigh of autumn before the long winter arrived.

I had never heard of so much meat for one feast alone! Your father, King Christian, seemed determined that no one would go hungry. Butchers were slaughtering for days before the wedding and I heard near one hundred oxen, a thousand sheep, dozens of turkeys and chickens were prepared, along with giant blood sausages, huge smoked hams, baked pheasants and doves.

As the king's physician, my father was considered important enough to be invited to the wedding. My whole family were to attend, but I did not want to go. My mother had to cajole me; I was a bashful maid of nineteen years and knew well my appearance would be scrutinised by every man in the room, my value judged for marriage potential; for it was about time I was wed.

I had no interest in parading with all the other young ladies decked out and on display, for my preferred place was in the library or my father's cabinet of curiosities, or better still, in my father's botanical gardens. To sit at the table and dine off silver platters and drink out of Venetian glass with the nobles of not just Copenhagen but all of Europe and their kings, queens, princes and princesses filled me with such nerves I was fairly shaking with them.

'Please, Father, let me stay at home,' I had begged.

'We can't countenance the idea, Anna. The king has taken a personal interest in your marriage,' he said.

'Does he not have enough of his own daughters to marry off?' I protested.

'I believe he never tires of the marriage game,' my father said, in a dour voice.

As you know, your father, King Christian IV – whom my father was in daily attendance of, with all his various ailments besieging him in those later years – had fathered over twenty legitimate children, let alone the illegitimates. I had grown up in a house close to Rosenborg Palace, and though not allowed to play with the royal children I had watched all the little princesses on their daily walks with the governesses.

I had watched you as a young prince, too, with your tight curls of shiny black hair, grow taller and taller. With each year, your shoulders broadened, your legs became stronger beneath breeches and stockings, and the hairs gathered upon your chin. I was delighted by the sight of your distinguished moustache, and your big brown eyes as entreating as a gentle hound. You held yourself with poise and presence, possessing a resolute calm, unlike your boisterous older brother who had such a reputation for wildness.

I watched you, but I believed I was not seen by you, even after the day we met in the library all those years before, or in my father's cabinet of curiosities. I believed you'd forgotten me as quick as the snap of your fingers, for who was I compared to you?

Ah, but let us return to my memories of the night of your brother's marriage celebrations. He was the future king of Denmark – or so we all believed at the time – Prince Christian, named after his father, dressed in silks and brocades and filled to the brim with wine and good food, patting his well-filled belly with a grin as wide as a crescent moon. His wife could not have been more different for she was a neat, reserved woman and though dressed in a resplendent golden brocade gown, her dark hair braided and decorated with tiny pearls as if stars in the night sky, there was an air of austerity about her. The louder her new husband became, the tighter she clasped the cross around her neck, only picking at the silver platters piled with delicacies.

I knew Magdalene Sybille to be a very devout young woman, and indeed in my library in Bergen, I possess an edition of the prayer book – an exquisite volume – she wrote not long after your brother passed away. How disapproving this pure Lutheran girl must have been of all the extravagance of her wedding, with endless courses of rich foods announced by trumpeters and kettledrums.

As we sat around the tables, brimming with all the opulence of this grandest of all wedding feasts – meats, breads, cheeses, towers of marzipan and cones of sugar – I felt your gaze upon me. I was dressed in the best we could afford, but I knew well which colours suited me, and had selected a gown of cornflower blue silk, with my mother's pearls wound tightly around my neck. I possessed a beautiful fan made of peacock feathers that had once belonged to my grandmother, behind which I hid most of my face; not to be coy, but because my cheeks had turned crimson to feel your eyes upon me.

I snuck a furtive look at your mistress, Margrethe Pape. She was a magnificent creature, haughty and proud, and I wondered how your eyes could stray from such a beauty.

What agony the marriage feast became, for after the first few delicacies my stomach was full, but hours went by and the courses were endless, each dish richer than the last; on and on, my corset digging tightly into my sides, the wine tasting sour in my mouth from the excesses of flavours on our platters.

At last, the Royal Ballet was announced in the great palace ballroom, and we all gathered, crowded and hot, trying not to belch from our excesses while watching the dancing. Ah, now this was lovely indeed, and the grace of the dancers lives forever in my memory.

Afterwards – do you remember? Your father led the first dance with his new mistress, who had been the maidservant to his second wife.

As I watched them, I mused upon how expendable women are in the world of kings, nay of men, all of us appendages: wives and mistresses, and those not even worth the mention. Your father could hardly move, but his mistress was nimble upon her feet. None at court liked her and I sensed the hostility in the air, sharp and brittle, for it was one thing for a noblewoman such as his second wife to be a king's mistress first of all, but for a common servant to elevate herself was unthinkable. And yet it appeared that the king was besotted with her, though I could see no pleasure writ upon her face, and I wondered whether she had wanted the king as her lover. Of course, no woman would refuse – it had to be the greatest of all honours.

The flames of the candles were flickering in the crystal of the chandeliers as if magnified into a fire burning above us. The air was thick with the smoke from their wicks, and the scents of all these noble people – the sweat in the silks and their breath full of spice from our feast – but worse was the air of malevolence, for I could sense it even then. These nobles of Denmark pranced around the king and the prince elect, all bowing and scraping, but their eyes were as snakes'. They would wish to destroy you, all these nobles.

Well, this you learnt not so long afterwards – for see what happened to the English King Charles! But I have always been on your side, you know this, forever and ever. My wish is to elevate the monarchy.

I was asked to dance by a prospective suitor so insignificant that now I do not remember who he was, though he spoke German to me. I knew the language well enough, though the strain of turning it to Danish in my head made me feel dizzy, while the feeling of being on show as every unwed girl was held me rigid in my tightened bodice, and I struggled to breathe. Was it better to be in the dance, where at least there was order and space in the formality of it? Or crushed in the crowd of onlookers?

I saw my father talking to a group of young nobles, and their glances towards me. My throat tightened with dread, for the idea of being married to a noble and leading a life of idle leisure was not appealing to me, let alone the dangers of childbirth. I desired to have purpose beyond the role designated to me as wife and mother. I wished to leave a mark upon this world, my king, and for my legacy to be more than offspring.

We changed partners and, much to my surprise, I was holding your hand and doing a turn while looking into your umber eyes.

'Anna Thorsteinsdatter,' you said in a quiet voice and no more. Just my name, but to hear you say it sent a tremble through my whole body, for you remembered me though it had been four years since you had visited my father's cabinet of curiosities.

I felt the penetrating gaze of Margrethe Pape upon me as she spun in the line of dancers next to us.

'Your highness.' I bowed my head to you, feeling a glow upon my cheeks.

There was no opportunity to speak further as you swept on, linking hands with your next partner, and I was carried on to another noble.

When the dance was over, I slipped out through the crowd for I had no desire to dance with any other man. A window was opened out onto the veranda, and I escaped into the cool October night. It was against etiquette for an unaccompanied young lady to wander in the king's garden, but I couldn't bear to spend one more minute in the glare and noise of the wedding party. I decided I would take a little air and return to the feast before I was missed.

I wandered along the serene pathways lined by trees, listening to the soothing sound of the water fountains and the night call of a lone owl. I paused to look at the water as it caught the light of the moon upon it.

I stopped to gaze at the fountain which, though beautiful, did not raise the low feeling in my heart, for I was thinking what my destiny would be. Soon, no doubt, I would be married to a bore of a man who might not even allow me to read.

My thoughts were disturbed by the sound of footsteps behind me, and I turned around in alarm, worried that it was my father come to chastise me. But it was not he, no indeed, for you stood before me.

I was so speechless with shock, my mouth nearly fell open in a gape.

'We might as well be at the French court, do you not think?' you said, a familiar tone to your voice, as if we had been conversing the whole night long. 'For this night reeks of the Catholic Baroque!'

'It is quite sumptuous,' I agreed, in a timid voice.

'One would not think us Lutherans at all,' you declared. 'But my brother must show the rest of Europe he is the richest prince of all!' You sighed, and it was clear your disapproval was great.

I did not know what to say in return, as it would have been foolish to make any criticism of the prince elect.

'Where are you going, Anna Thorsteinsdatter, daughter of the king's physician?' you asked, your tone a little mocking. 'Are you running away from the biggest party Copenhagen has ever held?'

'I feel a little faint, your highness,' I said in a nervous voice.

'I am sorry to hear it.' You offered me your arm. 'Come, let me accompany you through the gardens.'

I slipped my arm through yours, delight bursting in my heart.

'Tell me, has your father added much to his cabinet of curiosities since I last saw it?'

A huge thrill swept through me to think you remembered the day you had visited the cabinet with my father and me as guides.

'He collected a snake's skin, all the way from the Africas,' I said, thinking again of the nobles at the wedding party: snakes beneath their fine attire. 'But this past year he has been preoccupied with his botanical garden and apothecary.'

'Oh, yes, indeed, I am most interested in this,' you said. 'To learn the medicinal value of our herbs and plants is a wondrous occupation.'

'We now have over two hundred different species in our botanical garden,' I said, proudly.

'You said "we", Anna Thorsteinsdatter. Am I right to presume you have a personal knowledge of the botanics in your father's garden?'

I blushed. 'Why, yes. It is a passion of mine.'

You looked me in the eyes, and I couldn't see your expression clearly for though the moon shone, the shadows had turned them such a dark shade of brown they appeared almost black.

'I would very much like to see this garden,' you said.

'It is not as beautiful as the king's garden. And you have many fruits, vegetables and herbs in this very place which are of benefit.'

'Might there be something nearby you could take to improve your condition this evening?'

I swelled with pride, for you were asking me to share my knowledge with you. 'Why, yes. I believe here is some mint.' I bent down and plucked a sprig.

'You are feeling a weakness in your stomach?'

I was pleased you understood the properties of the herb. I smiled and nodded, though in truth, it was because my stomach was in a tumult of nerves to be so close to you, and alone.

I handed you a mint leaf and you took it. I inhaled its refreshing scent and how it made me feel calmer, and soothed; ah, mint always takes me back to that night with you.

'I would like to show you my favourite place in my father's garden,' you told me.

I hesitated, for my behaviour was very unseemly for a young lady, but I could not turn you down, for you were a prince after all.

You led me through a gate and into an orchard of pear trees, the last golden pears hanging heavy in the autumn night. You plucked one from the tree, so tall you were, took a bite and then handed the pear to me.

Nothing in my whole life has tasted as this pear did – so sweet, and juicy with temptation.

'I have been watching you all night, Anna Thorsteinsdatter,' you said.

'But why, my prince?' I blurted out. It seemed strange to me that I would catch your notice among all the wondrous beauties of noble Europe, and beside your bewitching mistress, Margrethe Pape.

To my utter surprise, you leaned forward and stroked the side of my face. 'You possess a rare quality at court in these days.'

What is this quality? I thought, but I said nothing. Beyond shocked by your action, my stomach churned with the sensation of your fingers touching my cheek.

Nevertheless, you answered, as if reading my mind. 'Innocence,' you said.

I bloomed pink, the scent of mint still on my palm rushing up to me, the taste of sweet pear in my mouth. I had admired you for so many years, for you had been the Prince of my dreams but now here you were before me, lavishing praise. I was in conflict too, because I was alone with a man who was not my kin and it was not seemly, and yet, it was so delightful.

'Tell me, Anna, do you still possess your virtue?' you asked me.

The question felt brutal after your gentle touch, and it hurt my heart a little, but all the same I was dazzled by you.

'But of course, you are virtuous, Anna Thorsteinsdatter,' you replied for me. 'And has your father arranged a marriage for you yet?'

I shook my head.

Your hand trailed my cheek again, then to my neck and to my bosom, squeezed into my bodice. 'How I would wish for you to be my mistress.'

I widened my eyes in wonder at his words. 'But Margrethe Pape—!' I gasped out.

You sighed. 'She is a handsome woman, but she does not possess your intelligence, Anna. I would wish for a mistress I could discuss the properties of these plants with, and a mistress with an interest in books which you displayed the first time we met. I wish for a companion in my private chambers who is my match in mind. Would you like this position?'

I was overwhelmed. He had made mention of his private chambers, and yet though reserved, I was also bold and did not hesitate with my reply. 'Yes,' I whispered.

You smiled, and my heart curled around itself. Ah, yes, always your smile made my legs weaken.

'Your answer pleases me greatly, Anna Thorsteinsdatter,' you said, leaning down to kiss me.

I was lost in your lingering kiss – oh, so lost – and I let you bring me down to lie upon the chill grass of the orchard, and right beneath one of the laden pear trees we consummated our arrangement for the very first time. You were gentle, but still it hurt, and I gave a little gasp of pain, but to hear my cry, I believe, ignited your passion further. You buried yourself deep in my skirts as you drew your lips away from mine and uttered a deep sigh of pleasure, which filled me with such pride.

I will never forget our first time, for guilt and pleasure warred within me. I was sinning, and yet the son of the divine king had chosen *me*, the plain daughter of a physician. You had chosen me not for my stature nor my beauty, but for my mind.

Chapter 22

Ingeborg

Such cruel beauty took Ingeborg's breath away: cloud-white fur so soft she longed to put her hands upon it, but of course that would have meant instant death. Magnificent jaws and sharp teeth, but it was not snarling at them. The paws were huge, sheathing deadly claws, Ingeborg knew. Its white coat was spotted with dark brown smudges, and its magnificent head possessed pointed ears with long tips of fine fur. Her eyes were drawn to the great lynx's, full as they were with rich, warm colour: gold, amber, flashes of sea green and flecks of deep brown.

The lynx circled where they stood, slowly, almost languorously. Ingeborg caught the glint of Zare's knife in his hand, but what good would his small blade be against such an adept predator? They held their breath.

Suddenly, as if they weren't worth its interest, the wild cat turned away from them. It crept across the snow in silent stealth, and then broke into a run, back the way they had come, to the west.

'It's heading inland to find some woods,' Zare said, sheathing his knife again. 'I am surprised to see it on the mountain, as it will find little prey.'

'Why did it not kill us?' Ingeborg said, in a shaky voice.

Zare turned to her. 'It is very unlikely a lynx would attack us, more likely a wolf or bear, though they are asleep still,' he said, but beneath his words she could see he was as shaken as she. 'You are trembling with the cold.'

He pulled her to him and hugged her. His action was so intimate, so shocking, she didn't know what to say. *He is just warming me up, so I don't die of the cold*, she told herself, but she could not help but inhale his scent. Longed to remain in his embrace when he let her go.

'We had better catch up with Maren!'

Maren. Zare's mention of her name created an unsettling jolt within her. The eyes of the lynx, all those colours within them. The umber and gold, shards of sea green . . .

She shook herself. What a foolish notion. Maren would be sorry she missed seeing the lynx.

They flashed across the frozen white summit of Domen, propelling themselves faster, speeding down the other side of the mountain. The snow sprayed up around Ingeborg and stung her face.

A sudden squall obscured them within a fog of driving snow, yet on they went.

When the blizzard eased, they were at the bottom of the Devil's Mountain. The clouds dispersed to reveal the Varanger Straits. By the sea's edge, a small settlement of coastal Sámi was living in a cluster of turf-clad *goahti*. On the other side of the frothy water rose the rocky island of Vardø.

There was a huge whoosh of snow, and Maren skidded to a halt beside her.

'Where have you come from?' Ingeborg asked her.

'I lost my way, but here I am now.'

'Where did you go?'

'What does it matter?' She put her mittened hand on Ingeborg's arm. 'I will not leave your side again.'

Maren was staring at Ingeborg as if searching for something she had lost inside her. The air felt thick and hot between them despite the cold.

Ingeborg looked at Maren's cloudberry lips, the glow of her skin – warm from her long ski. She could see the power Maren spoke of brimming out of her.

Ingeborg did not feel her equal.

Maren turned her face away suddenly, but the feeling between them remained: something strange and unspoken.

'I will ask for shelter in the village.' Zare spoke up. 'My father's cousin is married to one of the Sámi here. It is many years since we have seen Morten, but I remember him as a good man.'

'How will we cross the water to Vardø?' Ingeborg asked, aware of the wind picking up around them and conjuring squalls of loose snow in the gathering gloom.

'We will trade for use of a *bask*,' Zare said. 'None will want to row us to the governor's domain on Vardø, but Morten might allow me use of his.'

'And what are we trading?' Maren asked Zare. 'I have nothing with me but a pocket full of feathers, and I doubt Ingeborg has little more.'

'My mother gave me some items to trade. The coastal Sámi are always keen for reindeer meat, skins, and antler for tools. And I've sinew thread for his wife.' He patted the pack on his back. 'Instead of fish, we will ask for use of the boat.' Zare pulled his hat down over his brow as the snow began to fall heavier. 'Wait here,' he instructed them, before setting off for the settlement.

The dusky brief hours of light had subsided into deepening darkness, the moon and stars concealed behind boulders of clouds as snow swirled around Ingeborg and Maren.

'Zare likes you,' Maren said lightly, but Ingeborg heard the edge to her voice.

'As you!' Ingeborg turned to Maren.

Maren shook her head knowingly. 'Do not be coy, Ingeborg Iversdatter. I can see well enough what passes between you.'

'Nothing!' Ingeborg declared, affronted. 'I am a God-fearing Christian, and he is Sámi!'

'And what of it? Sámi can play at being Christian. We know of fishermen in Ekkerøy who have taken Sámi wives and reared children. Remember Einar Robertson and his wife Ragnild? Was she not Sámi? They had many fine children, all raised as God-fearing Christians!'

Ingeborg looked at Maren, startled. What was this talk of children? 'Zare is your friend, not mine, Maren.'

In the darkness, concealed by the snow, Ingeborg had lost all sight of Maren's face. All she could see was her silhouette, hazy and almost without form. She had the urge to catch hold of the other girl's hands and pull her close. She longed to gaze into her jewelled eyes and take from her some little part of her strength; rub it onto her skin like the cod liver oil her mother had done when she was a little girl.

But Elli had told Ingeborg to take care of Maren because it was she who was vulnerable, not Ingeborg.

'Why do you help me?' she asked her now, as they waited for Zare to return.

'Because it is my desire to do so,' Maren said.

'But why?'

Maren didn't answer. Snow fell in silent curtains and the only sound Ingeborg could hear was the sea beginning to churn. The wind pushed against her back, and she felt her heart beating faster and faster. The storm was coming. She needed to cross the Varanger Straits soon, for how many days might the storm take to abate? Days and nights when her mother would be all alone and frightened, in the witches' hole.

'I wish for vengeance against the governor of Vardø,' Maren said softly.

'But this is impossible,' Ingeborg warned her. 'He's the most powerful man in the whole of Finnmark. He has soldiers at the fortress. How can you—'

'Hush,' Maren whispered. 'I wish I hadn't confessed my wish to you now. Do not assault me with doubt. All you need know for now is I am intent upon the rescue of your mother.'

Maren moved closer to her and as the snow clouds raced above, a streak of moonlight lit upon the side of Maren's face. Her skin gleamed copper and looked as if polished. Ingeborg wanted to pull her hand free of its mitten and place her fingertips upon it to make sure she was a real, flesh-and-blood girl.

Zare returned with the news that his cousin Morten welcomed them to his *goahti* to rest before the final part of their journey. The trading had gone well and in return for the reindeer meat, skins, antlers and threads Zare had brought with him, Morten would allow them use of the boat.

'I can stay no longer than one forenoon upon the island, for he can only spare his vessel for one day's fishing.'

'Is it enough time to find the tunnel and reach my mother?' Ingeborg asked nervously.

'It will have to be,' Zare said.

As they entered the peat-clad hut of Zare's cousin Morten, Ingeborg was struck by how different it felt from Zare's home in the *siida* by Andersby-vatnet. There was no Elli to welcome them with cups of warmed reindeer milk and sorrel. Morten and his wife were wary of them, not raising their eyes to look directly at them, and keeping their children hidden in the far corner of the *goahti*.

Even when Maren spoke to them in Sámi, they turned their heads away.

'Why don't they wish to speak with me, Zare?' Maren said in Norwegian, as they huddled in the guest area of the *goahti*. 'I wish to thank them.'

'They are not so happy to have you in their home,' Zare admitted. 'It took much persuasion, for they view your people as having stolen their fish away. I was told at first to take you to Svartnes, the fishing village down the way.'

'But we can't go there. They would give us up to the governor,' Maren said.

'This I explained, and passed on my mother's message to help us,' Zare said. 'Morten has great respect for my mother and my father.'

The wind howled outside the *goahti* despite the solid peat walls.

'We need to leave now,' Ingeborg said urgently. 'Before the storm.'

Zare turned to her. The firelight had softened the ice blue of his eyes to the soft shades of their northern summer skies. She ached for those days of light, not so long ago, and before the terrible arrest that had broken up her little family.

'I am sorry, Ingeborg, it's too late. We must wait,' Zare said.

Ingeborg's heart plummeted. She dared not count how many days it had been since her mother's imprisonment, as each one placed her in more peril.

The storm blew wild and furious for two days and nights. Most of the time they remained huddled in the *goahti* with Morten and his family. His wife fed them dried cod and *flatbrød*.

There were three girls. The eldest was the same age as Kirsten, while the younger two were little more than babies. The bigger girl had a face akin to an Arctic fox with pointed chin and bright, inquisitive eyes. With the thought of Kirsten, Ingeborg felt guilty again about how long she had been gone. She missed her sister. Ingeborg smiled at the girl as if it might ease her conscience, but the child pushed her face into her frowning mother's side.

It was a strange feeling to be the object of fear.

Zare and Morten shared a pipe and spoke a little in Sámi. Once or twice, Maren spoke up in Sámi but each time she did, Morten fell silent and shook his head at Zare.

'What are they speaking about?' Ingeborg asked Maren.

'Morten is warning Zare not to get involved in the witch hunts, because it will be bad for the Sámi people.'

'He is most likely right,' Ingeborg said, with a heavy heart.

'The Sámi have been accused before and will be accused again,' Maren said. 'What we do makes little change for them.'

Ingeborg woke stiff, but warm, curled beside Maren. It was the third day. As soon as she took her first breath she listened. Her heart sank, for she could still hear the low moan of the wind and the crashing sea. She squeezed her eyes shut and prayed to the Good Lord. *Please, dear Father in Heaven, have mercy upon my mother. Let the wind abate. Grant us safe passage.*

Maren stirred beside her, stretching like a cat, but didn't awaken. A week ago, the girl had been near a stranger to her, but now they spent every night hitched to each other for warmth. Maren's scent was upon her skin, woody and sharp, like the winter forest. It felt like something special to be close to a girl so different from any other. She longed to ask Maren about her father. Was it true he was a Barbary pirate? What was his name? How had her mother met him? But these questions might lead to another: was it true, as all the women at Ekkerøy had said, that Maren's father was the Dark Lord?

Was the pleasure Ingeborg felt to be by Maren's side, to be seen by her, and helped by her, all a temptation that would do Ingeborg and her mother more damage and add more evidence to her charges of witchcraft?

Ingeborg's head ached with her questions. She longed to get out of the *goahti*, even if to be pushed back inside by the storm. She glanced over to the other side of the *goahti*. She could see the outline of Zare's hat and his folded arms across his chest, as well as make out the cluster of his father's cousin and his family. It must be night still, for all to be so deep in their sleep. Who was to tell? For the morning was dark as the midnight.

She crawled out of the *goahti*, pushing hard against the wooden door to get outside. As soon as she made her way through, the wind knocked her backwards against its solid walls. Black, so black. She could see no light in all the wild stirrings of nature apart from dizzying whirls of snow, its icy little daggers stabbing her skin. The wind could destroy any mortal if it so wished.

She tried to pray but it was all she could do to stay upright.

Ingeborg stopped praying, she stopped trying to breathe. In her surrender it felt as if the wind was breathing for her. She softened her body and let the wind pull her this way and that. She turned to face the *goahti* and then opened her arms wide, falling back against the wind. It held her up, almost so her feet left the ground.

How would it be to fly?

The door of the *goahti* opened. It was hard to see who it might be in the darkness, but instinct told her it was Zare. Poking out his head as if a bear coming from his cave. She found herself laughing at the thought of Zare the bear, although the sound of it was lost in the fury of the wind. The door pushed open further, a gleam of light from the fledgling morning fire within lighting up Zare's face.

It slammed closed behind him, but she could make out his broad contours moving towards her, pushing against the wind through the spins of snow. He called something to her, but she shook her head because she couldn't hear him against the raging of wind and sea in her head. Then he turned his back to the wind and spread his arms too. They were side by side, a fingertip's space away from each other, feeling the uplift of the wind beneath them and the power of nature.

A sudden violent blast knocked Ingeborg sideways and she fell into the thick snow, sinking down in it. Zare crouched down beside her. It was as if they were beneath the wind now, in the snow. A small, low space of stillness and silence.

'Are you hurt?' he asked her.

She shook her head. 'When will the storm stop?'

The joy at her wind-borne flight had fled. Her fear for her mother was returning.

'Bieggagállis the wind god will shovel his wind back into his caves soon, as he always does,' Zare said.

'There is a god for wind?' she asked, thinking of her prayers to a god of all things.

'Yes.' Zare looked at her. 'In our tradition all things have a soul, and thus we have reverence for everything in the world around us. We have many gods such as the sun, the moon, the thunder, the primeval mother and her daughters. Bieggagállis, the god of wind, is one of the most powerful,' he said. 'If he doesn't stop blowing today, we will *yoik* to him tonight,' Zare said. But he licked his lips, and then frowned.

'What is it?' Ingeborg asked, sensing his unease.

'Morten has missed two days' fishing. I am not sure if he can spare us his boat now—'

'Oh no! But when?'

Zare took his hands in hers. 'I have given him and his family a great deal of reindeer meat. If the wind drops today, he will let us go.'

Ingeborg looked down at Zare's rough hands around hers. Neither of them wore their mittens, and their skin were different shades of blue from the cold. The feeling of his presence was different from Maren's, but Ingeborg wanted to be by his side as much. There was something about Zare that reminded her of Axell. He made her feel safe. She didn't know how.

Maren made her feel the opposite, as if she were playing with fire. But still she craved it too. Why did she want both to touch her and look with care upon her? Could it be she had been so starved of affection from her mother she wished it from whoever took notice of her?

Zare squeezed her hand and whispered to her beneath the tumult of the wind above.

'Let us lie in the snow. It is quite dry, and I will *yoik* to Bieggagállis now, although you must tell no one I do so and in front of you.'

'I promise,' she said, feeling honoured he would do such a thing.

Beneath the storm they lay, hand in hand. Ingeborg closed her eyes to listen to the *yoik* Zare made, similar to the sounds she had heard when she and Maren had watched his father, the *noaidi*, fall into the trance. Strange, ethereal notes like no other; so far from their tightly wound kirk's hymns that they had to be from another different world.

On their bed of powdery white, the dome of the world beneath her, Ingeborg squeezed her eyes shut, trying to not worry about whether she was taking part in dark magic. All she wanted was to be with her mother, and to save her.

She listened to Zare, feeling the sturdy, grounding touch of his fingers interlaced with hers. How long they lay this way she could not say, for despite the deep cold she hadn't become chilled.

When she opened her eyes again, Zare was no longer *yoik*ing, and the wind was gone. The sky above was dusky blue for a mid-winter forenoon; a brief glimmer of less than dark.

She turned her head to Zare.

'We should go.' They spoke at the same time, the same words. Zare's eyes opened wide, and Ingeborg found herself smiling.

There in the half-light she saw a thread between them, silvery and fragile as a spider's web. She blinked and it was gone.

The door of the *goahti* creaked open and she could hear Maren puffing across the snow. 'There you are!' Maren towered over them. Hands on hips, dark hair unbound, her eyes narrowed.

Ingeborg quickly let go of Zare's hand.

'What are you doing out here? Or need I ask?' she sneered.

But Ingeborg saw the hurt in her eyes. They had left her out. She wanted to explain it was not what it seemed, that she hadn't meant to exclude her. Maren had been fast asleep when she had ventured out into the storm. She didn't know Zare would follow her, and well, this was magic, what had happened with him in the snow. But Ingeborg didn't know how to begin.

Maren spun around and stomped back towards the *goahti*, hair flying behind her.

Ingeborg scrambled to her feet, guilt-ridden. Zare was standing now too. There was a new awkwardness between them.

'Thank you,' she whispered.

Zare nodded. 'It is an opening in the storm, but Bieggagállis will return soon. He will take his shovel out and blow the wind again.'

Together the three of them launched the small *bask* Morten had lent them into the choppy sea. Ingeborg rolled her breeches up and icy water slapped against her bare legs as she clambered into the boat. Zare grabbed her hand and pulled her in, while Maren deftly climbed in behind her.

They rowed past the fringes of the Sámi settlement and out across the straits. The power of the sea rocked their little craft dangerously. Ingeborg felt her stomach churn. Her fear was strong, but so was her determination. It was too late to go back now.

As they approached Vardø, the sky dripped grey over the turf cottages, darkness clutching at its edges. Water slopped over the sides of the *bask* as Zare wrestled to keep them on course.

Ingeborg looked down at his broad hands as they gripped the oars. The memory of an old dream came to her. In it, a pair of hands such as these were cradling her face with such tenderness. The thought of it made her blush. In her dreams, Ingeborg had encountered the kind of love she had never felt in her waking life. She had felt a deep brotherly love and trust from Axell but this was different. These were not her brother's hands.

The tug and pull of the small boat set her heart pounding. Zare was looking at her again with his sharp eyes. She shrank back, pushing her hat down over her brow. Maren glanced at her and frowned.

Swathes of silvery mist created a haze above the straits, as the wind began to stir again. Cracked ice swirled upon its surface like the thick strokes of glaze upon the oil painting of the Brasches in their village kirk. Beneath her, a shard of floating ice and her reflection: a flashing oval of pale skin, a reindeer skin hat, one stray strand of brown hair.

The little *bask* bucked across the choppy water, and Ingeborg gripped onto its sides. Zare stopped rowing. He lifted the oars up as glassy droplets of water spattered upon the ruffled sea.

'Why have you stopped?' Maren asked him.

'I am feeling the currents,' he said. 'Working out which way to go to land.'

The sea was in Zare's eyes. The crash and drag of it.

He seemed about to say something to Ingeborg, but then he picked up the oars again and continued to row.

The wind was growing stronger now, and he had to push with all his might against it. Maren picked up the other oars lying in the bottom of the craft to help him. The sea churned around them like boiling broth.

At last, they were through the currents and in calmer waters. They grounded with a bump on the stony shore.

'One of us should remain and make sure the *bask* is not lost or taken,' Zare said. 'Ingeborg, will you stay?'

'No! It's my mother imprisoned in the witches' hole,' she said, clenching her fists.

'It would be safer to stay—'

'No!' she said, furious he would expect her to wait by the boat.

'Well, then – Maren? Because I have to show Ingeborg where the tunnel is.'

'My mother's spirit is trapped on Vardø between the living and the dead,' Maren said, bitterness lacing every word. 'I am not staying behind with the boat. That is not why I came all this way with you.'

'Very well. We need not waste time arguing,' Zare said, indicating for the girls to get out carrying the oars between them. Once they had waded through the water to the rocks, Ingeborg turned to see Zare lifting the boat over his head and carrying it to a slab of flat dry stone to place it down. The *bask* looked like the shell of a giant turtle, and it was hard to imagine such a light craft had been able to transport them across such choppy water. 'Let fortune be on our side and it will still be here when we return,' Zare said.

Ingeborg glanced up at the storm clouds gathering against the dark sky. 'Do we have enough time?'

'Let us believe so,' Zare replied. 'There is no going back now.'

Ingeborg scrambled over the slippery rocks, after Maren and Zare. They seemed to be moving so fast it was hard to keep up. Zare began to head inland, and she glanced up to see the sheer white walls of Vardøhus rising above. They scrambled up a steep cliff, and then crouched behind an outcropping of rocks.

'It's unlikely we will be seen, as my mother told me the soldiers prefer to smoke their pipes in their hut rather than stand guard outside, but we should be careful in case,' Zare said.

They continued to climb up the rocks until they came to the foundations of the castle. Zare felt his way along it with his hands, then turned to look back, assessing the way they had come. 'The tunnel is around about here. I am certain of it.'

He tugged away on the rocks around the base of the fortress and, eventually, one moved beneath his hands to reveal a small hole.

Zare went in first, then Maren, and finally Ingeborg. They wriggled on their bellies, Ingeborg's chest so constricted by fear that her breath was short and throttled. They were in complete blackness. She could see neither Zare nor Maren, just heard their shuffling and heavy breaths in front of her.

Suddenly, she heard Zare exclaim in Sámi, before she banged into the back of Maren.

'What is it?' she whispered.

'They have sealed the tunnel,' he said, and then cursed again softly under his breath. 'But, of course, how foolish we have been. Of course, they would do so!'

'Can we break through? Or tunnel around it?' Maren asked.

'No, it's solid rock,' Zare said. 'It took days for my father and I to do it before, and we don't have the time.'

'But we have to,' Ingeborg pleaded. On the other side was her mother, desperate and alone in the witches' hole. They were so close.

'It's impossible,' Zare said.

Ingeborg slapped her hands against the hard stone on either side of her. Her palms were stung by the icy rock. 'No! No!'

'We'll find another way,' Maren hissed to her.

Back outside, dark clouds were billowing in the inky sky, and the wind was moaning in warning.

'We should go, the storm is coming back,' Zare warned. 'Morten needs his boat. Besides, we can't get trapped on the island. We'll either freeze or get caught.'

Ingeborg looked up at Vardøhus fortress, at the cracks and crannies of the old wall. She pressed her hands against it, seeking with her fingers. There, right in front of her, was a foothold. She looked up to see more tiny ledges all the way up the fortress walls.

Axell's words from summers past surfaced in her mind. *Imagine you are a cat.*

'I can climb the wall,' she said, turning to Zare.

He looked at her, aghast. 'You will fall and die,' he said, roughly. 'You're not strong enough, Ingeborg.'

But Maren was by her side and squeezed her hand in hers. 'Yes, she is, and I will climb it too. We will manage it.'

He looked at the girls, incredulous.

'Go back and mind the boat,' Maren said, a command in her tone.

Zare shook his head. 'This is madness.'

'I have climbed worse,' Ingeborg said, thinking of the bird cliffs at Ekkerøy. 'If we don't return in time, get back to Morten and his family on the other side.'

He reached out and placed a hand on her arm. 'Don't do it, Ingeborg.'

'I have to.'

He looked into her eyes and she could see he understood, his expression softening in sympathy. 'Very well, I would do the same for my mother. But I can't wait long. The storm is coming, and I will not let them throw me in their dingy cells!'

Ingeborg faced the fortress walls again, Maren by her side. She slackened the limbs of her body before gathering them up, taking a deep breath, inhaling her strength. With a rush of energy, she pulled herself up, digging her fingers in and clinging to the rough wall. Then she found her footing and hoisted herself up again. *Never look down.*

Maren was just below her. She could hear the breath of her exertion.

Ingeborg felt her way with her senses. She slunk up the fortress walls with a sense of something other than herself within her. Her nails felt as if they were claws as they dug in; she was stuck so fast to the wall. She knew instinctively she would not fall.

The wind was tugging at her but still she kept on climbing. At last, she had reached the top, and slipped over the other side. She peered over the battlements to see where Maren was, but she saw nothing. Her stomach lurched, but then a voice whispered by her side.

'We are here, my feline friend,' Maren said, grinning at her.

Ingeborg took one last look from where they came. Saw the tiny figure of Zare waiting by the boat as the sinking winter sun hidden beneath the horizon burned magenta reflections upon the snow; a line of crimson bleeding heavenwards, pooling mauve upon the sea before succumbing to utter darkness.

The two girls crouched down by the side of one of the cannons to shelter from the rising wind. It was so rusted and iced up Ingeborg doubted it had ever been used.

'What do we do now?' Maren asked her, green eyes bright with antici-pation. She did not appear to be at all afraid.

Ingeborg looked below them. It was not quite complete darkness yet, and there were torches lit in braziers around the inner walls of the fortress casting shadows and light. There was the soldiers' turf hut. She could hear the low mumble of voices, smell the peat fire. To one side of the hut was the castle itself. She spied the lit square of one small window, but the rest of the building was in darkness. She turned her head and saw the gatehouse and the fortress gates. This would be where they would have to get out, unless they could find a rope and tie it to the top of the battlements. Why had they not thought to bring a rope?

'Look, is that the witches' hole?' Maren whispered, pointing past the gatehouse and a long, low house to a tiny, windowless hut.

'It looks desperate,' Ingeborg said.

Maren pulled Ingeborg around to look out across the island. 'Do you see the jut of land, past where Zare waits for us?'

Ingeborg nodded.

'Well, that is Stegelsnes, the execution site. It was where my mother was burned.'

Ingeborg's chest constricted again. She couldn't conceive the same end for her own mother.

'One of us needs to go to the gatehouse and try to get the key to open the castle gates,' she said to Maren. 'And the other to somehow get into the witches' hole.'

'Two rather impossible tasks,' Maren said, raising her eyebrows, but she didn't seem disheartened. 'I will get the gatehouse key.'

As they whispered, there was movement in the courtyard below. The door to the witches' hole opened. To Ingeborg's surprise, it was not a soldier who exited, but a woman, tall and straight-backed. The woman locked the door to the witches' hole and slipped the key into a pocket beneath her cape. The girls watched her as she daintily picked her way across the snow and entered the low longhouse.

'Well, there's the way into the witches' hole,' Maren said to her.

'I will go and get the key from her,' Ingeborg said. She didn't know how she would do it, or who else was in the longhouse, but it seemed an easier proposition than tackling the soldiers.

They clambered down the steps to the courtyard. The icy wind cut into them, but Ingeborg was glad because it meant the soldiers were unlikely to venture out.

Ingeborg turned to Maren to tell her to be careful, but she had quite disappeared. The courtyard was empty apart from a large rat scampering across it.

Ingeborg slipped across the icy ground to the low longhouse. A thin spiral of smoke spun up from its sagging roof. She put her hand upon the door and pushed it open.

Chapter 23

Anna

I was your secret mistress. We met clandestinely in the places we loved: the royal library, the botanical gardens, the pear orchard, in my father's cabinet of curiosities – gazing up at the snarl of the baby polar bear as your long, dark hair cascaded over my naked breasts.

Four years I waited for the invitation to attend court at the palace as your official mistress, but it never came.

Four years is a long time for one so young but, now, it is but a blink. Ah, how naive and in thrall to you I was, for surely if you had instructed me to meet you in the chicken coop I would have!

You ate up every little morsel of me, from my toes to the crown of my head, into my loins, my heart, and every corner of my mind. I lived and breathed for my prince, awaiting the daily arrival of a little square of parchment and your royal seal. Breaking open your love letters, your words of endearment intoxicated me, and I would run breathless to our meeting point, with only time to dab my breast with rose oil. How dizzy I became in our embraces, as you peeled me from my gown, my petticoats, and buried yourself in my young flesh.

I was not taken advantage of: I wanted you. It is shocking for me to acknowledge the truth of this, but I know well the lasciviousness a woman can let herself surrender to. I was possessed by the desire for coupling, for as soon as I returned home, I craved our next tryst.

My king, I wonder, are your memories as crystal-clear as mine?

I think not, for you said such sweet, loving words to me, and held me with much affection when I was a young woman. And you were so different the time we saw each other last, when you had become quite another man. I may look different for my skin is duller, my waist thickened, and my black hair streaked with grey, but inside I have never stopped being the young girl in love with her prince. I had separated the sins of the flesh from the pure love embedded in my heart.

Here on my own, with little to distract me, I brood too much upon those early years. I wonder, had our circumstances been different, could I have become as Margrethe Pape, your official mistress and mother to your illegitimate son? But in the end even Margrethe Pape was cast aside for your marriage to Sophie Amalie of Brunswick-Luneberg, not a woman to cross as your sister Leonora Christina knows so well.

Is Queen Sophie Amalie behind my unjust exile too? I wonder, for she looked upon me with much disdain when I met her in later years. But that was when I had been long-gone from Copenhagen, and I was then married, too.

Chapter 24

Ingeborg

In the longhouse, Ingeborg smelt the woman first – the cloying scent of rose oil mixed with turf smoke filled her nostrils – but she couldn't see a soul. Smoke belched from the sputtering fire, filling the rafters until it slunk out of the smoke hole. There was a lopsided table with a lantern upon it, two rickety stools, and one straight-backed chair with a thread-bare tapestry cushion. All were positioned by a tiny window that was sealed tightly with a flap, as if grasping for what little light might enter the room.

Where was the woman with the key? On the other side of the chamber there was a door, ajar. Ingeborg crept across the uneven floorboards, and gently pushed it open.

The woman had her back to her and was kneeling by an opened trunk. She withdrew a small hardback book from it and placed it upon the floor, before slowly standing up. It was as she turned around that she saw Ingeborg and gave a little start in fright.

Ingeborg imagined she must look very strange indeed in the eyes of this woman – half-girl, half-boy in her breeches and buckled skirt, with her big hat and wet brown hair framing her face in straggles. In contrast, Ingeborg could see this was no ordinary woman, but one of noble birth. Although she was possibly not much younger than Widow Krog, she held herself as tall as a young woman, and Ingeborg could see a glimmer of crow-black hair beneath her white coif. Her slender frame was bodiced in a sumptuous blue gown, and the skin upon her cheeks was pale and smooth. But a faint nest of creases around the corner of each of her eyes belied her years.

'Who are you?' she asked in an imperious voice. 'And what are you doing in my chamber?'

'No harm will come to you. Just give me the key,' Ingeborg said, sounding more courageous than she felt. Her heart was rattling against her chest, and her hands were clammy, but she was determined not to show her fear to this grand lady. She must get the key.

The woman arched her eyebrows. 'What key?' she challenged Ingeborg.

'The one in your pocket, under your skirt.'

'And why would I do such a thing?' she said. 'Tell me who you are.'

Ingeborg drew Axell's small hunting knife from her belt and brandished it before her as she took a step forward, but the woman didn't look afraid. 'That is none of your concern. For the last time, give me the key.' Ingeborg brought the tip of the knife to the soft pulsing throat of the gentlewoman.

'Very well,' the woman muttered.

Ingeborg lowered the knife as the woman pulled the key out of her pocket. She fingered it as if to goad Ingeborg.

'Give it here.' Ingeborg was close enough to the woman to see that her eyes were icy as the glaciers. She brought the hunting knife back up to the woman's slender throat praying she would not have to use it.

'It will not end well,' the woman said, handing it to her. 'How do you think you will get away?'

As she spoke, Ingeborg heard movement in the other chamber. She backed away through the door and was relieved to see Maren swinging the big fortress gate key in her hand.

'Easy. The dozy old bailiff was fast asleep!' Maren sighed. 'I was tempted to cut his throat but thought it would take too much time.' She looked very pleased with herself as she swung the big key by her side.

'You!' The noblewoman had followed Ingeborg and now she stood, pointing at Maren. 'I saw you!' she declared. 'With the lynx!'

Maren grinned at the woman. 'That was indeed I!'

Ingeborg had no idea how Maren could know this woman, but she didn't have time to find out. 'Tie her to the chair,' she said to Maren.

'You tried to kill me.' The woman continued to address Maren.

'Not you, mistress!' Maren said, wrenching off her belt and strapping the woman to the old rickety chair.

At that moment, the door to the longhouse opened again, and a maid carrying a stack of turf stood on the threshold. She gave a small scream, dropped the turf, and ran shouting from the longhouse.

'Flee, girls,' the noblewoman whispered.

Ingeborg and Maren tore out of the longhouse, but already the soldiers were streaming from their hut with muskets in their hands. Lockhert came charging from the gatehouse, his face purple with fury.

'We can still escape, Ingeborg,' Maren whispered to her.

Ingeborg couldn't imagine how. They were surrounded. 'I'm not leaving my mother.'

'Very well, we stay,' Maren said, as if they had a choice.

Ingeborg dropped her small knife. What good was it against a musket aimed right for her heart?

A soldier grabbed her and pulled her arms tight about her back. Her shoulders were wrenched, and Ingeborg cried out with pain.

Bailiff Lockhert grasped Maren by her long black hair while snatching the gate key from her hand. He slapped her so hard she was flung to the icy ground.

The maid fled back into the longhouse.

'What are you two thieving bitches up to?' Lockhert snarled at them. Then he looked at Ingeborg's face. 'I recognise you! You're the witch Sigvaldsdatter's daughter.'

Ingeborg shook her head, refusing to answer.

The noblewoman stepped from the longhouse, having been freed by her maid. She walked towards them. The key was still tucked into Ingeborg's palm, behind her back. The woman circled her and then Ingeborg felt the woman's fingers on her clenched fists prising the key out. She circled her again once she had the key, slipping it back under her skirts into her hidden pocket.

'So, you are the witch's daughter?' she asked.

Ingeborg looked into her chilling eyes. They held no expression. No hate, no compassion, no emotion whatsoever. Who was she? And why had she the key to the witches' hole?

An oval of golden light suddenly shone upon the group as the figure of a tall man in black walked across the courtyard from the open castle door.

'Your honour, we have apprehended these two girls trying to release the witch Zigri Sigvaldsdatter.' Lockhert addressed the dark figure.

'My mother's no witch, I swear,' Ingeborg spoke up.

'Silence!' Lockhert bellowed at her.

The tall man stepped into the light of Lockhert's lantern. Upon one of his cheeks was a long battle scar from the edge of his bushy eyebrows all the way to his chin.

'So, this girl is the eldest daughter of the witch Zigri Sigvaldsdatter?' he said, pointing at Ingeborg. 'And who is the other strange creature?'

'My mother was Marette Andersdatter!' Maren said proudly, standing up from where she had fallen.

The governor flinched.

'Yes, you remember her?' Maren challenged, walking towards the governor, but stopped by one of the soldiers who hauled her aside. 'She was otherwise known as Liren Sand.'

'Indeed, never an eviler witch have we been attacked by in these regions,' the governor said, flicking his hand at her. 'And now here you are, girl, clearly brought over to the Devil by your mother too.'

The governor turned to the noblewoman who was standing quite still, watching Maren as she struggled against the soldier. 'It is as I told you, Fru Rhodius. The witches sacrifice their daughters to the Devil.'

'I am not so certain of this, governor,' the noblewoman named Fru Rhodius replied quietly. 'I have never seen it with my own eyes. They are bold girls to be sure—'

'They are surely witches' gets,' Lockhert declared. 'I have seen it in Scotland. My homeland was besieged with witches and their daughters.'

The governor walked up to Ingeborg. He towered over her.

'The witches in Vardø threaten the whole kingdom of Norway and Denmark – the very king himself, through terror and plague. The witches, in league with the Devil, run amok.' He bent down and whispered into her ear: 'And I can see you *are* in a pact with the Dark Lord, girl.'

Ingeborg tried not to show her fear.

'Your honour, my mother did not put me in a pact. She's innocent—' she said, her voice shaking.

'Silence! I didn't give you permission to speak,' he spat at her, and she felt flecks of his spittle land on her frozen cheeks. 'There will be time enough to speak at the trial.' The governor stepped out of the light of the lantern. Now his expression was hidden by shadows. 'Put them in the witches' hole, Lockhert,' he commanded.

'Would they not be better lodged with me, your honour?' Fru Rhodius intervened. 'They're so young—'

'—but old enough to be witches,' the governor snapped. 'It is where they belong.'

The soldiers pushed Ingeborg and Maren across the courtyard. Ingeborg thought of Zare. How long would he wait for them? She prayed he would not be caught as well. Already the wind was howling through the fortress, and the clouds racing above. Hard bites of hail began to fall. The storm had returned, the Sámi wind god, Bieggagállis, blowing hard. Zare would be rowing back, thrust forward towards the mainland by its force.

Lockhert unlocked the witches' hole with his key, and the soldiers threw Maren and Ingeborg inside. As they did so, Ingeborg caught a glimpse of the noblewoman Fru Rhodius shaking her head, as if they were two naughty girls who had forgotten their prayers. But their predicament was way beyond any childish misdemeanour.

She and Maren landed in a tumble together on the rough floor. She reached out in the pitch black and felt a wall slimy with filth. It was impossible to see how big the hole was, or what was in it. What was certain was there was no light, no fire, and no comfort whatsoever. But this she didn't think of as she scrambled to her feet and called out: 'Mother!'

A sharp intake of breath in the shapeless dark.

'Mother, it's me!'

'Ingeborg?' Her mother's voice returned to her, faint and cracked. 'Oh, the Good Lord, Ingeborg, what happened?'

She sensed Maren moving next to her, and then heard a sound. Saw a spark between two stones. Then a light.

Maren had a tiny nub of candle upon her palm. Its small flame flickered but it was enough to see the huddled form on the other side of the tiny cell, that was no more than seven paces by six. The wooden walls were cracked and grimy, the earthen floor was hard from protruding rocks and clumps of dried turf, with no sign of the tunnel that once had been. There was a terrible stench of excrement and the metal tang of old blood. The cell was so cold her throat was tight with the bite of it. None of it mattered though, because here was her mother, and she was alive.

'We came to save you,' she said to her mother.

'Oh, Ingeborg,' her mother wailed. 'How very foolish of you.'

Ingeborg went over to her mother, hunting for her hands beneath the pile of skins upon her. With the light from Maren's candle, she could see her mother's face.

Her eyes were blazing with anger.

'You stupid girl.' She stood up, lashing out and slapping Ingeborg on the cheek.

Tears welled in Ingeborg's eyes at the shock of her mother's anger.

'You've made this worse!' her mother said. 'I told you to get Heinrich. He will speak for me.'

'Heinrich Brasche is in Bergen, Mother,' Ingeborg said, her voice harsh with hurt. 'His father sent him there for trade.'

Her mother looked horrified.

'He was sent away the day after you were arrested.'

'No, no!' Ingeborg's mother said, her anger dissolving as she collapsed. 'He promised me.'

Maren's candle stub was nearly gone. 'We can save you, Zigri Sigvaldsdatter,' Maren said, her eyes amber from the candle flame.

'How?' Ingeborg asked Maren.

'Did you see how fearful the governor became when I mentioned my mother to him?' Maren said, her voice high with excitement. 'We will make him frightened of us. We will threaten curses upon him and his wife.'

Ingeborg's mother was no longer listening, sobbing hopelessly in her pile of skins.

'He's the governor of Vardø, Maren! He has soldiers with guns, and more power than we could ever dream of!' Ingeborg said. 'Our only hope is his mercy.'

'Well, he possesses none,' Maren said, crouching down on the other side of Ingeborg's mother. 'But we will find a way.'

Hopelessness gnawed at Ingeborg's heart. She sank down next to her mother. Took her hand in hers. 'The truth will come out, Mother,' she tried to reassure her. 'You're innocent, and it will be proven in court.'

But her mother continued to cry, curling up with her head upon Ingeborg's narrow lap.

'And Kirsten is safe, Mother. She's with Solve.'

Her mother stopped crying, wiped her tears, and stared up at Ingeborg. Her eyes were hard. 'There's something not right about Kirsten,' she whispered. 'It's her fault Axell drowned.'

Ingeborg looked down at her mother in astonishment. 'No, Mother!'

'Her lamb she calls Zacharias is a little devil,' her mother whispered.

'Kirsten is only twelve—'

But her mother interrupted her. 'Kirsten's a bad girl.' She sniffed. 'Evil.'

Chapter 25

Anna

The northern storms smashed into the island of Vardø, and the wind howled as if a horde of devilish creatures were flying above my longhouse prison. I huddled beneath the covers of my bed, pulling the hangings shut to keep out the cold. There were ghosts all around me, and not only of the poor souls who had died as prisoners here, like the old priest expired upon the very bed I lay upon.

There were other ghosts from my past. The faces of those I had tried to heal during the Great Plague, of whom I didn't remember names, but would never forget the number of the souls departed: three hundred and four dying souls I tended to during that one terrible season of sickness, and, my king, I was not afraid to hold them. The suffering of the common folk was immense, the pain and fear of the dying as if a rawness in my eyes so I was beyond tears. But now and then there would be a pure fragment on the edge of the last rattle of breath when the soul dislodged from within the body. I would see ether rising, misting my vision so all I could do was feel the passing with hairs rising upon my skin, and the soft whisper of departure in my ears. The weight of whoever had just passed would be, all of a sudden, light in my arms, as if the shell of an egg, and deep serenity filled me as thick as the yolk.

Truly this crossing between life and death became a force I grew used to. It made me feel heady; it was intoxicating to see the struggle cease and peace flood into their closing eyes, the grace of God upon them at last.

These ghosts swirled around me in my lonely prison bedchamber in the longhouse in Vardø fortress, and they wished me no harm. Those lost dead from my plague year came to comfort me in a way no mortal had.

And yet I couldn't quite catch hold of my own babies, all lost in my quest for motherhood.

Let us return to July 1638 and back to my twenty-third year, and my first pregnancy.

Yes, my king, the babe was yours, but you never knew, no, never.

You had been away in France visiting Louis XIII's court while I had been sick in the mornings for the nine whole days of your absence. In my foolish innocence, I believed myself terribly ill and I asked my father to examine me.

'You are not sick, Anna,' he had deduced, looking very grave as he dipped his hands into a basin of water to clean them. 'You are with child.'

I gasped with shock, though a little part of me was pleased, for now I thought my prince must claim me as his official mistress and bring me into the light, show me off to all at court. Surely King Christian IV would be pleased that his favourite physician's daughter had become favourite to his son?

'Anna, tell me how this happened,' my father asked. Colour was rising in his cheeks, the anger gathering like storm clouds, for now he knew why I had turned down all the suitors presented to me for marriage.

'Father, I am carrying Prince Frederick's child.'

His reaction was not what I expected. For the first time in my life my father exhibited force, grabbing me by both my arms and shaking me. 'Stop speaking such nonsense, girl, and tell me the truth.'

'But it is the truth, Father. I am the prince's mistress!' I announced.

'The prince's mistress is Margarethe Pape, and she is a baroness.' My father looked quite despairing. 'Tell me, is it my student, Ambrosius, who has taken advantage of you? I have seen the way he looks at you.'

'Oh, no!' I said, almost laughing at the suggestion.

Ambrosius Rhodius was a young German student of medicine who had been lodging with us for the past three months. I had barely taken any notice of him, so enrapt was I in my affairs with you. Now it seemed this lanky German youth had eyes for me, for he was always tripping over his feet and dropping his dinner bowl in my presence. I had believed him merely clumsy for the young man had barely said a word to me since we'd been introduced.

'It would not be the worst thing, Anna,' my father continued, ignoring my denial. 'Ambrosius has good prospects. He comes from old German nobility, although they have lost all their lands.'

'Father, he has never so much as kissed my hand!'

My father paused, his face darkening. 'But who then, Anna? Tell me now, don't lie to me.'

'I told you. This baby' – I placed my hand on my belly proudly – 'belongs to Prince Frederick. Surely he will move me to court once he discovers—'

'Dear Lord.' My father buried his face in his hands.

'Father, have you never once thought it? All the letters that came from the royal palace, addressed to me? I have been his mistress these past four years.'

My father raised his head with an expression of absolute horror. 'I thought they were from the Princess Leonora, for I know how she likes to take strolls with you . . .' His voice tapered off. 'It was not Leonora who you walked with?'

'No, Father.'

'You must not tell your mother,' he instructed me, eyes drawn in a thin line. 'Have you any notion of the position you've put us in?'

'But I shall speak to the prince when he returns from France.' I reached forward and took hold of my father's cold hands. 'He loves me, Father! Allay your fears. He is the prince, and he will look after me.'

'Oh, Anna.' My father's voice broke, and he pulled his hands away.

He knew, of course – my father had the wisdom I did not that my words were but an illusion, but I was young and in love and, I believed, so were you.

When you returned from France, I waited one week before I received a letter from you. By this time, my father was a constant nag at my side, assuring me a marriage could be arranged with Ambrosius Rhodius. It was still so early there was no sign of my condition, but I refused to listen to him.

At last, I received a few lines in your beautiful script I loved so well, inviting me to a meeting in the king's garden so early in the morning none of the servants of the palace would be awake. You told me to make my way through the lavender and wait by the mulberry tree, its berries pale and not yet ripe.

How I loved the month of July, the season of summer in the north, with the eternal sun still high in the gentle azure skies. My heart was pounding in my chest with anticipation as I slipped out of my father's house, a hooded cape concealing all but my eyes. I picked my way through our stinking alley, my kid shoes thrust into wooden pattens, until at last I entered the king's garden and breathed in the floral air. Now I ran as if floating on air, beyond excited to be on the cusp of a new adventure with you at my side.

You were not at the mulberry tree when I arrived, and I waited impatiently. The bees droned around me, and the air thickened with morning warmth. At last, you came, walking slowly, not rushing into my arms as I had expected. I felt a little dislodging of my confidence, for I sensed all was not as it had been. Gone was the gold earring, gone the scarlet stockings and golden brocade doublet. You were dressed entirely in absolute black with a tall, high-crowned black hat, and it felt as if a dark cloud had covered the sun in the sky.

'My love—' I gushed, but you took a step back before speaking over me.

'Dear Anna Thorsteinsdatter, thank you for meeting with me this morning.' Your tone was so formal it confused me, and your head was turned from me as if you could not bear to look in my eyes. 'I am duty bound to inform you our arrangement must from herein cease. I have enjoyed your company immensely, but Margrethe is with child. It is she I must attend to. I have promised her.'

Your words cut deep into my heart.

'But she's not your wife,' I protested. 'You are unwed, my prince, and you're free to choose—'

'Ah, no, dear girl, I am not at liberty to make such choices.' You shook your head. 'I must set a standard. And we both know you could never appear at my side in court, because you are not high nobility.'

I stood in shock, shaking and cold, although the sun was warm upon my skin.

'You have your whole life ahead of you, sweet Anna,' you said finally, looking at me. 'A husband fitting to your class, and a family of your own to be got. You will thank me for setting you free. But I am a caged bird, and always will be.'

'But, my prince, I love you—'

You raised your hand to stop me from saying more. 'You're too young to understand the kind of love I share with Margrethe. What I gave to you was an education of the senses; what you gave to me was an appreciation of my learning.'

I stepped back, reeling with hurt.

'I brought you a gift,' you said, pulling a thin gold chain out of your pocket. On its end dangled a tiny black cross. 'It's onyx. I found it in Rome.'

You handed me the cross and I took it with stiff fingers.

'Black as your hair,' you said, shaking your head and looking rueful, as if it were I who was breaking off with you. 'Wear it, and pray for forgiveness.'

It dangled through my fingers, for you did not even bother to clasp it around my neck.

You then walked away from me through the green vibrant haze of the king's garden, butterflies fluttering above the lavender and the scent of our love suffusing me.

I wanted to throw the cross back at you, but instead I fell to the grass and retched beside the roots of the mulberry tree.

What should I do? Panic rose inside me, like one of those butterflies trapped inside my chest.

With shaking hands, I lifted the black cross. It glinted in the light, the onyx shiny as a beetle's shell. I had been yours for four years, and my reward was one small cross. I could not help thinking upon all the jewels I had seen bedecked upon the neck of Margrethe Pape, but not one ruby or sapphire for me.

Ah, but there *was* more. For you had given a life inside me, and you would never know.

Chapter 26

Ingeborg

Day and night became one long icy darkness. The cold penetrated every part of Ingeborg as she huddled beneath the reindeer skins between her mother and Maren. Without a fire in their hovel, the air was as stinging as frozen iron. They sank into each other, one suffering creature with three hurting hearts. Hunger gnawed at them. Once a day, their guards brought a pail of water from the fortress well, scudded with slime, not like the pure spring from their village well. But it was water nonetheless, and they gulped it down, flies and all. Into a second pail, they released their waste. But there had been no opportunity to empty it yet, and in their small cell the stench was unpleasant. The only food they had been given was a watery broth of fish bones so salty it felt to Ingeborg as though she had been swallowing the sea. It made her want to vomit.

Even Maren became irritable, confiding in Ingeborg her monthlies were about to arrive, and what would she do with no rags?

Ingeborg's mother was in constant tears, in anguish over Heinrich Brasche. Ingeborg had never seen her shed one tear over her father. And yet for this man, who she must have known could never have been hers, she wrung her hands and sobbed as a lovestruck girl. It was up to Ingeborg to hold her mother and soothe her.

There was something else too. Something about her mother's face: a heaviness in her jaw, and the way she moved – clumsy and unbalanced when she shifted to stand up and stretch in their tiny hole. They'd been parted barely one cycle of the moon, but her mother had shed her outer shell. Now she clutched on to Ingeborg, asking in a cracked whisper if there was any hope for them.

Ingeborg thought of Zare, the Sámi boy. But even if he had made it back to his settlement and his mother, Elli, there was nothing they could do for them. She had hunted for the entrance to the tunnel in the witches' hole, and it had been covered with heavy rock she couldn't budge.

Maybe three days had passed – or four, it was hard to tell – when the key turned in the prison door. This time it was not a soldier with broth or water, as the light from the lantern illuminated Bailiff Lockhert.

In the tiny cell he appeared even more monstrous as he stooped to fit beneath the low rafters. Behind him was the noblewoman Fru Rhodius, picking her way through their dirt, a handkerchief held to her nose.

To see her disdain made Ingeborg angry. How would *she* like to sleep beside a pail of her own excrement?

'Smells like my father's hogs in here,' Lockhert commented, sounding pleased about it.

'Has their waste bucket been emptied?' Fru Rhodius asked him.

'The soldiers won't touch it. They're afraid of the witch.'

Fru Rhodius tsked disapprovingly. 'Her guilt has not been proven yet, Lockhert. Can the two girls not carry it out, and throw it over the fortress walls?'

Lockhert barked instructions at his soldiers, and Ingeborg and Maren were ordered to carry the heavy bucket of waste between them.

Ingeborg was retching as they carried it out of the witches' hole. But the sweet, clean air and fresh spinning snow was bliss upon her cheeks.

They lugged the bucket up the steps along the fortress walls and threw it over the side. Saw its brown muck land on the pure white. Soon the falling snow would cover it with a thick pelt.

'Ah, taste the clean snow on your tongue, Ingeborg,' Maren murmured, as they both tipped back their chins and opened their mouths. The snow falling on her dirty skin, so gentle and tender, made her heart ache.

Their guard got impatient, thumping his cold feet on the ground and pushing the girls back towards the cell.

'Look, Ingeborg,' Maren said, pointing up at the swirling snow. A black crow was circling above the fortress, cawing loudly. 'What think you? Is she one of us, calling to our sisters?'

'Shush,' Ingeborg hissed. Maren's talk would send them straight to the stake. And yet, a part of her wished so much she were right.

When they got back into the cell the air was charged with menace.

Fru Rhodius was between Lockhert and her mother, who was leaning against the filthy wall. The noblewoman had the Bible outstretched in front of her and was shoving it in Lockhert's face. 'Think on the Good Lord's word, Lockhert,' Fru Rhodius declared passionately. 'And the laws of this kingdom.'

'The governor placed his trust in you to extract a confession from the witch, but you have been unsuccessful. It is now time for other methods,' Lockhert snarled.

Ingeborg saw something glinting in Lockhert's hand. It made her heart thud slow, slow, slow with terror and dread.

'It is against the law to torment a woman accused of witchcraft in the kingdom of Denmark! She must freely confess,' Fru Rhodius said to him.

Lockhert waved his instrument of torture in front of Fru Rhodius. 'You stop meddling else I might have need of my pinniwinks on you,' Lockhert said, as Fru Rhodius flinched at the sight of rusted blood on the metal. 'We have our own laws here on Vardø.'

Ingeborg watched closely. The image of Elli's broken hands surfaced unwelcomed in her mind.

Fru Rhodius drew breath. 'It is the governor who has asked me to "meddle".'

'Which has been unproductive! The witch has told us nothing of worth. Get out of my way, woman!' Lockhert bellowed at Fru Rhodius.

But she didn't move. And then she spoke so quietly Ingeborg barely heard her. 'You can't touch her,' she said. 'The woman is with child.'

Ingeborg took a step back in shock, banging against Maren, who was standing behind her.

'How do you know that?' Lockhert asked, grumpily.

'Just look at her!'

All the while Ingeborg's mother had been whimpering by the wall, covered in the reindeer skins, but Fru Rhodius turned and gently removed them from her shoulders.

Ingeborg gasped. There it was, plain to see. The bodice straining over the small bump.

'Whatever your laws are here in the north, they cannot be to torment a woman with child.'

Lockhert looked furious.

'And neither can she be put to the stake in such a state,' Fru Rhodius continued, rounding on the bailiff.

'But the witch is a widow!' Lockhert fumed. 'She must have fucked the Devil—'

'No! It's not true!' Ingeborg's voice came bursting from within her. 'It can't be. Mother, tell them.'

But Ingeborg's mother was sliding down the wall with despair, her face wet with tears.

Lockhert spun around, looking at Ingeborg and Maren as if he'd forgotten they had been sent out with the waste pail.

'Well, if the mother can't be talked to, then I shall question her daughter,' he said, shaking his fist with the thumbscrews at her.

'Absolutely not, Bailiff!' Fru Rhodius declared with such an imperious tone the bailiff dropped his fists. 'They are too young, as you know.'

'They look like women to me.'

Fru Rhodius approached Ingeborg and Maren. Looked at Ingeborg, and then rested her eyes on Maren's face. 'How old *are* you, girls?' Fru Rhodius asked, the bailiff glowering behind her.

'Sixteen summers,' Ingeborg said, looking beyond Fru Rhodius to the crumpled form of her mother.

'And you?' She turned to Maren, and Ingeborg could see her staring at the girl's skin, and black hair, wild and unruly.

'The same. I am tall for my years.' Ingeborg could hear the cheek in Maren's tone. 'It comes from my father.'

'And who might he be?' Fru Rhodius asked softly.

'You may well ask,' Maren said, grinning like a cat about to draw blood. 'Though some say he was a Barbary pirate and the Dark Lord of the eastern seas.'

What was she *doing*?

Lockhert took a step towards Maren, glared at her. 'Black inside and out,' he commented, before releasing a big glob of spit at her feet.

They were all pressed up so close together Ingeborg was holding her breath, stuck to Maren's side, and yet all her focus was on her mother. Pregnant with Heinrich Brasche's child. Was it such a disaster? Fru Rhodius was right. It might save her life. But Ingeborg felt anger swelling inside her. Her mother had given all to Heinrich Brasche, and in the doing had neglected her and Kirsten.

Lockhert stomped out of the witches' hole, leaving Fru Rhodius and the lantern.

Ingeborg went over to her mother, tugging on her arms. 'Mother, Mother, why didn't you tell me?' She couldn't help the outrage in her voice.

'I was hoping,' her mother whispered. 'I was hoping for Heinrich to come—'

'None will believe you,' Fru Rhodius said, sounding sad. 'They will say your child is the Devil's. It will count as evidence against you, Zigri Sigvaldsdatter.'

'But it's not true!' Ingeborg declared hotly, although her mother remained silent.

'Come, I have brought you a little *flatbrød* and salted herrings from my rations.' Fru Rhodius drew some sheaves of bread and a small pot of herrings from her cloak. 'Some sugared almonds too.' She pulled out a palmful of almonds from her pocket and offered them to Maren warily, as if she were feeding a wild animal.

Maren snatched them off her palm. 'Try them, Ingeborg,' she said, munching on the nuts.

As they ate the provisions, the sugared almonds a taste like none other, Fru Rhodius circled their dingy cell. 'I have come tonight to read some prayers with you,' she said.

Maren crouched on the filthy floor, licking the sugar off her last almond before dropping it into her mouth. 'I don't see the preacher's cassock on you, Fru Rhodius,' she said. 'Never mind prayers. Would you not like to hear one of my stories?'

Fru Rhodius hesitated. She wore a pair of pearl earrings that gleamed in the lantern light as if two drops of moonlight. Ingeborg thought she was going to admonish Maren, force them all on their knees. But instead, she took a great big sigh. 'Well, as you wish, Maren Olufsdatter.'

Ingeborg squatted next to Maren. Why would Fru Rhodius allow Maren's stories? Inside Maren's head lived trolls, sorcerers, bandits, and the Devil himself. But it was a make-believe world.

Her mother had stopped crying at last and was chewing mournfully on a herring.

'Forgive me, Ingeborg,' she whispered in a cracked voice to her daughter.

But Ingeborg turned her face away. Her mother had betrayed her and Kirsten, and what they had once been. A family. Ingeborg clenched her teeth, memories of her father resurfacing.

Elli had said the spirits of the dead lived among them in their own special world, where food was bountiful, and they never suffered. Ingeborg wished she could believe it but no matter how much she tried, it was impossible to imagine her father and Axell among the *huldrefolk*. Here in the witches' hole, there was no air, no light and no space for another spirit realm. They were trapped in the squalid confines of fallen women.

She blinked away tears of shame at what her father would think of her mother. Maybe her father hadn't drowned. Maybe he had sailed to a place beyond the grief of his wife, and now he couldn't return?

Maren reached out, took hold of Ingeborg's hand, and gave it a reassuring squeeze.

'This is a story I heard the Sámi tell,' she said to Ingeborg, warming her with a look of sympathy. Ingeborg could still hear her mother's sobs, and the rustle of Fru Rhodius's skirts as the woman came closer to listen, but all these sounds faded as Maren began to speak. Her story created a little pool of comfort around them, a few moments where they could be somewhere else.

'My story is set on the *vidda* in the spring, when the snow is at its thickest, and the daylight skies are filled with delicate pinks and brilliant orange,' Maren began. 'Once a group of bandits came upon a rich widow, her reindeer herd and two daughters. The bandits tied up the widow but left the two girls free to tend the reindeer herd. As she was taken away, the mother thrust a bag of feathers into the hand of the eldest girl and whispered something to the youngest girl. The rich widow was in fact a sorceress and she was passing on a magic spell to her daughters.

'These men were big and cruel, tying the widow to a rock where she shivered all night long, and making the Sámi girls stay outside to mind the reindeer herd while they remained within the widow's *lávvu*, eating all her reindeer meat and digging up her reindeer milk from its store beneath the earth, to drink. They also had ale with them which they drank to their fill. Every time one of them went out to have a piss, he jeered at the two girls. The bandits had thought it amusing to plait the girls' hair and bind their plaits around their arms so they could not be free of each other. But, in fact, this gave the girls greater strength because they were able to move as one being together in harmony.'

Maren picked up Ingeborg's long straggle of hair and began to smooth it in her hands. Ingeborg closed her eyes as she continued to listen to the story.

'When the bandits settled down to sleep the girls told them they would call if the wolves came for the reindeer for, unarmed and weak as two girls were, they would be unable to fight off the wolves alone.'

Maren parted Ingeborg's hair with her hands and began to plait it as she spoke.

'Once outside with the reindeer herd, the girls appealed to the reindeer bull, who was their guardian. With his great antlers he cut the ropes binding their mother to the stone, so she was able to fly free. Their mother turned into an eagle and spun up into the dark night. Next, the girls called out pretending that the wolves had come while they opened the bag of feathers, saying the magic words their mother had taught them. Immediately the feathers turned to snowflakes, and as the bandits ran out of the *lávvu*, they were swept up in a vicious blizzard, unable to see or hear where the girls or the reindeer were.'

Maren's deft hands had finished plaiting Ingeborg's hair and she let it softly land upon her back.

'The reindeer bull bowed down to the two Sámi girls who clambered upon its back together, plaits binding them for all eternity. They rode off into the west, as their mother eagle circled above them. And the bandits froze to death.'

Maren clapped her hands together in glee as she finished the story.

'Who told you this tale?' Fru Rhodius asked, her expression sharp as she surveyed the two girls.

'It is a well-known story among the people of the north,' Maren told the Danish woman.

But Ingeborg had never heard the story before. She liked the idea of two sisters bound together in strength, but she couldn't picture her and Kirsten as one and the same, ever. Where was her little sister now? She prayed she was safe and sound, but there was a worm of doubt wriggling inside her, making her feel sick to the stomach. She shouldn't have left Kirsten behind.

Chapter 27

Anna

My transformation from mistress to the king to the respectable wife of a doctor occurred within one week. After our meeting in the king's garden, I had returned to my father's house and taken to my bed. The smells from the sewer beneath our street wafted up into my open window but I could not be bothered to close it. My mother had no idea why I refused to leave my cocoon of misery while my father guessed all and took quick action. He didn't feel the need to ask me what I wanted because in his opinion my behaviour precluded any kind of choice. I must be wed, and quick, so my husband might have no clue as to the identity of my baby's real father.

I was going to have a child. I should have been filled with terror at the thought, shame at the least, but I was grateful for the babe within me, for I would always have a little part of you. It was this thought only that soothed my heartache at your abandonment.

Whatever transaction occurred between my father and Ambrosius Rhodius I was never privy to. All I do know is that within the week, Ambrosius and I were wed in Sankt Petri Kirke, but a few streets away from my father's university. My father was very well connected in academic circles, which is likely the reason Ambrosius also received a new position at the Latin Skole in Bergen. We were to board ship for Norway within a few days and travel a great distance away from Copenhagen, to the western edges of your kingdom.

I remember standing on the steps of the Sankt Petri Kirke, on my wedding day in late July in 1638, now as a wife, and glancing up at the skyline of Copenhagen. I could see the green-roofed turrets of your

Rosenborg Palace and could not help wondering if you ever looked out of your window and missed me. More likely, I had belonged within one short era of your life, for you had moved on to another era with Margrethe Pape and your child to be.

Over the years, I have tried my best to love my husband. There was much to like about Ambrosius Rhodius for he was passionate about his studies and had many very unusual and interesting ideas. He was, and I can only imagine still is, obsessed with the teachings of Paracelsus, the alchemist. Ambrosius believed in the predictive worth of dreams, and his ability to prophesy. I dare say if I had spouted forth such opinions, as a woman I would be branded a heretic or a witch, but my husband, as nobleman and a less talented doctor than I was never at any risk. Best of all, Ambrosius allowed me to read, and collect books. It was I who introduced him to different theologians and teachings from the whole of the Protestant doctrine. I believe you might disapprove of some of the texts I collected, but my husband and I were always loyal to our Lutheran faith, I promise you this.

My life in Bergen was a good one. My husband consulted me daily, and I made valuable contributions to his work as both physician and scholar.

With his new position came a house in the Sandviken district of Bergen with land. When I proposed we create a botanical garden, he was enthused with the idea and thus I was tasked with its design and the plants we would put in the garden. This was the greatest gift my husband gave to me in all our years together; truly, no number of jewels matched my joy in our garden. How it aches my heart to think of it now. Has Ambrosius managed to take care of it? We had two gardeners, but would he manage them as well as I did?

And why does he not write to me?

It hurts too much to think upon my husband because, in the end, he betrayed me.

Instead, let me remember the first weeks of my new life as a young wife in Bergen in the autumn of 1638. I was mistress of my own house, and although twenty-three years of age, I slipped into the role with ease. I employed three goodly women as my servants. Sidsel was gifted in the art of keeping house and, along with Kjersti, she cooked for us, kept the windows clean, the floors polished and organised the weekly visit to the washhouse. My third servant, Hege, was a very gifted seamstress, a skill my mother was always irritated I lacked. We had a large loom in the upper storey of the house, and it was here Hege spent most of her days spinning wool, or mending, sewing and knitting. She even had a flare for fine embroidery.

My three serving women gave me the time to learn about my plants. I had already studied much under my father and read medical treatises by learned doctors such as the Bartholins. In Bergen, I talked to the market women about their uses of herbs and plants, as well as consulting with the apothecary, and thus I began to learn each plant and its properties aligned with the Zodiacs. This interested Ambrosius immensely, for he was a great believer and follower in the planetary movements. I read all I could find on botanics and as I did so I found myself questioning some of the medical teachings my father had passed on to me.

From my perspective, I had always felt bloodletting weakened patients, and when I saw how Sidsel used herbs in our cooking, I understood that the use of these herbs and plants nourished patients, rather than took away from them. Surely this was how balance could be regained? But who was I to contradict the learnings of so many great men? Even so, I put down my books for a while and I sat in the kitchen asking Sidsel her knowledge of herbs. Why, it was encyclopaedic, and I asked her how she had learnt so much for one who could neither read nor write.

'From my mother, mistress,' she informed me. 'And her mother before her.'

The matriarchal lineage of healing was a revelation to me and gave me confidence: not just learned men as my father could heal. I hung upon the words of Sidsel taking copious notes and experimenting with remedies.

Ah, my king, I have been rambling and allowing happier memories of the past to fill me with images of herbs and plants, of the years I spent in my study of plants and cultivating the most magnificent botanical garden in the whole of Norway.

I had not forsaken you in my first months in Bergen – how could I, with the growing awareness of your child within me? What comes to me now is a happy scene of Hege embroidering my red bodice with green thread and I spinning a slow and careful circle for her, my hands upon my thickening waist, anticipation bubbling within me.

I believe by now mystification must have taken hold upon you – *What of this babe?* Yes indeed, for you know me as a childless woman, so where is your progeny?

I was yet to share the news with Ambrosius that I was expecting. I had been busy every night in the bedchamber to ensure there would be no doubt in his mind, and when the child came early, I would declare it keen to make an entrance into the world and distract my husband with what the planets had forecast.

But my lies were never necessary.

It was the month of September. Chill air and hazy light streamed through our open latticed window, and I awoke with a cold face, shivering under the covers, knowing almost at once all was not right. Ambrosius had already risen and left for the Latin Skole, which had been one saving grace.

Cramps were assaulting me, deep and urgent. Taking a deep breath, I reached down with my hands. As I lifted them to my face the fingertips were touched with my blood.

In that moment, how did I feel?

A huge confliction of emotion, for I did not want to let go of this child, and yet did it not make my life so much simpler? I was young and there would be many years ahead for children with my husband. But it was this thought that brought me to tears, for I had a husband now, and all for nought. Kind as he was, I did not love Ambrosius.

Only my women knew the truth of my menses the third month of my marriage. It was they who saw how heavy the bleed was and what my body purged from me. Sidsel brewed me a tea of comfrey root, sweet with honey, while Hege tucked me into the bed.

Ambrosius remained aloof, wishing to know nothing about the menses of his wife.

And so, it transpired within the ringing of ten and then eleven bells, that I no longer carried your child. As the blood gushed from between my legs, as the tears dripped from my chin, as my belly cramped in agony and the life we had made within me perished, my hope for us died too.

I believed never again would I feel your touch.

Chapter 28

Ingeborg

When the others arrived, the fortress was deep within *mørketiden*, the dark time. The sun had disappeared and would not return for weeks. Ingeborg had been sent out to the well on her own. How many days had she been confined in the dark? She had no idea, but during the time of her captivity so much snow had fallen upon the witches' hole, the soldiers had to dig out the doorway for her.

She walked through a tunnel of snow; the light, a watery green, fleetingly making her feel as if she were underwater. Out of the tunnel, she was high up on banks of white piled around the fortress, all the way up to the roof of the old longhouse, where Fru Anna dwelled.

The snow fell straight, and it fell sideways, teasing Ingeborg's skin with tiny flakes of ice, lacing her eyelashes and covering her reindeer skins in white. How she wanted to fall into the kindness of its oblivion and disappear.

The sky forever dark. Ingeborg only knew it was night by the tolling of the church bell and the northern star winking above her. She made her way to the well, thigh deep in snow, and took up the wooden stick to break through the skin of ice.

As she was filling her pail with the freezing water, the fortress gates swung open with a loud rattle. In swept a sleigh across the stacks of snow, followed by two more. At the sound of the reindeer bells, the soldiers of the fortress scrambled out of their turf hut in a ramshackle muster.

The first sleigh was driven by the hulking figure of Lockhert. Behind him was a figure, hidden in a bundle of skins and chains. Lockhert ordered the soldiers to pull the person out of the sleigh, and another figure out of the second sleigh.

Governor Orning got out of the third sleigh, along with a small, pale girl whom Ingeborg guessed must be his wife. He looked like a bear he was covered in so many furs, while she a tiny mouse.

There were two other figures behind them and, as the snow briefly stopped and Ingeborg moved a little closer, she was astounded to see the stout figure of Reverend Jacobsen, and next to him Kirsten. She froze, dropping her bucket, her heart in her mouth.

Her little sister was squeezed in next to the fat priest, her face pinched with cold and fright. Every part of Ingeborg ached to call out to her sister, but if she did, the governor would see her, and have her beaten for no other reason but that she had spoken. She had to bide her time. Wait and see what was about to unfold.

As the bundled figures were dragged out of the sleighs, Lockhert raised a lantern to cast light upon the two fettered souls: Solve, white-faced and blinded by the lantern, and Widow Krog, standing as tall as she could without her walking stick.

Ingeborg's breath quickened, pluming from her mouth in short, panicked puffs. Neither Solve nor Widow Krog had seen her.

Lockhert stomped across the courtyard to bang on the longhouse door. Fru Rhodius stepped out as if she had been waiting by it, for the knock. She was bundled up in a fur-lined cape with her hands thrust into a muff. She approached the governor across the thick snow while he tugged on the end of his grey beard, a cruel smile on his face, as his wife hurried into the castle.

Ingeborg shifted yet closer, her eyes still upon her sister. Kirsten was clutching the sides of the sleigh, staring around her, but not seeing her own kin. Ingeborg strained to hear what was being said.

'Fru Rhodius, accompany these new prisoners to the witches' hole and impress upon them the need to confess,' the governor was saying to the Danish woman.

'Yes, your honour.' She nodded in compliance.

'Remember what is at stake if you fail me,' he said in a low voice.

Ingeborg saw the effect of his words on Anna Rhodius as she stiffened: a mixture of fear, and what Ingeborg thought might be dislike.

The governor turned to Reverend Jacobsen, who was huffing and stamping his feet next to him. 'Reverend Jacobsen, assist Fru Rhodius, and attend to these women's damned souls.'

'And what about the girl?' Jacobsen asked.

'I shall put her in the witches' hole with the others,' Lockhert said.

Ingeborg felt her heart lurch. She wanted to hold Kirsten so dearly. They would all be together, but at the same time she didn't want her little sister to experience the horror of the stinking black witches' hole, with rats scampering to and fro all day and night. She would be so scared.

'Surely it's not a suitable place for such a young girl?' Fru Rhodius spoke up.

The governor considered her for a moment. 'She may well be intimidated by her witch mother not to tell us the truth. You can take the girl into your prison house, Fru Rhodius.'

Anna Rhodius called for Helwig, who appeared, shivering, in a thin woollen shawl.

'The stories this Iversdatter girl tells interest me,' the governor said to Fru Rhodius. 'Make sure you relay everything she says to me.'

His words filled Ingeborg with alarm. What had Kirsten been saying? She remembered Kirsten's words: *I saw Mother with the Devil, Ingeborg. Just like Fru Brasche said.*

Dread spread thick upon her chest. She had to warn her. 'Kirsten!' She ran across the snow, slipping and sliding, reaching out. 'Kirsten, hold your tongue, sister!'

Ingeborg was wrenched from behind and flung to the ground by one of the soldiers.

Kirsten saw her now. 'Inge! Inge! They told me Mamma is a witch!'

'No, she's not—'

Lockhert's rough hand was slapped over her mouth, and she was dragged away, while Helwig took Kirsten by the hand and tugged her towards Anna Rhodius's longhouse.

'Ingeborg!' Her sister's voice was high-pitched with fear. 'They killed Zacharias! They said she was my familiar. But she loved me!'

Ingeborg struggled to get away from Lockhert, but he threw her on her knees. 'Pick up your pail, witch's get, refill it and back into the hole you go. After these other witches.'

His words felt like a brand. *Witch's get.* Her mother was not a witch and nor was she. But it was pointless to fight against the brute. She caught sight of the shocked, glazed eyes of Solve, and the haggard face of Widow Krog watching her.

Picking up her empty bucket, Ingeborg refilled it with shaking hands, tears stinging her eyes as she watched Helwig take her little sister into Fru Rhodius' longhouse. One soldier remained watching over her, while the other, along with Lockhert, shoved Solve and the hobbling Widow Krog through the archway of snow and into the tiny witches' hole. Behind them stumbled stout Reverend Jacobson while Fru Rhodius stalked in last, head held high.

Now there would be five of them from the village of Ekkerøy crammed into the tiny cell. Ingeborg's breath came short and tight with panic once more. She had seen the hunger in the governor's eyes when he had ordered Fru Rhodius to get their confessions.

But she was Ingeborg Iversdatter, the resourceful daughter. Always finding a way. Her father had often said it when she had mended his old fishing nets for yet another year or collected great heaps of seaweed to give them nourishment, or found the best patch of bog with the driest peat; Ingeborg, always carrying on, and finding the best there could be when her father or her mother or her brother and sister had wanted to make do. Ingeborg had never given up, ever. Not like her father.

But now she was lost. They were in a deep pit, and she had no idea how they would get out.

Chapter 29

Anna

The governor and Bailiff Lockhert returned with two captured witches from the Varanger Peninsula, along with a village priest, Reverend Jacobsen. I had been unsuccessful in extracting a confession from Zigri Sigvaldsdatter, and Governor Orning was not pleased to learn of this, nor the fact she was with child, for her condition protected her from any harsh treatment as well as the stake.

'She claims the babe's Heinrich Brasche's, but his father sent him away to Bergen,' I told the governor, the first night of his return. 'Might we wait for him to return and confirm the truth of this?'

I had been sent across to the governor's house as we were about to eat our broth, leaving Helwig to feed the child Kirsten Iversdatter. Slipping and sliding across the icy courtyard in my pattens, my stomach had rattled with hunger and dread, for I was not looking forward to the governor's chagrin.

My initial questioning of the Varanger witches had not gone well. I had not managed to illicit any useful information, let alone a confession from either of them. The stooped crone, grey-haired and with a whiskery wart upon her chin, looked every bit a witch. I have lived in dread of grey hairs and every night inspect my jet-black hair for offending streaks, plucking them out. The old hag, named Widow Krog, had refused to say one word to me.

The other one, Solve Nilsdatter, was the cousin of Zigri Sigvaldsdatter, as well as the aunt of the dark girl, Maren.

As soon as Solve Nilsdatter had laid eyes on her cousin and niece, she had gone into a tirade of harsh words at them for denouncing her.

'I've confessed to nothing,' Zigri had said to Solve tearfully.

But when Solve had seen her cousin's protruding belly, she had gone into another flurry of curses. 'Look what you have done, Zigri!' she said. 'I warned you, and now we are all locked up. You have done this to your own daughters.'

'Kirsten, too?' Zigri had asked, narrowing her eyes.

Zigri's elder daughter, Ingeborg, appeared from behind me, carrying her pail of water. 'She is to be kept with Fru Rhodius in her longhouse,' she said putting down her bucket.

'She will be cared for as if one of my own,' I said.

There was a shocked silence as the mother took in the information that her little girl was also within the confines of the fortress walls, but her reaction was not what I expected. 'The little wench will surely fill you with lies!' Zigri shouted shrilly.

Her words hardened my heart towards the woman, for what kind of mother says such things about their own child?

'This is all your fault.' Zigri rounded on Maren. 'Filling Kirsten's silly head with your imaginings and folk tales about trolls.'

'They're not imaginings—' Maren had responded, but at this point the Reverend Jacobsen had stepped in and told the women to be silent.

'On your knees,' he said in a stern voice. 'We must pray to the Good Lord to guide you to speak the truth to Fru Rhodius.'

The priest had given me a cold, unwelcoming look as he said this for he clearly disapproved of my involvement, but I had the measure of him through the few words we had already shared. Reverend Jacobsen was of limited intellect. He was one of those dogged servants of God who have no means to inspire their brethren. For surely, was it not on his head that some of his flock had wandered?

After the prayers, the women had been even less inclined to speak to me, for Reverend Jacobsen had filled them with impending doom. They were exhausted from their long, brutal journey in the sleighs across the Varanger Peninsula. I was not in the heart to push them.

Now I stood in the governor's great chamber watching him demolish a platter of roasted seal meat, his lips slick with oil and his beard greasy.

The scent of the meat wafted over me and made my mouth water but I was not invited to dine with the company, nor even to sit and take my ease by his fire. Clearly the governor's gratitude for saving his wife's life was now spent.

As I spoke, all eyes were upon me: the governor's bloodless expression, the cruel gaze of Lockhert, the chill eyes of Reverend Jacobsen, and the flitting eyes of the governor's jittery wife.

'That is quite out of the question.' The governor belched as he responded to my suggestion we awaited Heinrich Brasche's return from Bergen. 'Fru Brasche is adamant she saw the accused with the Devil and has sent written testimony, as well as Merchant Brasche's account of the sinking of his ship. Furthermore' – the governor paused to help himself to a roasted quail – 'we will have the testimony of the child, Kirsten Iversdatter,' he said, as he crunched tiny bird bones between his teeth. 'She told me she saw her mother with the Devil, just like Fru Brasche said. It is your task to ensure she must not change her story.' The governor glared at me.

'The mother's conviction will have to wait until after the birth of the—'

The governor waved his hand.

'Devil's spawn,' Lockhert boomed, a look of pure hatred on his face.

I could hear Lockhert's heavy breath, his panting like a vicious dog on a leash waiting to be let off.

'We need confessions from the other two women, Solve Nilsdatter and Widow Krog.'

'Why have they been accused of witchcraft, governor?' I ventured to ask.

'Solve Nilsdatter drinks too much ale for a woman,' Reverend Jacobsen spoke up. 'Not only this, but she gives it to other women, even young girls, and encourages them to dance.'

He paused for effect, but I refused to show any reaction.

'And?' I asked in a cold voice.

The reverend looked a little excited. 'She has been seen going up the mountain on her own to meet the Devil.'

'I believe she is one of the witches who joined the diabolical coven with Zigri Sigvaldsdatter to sink Merchant Brasche's ship,' the governor interjected.

'And what about the older woman?' I asked.

'Widow Krog encouraged dancing on Midsummer's Eve, and she was given the craft of witchery by the Sámi Elli,' Reverend Jacobsen said. 'Fru Brasche saw the widow receive a fish from the Sámi witch, which made Widow Krog sick. This is evidence of the fact the hag was infected with witchcraft.

'I am convinced Sámi Elli and Widow Krog were the other two witches involved in raising weather magic and destroying Merchant Brasche's cargo and all souls aboard,' Governor Orning concluded.

'I must find Sámi Elli again.' Lockhert scowled. 'She is behind all the wicked deeds on the Varanger Peninsula.'

'So, as you see, Fru Rhodius, we have our crimes, but I need confessions and names of other witches in the peninsula,' the governor said, helping himself to another quail. 'Impress upon these two women the consequences if they don't.' He paused to spit out some of the bird bones. 'They will be sent to Lockhert and he is keen to acquaint them with all our methods of interrogation.'

'Oh, Christopher, no!'

She had been so quiet I had almost forgotten Fru Orning was dining too, but now the young woman looked at the men in wide-eyed horror, the pox scars upon her pale face raised and red.

Governor Orning put his hand on his wife's. 'They're evil witches, Elisa. Remember, they cursed our son.'

Elisa's eyes filled with tears, but she said no more, merely sliding her hand away from that of her husband's and bending her head to her untouched plate of food.

I too felt horrified at the suggestion of torture, but my situation was precarious, and I sensed I needed to be careful how I voiced my protests.

'And what of the two girls, Ingeborg and Maren?' I asked. 'Should they not be separated from the older women? There is no space for all of them to remain in the witches' hole.'

I thought of those five bodies stuffed inside the dank confines of the witches' hole, where there was hardly room for one soul, let alone all five. I wished to remove the girls away from the hopeless cases of Zigri, Solve and Widow Krog and bring them back to our Good Lord.

'The niece, Maren Olufsdatter, is most certainly a lost girl,' the governor said. 'We shall follow Lockhert's Scottish method of waking the witches for six days. If none confess, the two girls will lodge with you, Fru Rhodius, and the younger one, so Lockhert can work with other ways of getting the older women to confess.' He wiped his greasy face with his napkin and smiled at me. 'The trial will be before the winter's end, and I expect you to glean the truth from these girls on all the witchery in the Varanger Peninsula.'

'Yes, governor.' I made a low bow, but my heart felt constricted. All three girls – Maren, Ingeborg and Kirsten – were in mortal danger. It was up to me to save them before the trial.

Chapter 30

Ingeborg

Fru Rhodius smoothed down her blue silk skirts, then looked up and spoke to them.

'I am here under the direct orders of the illustrious Governor Orning, and thereby under Royal Command. I encourage you to confess all to me.' She paused, licked her thin lips. 'You women of Varanger are in this cell for a reason, you well know it. There is no point trying to hide your guilt any longer, for it will be exposed.'

Widow Krog lifted her chin defiantly. Looking Anna Rhodius in the eye, she spoke up. 'Shame on you, Fru Rhodius, to condemn other women so easily.'

'Think upon your eternal damnation,' Anna Rhodius responded, her cheeks flushing. 'If you don't confess, your soul is condemned to Hell.'

'Worse than the men are women who hunt each other.' Widow Krog's voice was low with fury.

Fru Rhodius turned her back on Widow Krog and attended to the shivering Solve. 'You've been seduced by the Devil and his empty promises of a better life,' she said to her.

Solve looked up at her, beseechingly. 'Please, my boys are all alone,' she pleaded. 'I've done nothing wrong. I beg you—'

Ingeborg watched Fru Rhodius as she ignored Solve's words.

'You've been tempted by greed, rather than submitting to God's will and accepting this earthly life with its hardships,' she lectured. 'Now you must face the consequences of abandoning the Good Lord.'

'I made no promises to the Devil,' Solve declared. 'I'm not a witch.'

In the light of the lantern clutched in Fru Rhodius's hand, Ingeborg could see little beads of sweat upon her forehead. Despite the fact her breath plumed into the freezing cell, her cheeks were crimson with heat. *She doesn't want to do this*, she thought. Despite her preaching, she suspected the Danish woman was against forcing them to confess.

'Listen to me,' Fru Rhodius whispered. 'They will not let you go home.'

'But you promised we would await Heinrich's return,' Ingeborg's mother spoke up.

'It's not up to me to make any promises,' Fru Rhodius said. 'Let us pray he returns before the trial.'

Ingeborg felt her throat tighten at the word *trial*.

Solve cried out in horror. 'No, no, I can't be put on trial! I've had no dealings with the Devil.'

Fru Rhodius shook her head, her moon-drop earrings catching the lantern light. 'There are other witches out there. They must be caught,' she said, curtly.

'Who?' Solve asked wildly, while Ingeborg noticed Maren looking sharply at the Danish woman. Listening and still, like a cat about to pounce.

'Sámi Elli,' Fru Rhodius said. 'Do any of you know where she is?'

The women shook their heads.

'If you tell me nothing, then you will be sent to Bailiff Lockhert.' Fru Rhodius licked her lips again, this time nervously. 'And he has other methods of interrogation – terrible, painful ways, such as the rack. I wish to spare you all such suffering.'

Ingeborg's body stiffened. There was worse, much worse than the thumbscrews Lockhert called his pinniwinks.

Solve shivered, a terrified look upon her face, and her mother appeared dazed, but Widow Krog shook her head. Her thick crown of white hair was like a crest of owl feathers, as she spoke very slowly but clearly. 'I will not lie upon myself or any other woman,' she said. 'We are not witches.'

After Fru Rhodius had left, a soldier was posted with them who would not allow them sleep. Seven lanterns were hung upon hooks in the walls of their hovel and kept lit day and night. If one of them fell asleep, the soldier would hit them with a stick. The slap of the hard wood against skin hurt enough, but it was the jolt to the exhausted women's hearts – the knowledge they were all still trapped together in the witches' hole – which was worse.

As the days wore on, her mother's accusations about Kirsten grew.

'She is a wayward sly child. See how she has sneaked off to tell all sorts of tales to the governor!'

'Mother, it's not true! She's a captive too.' Ingeborg defended Kirsten, although she worried about her sister's want to colour their dour village life with make-believe.

Solve, on the other hand, never ceased berating Maren for her own witch mother: how it had marked Solve with misfortune since the day Maren had arrived at her home. Or else she was at her cousin for being a slut; Zigri would retort that at least her husband had never battered or raped her, which led to more curses from Solve.

It took stern words from Widow Krog to silence the two cousins. 'We are in this cell through the fault of no girl nor woman,' she admonished them.

'But where are the witches of Varanger?' Ingeborg had asked Widow Krog, in a low voice.

Widow Krog put her chill hand on Ingeborg's own. 'There are no witches in our village, Ingeborg, but the Devil does exist. Look into the eyes of our accusers and you will see him there.'

Despite her words, Ingeborg wondered whether Widow Krog was the true witch among them, for she showed little fear. Maren and Widow Krog huddled together exchanging stories. Were *they* two witches among them then? Ingeborg's head hurt from the worrying and the fear, while her stomach griped with hunger and her body ached from cold.

All she wanted was to go back in time to when Axell had been there by her side. His loss came upon her like the wildest storm, sweeping through her, making her curl up in grief.

When she raised her head again, the lanterns were still casting shadows upon the walls of the witches' hole. Ingeborg could see the Devil in their shapes. A high-crowned hat on his head, horns poking through it, claws for hands and hooves for feet. She pinched herself with such fury she drew blood.

*

The only way for them to keep their eyes open and avoid the soldier's beatings was to tell each other stories. Maren spoke of grumpy but kind trolls and clever, brave Sámi girls, while Widow Krog's tales came from the old religion.

In the telling of stories, the women stopped their bickering, and huddled together.

'These are stories that my grandmother told me,' Widow Krog whispered. 'And hers before her.' She scratched her whiskery chin. Her expression was pensive, her eyes heavy-lidded with nostalgia. 'All my children are scattered to the four winds, and I am glad to say my two daughters are a long way from Varanger.' She sighed. 'But I fret they might not remember these stories so well.'

'We won't forget them,' Maren promised.

The widow nodded at the girl's understanding. 'Before the Good Lord came to our land of Norway and before Jesus Christ was born,' she whispered although the soldier was sure to hear her anyway, 'there were gods and goddesses who held sway. At the centre was the huge ash tree, Yggdrasil, the great tree of life. It was so mighty it reached all the way to Heaven and all the way down to Hell. Within its branches dwelled gods and goddesses, elves and dwarves, and trolls. At its base were three twisted roots: one that passed into Aesir where the principal gods dwelled, one that passed into the land of the frost giants, and one that passed into the realm of the dead.'

Ingeborg's mother rested her head upon her shoulder, and Ingeborg stroked her hair as though her mother were her child. It was impossible to stay angry with her; despite the shameful thing her mother had done, she still loved her. Ingeborg closed her eyes. Imagined the tree of life cracking open the rocky, hard floor of the witches' hole, its branches bursting through the low rafters, up through the ammunition store too, and out of the turf roof.

Widow Krog was not as lively a storyteller as Maren, but Ingeborg found her tales of the old religion beguiling. There was good and evil in them, but there was no mention of the Devil. In Widow Krog's story of the three mothers, Ingeborg found a way to see her world in a different light. She remembered Zare's talk of the gods of everywhere in his Sámi faith, the gods the Sámi revered but could also touch.

What if the ruler of all was not God Almighty in Heaven?

It made her hands shake to think of such heresy. She pressed her palms together and tried to pray for mercy, but instead she would see the three mothers in her head. Urth, Verthandi and Skuld weaving her fate at the bottom of the great tree of life, Yggdrasil.

Take me across Bifrost the burning rainbow bridge in Widow Krog's stories, take me away from this earth to Asgard the realm of the Gods, her heart would plead. When she squeezed her eyes shut, and thought very hard, sometimes she would see a flicker of the old religion's burning rainbow bridge. Waiting for her at the other side was not her own family, nor even the ancient Norse Gods much to her astonishment, but Elli *yoik*ing, and Zare banging a *runebomme.*

Amid the moans, the coughing, the sobs of the imprisoned women, Ingeborg clung on to the thread of the *yoik* and the beat of the drum. It fed a little hope inside her, a stubborn refusal to believe all was lost.

Chapter 31

Anna

I journeyed through twenty-five years of marriage, and it was a war as filled with physical hardship for me as any soldier. My battle was not with my husband Ambrosius, for he was never harsh nor raised his hand to me once. Nay, my king, my fight was with my own flesh and blood, for my body would not surrender to my will.

My body, which bled, ripped and tore, assaulted me with such sufferings – and still I was not victorious. All I wanted was to have one son, but it was God's will my wish for a boy was forever denied us.

From time to time, I heard about the success of the son, your mistress Margrethe Pape bore for you. Within his very appellation – Ulrik Frederik Gydlenløve – you proclaimed to all he was the illegitimate son of the King of Denmark – *Gyldenløve* – ah, what an honour you bestowed on Baroness Pape! I heard of your son's rise through the nobility in Copenhagen, and his skill as a soldier, for his glory at the Battle of Nyborg is legendary. In some small way I felt ownership of his story for a voice inside my head often whispered, *Ulrik Frederik Gyldenløve could have been your boy, Anna, and you made a baroness as his mother was.*

But my life, though privileged, dwelled in more humble circles and I am glad for it now; truly, for my experiences among the common folk of Bergen brought me closer to understanding the injustices of our world. Once you were interested in the welfare of your subjects, but I believe, my king, you have long forgotten your duties, encased as you are in your protective shield of an absolute monarch not limited or restrained by the laws which govern your people. Ah, but for how long can you fend off those who seek the truth and justice? For all your dissenters cannot be exiled to Vardø.

I was a doctor's wife and walked among the ordinary people on the cobbled streets of Bergen. I listened to the herbal lore of the local women and collected with my own hands the roots and seeds found in the wooded hills surrounding the city. I brought them back to our garden and planted them myself.

On my travels I would see how the people struggled to survive, vulnerable to every slight ailment. Beggars who had once been soldiers, sitting along the quays or in the fish market with missing limbs and defeated souls. Despite their hardships, not once did I hear any fisherman, tradesman, baker, nor serving woman speak of anything but love and devotion for their king. No, the words I heard against you were within the higher circles, and how it boiled my blood to witness these aristocrats with Statholder Trolle at their head raising taxes and stealing hundreds of riksdaler from the people and from *you*, my king. But you know this, because many times I wrote to you on the matter over the years. Even though not once did you reply.

My passion to give birth to a living child never waned, although after losing our sixth child, Ambrosius begged me to stop.

'Anna, you will not survive another pregnancy,' he warned.

'Have you seen in it in the planets?' I challenged him. 'Am I to die in childbirth?'

'No,' he paused, his voice cracking. 'But we have buried so many. They are all born still and blue. Not one has uttered a breath of life.' A tear slid from his eye, and it enraged me.

How dare he cry, when I valiantly pursued my destiny of motherhood, for must not all men have a son?

'We will have our boy, Ambrosius, even if he is delivered with my dying breath.'

I meant these words with all my heart, believe me.

How I suffered during all those years of dead babies born, or short pregnancies terminated, in a flush of heavy blood and searing cramps and my heart breaking again and again. Was my sin with you so great I was never to be allowed a living child? Moments there were, in my fever of giving birth, knowing it was too soon, gritting my teeth in desperate agony, when I would see the Dark Lord watching me. He would be standing in the corner of my bedchamber and staring with lustful eyes at the most private part of me split open. The dead baby would slip out, unbaptised, and he would scoop them up into his arms and take them for his.

Oh, the agony of all those lost souls.

But then, oh then, my king, came the sweetest season in my life.

In April 1646, two years before you ascended the throne of Denmark, I became pregnant yet again. The world was in upheaval for nobles and kings were in combat with each other over all of Europe, but in my world it was calm at last, for the baby clung on within me, and on the very eve we heard of the death of your brother, the prince-elect, I gave birth to a living baby girl. We named her Christina, after your brother.

Christina. If I close my eyes, hold my breath, and think very hard, I can smell my little girl and I am no longer in the shuttered dankness of my prison longhouse but back home in Bergen, cradling my new baby in my arms. I can smell the scent of her skin upon my skin, feel my fingers curling her fine red hair and remember my heart fairly bursting with the joy.

'We have a daughter,' I crowed with delight.

Ambrosius beamed at me. 'You are magnificent, Anna.'

Never had I felt so happy as wrapped in my husband's arms, holding our baby.

Christina. She was such a pleasing baby – always smiling, and charming all who looked upon her. My serving women argued over who knew the best wet-nurse, but I refused all their advice for I nursed her myself. I had not suffered eight years of barrenness to let my baby drink from another woman's breast. My decision shocked the whole household, including Ambrosius, but I was adamant.

I remember still the sensation of her suckling, the tug on my nipple, and the pull in my belly as if still tethered to my child within the womb. Hege would sit with me knitting little blankets for the baby – so many blankets – her eyes gleaming with joy for me. How my women loved me and my little girl! Sidsel would bake cinnamon rolls laced with sugar because she said I had become too thin, and Kjersti made me tonics to heal my womb and give me strength.

The first year of Christina's life was within a bower of these three women's care, and Ambrosius became a shadow. He would come and sit with Christina and me, but when it came to night, he preferred to sleep in peace away from her cries and feeding.

Christina at three years of age was even more adorable; clinging on to skirts with her little fists as she waddled up and down our staircases. If not my skirts, then Hege's, Sidsel's or Kjersti's. She had milk-pale, soft skin, summer-blue eyes and red curly hair, with little likeness to my features. Ambrosius claimed she had the look of his sister with her spattering of freckles upon her nose. I counted all those freckles and there were twenty-five of them, as if a blessing of little stars upon her face. Each night, I told my little girl stories about baby Jesus as she fell asleep in my arms, and while she slept, I gave thanks to the Good Lord.

Christina at eight years old was as quick as a swift but as silent as smoke darting up and down the staircases. Unlike her parents, Christina was a quiet child, but she listened, drinking in every tiny happening with her big blue eyes. She watched Sidsel and Kjersti in the kitchen and learnt how to make our tinctures and decoctions, for when I asked her to bring any herb or leaf in from the garden, she knew what to find and what they were for.

I was so proud of my beautiful, clever girl, and I wonder now if pride was my downfall.

Christina was growing and needed a new dress; besides, it was my desire to have a miniature portrait painted of my girl, which, though costly, Ambrosius agreed to, for he doted upon Christina as much as I.

It was raining the day the package was delivered from the harbour to our house in Bergen. Sidsel unwrapped the wet paper from it and pulled out the length of brocade the same shade as emeralds. How I clapped my hands with delight, imagining my red-haired Christina in such a gown would look as if a princess.

When Hege saw the fine material, she went to work with a clapping of her hands too. Together, she and Sidsel hung it to dry in front of the kitchen fire. Steam rose from the damp material and filled our small kitchen with the musky scent of foreign lands, for I had ordered the brocade direct from Amsterdam, and been told it had traversed all the way from the north African city of Algiers.

When I returned from the fish market with Christina, Hege told me it was time to fit Christina for her new gown. Such excitement, my king, as the newly dried material was measured against my child's figure; Christina hopping from foot to foot in glee, and Hege cajoling her to keep still else she would be pricked with her pins.

These are the moments I roll over in my mind in my darkest, most lonesome thoughts. I believe what occurred next was to do with the package from Amsterdam that I had gone to such lengths to procure, out of my love for Christina.

Chapter 32

Ingeborg

Bailiff Lockhert swung the lantern backwards and forwards as Ingeborg's head spun. Her eyes were dry and tight, as if filled with tiny grains of sand. Her throat was parched, no matter how much of the icy water from their pail she scooped into her mouth. How many days had they all been kept awake? Even for northern women, used to the relentless light of summer nights, it was becoming too much to bear.

Solve's eyes roved constantly, her whole body shaking with exhaustion. Nothing was left of the dancing, jolly mother from Andersby.

As if detecting she were the weakest of them all, Lockhert directed his attention upon her. 'Tell me the truth, lassie, of all your heinous deeds terrorising the Christian folk of Varanger.' He continued swinging the lantern back and forth.

'I am innocent,' Solve's voice quivered. 'Please, my boys. I must get back to my boys.'

Lockhert gave a cruel laugh. 'First confess your part in weather magic, Solve Nilsdatter.' He poked Solve with his stick as her head nodded forward. 'You were all seen as birds by Merchant Brasche.' He pointed at Ingeborg's mother. 'She was a white dove, and the old crone a white swan, the Sámi Elli a black-headed gull and you were a plover, Solve Nilsdatter. The four of you cast a spell upon Merchant Brasche's ship and caused it to sink, taking all those on board down with it.' His eyes narrowed.

Ingeborg's head was thick with confusion. How had Merchant Brasche been able to tell Lockhert the birds he saw had been women, let alone witches?

But the bailiff was sure of it, and so very angry and outraged, that he began to beat poor Solve with his stick as she pleaded her ignorance.

'*Caw, caw, caw!*' Maren was on her feet and circling the tiny cell, her arms outstretched as wings. 'You would like to be a bird too, Deputy Lockhert!' Maren declared as Ingeborg stared at her in hazy wonder. 'The only time we are truly free is when we're up high, above all menfolk's filth and sin. When we are soaring in the sky.'

Lockhert took a menacing step towards Maren, but she did not leave off her goading of him.

'We circle the moon, catch the stars, dip into the sea to see the underworld kingdoms,' she told him. 'Aye, the glory of independence is what my bird self is to me.'

'Are you telling me, girl, that you can transform into a bird?' he said in a low voice, his eyes dark.

'Why, yes,' Maren said. 'But not these others.' She swept her hand wide. 'For you can't *choose* to shapeshift. No, *your* bird picks you.' She stopped spinning and clasped her hands to her heart. 'There it is – the glint of crow in my eyes when I look in the ice on the well top. And on top of the fortress, I see all through crow eyes.' She laughed. 'Put my hand on my face and there is a beak in place of my nose, the hard-shell cold to touch. I lift my head to look for my sister crows up above, and I call to them. *Caw, caw, caw!*'

She walked towards Deputy Lockhert flapping her arms, and it was then Ingeborg understood what Maren was doing. Upon the huge man's face had descended a look of fear. No amount of pleading, begging or praying for mercy would stop his tormenting, but Maren being a bird, ruffling her feathers, in preparation to curse him, had stopped him. His mouth fell open and he stared at the girl as if she had indeed changed into a big black crow.

'Crow perches in my heart and shifts my body into bird,' Maren told Lockhert. 'Spread my arms, my fingers, and watch black feathers grow,' she continued. 'Aye, it hurts, Bailiff Lockhert. Every single quill bursting my skin, taut and burning. All squeezing tight inside me. Smaller, smaller I become. My senses keen, my vision wide and forever, and I can be free whenever I wish.'

Maren's eyes glittered, and Ingeborg felt such terror for her. She wanted to pull her down, make her be silent. The more she said the more she condemned herself. But Maren appeared unafraid of all consequences. She approached the dumbstruck bailiff, and maybe he did see a big black bird as she cocked her head at him.

'It's me, Bailiff Lockhert, sitting on the window ledge of your gatehouse, looking in to get at *you*,' she said. 'And it was me sitting atop the mast of the boat which brought you to our island. The Dark Lord sent me and he's after *you*.' Maren gave a belch of wild laughter and began circling again. '*Caw, caw, caw!*'

At last, the bailiff recovered and bellowed, 'Enough!' But he didn't strike Maren, nor did he start again with his questioning. Instead, he ordered the soldier to put out the lanterns. 'Leave the witches in the black where they belong.'

The blessed black. The five of them fell like stones, unable to speak for exhaustion. They collapsed upon each other into the blissful oblivion of sleep.

Chapter 33

Anna

Remember, my king, the year 1654 when the Great Plague came to Norway and cast panic and terror upon every living soul whether noble or low-born. The 'Devil's Plague' was indiscriminate and brutal, and none of us were safe from its voracious appetite for death.

In our household in Bergen, it was Sidsel who took ill first, with a fierce, fast fever which left her calling out for snow. Kjersti and I looked after her as best we could. I gave her some of our Jenes treacle made from lung flowers, while Kjersti cooled her body with wet cloths. By the time Ambrosius returned from the Latin Skole, we didn't need to tell him what ailed her. Kjersti and I stared at each other in horror as we saw the black bubo swelling upon Sidsel's neck, then another under her armpit, and another. I roasted some white lily root, mixing it with hog's lard, and applied it to the sores to break them out, but all to no avail.

Poor Sidsel. She cried out for her mother, eyes wild with fear, but within the hours of one day she had passed.

'We must wrap her tight in a shroud, call for her to be collected,' I instructed Kjersti as she stood gripping her elbows, the expression on her face one of pure terror. 'Then we must fumigate the whole house with rosemary.'

'But will they confine us?' Kjersti asked, in a shaky voice. 'Board up the doors? Are we doomed?'

'No, we shan't tell them. Ambrosius will certify she died of the ague,' I said, my heart beating fast as I ran up the stairs to ensure all was well with Christina.

My daughter was with Hege, learning how to use the loom. I stood watching from the doorway, marvelling how her tiny fingers were so much more dextrous than my own. They both looked well, though Hege was shocked when I told her Sidsel had died.

'But Sidsel was well enough this morning,' Hege said, crossing herself.

I did not mention what she had died of, though I picked up the green brocade material we had ordered from Amsterdam.

When I returned to the kitchen, I threw the material on the fire as Kjersti looked at me in confusion. I did not know how to explain to her that there was something about the brocade's distant origins which disturbed me.

When Ambrosius returned in the evening he was most alarmed, though I saw no surprise on his face.

'I have heard three died of plague today. It will spread fast. We must leave the city with Christina at once,' he said. 'I have been able to procure rooms for us at the Rosenkrantzes Hatteberg farm on one of the islands. We will be safely away from the pestilence there.'

'But what about Hege and Kjersti?'

'They must remain in Bergen,' Ambrosius said firmly. 'We cannot bring them with us, Anna. There are servants at Hatteberg farm. It will be less of a risk.'

'Ambrosius, we cannot abandon them, they are women in our care!'

'Anna, the plague will rip through Bergen like fire. Our duty is to Christina, and we must take her out of the city as soon as we can.'

For my daughter, I was prepared to betray Hege and Kjersti, two dear souls who had journeyed with me through my years of barrenness and given me much solace.

Sidsel's body was taken for burial, and Ambrosius confirmed she had passed of ague – we had swaddled her so tight none examined her for signs of plague. As we watched her body being lifted onto the cart, it reminded me of my lost, swaddled babies and brought a lump to my throat.

Ambrosius and I were up the whole of the night packing our chests.

If we had not bothered with possessions and run with the clothes on our backs out of the pestilent city, would our story have been different?

The next morning, as I was locking our chests and preparing our travel wear, Christina appeared in my chamber in her nightgown and bare feet.

'Come, my child, we must prepare for departure.'

As I looked at her, I saw the flush on her cheeks and the glaze in her eyes. Truly, my heart felt as if squeezed by a fist, the scream in my throat strangled by a need to stay calm for her, for my darling girl.

'Mamma,' she whispered. 'My head hurts.'

My hand is shaking, and you will see this paper is buckled by my tears, for writing this letter to you is the hardest one yet. *I lost my daughter –* the four words so bitter and acrid in my mouth as the memories come hurtling back to me.

The plague swept through our city of Bergen and destroyed those I loved. Kjersti, Hege and I soothed and cared for our little girl with all the healing we possessed. We ladled Jenes treacle into her little rosebud mouth while dismissing the warnings of Ambrosius, who would enter the chamber with his face covered, telling us to stay back, stay back, but we would not. How could I let my Christina die alone? We held her hot hands and told her stories about sweet baby Jesus. When her time came, the black buboes were swollen monstrous on her little body, despite the poultices of white lily lard I had applied, but her eyes were the bluest forget-me-nots in all the world.

She could see a long, long way, further than any mortal soul. 'Baby Jesus is here, Mamma,' she whispered, through cracked lips. 'He is with me.'

After Christina's little body had been wrenched from my arms, swaddled by my sobbing husband and carted away, Hege took sick. Kjersti did her best to ease her suffering, but dear Hege was not long behind my daughter into the shadows. I felt not of the world. Did I shed tears for Hege? I cannot remember rightly, though what I do know is I touch her stitching every day and say a prayer for her sweet soul.

Kjersti, ever the most practical and stoic of serving women, made more Jenes treacle with the lung flowers, and leaves from the bay tree, in our garden. She instructed me to administer it to Ambrosius and myself after she was gone. Then she took to her bed and never rose again.

I waited my turn. But I did not take ill, and neither did Ambrosius. Our home, once full of joy and laughter, had become a house of death.

After Kjersti and Hege's bodies had been taken, Ambrosius urged me that we should go away to the country. All the nobles had left, and people were dying on the streets; the authorities were boarding up the houses of those infected, and we would become trapped. But I would not leave. I had no wish to live. For all I desired was to be with Christina.

Yet it was God's will, a cruel punishment for me to endure, and Ambrosius too. Upon reflection, I believe our suffering was God's design for Ambrosius and me to understand we must help others in pain.

During those dark days in our house in Bergen we finished the pot of Jenes treacle Kjersti left us, scooping up spoonfuls and filling ourselves with its bitterness. Maybe this is what saved our lives; but why ours, and not the others'?

All I know is I made more of the treacle with our lung flowers and bay leaves. I filled all the vessels I could find with it, the herby, floral scent sinking into my skin and bones.

'What are you doing, Anna?' Ambrosius asked me, his eyes red-rimmed with grief for our daughter. 'Please.' He held out his hand to me. 'We must leave at once. Please, wife.'

'No,' I replied, the first remembered word I had spoken to my husband since Christina had died. 'We are staying, and we are going to help.'

He looked at me in disbelief.

'We are physicians, and our work is to attend to the sick, husband,' I said to him.

'But we will die,' he said in a hoarse whisper, terror flicking through his eyes.

'And if we do, the sooner we will be with our dear daughter.'

He understood then, his eyes opening wide as he stared at me. 'They all say Christina looked like me, but it's not true, Anna. She's in you.' His voice broke and he wiped away a lone tear.

'Very well. I will stay. Very well, wife,' he said, his voice soft with resignation.

For the length of the wet summer and grim autumn in 1654, my husband and I worked with little rest, attending to the sick and dying of Bergen. Relentlessly, we spooned Jenes treacle into children's mouths.

For one already with fever there was little it could do, but I began to discern for some not yet infected it protected them. I scrubbed the floors of the poor with boiled water and birch lyre, for I had also concluded the pestilence did not like cleanliness: the more I cleaned and scrubbed, the more of the poor of Bergen lived. They called us saints – the physician and his wife – for staying to heal the needy, the abandoned citizens of your great western city in Norway, while the likes of Statholder Trolle had run for the hills. But in truth my intentions were not as honourable, for I was waiting for the day I would awaken with a hot head and swellings upon my skin. I was waiting to find Christina in the next world with all the other angels, but that day never came.

Chapter 34

Ingeborg

From deep within the surrender of sleep, Ingeborg heard a tapping on the wall behind her. *Tap. Tap. Tap.* A voice calling her name. 'Ingeborg! Ingeborg Iversdatter, where are you?'

Her shadow-self separated from the weight of her dead-tired body and mind. It emerged strong and lithe, pulling on the plank of wood. Her nails breaking, splinters piercing her fingertips, until she'd wrenched free one of the boards. Bending down, she looked out.

Whom should she see but Maren Olufsdatter! How had she broken out of the cell? But there she was dancing in the Christmas snow with the Dark Lord. Not as gross as Reverend Jacobsen described him, but tall with lustrous black hair, skin burnished as copper, and eyes the blue of mussel shells.

Maren let him spin her before leaping into the air. Instead of landing in the snow, she took flight. Ingeborg felt a surge of wonder as her arms spread into two magnificent black feathered wings. How beautiful she looked!

'Come, fly!' Maren called to her.

Ingeborg wanted to share the magic with the others. So, she woke them all up, showed them the hole in the wall.

'Let's go, let's go,' she urged, and they all squeezed through.

Outside the snow was falling, but they were not cold. The women held hands. At last, all of them were united. They looked up at Maren the crow soaring in the sky. She landed outside the closed door of Fru Anna Rhodius' longhouse and knocked on the door with her beak. As if by magic, it swung open and there was Ingeborg's sister standing upon its threshold.

'Kirsten!' Ingeborg called to her.

Kirsten waved before wading across the snowy courtyard and joining the women as they climbed up the steps of the inner fortress walls.

'Mamma, I am here,' Kirsten told their mother, and for once Zigri did not turn away, but took her youngest daughter's hand.

In a row, they balanced on the top of the fortress walls – old Widow Krog, Solve with her ringlets of brassy hair, Zigri with the unborn babe within her, holding the hands of Kirsten and Ingeborg herself. They could see the whole of Vardø before them: the island blanketed in white, and the sky a dome of dizzying colours: green in all its power, red with its fury and violet from the deep dark. Swathes of the shifting lights calling to them, the bright northern star beckoning to Ingeborg.

Ingeborg watched as Maren the crow caught the wind and swooped spectacularly in a circle. Now was the time to follow her. Ingeborg, Kirsten, and their mother stepped off at the same time. Plunging towards the ground, bumping on the wind, until they spread their arms and began to glide.

Her mother was laughing. 'Look, girls!' she exclaimed. 'They cannot touch us now.'

The governor and his men were staring up at them in astonishment: Reverend Jacobsen open-mouthed in shock and Bailiff Lockhert shaking his fist, though his face was streaked with terror.

Solve and Widow Krog followed them off the wall. Dropping upon the air and circling the town of Vardø. The sexton rang the church bells, and all the folk were pointing and looking at the six of them as they sailed the sky. Ingeborg was intoxicated by the rush of wind through her feathers, her speed and power as she glided above.

Why had she never flown before? Ingeborg was as light as a feather, as poised as an arrow. They had all turned into birds. Zigri the dove, Widow Krog the swan, Solve the plover, Maren the crow, and Kirsten had become a bright-eyed sparrow. And what bird had Ingeborg become?

They hovered above the fjord's thin glaze, shifting between ice and ripples. Her shadow upon it was of an eagle. Ingeborg felt the power of the bird within her: its majesty, its wisdom, and its might.

They flew to the top of Domen, and when they arrived, the Dark Lord greeted the women with a great feast: slices of hot gingerbread for them to devour, and jug after jug of creamy cinnamon milk. They danced in a circle, and the Devil played a song on his red fiddle. How could he be evil when he made them all so happy?

Ingeborg awoke in the stinking pitch black, clinging to her pregnant mother. It had all been a dream. They were no more birds than the fleas crawling on her dirty skin. Moreover, Kirsten was not with them, and her mother had shown her youngest daughter no love. She stifled a sob and closed her eyes again. *Take me back, take me back to the big sky with my sister and mother. The three of us harmonious and in liberty.* But she couldn't get back. She'd lost her bird self, her family, and her freedom.

Chapter 35

Anna

It is a common saying, is it not, that even during the darkest night, there is a glimmer of light, a lost star, a sliver of moon, a lit candle?

My lost star was Kirsten Iversdatter.

I remember the night of her arrival. I had returned from questioning the new prisoners, and when I entered the longhouse, Kirsten was sitting on the stool by the table, gobbling down the fish broth Helwig had given her.

The maid was watching from the other side of the chamber, with arms crossed and a critical eye. 'There's something not right with her,' Helwig said to me in a loud whisper.

Kirsten paused from her repast, having clearly heard Helwig, her spoon half-lifted, broth dripping from it. She looked directly at me as if Helwig was not in the room.

It was in that moment that I took note of the girl's appearance; the likeness hit me as a thunderbolt. I staggered back and grasped Helwig's arm.

'See, she's strange-looking, those eyes,' Helwig whispered, misunderstanding my reaction.

I let go of Helwig's arm, embarrassed by my sudden loss of composure. 'What nonsense.'

Helwig scrutinised me. 'I warned you this is a bad business, Fru Anna. Better you don't get mixed up in it.'

'I have no choice in the matter, Helwig,' I said huffily, my eyes still fixed upon Kirsten, who had continued eating her broth.

I moved across to Kirsten and spoke to her gently. 'There's nothing to fear, Kirsten,' I said. 'I will look after you.'

She looked up again, and the image of her skewered my heart. How could this girl *be*?

Kirsten had the same big blue eyes, with such familiar long black lashes, as if painted upon her porcelain skin. There was a spattering of freckles upon the bridge of her nose, and I wondered if there were twenty-five of them. Her hair was the same vibrant red in a confusion of curls, and her teeth had a slight protrusion over the bottom lip just like Christina had.

This fisherman's child, Kirsten Iversdatter, was the image of my dead daughter. The only difference was their age: Christina died when she was eight years old; I had been told Kirsten was twelve, and she was indeed taller, though her face was babyish.

'They killed my lamb,' she said, her eyes welling with tears. 'They killed Zacharias.'

'Lambs are meant to be killed,' I told her. 'It is their purpose.'

My words surprised her. She stopped eating, her mouth open.

'*Agnus Dei*,' I told her, sitting down next to her.

'What does that mean?'

'It means "Lamb of God" in Latin, the language of our Church, and it is what we call Christ sometimes. *Agnus Dei, qui tollis peccata mundi, miserere nobis. Lamb of God, who takes away the sins of the world, have mercy upon us.* He sacrificed His life for us.'

She put down her spoon and wiped her mouth with her sleeve.

I would have to teach her how to use a napkin.

'Zacharias sacrificed her life for me?' she asked, frowning. 'She was bleating a lot. I don't think she wanted to die.'

'Well, Jesus Christ didn't want to die, either, but he did it to save us,' I said, wanting so much to touch her, and ensure that this living evocation of my Christina was truly of a beating heart, flesh and bone.

Her first night in my longhouse, Kirsten was put to sleep with Helwig on her pallet. But in the middle of the night, the maid woke me. 'She's walking in circles and her eyes are open, but she ignores me when I tell her to go back to bed,' she protested. 'I can't put up with this, Fru Anna.'

When we went back into the main chamber, Kirsten was trailing around and around the cooking fire in her nightgown, bare feet black from dirt. Oh, it was a like a lance to my heart, for it reminded me of the last morning Christina had walked into my bedroom. Her last words before the fever descended surfaced in my mind. *Mamma, my head hurts.*

I knew at once what was occurring, for it was clear to me Kirsten possessed somnambulism. I had seen it before in my days as a physician's wife in Bergen.

'She is somnambulating,' I said.

Helwig glared at me. 'I don't know what that is but looks to me like the Devil himself has her!'

'Not at all. It is a medical condition,' I said. 'Not so uncommon. She is merely walking while asleep.'

'But her eyes are open, Fru Anna! And look at them!'

Kirsten's eyes were round and staring off very far away, or down deep, like eyes open underwater.

'I will wake her. There's nothing strange going on,' I said.

Helwig shook head. 'The girl's not right, Fru Anna, she's trouble—'

'Enough!' I snapped. 'I would ask you not to mention this to anyone in the fortress.'

Helwig looked very cross but lay back down on her pallet while I guided Kirsten into my bedchamber and gently woke her up.

She looked at me in a daze. 'Where am I?'

'You are here, with me, in my bedchamber, Kirsten. You were walking while still asleep.'

She looked confused. 'I don't remember.'

'Get into my bed, and back to sleep.'

The girl did as she was told and fell fast asleep again.

I lit a candle, clasped my hands, and prayed to the Good Lord to protect Kirsten. I had been disturbed by the girl's behaviour, and Helwig's warning was lodged in my head. I would not let the Devil take my girl.

I reasoned with myself that Kirsten had been very upset over her lamb, and this was most likely the cause of her somnambulism. But it was odd indeed that she was uncommonly distraught over the lamb, and yet had not said one word upon her sister Ingeborg or her mother, both of whom she knew to be imprisoned and suffering in the witches' hole.

After this first night, I told Helwig that Kirsten would sleep in my bedchamber permanently. I instructed her to make up a cot at the end of my bed with birch twigs and reindeer skins, but most nights, unknown to Helwig, I allowed Kirsten into my bed.

I noted it was the waning moon, and upon the days following it Kirsten somnambulated every night, but as soon as it was the dark moon, she stopped. However, she would then wake up in the middle of sleep weeping for her lost lamb. I let her slide in next to me, her toes cold from the floor, and warm her feet between mine, for I was never cold. During the time of watching between first and second sleep, I might read to her stories of baby Jesus from the Bible, or other times, I would give her tea of borage flowers and sweetened rosewater to aid sleep. She would drop off while I stroked her hair, marvelling at its soft, silken texture, the brilliance of its red.

How hungry I was, my king, to love another soul.

But Kirsten's night terrors could be terrible, and I would wake to see her face above mine, eyes wild with fear. When I asked her what the matter was, she would tell me she had dreamed she was in the sea and drowning, just as her father and brother had done.

'You are safe here with me,' I comforted her.

'I miss my father,' she said to me. 'He loved me the best.'

'My father is dead too,' I told her. 'But I like to think of happy memories of him. Can you think of any of your father?'

'Yes,' Kirsten said. 'He would sit me upon his knee and tickle me under the chin.'

Ambrosius had never set Christina upon his knee, and I tried to imagine the lost father of Kirsten Iversdatter as a strong fisherman with gentle hands.

'Papa would tell me stories about the big blue whale and her kingdom under the sea where all the lost fishermen live. Have you ever seen a whale?'

'No, but my father possessed the horn of a narwhal.'

I told Kirsten about my father's cabinet of curiosities, and she was captivated. Every night she asked me to describe one more item and where it had come from.

'But how do you know it wasn't a unicorn's horn?' she asked me of the narwhal horn yet again. 'How do you know unicorns might not dwell in a land we have never been to?'

'Because no soul from any domain on our God Almighty's earth has ever seen a unicorn, but my father saw a real narwhal skeleton.'

Kirsten shook her head. 'Just because you can't see something doesn't mean it does not exist, for I have never seen God.'

She was a clever child, though Helwig claimed she was simple because she would sit for hours staring into the cooking fire, letting the potage burn right in front of her. But I knew Kirsten Iversdatter did not see what was up close, for she possessed the long gaze to distances very far away, or through the flames into the valley of Hell, or up above where God, the angels and my Christina dwelled.

I believed Kirsten Iversdatter could see behind the veil.

And yet at other times, she was merely a little girl who wished to make light of life. Adding even more to Helwig's dislike of her, she named all the rats, though I do not know how she could tell the difference between our vermin lodgers. She gave them names from stories her father had told her: Big Per and Little Per (although they were both the same size), Ash Lad, Ganske, Kari Stave Skirt, Lillekort and Haaken Specklebeard. She tried to pick them up and sing to them, as I expect she had once done with her lamb, but of course the rats ran away.

'See, at least it is one way of getting rid of them,' I said to the disapproving Helwig.

One morning, I awoke to feel Kirsten's fingers upon my face, prodding my cheek and staring intently at me. 'What is that on your face, Fru Anna?'

I tried to keep my voice calm. Could I have the pox? Or worse. 'Get my mirror from my trunk, Kirsten,' I asked her.

Often I have wondered why you put a precious hand mirror in my trunk. Was it a gift to show your esteem for me? Or, in my heart as I know it to be true, did you want me to be tortured by my ageing reflecting year after year?

What I saw in the mirror filled me with as much horror as the pox, for it was a large brown mole upon my cheek, larger than any Widow Krog possessed.

'Will it wash off?' Kirsten asked.

I shook my head, tearful as I imagined Lockhert's reaction: 'Fru Anna Rhodius has the Devil's mark upon her face!'

Kirsten looked at me with curious eyes.

'Open up my medicine chest, Kirsten,' I ordered her, as I slipped out of bed and pulled my cape around me.

Kirsten loves looking in the medicine chest. As I have already written she is clever, because already in just two weeks she can remember all the names of the herbs and potions, and what they could be used for.

'Can you get rid of it?' she asked.

'No, but I can hide it,' I said. I took my small phial of powdered arsenic. 'What is this?' I asked her, testing her knowledge.

'It is arsenic, and I must never, ever touch or taste it because I will die.'

'Very good. But I can use a little of it, mixed with some vinegar in this small bottle, and some white chalk, and put it on my skin. A tiny amount is safe and worth the risk.'

Kirsten watched me with fascination as I proceeded to make the mixture I had made for other ladies in Bergen so many times – those who woke with moles such as these or were merely vain and wanted paler skin. I had considered them rather sad creatures, but now I was joining their ranks.

When I had finished my work upon my face, the mole was gone.

Kirsten clapped her hands in delight. 'Magic!' she crowed gleefully.

'No, Kirsten, this is science.'

Yesterday I watched from my longhouse prison window as the prisoner Solve Nilsdatter was led to the governor's house for questioning. I did not wish to think of the horrors she would be subjected to, and prayed she was a witch, because then the tortures would be justified, but I feared Lockhert was committing a great sin by breaking your laws.

An hour passed, then another, as I waited by the window. Kirsten stood beside me and held my hand, and we watched silently together.

The January moon was fulsome, and the snow glared white beneath it when at last Solve Nilsdatter was returned to the witches' hole. I caught sight of her, told Kirsten to turn away.

Oh, my king, what had been done to the pretty young mother? One arm hung by her side like a broken wing, and blood dripped from broken fingers, but worse were the burns. I saw her bodice had been torn off and she was almost naked in her shift in the stark Arctic moonlight. The skin of her chest was red-raw and I could smell the scent of sulphur wafting into the longhouse. The odious Bailiff Lockhert had poured it upon her breasts.

Solve's head was bent over so I could not see her face, and her back was hunched, as if she had aged a hundred years. She dragged her body across the courtyard, pushed by a soldier, and crammed back into the witches' hole.

I watched Bailiff Lockhert march back to his gatehouse, an air of satisfaction around him, and I felt my stomach heave with loathing.

'Get me my medicine chest, Kirsten.'

She obeyed without a word and watched as I hunted through it for my small bottle of distilled coltsfoot and elderflower water, which I intended to apply to Solve's burns with cloths.

Despite my failure in getting any of the women to confess, I still had the key to the witches' hole in my possession. I put on my cape, and hat.

'Can I come with you, Fru Anna?' Kirsten's blue eyes tugged on my heartstrings.

'No, child.' I did not want her to see her mother or sister in such a place, let alone the state of the other prisoners. 'It's late. See, Helwig is already asleep. Get into my bed and warm it for me.'

'Will you bring Ingeborg back with you?'

'I am not allowed tonight, but soon – the governor has promised me that she and Maren will be removed from the witches' hole.'

It was the first time Kirsten had mentioned her family since residing with me. Her question upon Ingeborg unsettled me somewhat, for I was beginning to believe Kirsten belonged to me and no other, and that she desired to be by my side.

I slipped into the dark gloom of the witches' hole. The faint scent of sulphur I had caught on the wind before almost overpowered me, and I brought my handkerchief to my nose and inhaled deeply. I hung my lantern on the wall hook and clasped my medicine chest to me.

The three women and two girls were huddled together.

'Look what the bailiff did to her.' Widow Krog spoke, her eyes accusing, as if it were my fault.

'There's nothing I can do about his methods,' I said, brusquely. 'I am here to help soothe her pain.'

I examined the poor woman Solve, but there was little I could do to ease the damage done to her skin. I applied cloths wet with coltsfoot water to the affected areas and gave her a beaker of wine with a few drops of lavender oil to soothe her. She had her head upon her cousin's lap – clearly there was no longer any blame between them.

'He forced her to confess,' Zigri said in a frightened whisper. 'She has denounced us all.'

I shook my head, my heart heavy for the suffering of these women, for now the governor had his evidence for the witch trial.

'We must not show our fear,' Maren said, as though I wasn't standing right there beside her. 'Do not be afraid. We can have great power.'

When I left the witches' hole, I did not return to my prison house for, despite his threats, I did not fear Bailiff Lockhert. I had suffered too much in my past to ever be afraid of what lay in my future, and thus I knocked loudly upon his gatehouse door.

He had clearly been drinking, for I could smell the stink of ale off him. There was blood still on his tunic and, moreover, he hadn't even washed the poor woman's blood from his hands. 'Well, Fru Rhodius,' he said. 'I am very flattered by your visit, but you are a little old for my tastes.'

I wanted to scream my affront at his implication, but I held back.

'Come in if you will!' he said, when I didn't move from the threshold.

'No,' I replied, for I had no intention of taking one step inside his lair. 'I am here because—' I hunted for the right words. 'I entreat you to desist from your tormenting of the women.'

His eyes gleamed at the mention of his vile actions. 'But why would I do so? In one day, the bitch confessed, whereas you spent weeks pandering to the witches and got not one word of the truth from them.'

'It's against the law—'

'Are you able to keep your tongue, woman?' he snapped at me. 'In my home country you would be long hung from the gallows for your constant haranguing.' He placed a big hand on my chest and pushed me back. I fell into the snow, dropping my medicine chest.

'Who do you think you are?' he said, glowering over me. 'Well, let me tell you who *I* am, if it's not already clear. My purpose, until my dying day, is to hunt witches. This was why I was sent for by the governor of Finnmark. You people don't know how to deal with witches, but the Scottish do!'

I sat up in the snow, pulling my chest to me, relieved it had not broken open.

'Witches took my family from me. Four of us set sail from Scotland for Norway but my wife and two children were drowned.' He bent down over me, his spittle showering my cheeks. 'Just as Merchant Brasche, I too saw witches as birds flying around our ship, and then the storm came in. They knew what I was coming here to do, and they tried to drown us all by wrecking the ship. But I survived!'

He spat at me then, a thick blob landing on my forehead before he straightened up and went back into his hut, slamming the door.

I wiped the spit off my face, feeling sick, and picked myself up.

The man was vile. And I ask you, my king, why did such a soul live on, when so many others were cruelly taken, sometimes within a heartbeat?

And yet I had caught something in his eyes – a deep, haunting sorrow I recognised – for Bailiff Lockhert possessed the look of one who had lost all he had ever loved.

Chapter 36

Ingeborg

The morning after Solve returned broken and in agony from her questioning with the monster Lockhert, Ingeborg and Maren were ordered out of the witches' hole.

'I would rather keep you all penned in together,' Bailiff Lockhert declared. 'But the governor wishes you to be split.' He bent down and gave Ingeborg a cold stare. His eyes looked like those of a cow gone mad with sickness – open wide and skittish. 'Aye, think yourselves lucky, lasses, to be under the care of Fru Rhodius. You'd best tell her the whole truth.' He poked his dirty finger in Ingeborg's chest. 'Else I shall have you back in my domain.'

Ingeborg fought not to show her fear and curled her shaking hands into fists by her side.

'Aye, the governor believes away from the influence of your witch kin, the truth might be got from you.' He turned to look at Maren, his expression more wary. 'If it were up to me, I'd wring it from you with my hands, for there's no doubt of your witching ways.'

Ingeborg's mother sobbed to lose her as she clutched her swollen belly. The last of Ingeborg's anger at her mother's wantonness turned to pity. She promised her yet again she would do all she could to help her.

They were marched across the slippery courtyard and received by Fru Anna Rhodius and her surly maid Helwig in her prison house. Ingeborg had lost her mother, but here at least was Kirsten safe.

'Hello, Inge,' Kirsten said, with lowered lashes, sitting at Fru Anna's table on a stool and swinging her legs, as if it was only the day before they had been out on the bog together, collecting turf.

'Sister!'

Ingeborg ran over, but Kirsten drew back. 'You smell!' she said, wrinkling her nose in disgust.

Ingeborg and Maren were sent to the washhouse with Helwig, who scrubbed them mercilessly as if she meant to purge the evil out of them.

'You can't wash the colour off my skin!' Maren pulled away from the vigorous maid. 'I am always this shade!'

Helwig went red in the face. 'I have never seen the like of it.'

Ingeborg thought Maren was beautiful. She herself was faded, and flimsy, compared to her tall and glorious friend. What would she do without Maren's refusal to give in to the threats of Lockhert? The girl gave her courage; a strange sense there was more to things than she could see with her own eyes. If she let herself believe she had power then maybe, maybe it might be true.

Once they had been washed, they were dressed in old bodices of grey wool and heavy black skirts discarded by long deceased maids. Both were too big on Ingeborg.

'You look like one of Widow Krog's elf dwarves!' Maren laughed at her.

'I am sure I do not!' Ingeborg said, indignant.

'Come, come and you will see.' Maren grabbed her arm and pulled her out of the washhouse. She led her to the edge of a sheer stretch of ice that had been created by all the water run-off from the washhouse.

'See for yourself!' Maren said, still laughing and indicating for Ingeborg to look down.

She shuffled forward in her old boots, and peered into the ice reflection, a little dread in her heart. What must she look like after so many weeks in the witches' hole? But Maren was right. She did look ridiculous. A tiny mouse of a girl swamped in grey and black wool. Oh, such a dramatic pinch to her face, and big baby-deer eyes. Laughter burst out of her mouth. Washing through her tense body.

It was wrong to laugh in all their misery, but she could not stop herself. Especially when she saw Maren's reflection too, and the faces she made into the ice to make her laugh all the more. And look how short

Maren's skirt was on her! Not only her ankles but her calves were on display, thick with dark hair.

The two girls laughed until they cried. And then the earlier mirth slid off their shoulders. They looked at each other, one so tall, and the other so small. But still, just two girls. Maren opened her arms to Ingeborg. They wept against each other's rough woollen jackets, shaking, holding each other up, until Helwig roared at them to stop their caterwauling.

After days and nights with no beginning and end in the witches' hole, Fru Anna imposed order and routine in the longhouse prison. After morning prayers in darkness, a candle was lit for them to learn their letters. Fru Anna had a Danish edition of the Lutheran Bible. It had a picture of King Christian III, the grandfather of King Frederick, on the front of it. It was the first book Ingeborg had ever touched.

Fru Rhodius sat before the girls and instructed them in reading skills. She allowed them one at a time to trace the Bible script with their fingers – if they were clean. Ingeborg traced the pregnant 'B' again and again. And then the snakish 'S' dancing upon the page. She learnt the word *SATAN*.

A snake, a Sámi lávvu, a tree, another lávvu, and the mountain on the other side.

'When you can read the Bible, you're closer to God,' Fru Anna told them. 'Sometimes God may not choose a woman to be a mother. Sometimes it's her duty to spread the teachings of Jesus Christ.'

Fru Anna told them Bible stories about Jesus, and for a few moments Ingeborg could forget where they were. Jesus had been very poor too. Born in a stable with animals all around him. He had loved the animals, like Maren, and refused to treat women differently. Ingeborg hungered to hear the stories about Jesus and Mary Magdalene. But after these Bible stories came the catechism: weary hours when Fru Anna would ask them questions and they must reply word for word as laid down in the copy of Luther's Catechism given to her by Reverend Jacobsen, for their instruction.

'What is baptism?' Fru Anna asked the girls. Although Ingeborg had learnt her catechism from Reverend Jacobsen back in Ekkerøy, now the words had unfettered themselves from her memory. But Kirsten had learnt well from Fru Anna during the time she had spent with her alone.

'Baptism is not simple water only, but it is the water comprehended in God's command and connected with God's Word.'

Fru Anna placed a hand on Kirsten's head of red curls and gave her a beneficious smile. 'Good girl,' she said, removing her hand and picking up the catechism book before reading from it. 'What does baptism give or profit?'

'It works forgiveness of sins, delivers from death and the Devil, and gives eternal salvation to all who believe this, as the words and promises of God declare,' Kirsten recited.

'What are such words and promises of God?' Fru Anna continued.

Maren gave a big yawn and scratched her leg underneath her woollen skirt.

Fru Anna glanced at Maren with disapproval, before waiting for Kirsten to reply, an expectant smile on her face.

'Christ, our Lord, says in the last chapter of Mark.' Kirsten paused and closed her eyes before continuing: 'He that believeth and is baptised shall be saved; but he that believeth not shall be damned.'

Ingeborg looked at Kirsten in astonishment. She had never professed such an interest in the catechism when they had been made recite it every week with Reverend Jacobson. But there was something different about her sister when Fru Anna spoke to her. As if a light had been lit within her. When she thought about it, this light had existed before, but had blown out the night their father was given as lost.

'How can water do such great things?' asked Fru Anna, all her attention on Kirsten, as if Maren and Ingeborg were invisible to her now.

Kirsten tilted her face towards Fru Anna, and spoke, her voice bright and singsong as she repeated the words taught to her.

Does she even understand them?

'It is not the water indeed that does them, but the word of God which in and with the water, and faith, which trusts the word of God in the water. For without the word of God the water is simple water and no baptism. But with the word of God, it is a baptism—' Kirsten faltered.

'—a gracious water of life . . .' Fru Anna intervened.

'A washing regeneration of the Holy Ghost.' Kirsten finished.

'Yes indeed, as St Paul says, in Titus, chapter three.' Fru Anna took a dramatic breath as Maren rolled her eyes at Ingeborg.

Maren's lack of reverence was shocking, but a part of Ingeborg wanted to roll her eyes too. She had thought she was a good Christian girl all her life – once, she had been able to recite her catechism word perfectly. Yet still she had been imprisoned and told she was unchristian, a bad, bad girl.

She sighed as her heart ached, feeling conflicted by her sister's devout recitations of the battered copy of the Lutheran catechism.

'So, Ingeborg.' Fru Anna directed her cool gaze upon her. 'What does such baptising with water signify?'

Ingeborg scrambled for the right words. The water drowned, yes, the water drowned the evil, and then all was pure. This she knew was in the answer, but she didn't know how to say it, and so she shook her head.

Fru Anna tsked. 'Maren? Do you know your catechism?'

Maren shrugged. 'Of course, but it bores me to repeat such dull words. Might I not tell a story, Fru Anna?'

'Later. Though, child,' Fru Anna warned, 'your stories will do you no good. If you learn your catechism, it will aid you—'

'The water signifies the old Adam in us should by daily contrition and repentance be drowned and die with all the sins and evil lusts, and again, a new man daily come forth and arise who shall live before God in right-eousness and purity forever.' Maren whisked through the words, before leaning forward and pointing her finger at Fru Anna who looked at her in astonishment. 'But, mistress, what about us, the maids, the mothers, even the noblewomen such as you? Why no mention of Eve? Tell me now, how could Luther forget all about us, when his way into this very world was *through* one of us?'

Fru Anna's eyes opened even wider in shock at her words, but she didn't admonish her. Instead, she got up and placed the book down on the table. She put her hand into her pocket. Ingeborg imagined her fingers grazing the key to the witches' hole and longed to thrust her own hand in the pocket and have it from her.

When Fru Anna drew out her hand it was clasped. She stepped towards the girls and opened her palm. Upon it were three almonds bigger than the ones she had given them in the witches' hole many weeks ago, the sugar upon them as if glazed by snow dust, and her mouth was watering at the thought of eating one of them.

'Would you like one of my sugared almonds?' Fru Anna asked, before continuing without waiting for a reply. 'They were sent to me as a gift from the King of Denmark, and I will share them with you as rewards if you're good girls,' she said, looking tense. 'All you need do is answer one question – did your mother, Ingeborg and Kirsten, or did your aunt, Maren, baptise you over to the Devil?'

Only one question she says, but what a question!

'My mother—' Kirsten began as she stared at the almond but Ingeborg placed a warning hand on her sister's arm. 'Our mother did nothing of the sort,' she intervened, looking over at Maren.

When Maren said nothing, but rather gave Fru Anna a menacing look, Ingeborg answered for her: 'And nor did Maren's aunt baptise Maren.'

Did Fru Anna look relieved by her answer? It was as if the lady had been holding her breath and now, she let out a big sigh. She proffered the sugared almonds one by one even though they had confessed nothing.

Such sweetness in her mouth, more than the sweetest summer berry, but then she bit into the nut, and the taste was of another life. Not the fishy repasts of her Ekkerøy home, but of the world she had wished to sail to with her brother, Axell.

Some afternoons, Fru Anna taught them a little about the healing herbs in her medicine chest, warning them not to go near them as some could be poisonous if too much taken. Ingeborg's mind swam with all the different names and uses, but Kirsten and Maren picked up the knowledge quickly.

Before dinner, the girls practised writing with their fingers in the dust in the corners of the longhouse.

'Look, Ingeborg, your name is the longest,' Maren said, as Ingeborg slowly read out the three names scrawled in the muck: *Ingeborg, Maren, Kirsten.*

'All together,' Maren said, looking pleased.

After the kirk bell pealed twelve times, they had their dinner. Most days it was potage and salted cod. Maren refused to eat the fish, and Ingeborg worried she would become too thin. But the girl always produced a pocketful of root tubers or stems she could suck upon. Fru Anna never asked her where she got them from.

As the weeks passed, the sun snuck back above the horizon, a few short hours of light each side of noon. A rich haunting blue emerged from beneath the crusts of snow and filled the sky. When Ingeborg raised her hand outside, it seemed as if taken into this gloaming light, and she imagined the sky would wish to drag her behind its curtains. Gladly she would go and hide, yet her exposure was relentless, for life in the prison longhouse carried on its usual round of prayers, chores, catechism and daily questioning. How had her mother and Solve found the craft? Met with the Devil? Partaken in weather magic? Always she and Maren refused to answer and were never punished for it. But what worried Ingeborg most were the long hours Kirsten spent with Fru Anna in her bedchamber. It was where she chose to sleep – at the end of her bed on a tiny pallet – whereas Ingeborg and Maren shared the maid Helwig's pallet.

'What have you been telling Fru Anna?' Ingeborg asked her sister.

Kirsten looked at her with a blank expression. 'Nothing,' she said. 'She gives me sugar to eat, with lemon, and more sugar almonds too.' She paused. 'She likes to call me Christina. I think it was the name of her daughter.'

Ingeborg frowned. 'But you are not her daughter, Kirsten, remember.'

'Mother has never loved me, Inge!' Kirsten flounced off.

The trial was almost upon them, and her sister was under the influence of Fru Rhodius. Time was running out.

Soldiers guarded the witches' hole, and Ingeborg could not get near it. In the evenings, by the cooking fire, Ingeborg's gaze would fix upon Fru Rhodius's skirts. Beneath her petticoats in her pocket was the key to the witches' hole. She had to get it from her. But the Danish woman always had the key upon her and hid it under her pillow at night.

257

Ingeborg would lie crushed between Maren and Helwig on their pallet, pushing her fists into her temples. *Think, Ingeborg, think. There has to be a way.*

Ingeborg had been called to the castle to be questioned by the governor. Bailiff Lockhert pushed her into the governor's chamber, before turning on his heel and stomping off again. She stood uncertainly in the doorway, her shoulders sore from Lockhert's grip, awed by the grandeur before her. Even larger than Heinrich Brasche's living chamber, the walls were hung with rich tapestries and oil paintings, and a fire blazed in the hearth. Not turf but precious wood sparked and spat in the huge fireplace. Her nose was running from the warmth in the room, and she wiped it with her sleeve, daring not to imagine how vile she looked.

Seated in one of the big wooden chairs at the end of the room was Governor Orning, his long battle scar splitting his craggy face.

Next to him was a young woman, who Ingeborg supposed was his wife. She had hair so pale it was almost white and was dressed in a black satin gown; her white lace collar was off the shoulder and decorated with a crimson silk rose in the centre. The red was a startling shade against her white décolletage. A big black cat was curled upon her lap, and Ingeborg could hear its loud, rhythmic purr. Most of Fru Orning's face was concealed by an enormous black lace fan that she grasped in a tiny white hand to protect her from the fierce fire raging in the hearth.

The governor stood up, disturbing two wolfhounds sprawled at his feet. The cat gazed with cold indifference at the dogs as it continued to purr upon the woman's lap.

'Come with me, girl,' the governor said, hooking his finger.

His wife paused in her fanning. There was a warning in her eyes. But what could Ingeborg do? She couldn't refuse the governor of Finnmark.

Ingeborg followed him to the other side of the chamber, and into a huge hall. It was empty of furniture apart from a grand chair with elk antlers hung above it, and a big chest. On the walls were hung tapestries and oil paintings and the glazed windows were undraped. There were no fires lit and it was very cold. Ingeborg could see snow falling outside the windows.

'Do you know what room this is?' Governor Orning asked her.

Ingeborg shook her head, shivering with the cold and a sense of foreboding.

'It is the trial chamber at Vardøhus,' he told her, eyes glinting. 'Very soon, it will be filled with people. Me, my loyal Bailiff Lockhert, and a jury of twelve good men. And the accused witches.'

Dread prickled down Ingeborg's spine.

'Yes, in just a few weeks we will be rid of witches!' he declared, sitting in the big chair, and indicating for her to come closer.

Ingeborg took a reluctant step forward.

'I must ask you about an incident that has recently come to light,' the governor said, looking at her sternly. 'Merchant Brasche has sent me a letter to tell me what happened at his cousin Anders Pedersen's house in Kiberg on Christmas Eve.'

Ingeborg clasped her hands, bracing herself for his interrogation.

'Witches arriving in the form of birds that transformed as cats and crawled into his cellar. They met with the Devil and drank all Anders Pedersen's beer. What can you tell me upon this, Ingeborg Iversdatter?'

Ingeborg looked back at the governor in astonishment. 'I know nothing of these events, your honour.'

'You lie,' the governor hissed at her. 'Merchant Brasche saw you himself, for he and Anders Pedersen came upon you along with the other witch's get Maren Olufsdatter, her aunt Solve Nilsdatter and your own mother.'

'No.' Ingeborg shook her head, panic flaring through her. 'It's not true. Why, we were prisoners here on Christmas Eve—'

Her voice trailed off, as the governor stood up and shook his head. 'Solve Nilsdatter has confessed to it. She said you all turned into cats and dug your way out of the witches' hole with claws. Then became birds and flew across the Varanger Straits to the village of Kiberg.'

'She doesn't know what's she's saying—' Ingeborg protested.

The governor walked over and poked her chest with his finger. Ingeborg backed towards the wall on the other side of the chamber.

'Do you understand what a serious crime this is?' he said. 'For women to sneak into a man's cellar, drink up all his beer?'

'Merchant Brasche is mistaken. Maybe he and Anders Pedersen drank up all the beer.'

'Is this slander I hear?' the governor said, raising his eyebrows and suddenly looking amused. 'You might be young, but you're not easily cowed, are you, girl?'

She said nothing, willing him to leave her alone.

'How old are you, Ingeborg Iversdatter?' the governor continued, clearly with no intention of letting her go.

'Sixteen years now, your honour.'

'You are a mere year older than my wife when I first bed her,' Orning said.

Ingeborg thought of the pale girl in black, with the red silk rose, her face hidden by the big fan.

'What a fuss was made. Had to get a pardon from the king, for I'd taken her away against the will and approval of her family. How angry Elisa's father was!' Governor Orning gave Ingeborg a dark smile, reaching out and brushing the hair from her face so that she started as if a spooked creature. 'It's a shame your hair is the colour of dirt, but I like your eyes. Warm cinnamon, with a "come hither".' The governor looked down the whole of her body. 'And your clothing is too big for you, but underneath you are what I like.'

He bore down upon her, and she stepped back again. Her shoulders pressed into the wall.

'In truth there's no comparison, for my wife is a nobleman's daughter and you're the common spawn of a Devil's whore but, all the same, you belong to me now.' He leered over Ingeborg as the tone of his voice changed.

Ingeborg pressed her hands into the cold wooden walls of the trial chamber.

'We shall see now if you carry the Devil's mark,' the governor said to her. 'Give me your hand.'

She had no choice but to raise her hands to him. He examined one, and then the other.

'What is this scar?' He glowered at her.

'I was bitten by Merchant Brasche's dog,' she whispered.

He cocked his head at her. Eyes unbelieving. 'Take off your boots,' he ordered her.

She stepped out of her worn reindeer skin boots. Her old wool stockings were filled with holes, her toes poking out.

'Take off the stockings.' The governor pressed his hands together. 'And your bodice and skirt.'

She froze in horror.

'Do as I say,' he said in a rough voice. 'How else can I examine you for Satan's mark?'

'Your Honour, I beg you, I have no knowledge of the Devil—'

'Take your clothes off now, girl, else I will have Lockhert tear them off you!'

She swallowed the lump in her throat back down. She would not cry in front of the governor. Closing her eyes, she began to unlace her bodice, her cheeks burning crimson with humiliation as the stays loosened.

Once she was shivering in her shift, the governor began to examine her. He raised her arms and pulled back the shift from her neck, reaching into it and touching all around her breasts. He placed his hand on her tiny left breast and squeezed her nipple. She let out a whimper of pain.

'All normal here, although you have the physique of a boy,' he said, giving her a nasty smile. 'Stand up on the chest.'

She clambered up onto the chest next to the big chair. Out of the high window, the blizzard swirled wildly.

'Raise your shift all the way to your waist.'

She swallowed down another lump and shook her head.

'Raise your shift, I said.'

Upon the chest she was as tall as the governor. She could see right into his dead-fish eyes. She shook her head again.

'Then I will do it for you.' He roughly yanked up the ends of her shift.

Instinctively, Ingeborg pushed him away and jumped down, running through the trial hall towards the big door at the other end.

'Come back here, you little bitch!' he called after her.

She wrenched the hall door open. Snow was cascading down, but though she was still barefoot in her shift it didn't stop her.

Out into the blizzard, but he came after her. His breath upon her neck, his stink of old wine and woodsmoke. He caught her by the arm and twisted it behind her back. Ingeborg cried out, but her voice was muffled by the falling snow. He pushed her down, and she landed upon the packed wet ice. Her hands were out in front of her but he was over her, pulling them aside. Slapping her hard across the face, yanking Ingeborg's shift up above her waist.

'You're as much a witch slut as your mother was,' he snarled.

His spit landed on her cheeks. The fury in his body, his hatred pinning Ingeborg to the snow.

'Don't resist, else I'll have all of you burnt, even your little sister.'

Ingeborg stopped fighting. She couldn't risk the others' lives, not for this.

Do not be afraid. Maren's voice was inside her head. *We can have great power.*

Ingeborg closed her eyes, heard him unbuckle, his rough hands pushing her legs apart, the heat and horror of his breath on her cheeks.

He broke her.

His weight on top, crushing her. As if he had thrust his sword between her legs, right up inside. Pain piercing her.

Ingeborg went as limp as the dead. Thought of Axell sinking to the bottom of the sea, how long it took him to drown. Counting. *One. Two. Three. Four. Five. Six. Seven. Eight. Nine . . .*

She felt herself rising off the frigid ground. When she opened her eyes, she was looking down upon the governor, his breeches around his knees as she lay beneath him and he assaulted her.

Drifting higher and higher, she transformed into her bird self. Flew up and away, out of the fortress and across the Varanger Straits.

Beneath her, waves washed over sheets of ice. Ingeborg saw rocks protruding, bubbles of water locked beneath the frozen surface. The imprisoned water was the love she sought.

Ingeborg flew towards the mainland. Closer to shore the ice was thicker, threads of white frost scattered upon its surface in random patterns. She flew over the white heights of Domen Mountain but did not see the Devil upon its summit. Then she flew on, fast, furious, above the white, desolate stretches of the Varanger Peninsula. Below her a pack of wolves, its leader looking up above and howling. The whole pack feeling her pain.

Ingeborg flew all the way home to Ekkerøy, circled her village, watching her old neighbours about their tasks. None saw her though she called to them, but they were deaf to her appeals. Gliding above Merchant Brasche's house, she spattered his front step with bird shit, before doing the same to the son's house.

In a field of frozen bog she landed, and there she found the Devil as a black dog. She whistled to him, and she made the dog bow to her. As soon as she did, she was back inside her body, assaulted by the governor's last, hard thrust inside her.

'By the Good Lord!' A woman's voice cried out in Danish. She knew that voice. 'Governor, I must protest!'

Anna Rhodius's face, white with shock, appeared, her hand upon the governor's shoulder.

'How *dare* you?' The governor pulled back. His expression was furious as he swiped Anna Rhodius's hand away.

'Governor Orning, she's but a young maid!' Fru Rhodius continued in an imperious voice, and Ingeborg was strangely impressed. How this woman stood up to the most powerful man in Finnmark!

'She is the daughter of a whore in service to the Devil—' The governor continued cursing Ingeborg and her mother.

'It has not been proven yet, your honour,' Anna said, in a low voice, looking away from him.

The governor stood up, his face purple as he buckled his breeches. 'Yes, indeed, the Devil took possession of the girl, tempted me to touch her,' he claimed. 'Thank the Good Lord you came along, Fru Rhodius.'

Fru Rhodius ignored the governor and bent down to Ingeborg. Gently, she pulled her shift down and smoothed the material out. Held out her hand for Ingeborg to take.

But she would not take it. No, this woman, who appeared so kindly, was no friend to her. Fury surged through her as Ingeborg stumbled to her feet by herself, then stalked off into the falling snow.

'Come back, Ingeborg! You've no clothes on, no boots! It is most improper, and besides you'll freeze,' Anna called after her.

'Leave her,' Ingeborg heard the governor say. 'The fortress gates are locked. She can go nowhere. A cold walk in the snow may persuade her to confess all she knows.'

Shame was in every burning step Ingeborg took. Her bare feet stinging in the cold. Passing by the soldiers' turf hut, trying to ignore their naked staring. Between her legs she was in pain, as if on fire. Nevertheless, she was determined not to cry. There was the witches' hole obscured by spinning snowflakes. How she longed to be back inside with her mother. She didn't care about the hunger and filth and the stench, because at least in there she was not alone.

She climbed up steps thick in snow to the top of the fortress walls. Walking their perimeter, balancing upon a ledge of snow, not caring if she plummeted to her death. In the corner battlement, Ingeborg looked out across Vardø. The wind was so wild not one bird was in flight. The sky swirled with snow against the darkness, and she wished it would take her in its grasp and hurl her out to sea.

She looked down at her feet. Blood was spattered on her blue toes. Turning around, she spied a trail of blood from the way she'd come. Ingeborg crouched down in the battlements, hid behind one of the cannons, while she lifted her shift and looked.

Her legs were smeared red, and when she put her hands between them, they were covered in blood. There was blood smeared onto her white shift, too.

The disgusting governor had snatched away her maidenhead, and now she was ruined forever.

A voice was singing. It drew her away from the edge of the battlements. She crawled along the top of the wall towards the sound. The words being sung were not Danish or Norwegian, and certainly not one of the hymns they sang in church. A mumble, a murmur, a soaring twist of notes. Rising and falling as the birds dropped and dived in the sky.

She knew this sound; it was *yoik*ing.

Ingeborg peered over the edge of the wall. Positioned by the back of the governor's house was a narrow corridor between the building and fortress walls. A servant boy stood there with his back to her. He was Sámi, dressed in a dark blue *gákti* edged in red braiding, woven with green and yellow threads, and belted around his hips. The colour of his attire was vivid against the white snow. He was feeding the governor's two wolfhounds slabs of reindeer meat – Ingeborg had never seen the creatures so docile. It was to the dogs he sang.

And something in his *yoik* soothed her too. As if he were calling her to him, as if she were part of his pack.

There was something about this boy.

Ingeborg leant over further to hear him the better, but the snow was soft beneath her, and she slid off the wall, landing on a pile of snow below. The dogs pulled back and growled as the boy turned around.

It was him.

'Zare!' she called out, as she struggled to get up out of the snow.

'Are you hurt?' He spoke in Norwegian, patting the dogs so they calmed down and returned to their meat.

Ingeborg shook her head. What was he doing there?

'But you're bleeding.' He took a step towards her.

'No!' She put her hand out in panic. Despite her joy at his appearance, she didn't want him to see her shame. 'Go away!'

He stopped in his tracks. 'Ingeborg, what's wrong?'

Ingeborg saw the pity on his face, and it made her cry. She put her hands to her hot wet cheeks, for she couldn't stop the torrent of her grief.

Zare came closer, placing his reindeer skin around her shoulders as Ingeborg wept. The kindness of his gesture made her fall to bits.

'The governor attacked me.' Ingeborg patted her bloodied shift. 'Here.'

Zare's eyes turned dark as ink. She heard a long low hiss under his breath; the same sound the cat made before he pounced on a rat. Then he scooped up some snow and cleaned Ingeborg's bloody hands with it.

'He will leave you alone now.' He rubbed her hands warm and dry.

'How do you know?'

But Zare didn't reply.

'How did you get into the fortress?' Ingeborg asked him. 'Why are you feeding the governor's dogs?'

'Because it is my job,' Zare said, an edge to his voice. 'The governor always hires Sámi boys, as we are the best with dogs – and he can treat us like animals too.'

Ingeborg felt overwhelmed with gratitude. This boy, one she hardly knew, had found a position in the fortress so he could help. He a Sámi, and yet none from their village had come to their aid.

'What were you singing to the dogs?'

'The *yoik* of the wolf,' he said. 'It makes them calm, for he's their ancestor.'

The big wolfhounds finished their meat and padded over. Zare stroked one's head and it wagged its tail. The other looked at her with piercing, wolfish eyes.

'This one is a girl dog and I call her Beaivenieida, the sun daughter, because she has a happy pant, this one is Gumpe, wolf, because he is a wolf in his heart.'

Ingeborg reached out and patted Beaivenieida's head, her fingers touching Zare's as she did so. Gumpe sidled up to them, pushed his muzzle into the palm of her hand and licked the last of the blood off her fingers. The hot tongue on her skin tickled and it made her feel better.

Zare looked at her, his expression thoughtful. 'I am here every morning feeding the dogs,' he said. 'This is where you will find me if you need me.'

'Will you help us escape, Zare?'

He looked troubled. But surely he had a plan, if he had got work in the fortress?

'What have you heard about the trial?' he asked her. 'Who is accused?'

'My mother; her cousin Solve; and Widow Krog from our village.'

'Just those three?'

Ingeborg remembered the talk of his mother Elli. 'I believe they're suspicious of your mother too.'

Zare squeezed her hands in his. 'Will you listen for me, Ingeborg? Come and tell me, when you can, what you hear?'

'Yes, but how will we escape? The fortress gates are always guarded and locked, and we have no rope to climb down the fortress walls. Besides, we will be seen—' She had spent night after night trying to work out how they could get away.

Zare rubbed her hands with his again, as if to make sparks for a fire. 'I will think on it. But, Ingeborg, hurry back. It's too cold and you've no boots on, and very little to keep you warm.'

*

That night, in her dreams, Zare came to her. Wordlessly he offered Inge-borg his hand, and the two of them ran with the wolves. They were part of the pack, side by side, their breath as mist before them, the moon lighting their way upon the sparkling snow. Safety in numbers. Wild and fierce. They had to get away from Vardø before the witch trial.

Despite what the governor had done to her, Ingeborg woke feeling more hopeful than she had in days. Zare would find a way.

Chapter 37

Anna

My daughter Christina talks to me. 'Save the girls,' she whispers.

I can feel her sweet breath upon my cheek, smell the smouldering rosemary in her pestilence-struck chamber and, oh, the softness of her fingers upon my brow.

Save the girls. This is my task, for the women in the witches' hole are beyond my help. This I knew for certain when the governor informed me the jury had been selected for the trial in four weeks' time.

'Twelve good and honest men of the island of Vardø,' he said. 'I will preside as magistrate, and Lockhert will present the evidence, along with confessions from the witch, Solve Nilsdatter.'

I had been called to the governor's private chamber to discuss the matter of the witches' gets.

'It is up to you to get these girls to declare their mothers sold them to the Devil,' he said to me.

I was uncomfortable to be in his presence after what I had seen him do to the girl, Ingeborg Iversdatter, but he appeared completely unabashed.

'But, your honour, I am not sure of the truth in the claim these girls were brought over to the Devil—'

The governor slammed his hand down on his table and glowered at me. 'Of course, it's true. We just need to make them confess to it.' He sat up straight. 'This one – Maren Olufsdatter – is the daughter of Liren Sand. And where is her father, pray? For she is no pale-skinned Norwegian. He is the Devil, to be sure. As for the girl, Ingeborg Iversdatter, well.' He gave me a hard stare. 'With your own eyes you saw she is a wicked temptress.'

I felt myself colouring at the perversion of the governor's words. I had witnessed him attacking the girl, but I had to be careful not to turn him against me, for I was the only hope these girls had.

'I need you to prepare them for trial. Make sure they provide enough evidence to convict the witches.'

'And if I turn them back to God, they will be freed?'

'If they are able to recite their catechism with perfection it is evidence enough that they have been returned to the Good Lord and I will ensure they live,' he conceded.

'What of the youngest girl, Kirsten?' I asked the governor, a tightness in my chest as I spoke of her.

A thin smile broke out upon the governor's face. 'Ah, yes, she must be persuaded to denounce her mother in court.'

I felt a deep ache of longing in my belly and heard my dear Christina's tinkling laugh behind me. Oh, yes, my love, I am here for you always and forever.

My decision was immediate and with all my heart I felt it was for the best. 'I will. But, after, you must give her to me. For good.'

'How so?' The governor frowned at me.

'I will do as you bid me, but when the trial is over, Kirsten will live with me in the longhouse.' I paused. 'Until the king's pardon comes for helping you, and then she will leave with me.'

The governor raised his eyebrows in surprise. 'This fisherman's daughter is a worthless whelp.'

'Do you agree to my terms?' I pushed the governor, not answering his question, for how could he ever understand? 'You agree to get my pardon and let me depart thereafter with Kirsten?'

He sighed. 'You are a most tiresome woman with your demands. But, yes, you may as well look after her, for no one else will want her after her mother is burned.'

His words, said so flippantly, were appalling.

'However, if you fail, Fru Rhodius' – his voice took on a more menacing tone – 'we will burn your girl and you will remain here for the rest of your days.'

Anger flashed through me at his threat, but I held my tongue.

I was trapped upon his web, struggling with fury, but stuck fast, nevertheless.

Chapter 38

Ingeborg

The *Nordlys* would come this night. Ingeborg could sense their approach in the thin tightness of the air, and the azure brilliance sunk within the dark blue of the sky. The northern star already beaming bright.

'What are you looking at?' Zare had slipped in beside her on the fortress walls. This was their secret place where, over the past week, they had snatched time together away from all the fear and horror down below.

Up on the fortress walls, Ingeborg need only look at the sky and dream. Now she pointed to the big star, her constant guide in the dark months within the fortress. 'I am looking at the North Star,' she told Zare.

'We call it *Boahjenásti*,' he said, shifting closer to her. 'It's the only fixed star up high in the dome of the sky,' he told her. She felt his soft breath on her neck. A pull so strong to him. 'All the other stars move around it.'

'It is so much brighter than the others.'

'Every autumn we make a sacrifice of a male reindeer to the North Star,' Zare told her. His eyes reflected the light from the silvery moon. They gleamed as if made of crystals.

'A sacrifice?' Ingeborg asked. 'Like when Jesus sacrificed himself for mankind?'

'Yes, but the reason we do it is to stop the world from falling apart.' He smiled at her, and she noticed there was a tiny chip in one of his front teeth. 'The sacrifice keeps the balance in our world, and it stops the world pillar from falling down.'

'What is the world pillar?' Ingeborg asked him, thinking of the pillars on Reverend Jacobsen's altarpiece in Ekkerøy Kirke.

Zare shifted position, and Ingeborg could feel the strength of his legs as they brushed against her. 'It's a big tree, and it holds up the sky.'

Like Widow Krog's Yggdrasil, the old religion's tree of life, she thought. But Zare's beliefs were not like Widow Krog's old religion. They were different. Special to the Sámi people.

'If the pillar breaks, the sky falls down and it's the end of the world.'

'Like the Day of Judgement?'

'In a way,' Zare said. 'The world tree has an eagle as its messenger to remind you what great and good things can be done in your life. It sends a message to everyone.'

'Not me, I'm just a girl. There is nothing great that I can do,' Ingeborg said quietly trying not to think her life on this earth might end all too soon.

'That's not so,' Zare said, turning to her, the look in his eyes so intense she was transfixed by them. 'Sámi revere the girl child as much as we do the boy.'

Ingeborg was astounded by his words. Reverend Jacobsen had always spoken of the Sámi as savages and sorcerers. They were to be feared. Yet she'd never heard a boy or man – not even her own brother – speak as if girls and boys were the same. Even women did not believe this. Ingeborg could think of only one who held such an opinion.

'Maren says we girls can have great power.'

'She's right. Though not as a witch.'

Zare placed his hand upon hers. Through their mittens, his touch warmed her.

'Sámi don't believe women can be witches.'

Ingeborg tried to imagine a world without witches, but what else explained all the bad things that happened? The storm that drowned her father and brother? The famine when they could catch no fish? The sickness and death of cows and lambs? She was about to say this to Zare, but he put his finger to his mouth to warn her to be silent. He tipped his chin to the sky and Ingeborg followed his gaze.

'It's the souls of the departed,' he whispered.

Gigantic waves of yellow, green and scarlet travelled fast across the sky. They looked like the big 'S's in Fru Anna's Bible, though facing the other way. The light swirled in luminous draperies until they faded away as suddenly as they came. Ingeborg heard a crackling sound, and her whole body felt as if charged with power from the lights.

'*Guovssahasat*. The lights we can hear,' Zare whispered.

Silvery, green, edged in violet and pink, the lights radiated outwards as if a blazing crown. They were the coloured folds of a swirling skirt, a twirling troll princess in the sky. They were a circle of dancing women. Ingeborg remembered Midsummer's Eve. Widow Krog thumping her stick as all the women held hands and moved in one sinuous wave. They had been accused of dancing with the Devil that night.

'There're no such thing as the Devil and his witches,' Zare said.

'But the Devil attacked me,' Ingeborg whispered. 'And lanced me with his sword.'

'Ingeborg, it was not the Devil who abused you.'

Sitting on top of the fortress, beside the protection of Zare, Ingeborg let the sway and spin of the shimmering lights lift her. She saw herself again outside the governor's house, running in the snow. There was the governor violating her.

She squeezed Zare's hand in fright at the clarity of her memory. 'He took my virtue,' she whispered. 'I'm ruined.'

'Ingeborg Iversdatter, you're far from ruined,' Zare said, stroking her hand. 'For I see the light of our goddess Sáráhkká within you.'

Ingeborg looked into Zare's earnest blue eyes. She wanted so much to believe him.

The Sámi boy cupped her face with his hands, and then he kissed her. Gently, on her forehead. Ingeborg saw the North Star again but this time it was inside her, shining so brightly she thought she might burst with light.

Chapter 39

Anna

'How did Solve Nilsdatter bring the Devil to you?'

This was the question I asked Maren again and again, looking for the evidence to convict her aunt, but every day she replied with a different tale. Maren claimed she learnt the craft from an old Sámi woman selling her a charm, or a white hare singing her a song, or a tiny sparrow hopping up her arm. As the days wore on her tales became more fantastic: she met the Devil riding upon the back of a blue whale, or as she freed the elk from the governor's hunting pits, or when she was floating on ice with a baby polar bear.

Just when I believed the last tale was the true one, Maren would change her mind.

'I believe I first met the Devil when he came to me as a seal resting upon a rock by the seashore at Ekkerøy,' she told me, putting her head to one side in thought. 'Yes, indeed, Fru Anna. And he persuaded me to sell my soul to him for a handful of coins.'

'Desist your games, Maren Olufsdatter,' I commanded, frustration growing within me. 'Confess to me once and for all – how did your aunt Solve give you over to the Dark Lord?'

'Promise me something first,' Maren asked.

'What would that be?' I asked listlessly, for what could I, a captive as well, give this wild girl?

Maren looked at me with fierce eyes. 'Swear an oath – not a hair upon Ingeborg Iversdatter's head will harmed,' she said. 'Nor her sister Kirsten.'

'I will do everything in my power to protect *all* of my girls.'

'As a healer, do you swear it?' she insisted, taking my hand and squeezing it. She had a strong grip.

'Yes,' I said, pulling my hand away and clutching my onyx cross at my neck.

'Very well. I will tell you who gave *me* the craft,' Maren said. 'But only me.'

I waited as she crossed her arms and looked out of the tiny longhouse prison window up at the snow, which had been falling for days.

'It was not my aunt Solve, but my mother gave me the craft in a bowl of beer. Looked like mouse droppings in the bottom, but I knew it was Devil's brew. I tipped the black grains out on the floor, but it was too late. I could taste the burn on my tongue, the slide of evil down my throat.'

She stood up suddenly and spun in a slow circle.

'The first time the Devil came was as a black dog with goats' horns on his head, bounding into the cottage. He asked me to serve him, but I said no. He asked again but still I refused, so he ran away.

'Second time, in the middle of the night, he returned as a bearded man with horns on his knees and big black hat. Asked me to serve him, but still I said no.

'Third time he said if I followed him, I would never be hungry again. He would bring me sweet *lefse* thick with butter and sugar. How my tummy groaned. And he said for your mother she can have big bowl of *rømmekolle*. How pleased will she be?

'He smiled at me. Made me feel so happy and so I said, aye, I would serve him.'

'You must tell this to the governor at the trial,' I told Maren.

She cocked her head. 'Will it save me if I confess?'

'Yes, it will,' I said, feeling hot in my face. 'But you must also recite the catechism, so all know you have been returned to God. You were so young when your mother gave you over to the Dark Lord, you can still be saved.'

'Do you think all the hours we spend on our knees praying to God is enough to save my life, Fru Anna?' Maren yawned lazily, as if she had nothing more to worry about than recite a few prayers.

'Yes, yes,' I said clutching my Bible to my chest, because I couldn't consider otherwise.

Maren stretched with feline grace, arms above her head, her green eyes flecked with amber and brown on mine. I thought of the first time I had seen her, with the big wild lynx. Or perhaps it had been a dream?

Maren yawned again, showing me sharp teeth as she gazed at me with catlike calm. The girl possessed no fear of death, and thus we were not so unlike.

Chapter 40

Ingeborg

Ingeborg staggered under the weight of the turf as she and Maren brought supplies back to the longhouse. They were nearly at the threshold when she heard barking. She turned around, careful not to drop the turf, hopeful to see Zare with the wolfhounds, Beaivenieida and Gumpe. But it was Governor Orning, marching towards the well. In his right hand, he was grasping a small, wriggling sack that the dogs were jumping up at, barking with excitement. Fru Orning was upon his heels, reaching out for the sack, but the governor dangled it high above her. Her black cat was running behind the group, and it was making a terrible high-pitched screeching noise. The sound brought the soldiers from their hut, weapons raised, but as soon as they saw it was the governor and his wife, they put down their muskets. Watched with curious eyes.

Ingeborg stepped back against the wall of the longhouse, the load of turf shaking within her arms. She had not seen the governor since he had attacked her. She was only one step away from being able to hide inside the longhouse and yet she couldn't move. Frozen by a tumult of emotion. Pain. Anger. Shame.

Maren was transfixed too. Still and silently watching.

'I beg you, Christopher, they are innocent little kittens,' Fru Orning called out to her husband.

No longer concealed by her black fan, Fru Orning's face was paler than chalk, caked thick with white powder.

The governor skidded to a halt. He was in such a fury with his wife he didn't notice the spectators. Not even Fru Anna and Kirsten hand in hand as they appeared upon the threshold of the longhouse prison.

The sight disturbed Ingeborg. The bond between her sister and Fru Anna was not right, but no matter what she said to Kirsten, her sister pushed her away.

'Fru Anna is kind to me, Ingeborg.'

'But she's not your mother.'

Kirsten would look at her with guileless eyes. 'I know. She loves me more than Mother.'

'Kirsten!'

But her sister would listen to her no more and would skip off to watch Fru Anna prepare more tinctures to ease the suffering of Solve in the witches' hole. Already her sister possessed more knowledge than she and Maren of all the botanical properties of healing plants.

The governor had reached the well and he held the writhing bag of kittens over it.

'Please, no! Please!' Fru Orning pleaded, one tear of sweat sliding down the powdery surface of her white face. But Ingeborg could see the cruel smirk on the governor's face. He was gaining pleasure from his wife's distress.

The black cat jumped onto the edge of the well and stood on her hind legs, swiping at the bag with her paws. The governor pushed the cat away with his free hand and she landed on her paws in front of the big wolfhounds. But they didn't touch her. She arched her back and hissed at the governor.

'I should kill your cat too,' he said. 'It's possessed by the Devil. Even my dogs are afraid of it.'

'We need the cats to keep away the rats!' Fru Orning begged. 'The kittens will be good hunters, like their mother.'

'They are not cats, wife – have you not seen the strangeness of them? I am ridding us of their evil.'

'I swear you're mistaken,' his wife insisted, her eyes fiery within her stark face. 'How can you be frightened of two kittens?'

One of the soldiers let out a sneering laugh and the governor shot a venomous look at the gaggle of men.

In his pause, Fru Orning had reached the well, and was pulling on his arm.

Orning looked down at his wife. His expression darkened. With his free arm, he elbowed her in the stomach, and she fell back next to the black cat, which was still hissing at the governor. 'How dare you question me, wife? I order you to return to the house.'

Fru Orning stumbled to her feet, pressing her hands to her chest, gulping for breath.

Ingeborg began to shake with the weight of the turf, anger swirling around inside her. She held her breath. *Don't move*, she told herself.

But to her shock, Maren dropped her stack of turf on the ground.

Hearing the sound it made, the governor shot a look over at them. His eyes narrowed as he saw Ingeborg and she felt her cheeks flare red, her heart tightening in her chest. But he looked at her as if she were no more than dog excrement on his boot. His eyes passed on to Maren and opened wide in surprise as the girl walked towards him.

'I have a question for you, Governor,' she said, not a trace of humility or fear in her voice.

He was so astonished the witch's get would speak to him he didn't drop the bag of kittens into the well. Instead, he lowered his hand, still gripping the bag tightly. 'What, girl?'

'If I make a confession to you, will you let the kittens go?'

Governor Orning glared at Maren Olufsdatter. 'Do you dare make a *bargain* with me, girl?' he roared.

Maren smiled at the governor. Then she pressed her lips together and made a high-pitched whistle. The governor's wolfhounds stopped barking. She whistled again and they trotted over to Maren, sitting before her. She raised her hand and whistled a third time. The dogs lay on their backs in the snowy courtyard.

Maren knelt down and rubbed their bellies with her hands, as the dogs licked her. 'Yes, I do dare make a bargain with you,' Maren finally said, looking up.

The governor stared at her in astonishment, clearly unsure what to make of her audacity. He was not used to women, let alone girls, talking back to him. How had she such control over his dogs?

Ingeborg felt a swell of pride. Maren's actions were foolish beyond measure, but she was brave. Moreover, she had distracted the governor to such an extent the black cat was up on the well again, trying to reach her kittens. Her claws snared on the sack as she tugged on it.

Quickly, Fru Orning ran forwards and snatched the sack from her husband.

Governor Orning spun around in fury. 'How *dare* you?' he bellowed, drawing his pistol and pointing it at his wife.

The captain of the soldiers picked up his musket behind the governor's back. Although he didn't point it, Ingeborg could see his shock at his master's actions.

'Be calm, Governor,' Maren intervened. 'The cats will, as your wife said, preoccupy the rats.'

Governor Orning slowly lowered his pistol. 'Pathetic creature,' he snarled at Fru Orning as she opened up the sack to pull out two mewling kittens.

One was a tabby and one ginger.

'See? They are cursed!' he said. 'How can a black cat have kittens of different fur? It's dark magic—'

'Let them live, and I will tell you a confession,' Maren teased, pulling the governor's attention away from the kittens' fur.

Governor Orning's eyes narrowed, and Ingeborg could tell he was conflicted between cruelty and curiosity. 'Very well,' he said. 'Confess!'

Maren stood up again, and the dogs leapt up by her side. She gave a little twirl, clearly delighted to have captivated the attention of so many.

'I confess . . .' she teased. 'I do confess . . .' She walked over to the tiny Fru Orning and bowed deeply before her. 'I believe your wife is a princess and you are the troll keeping her captive.'

There was a stunned silence. None of the soldiers dared laugh.

Maren then curtsied in front of Fru Orning, who clutched the little kittens to her chest, staring at the other girl in undisguised wonder. 'What do you say, Governor? Do you have troll blood in you?'

The turf in Ingeborg's arms quaked dangerously, her heart racing wildly. The governor would surely have Maren killed. Indeed, he was glowering at her. But then, to everyone's surprise, the scowl on his face split and he let out a thunderclap of laughter.

Maren took a little skip, clearly delighted by his reaction. The governor laughed even more, his hands on his hips, and Maren beamed over at her. *See, show them your power*, her eyes seemed to say.

The soldiers began to laugh, and even the fearful Fru Orning's face broke into a smile.

But Ingeborg couldn't laugh – she could see dark fury in the governor's eyes. Beside her, Kirsten was giggling but Fru Anna stood silently watching. *She sees it too.*

The governor stopped laughing as suddenly as he had started. He took one swift stride towards Maren and slapped her hard across the face.

She staggered back, but she didn't fall.

'You may enjoy your jesting for now, Maren Olufsdatter, but believe me, I will have the last laugh.'

He turned on his heel and stomped back towards the castle, his hounds scampering behind him. Upon the steps, he turned and roared at his wife. 'Get rid of those kittens.' But Fru Orning made no move. She remained looking at Maren in awe.

The spectacle over, the soldiers wandered into their hut, while Fru Anna and Kirsten went back inside the longhouse prison. Ingeborg moved towards Maren the turf still in her arms. She was torn between chastisement and admiration. Maren had displayed such courage.

But before she had a chance to say anything to her, Fru Orning walked over to Maren. 'Thank you,' she said, placing her hand on the cheek her husband had slapped, as if to cool it.

Maren shrugged. 'He is a brute. It is better to stand up to him because he will hurt us anyway. But you will feel better in your heart.' Maren took Fru Orning's hand from her cheek and placed it on the girl's own heart. 'If you speak up. For how could it make your life any worse?'

'How do *you* know?' Fru Orning whispered, her eyes filling with tears.

Maren said nothing, but the two girls looked at each before she finally broke the silence. 'You had best give us the kittens, and we will keep them in Fru Anna's house,' Maren said. 'She will be glad of them to hunt the rats.'

Fru Orning passed Maren the kittens as her black cat wound between their legs. She bent down and picked it up. The two girls stood close so the mother could lick her kittens' ears.

'I will keep your babies safe,' Maren promised the cat.

Maren bowed to Fru Orning again, a kitten in each hand, as the other girl blushed.

'You are a princess in my eyes,' Maren whispered, before turning on her heel and walking past Ingeborg and into the longhouse. She had forgotten all about the dropped turf.

Fru Orning stared after her. Hugging her black cat to her tiny chest with one hand, she raised the other to her cheek. Touched the alabaster white of her face. Up close, Ingeborg could see it was cracked. Why would such a young girl cake her face in white chalk? As if sensing Ingeborg's scrutiny, Fru Orning looked at her before dropping her eyes.

'I am sorry for your troubles,' she whispered, before running back up the steps of the castle.

Chapter 41

Anna

I am at a loss what to do, my king, for I must confess it is the first time in my life I feel consumed by doubt. I have made a deal with the governor. If Kirsten testifies against her own mother, the governor has promised he will ask you directly for my pardon because I aided him in his task of ridding the north of witches. With my pardon, I can walk away from this wretched island of misery and bring Kirsten with me. Kirsten and Christina – for does not the symmetry of their names have meaning? We would be free together and I could return to my husband, our house and garden in Bergen with a daughter. I could bring Kirsten to Copenhagen and present her at court, and all would agree on her beauty. I would show you *my* girl and I would tell you, 'My king, see, here she is, and she is all mine,' and you would be present for my liberation right in front of your eyes.

As the snows sweep through the early weeks of March in Vardø, piling higher and higher on all the buildings in the fortress, I dream of Copenhagen in summer. I dream of the scent of lavender and honeysuckle in the king's garden, filling me with such longing to return and promenade once more with our younger selves as we looked up at summer swifts with forked tails flying low and fast, their piercing screams portents of the future. I want to go back into the past, and yet my body is stuck in the present, pressed up against the suffering of the Varanger women so that the swifts' screams become their torment.

Solve Nilsdatter was already broken and had denounced the other two, but she found no blame from them. When I visited, the three accused women would be trying to keep each other warm, and I would give them lavender-infused wine to help them sleep.

Each night, I slipped out of the longhouse past Ingeborg and Maren asleep on Helwig's old pallet. My maid had not stayed more than one week under the same roof as the witches' daughters. She had told me her mother was sick on the mainland and needed her daughter, but the look in her eyes told me she was afraid.

I had no need of Helwig now, anyway, for the girls could do all the chores necessary.

Outside the witches' hole I might talk to Captain Hans. The young soldier was from Copenhagen too, and not as cruel as the governor and the bailiff. Captain Hans would give me little gifts of food, or a tin bottle of rum-bullion from his soldiers to alleviate the suffering of the trapped women.

Inside the hole, I attended to Solve and Widow Krog's burns and lesions as best I could. They had also put the old woman Krog through terrible ordeals, but she would not confess. I had gleaned the governor wished to know the whereabouts of the Sámi woman named Elli, who had once been in cahoots with the great witch Liren Sand, Maren's mother. All Widow Krog had said, in a hoarse whisper, was she had bought a fish off Sámi Elli, but that was the extent of it. Every time she was pushed to confess to witchcraft or denounce others, Widow Krog was adamant she would not tell a lie on herself or any other women.

My awe for the old woman had grown as she withstood the torments of Lockhert, and in my heart I had begun to doubt her guilt.

After I had fixed up the two tormented women as best I could, I examined Zigri Sigvaldsdatter, listening to the baby's determined heartbeat with a wooden horn pressed to her vast belly. The child will come soon – maybe even before the trial, I fear.

What am I to do? What I need is irrefutable evidence these women are indeed witches who wish to kill us all in our beds. If I had such evidence, it would ease my misgivings.

Back in my prison longhouse I watch Kirsten and marvel how like Christina she is in her looks and in the way she moves. Kirsten often tugs on a curl, wrapping it around her little finger as my daughter once did, and the sight of this small habit always brings a lurch to my heart. Of course, Kirsten speaks in a different way, with the harsh northern dialect of Norwegian, but when she sings the psalms in Danish; why, then her voice is as sweet as my darling girl's once had been. It is both a joy and a torture to be with this child every day.

I have discerned a growing distance between Kirsten and her sister, Ingeborg; also the wild girl Maren, which pleases me, I must admit, for I overheard them arguing in whispers while doing their chores.

'You imagined you saw it!' Ingeborg's voice above the rest.

'Mother has always hated me,' Kirsten whispered back. 'Remember how she used to beat me, Ingeborg? Remember? She called me a devil's whelp!'

While the two older girls are out at the washhouse, or collecting turf, or sweeping the snow from the doorstep, I share my precious lemons with Kirsten, slicing them thin and sprinkling them with sugar. We look into each other's eyes with delight at the sensation of the sweet sugar fizzing against the tart lemon, and it is during these times I sow my seeds.

'Would you like to come and live with me in my house in Bergen?' I asked my girl. 'You will have your own bedchamber and lots of fine dresses. You will never go hungry again.'

Kirsten's blue eyes filled with awe, as she sucked upon the sugary lemon. 'Can I have a little dog?'

'Yes, you can,' I said smiling at her, and she smiled Christina's toothy grin.

'I will call the dog Zacharias,' she said, looking pleased.

'And I will bring you to Copenhagen to meet the king.'

She laughed at the idea, clearly believing I was quite ridiculous but, I assured her, I did indeed know the king.

'The first time I met the king he was still a prince, and I was little older than you, Kirsten,' I told her.

Kirsten stopped laughing and looked at me with respect. 'You are a great and grand lady, Fru Anna,' she said reverently. 'I wish one day to be like you.'

How her words filled the deep well of my grief with succour.

These few weeks are the calm before the storm and these moments with Kirsten, drops of light and joy. But we can all feel the trial coming as if folds of darkness tightening like nooses around our necks.

The winter blue drags at us within, lingering far into March, and I wonder if there is such a season as spring in the north. I am fearful we will never find light again and spend many hours praying to the Good Lord the governor will keep his word to me.

Chapter 42

Ingeborg

In the centre of the courtyard, Ingeborg looked up at the dark skies. Black crows swooped above her. The snow was heavy, penetrating her outer garments. Breathing in the frigid air, Ingeborg opened her mouth and let flakes of snow land upon her tongue. Points of ice pattered upon her upturned face, her skin tingling with the sensation.

Leaving the pail by the well, Ingeborg crept over to the witches' hole, slinking by the soldiers' hut. For once the entrance to the witches' hole wasn't guarded: the snow was too heavy, and it was too cold outside even for the soldiers. Ingeborg burrowed through dry piles of crystalised ice until she reached a patch of the dank old wood of the witches' hole. She took off her mittens and pressed her hands against it. Imagined her mother inside with Solve and Widow Krog. She put her cheek against the wall, strained to listen, and whispered, 'Mother?' But there was no reply.

A door slammed, echoing from across the other side of the courtyard. Bailiff Lockhert was leaving the gatehouse, his big belt of keys chinking around his waist.

Ingeborg slipped away, around the back of the governor's house and down the back alley where Zare had fed the dogs.

She came to the hidden steps and climbed up them to the fortress walls. The night was very dark. No moon nor stars were out, and she felt her way by memory. On the top of the walls it was windier than she expected, and she was buffeted this way and that as she walked along them.

A shadowy figure crouched down behind the wall. They never made any agreements to meet but most nights they found each other on the fortress walls.

'Zare,' she whispered.

'Ingeborg,' Zare whispered back, as she saw the gleam of his eyes in the dark.

'How are you?' he asked, laying a hand upon hers. She felt the warmth of his skin. They interlaced fingers. Nothing had happened beyond the kiss upon her forehead, but his touch brought a flush to her cheeks which she was glad he could not see in the dark.

'I am as well as can be expected,' she said. 'But Fru Anna says the trial is soon—'

She broke off, gulping as she thought of her heavily pregnant mother.

'Did you hear any news on my mother, Elli?' Zare asked her.

'Yes. Lockhert has sent three of the soldiers to hunt for her.' Ingeborg paused.

Zare squeezed her hand. 'I have to go and warn her. This is why I came to work at the fortress.'

Ingeborg slipped her hand from his, feeling a little aggrieved. So, he had not come to Vardøhus to help her. He had come to spy for his mother.

'But how will you get out?' Ingeborg's voice was hoarse.

'I am a servant, not a prisoner.'

'Of course,' she said, feeling hurt. She was the prisoner, not Zare.

'Every day I'm sent down to the harbour to collect fish for the castle kitchen. Tomorrow I won't come back.'

Ingeborg's heart floundered in disappointment. How she wanted to beg him not to leave her. But she could not ask him to choose her over his mother.

'I thought you had come to help me. I thought—' She couldn't keep the accusatory tone out of her voice.

'I did,' he said, the whites of his eyes flaring in the dark. 'But I must alert my mother. They will kill her outright, with no trial. As a Sámi woman, she has even fewer rights than you.'

'I have no rights,' Ingeborg said bitterly, her mind returning to the unwelcome memory of what the governor had done to her.

'At least you are offered a trial, Ingeborg.' His tone was a little cool. 'At least your ways and traditions are not suppressed.'

The wind pushed into them. Ingeborg closed her eyes, breathed in the scent of Zare. He was leaving her. She would be left alone.

Zare reached out and pulled the reindeer skins up around her shoulders.

'You understand I must warn my mother?' he asked her. 'We need to take her far away, to the grazing grounds in the western tundra, where the governor and his men will never find her.'

She nodded, but fear welled up inside her. How could she endure not seeing Zare every day?

'What shall I do?' she whispered.

Zare pushed his face closed to hers. 'Never give in to them, Ingeborg. Refuse to confess or denounce. They can't convict you otherwise.'

'But the governor wants to kill us all—'

'He is one man only. I heard the people of Vardø have written to the king himself to request he send another judge.'

Hope surged through Ingeborg so violently she found herself embracing Zare. 'Truly?'

'Yes, but *min kjære*,' he said, his lips so close to her cheek she could feel the whisper of them, 'it might be too late for your mother.'

Her heart plummeted again. Zare was right. The judge wouldn't be able to reach them for a long time. He would have to travel from Copenhagen to Bergen which was an arduous journey in winter. From there the boat journey up the northern coast of Norway would take weeks.

'But I *will* come back,' he promised. 'By the next dark moon, I will have made it back to the settlement and Svartnes. I will row across the Varanger Straits every morning and wait for you until dusk.'

'Then I must work out how to get out of the fortress,' Ingeborg said, with grim determination.

Zare stroked her hand. 'Ask Maren.'

What could he mean? Maren was a prisoner just like she. But then there were times in the night when she awoke, and the space on the pallet beside her was empty. In the morning, she'd see a black crow's feather tangled in her friend's hair, her eyes dark with shadows as if she'd not slept.

'Promise me you'll come back,' she asked Zare, panic rising at the thought of his departure.

'I will,' he said. 'You have my word.'

He wrapped his arms around her, and she closed her eyes. Tucked her head under his chin as he rested it upon her crown. He was Sámi. Different from her. But he was the only one she showed her heart to.

'Ingeborg, it is hard for me to leave you, believe me.' Zare paused as if deep in thought. 'But what if you could come with me? We can disguise you as one of the servant boys and you could sneak out with me tomorrow.'

Ingeborg shook her head, though her heart was screaming *yes*.

'Come with me, Ingeborg,' Zare urged. 'Live with the Sámi. Roam the tundra, run with the wolves, and always be free.'

'I can't leave my mother, and sister,' she said, unsettled he would tempt her so.

'Of course.' He dropped his head. 'I am sorry for asking. But I will come back for you. I will take you away, far away.'

She felt a flare of anger. He had made her feel things for him, made her believe he had come to the fortress for her. But he had come for his mother, not her.

'I can't live with you,' she said, harshly. 'I don't want you to take me anywhere.'

She felt his body shift away from her. A voice inside her head was begging her: *Stop. Don't say any more.* But her hurt was making her.

'I'm Norwegian and you're Sámi,' she said, her voice hard. 'We could never be together because I am Christian and you're—'

'A *savage!*' He moved away from her suddenly, and she toppled over. He was standing and she scrambled up. The wind howled around them. She couldn't see the expression on his face it was so dark.

'We're different,' she said, the words whipped out of her mouth.

'You're wrong, Ingeborg Iversdatter,' he said.

She wanted him to ask her to come with him again. To take her in his arms. Make more promises, and then she could believe in him. Then she *would* say yes.

But he didn't. He moved so fast, slipping off the wall and down into the dark alley.

'Zare!' she called after him in a hoarse whisper. 'Zare, forgive me.'

Tears began to sprout in her eyes. What had she done?

She climbed down after him. Ran along the alley, but he had disappeared. She stood in the courtyard hugging her sides, tears trailing her cheeks. He must despise her now for her narrow mind, and prejudice.

Out of the dark night, suddenly Maren appeared before her.

Ingeborg gave a little scream of fright. 'What are you doing here?' she asked Maren.

'I could ask the same to you,' Maren said, her face as dark as the night, her hair flying loose in the wild wind. 'But I already know you have been with our Sámi friend, Zare.' She sighed. 'I believe he is in love with you, Ingeborg Iversdatter.'

'No, it's not true!' Ingeborg pushed Maren out of her way, her smile strained, the edge in her voice making her furious.

But it wasn't Maren's fault. Maybe Zare had loved her, but she had ruined it if he had. And now he must think very little of her. She had lost her only chance to escape her wretched destiny. She would never be free.

PART FOUR

Spring
1663

The Young Reindeer Herder and the Wolf

Ever since the moment the young reindeer herder was born, they wanted with all their heart to be as powerful and strong as wolf, *Gumpegievra*.

When they told their father it was their dream to become a wolf, he told them it was as if they wished to be bad.

'The wolf attacks our reindeer,' their father said. 'He is your enemy.'

But no matter how many times one of their reindeer were stolen by wolves, the young reindeer herder held a deep reverence for the great beast.

'He is living his true nature,' they said.

'The wolf is dangerous,' their father warned. 'He has no pity for any creature.'

'He is not set against us, Father. It is the other way.'

Their father told his child they must forget about their dream of wolves. Their duty was to mind the reindeer herd and keep them safe from wolves.

But still they dreamed of wolves. They worried their free soul was captive, so they went to see the *noaidi* in the village, who was the healer, knower and seer of all things.

'I dream of a big grey wolf,' they told the *noaidi*. 'I follow him every-where. Is my free soul captured by the wolf?'

'I will find your captive soul and bring it back,' the shaman promised them. He entered a trance to search for the young reindeer herder's captive soul.

The young reindeer herder waited.

When the *noaidi* returned from his journey in the death-realm he told them their spirit was not captured. The shaman picked up his drum and began to play it, *yoik*ing as he did so. Upon the drum's surface, the young reindeer herder saw the grey wolf running fast, in circles, through all the pictures and symbols of the Sámi world.

When the shaman came back from the world of spirits, he told them their helping spirit was a wolf.

'Find the curved tree in the middle of the forest and pass under it in the direction of the sun,' the shaman told them. 'Then you can run with the wolves, because the wolf will give you power and wisdom.'

The young reindeer herder did as the shaman said, although they knew their father would not like it if his child became a wolf. But their helping spirit was calling to them and they could not deny it.

The young reindeer herder walked and skied and walked across the vast snowy *vidda* under the wide night sky. Sacred Mánnu, the moon, guided their way. At last, they came to a big forest. They walked through the trees along a silvery moonlit path until they stood before a huge tree with a curved trunk, its branches twisting up into the sky. They knew it was the tree the shaman had told them of.

They sat down and ate some dried reindeer meat and drank a cup of melted snow while they waited for the sun to rise. Moon slipped away behind them as the spring sun began to rise above the snow, reflecting cloudberry pink and orange in the sky.

The young reindeer herder took three steps back and then they ran under the curved trunk of the tree, towards the rising sun.

They ran and still they felt as a human. They ran, and they could go faster. They ran, and their hands turned to paws before their eyes and their arms covered in thick grey fur. They fell upon all fours as their spine arched and soft grey fur fleeced their whole body. Their heart beat faster and they felt the blood of a Sámi become the thick red blood of the wolf. They turned their head and saw their beautiful grey tail lifting in the wind. They opened their mouth wide, and gleaming fangs emerged, their eyes rolled in their head and when they looked again the world was different: the sky further away, and the snow beneath their paws drawing them down to the earth. The landscape was a cornucopia of smells and bursting with sounds; the scents of other creatures, the tiny snaps of twigs.

Truly, they had never felt so strong and powerful.

The shaman had warned the young reindeer herder they could run as a wolf for two weeks and through the nine valleys of the Sámi world, but if they did not return to the curved tree in time, they would forever be a wolf.

They were so overjoyed to be a wolf and so proud they wanted to show their father. They ran back to their village. But they were so excited they frightened the reindeer, which ran off in all directions.

'It's just me!' the young reindeer herder called out, but their words had turned to howls.

There was their father, and the young herder bounded towards him. 'Look, Father! See, I am a wolf! How strong and powerful I am!'

But their father was not smiling. No. And though there was something about the wolf that made him hesitate – a recognition between himself and the beast – their father suppressed his intuition and reminded himself that wolves were predators. He raised his bow and arrow and shot the wolf-child in the heart.

The father stomped over to the wolf. It had surely been very stupid to not run away. But the coat would make a warm fur for his family. He would make a hat for his young one out of it.

Red blood stained the white snow and the father cried out in alarm. For lying before him was not a big grey wolf, but his child with an arrow in their heart. He fell to his knees, begging the spirits of the death realm to bring back his child, but it was too late.

The young reindeer herder was running with the wolves, and they would never return.

Chapter 43

Anna

Upon the morning of the trial on the third day of April in the year of our Good Lord 1663, the wind moaned low outside the longhouse. The water snapped at the edges of Vardø island, while great flocks of gulls circled the sky. My husband Ambrosius would claim all these workings of nature were signs and, indeed, the harshness of weather laid upon me a deep sense of foreboding. The land lay sheer and icy, white opaque sheets stretching endlessly, for it would be weeks before the thaw of summer. I could not desist from shivering, no matter how many woollen garments I layered upon myself; nay, it was not cold which assaulted me but fearfulness for the predicament of my girls.

I dressed the three of them with great care, brushing down their woollen skirts and bodices, and fastening one of my own white collars about each of their necks. Despite their protests I had persuaded Ingeborg and Maren to wear coifs to conceal their unruly hair, while I had braided my own green ribbons into Kirsten's red hair, for she was my star on this dark day.

Outside the door to the trial chamber, I paused to check the girls were still in order. We could hear all the island folk on the other side of the door, crammed into the courtroom and waiting for the drama to begin. It had been so many months since I had been in company I was besieged with sudden and urgent nausea. I pushed it down, and with the sour taste of bile in my mouth, I addressed Maren, Ingeborg and Kirsten.

'There are going to be a great many people in the court all looking at you and listening to you.' I spoke as much to myself as them. 'It's important you speak clearly and stay calm, most of all. Do not cry. Do not shout, for they will not trust your words if you do so.'

'I have told you, Fru Anna, I will not testify,' Ingeborg said. Her eyes were loaded with fury, but I could see the fear in her as she bit her lips, and her worried, sidelong glance at Kirsten.

'I have told the governor this already,' I said to Ingeborg. 'But he insisted you were present.' I sighed. 'Girls, I do not know what will happen behind this door, but I urge you to speak the truth, no matter how frightened you are.'

'I am not frightened,' Maren said, giving me a haughty stare. 'I have been waiting weeks for this day.'

I looked at the girl in alarm. Despite her dour attire, Maren's dark looks were beguiling, and it seemed to me as if her glittering eyes were lit with a thousand lights as she slipped her arm around Ingeborg's waist and tucked her chin into her neck, whispering something into the other girl's ear.

'What are you saying?' I asked, but Maren merely smiled at me, though her eyes flickered with hostility.

'Nothing you need to know, Fru Anna.'

I had no time to push her further, for the big door to the chamber was opened.

All eyes were upon us as we entered the trial hall. It was lit up with a great many candles, all casting dramatic shadows upon the huge crowd of people. I noted the majority were women for most of the island men were not returned from the winter fishing grounds. I felt their glares upon us and turned to look at the hunting tapestry upon the trial chamber's walls. I now noticed a series of paintings of battle scenes brimming with men in combat, heroes, and death.

The girls walked with their heads bowed, as I had instructed them. The chamber was stifling, full of the sweaty smells of the crowd, an odour of rank fish from their labour; and hotness from their bodies, the heat from the candles, as well as a blazing fire at the very end of the hall.

I was no longer shivering but felt as if a furnace had been lit within me, and the sickness returned in the pit of my belly. How I wished for a calming beaker of wine laced with lavender oil.

To the side of the raging fire sat the governor, while monolithic Bailiff Lockhert stood behind him. At his side was seated a clerk with ink and quill to document the trial testimony.

I eyed the ink pot with longing, for how I wish to write clear script to you, my king!

On the other side of the governor was Reverend Jacobsen, dressed in a long black cassock, his fat face solemn as he watched the girls enter. All of the men were wearing ruffs, positioned high about their necks as if they wished to bring us back to the days of your father's witch trials in Denmark.

Along the wall sat a jury of twelve good men upon benches, all of them formally attired in black wool and white ruffs too. Through one of the small windows above the jury's heads, I could see pewter clouds racing across the deep blue sky, spits of snow blown this way and that.

Ingeborg was called to testify first, but the girl would not move from the bench.

'Your honour.' I spoke up, my voice sounding stronger than I felt. 'Ingeborg Iversdatter has no testimony to give.'

The governor narrowed his eyes. 'That will be up to me to decide.' He turned his ferocious glare on Ingeborg. 'The girl Ingeborg Iversdatter is called to give evidence.'

Ingeborg didn't bow her head for, to my surprise she glared back at him, causing his scar to glow red and angry on his cracked skin.

'Very well,' she hissed, in none too submissive a tone.

Chapter 44

Ingeborg

All were holding their breath, waiting for Ingeborg to speak. She turned to look at Fru Rhodius and Maren, both seated upon the bench. The Danish lady gave her an encouraging nod, and Maren's eyes spoke to her. Ingeborg heard her whisper again in her head.

Tell the truth. Make them scared of your power. They can't hurt you if you do.

But Ingeborg had already been hurt. She felt the heat of the governor's cruel gaze upon her and turned to the crowd of Vardø islanders. A sea of strangers' faces, most of them female, all of them staring at her intently. None from their village of Ekkerøy were there.

Hostility rose in waves from the women. She remembered her last embrace with Zare, and wished he were among the crowd. But he had abandoned her, and she was faced with none who cared for her. She dug deep within to find some strength.

'Relate to the court what happened on Christmas Eve,' Bailiff Lockhert ordered as he stood over her. 'Tell the court how you and the other witches transformed into cats and snuck into Anders Pedersen's cellar. Met the Devil there and drank up all his beer.'

Ingeborg shook her head. If the people of the Vardø wanted to hear her one and only meeting with the Devil, she *would* tell the truth.

'Only once did I encounter the Devil,' Ingeborg answered. As she spoke, the spits of ice outside turned into a storm of hail hammering upon the roof of the governor's chamber, making the candles flicker and near drowning out her voice. She felt the strain of the whole room as all leant forward. All believed her. Holding their breath to catch every single word she uttered.

Now she understood why Maren called this power.

'I was standing up on the big box.' Ingeborg pointed at the governor's chest next to the jury of men. 'The Evil One attacked me.' She turned back to look at the governor.

The governor's neck was red, his face drawn of light, while his eyes bore into her. There was warning in his look. But Ingeborg's fear had left her. She had nothing to lose, and something propelled her to speak out, no matter what the consequences.

'The Evil One put his hand here.' She touched her breast. 'I jumped off the box and ran down the hall and outside. The Devil chased me. He caught me, dragged me around the courtyard. Hit me and threw my skirt up.' Ingeborg took a breath, preparing for her final revelation. 'He lanced me with his sword.'

She reached down with her hand, placing it on her skirt in a place all could recognise.

A ripple passed through the crowd, but Ingeborg kept her eyes on the governor, his whole face crimson now, apart from the scar, which was a slash of silvery white.

She could hear some of the island women muttering, for all knew what violation she spoke of.

'This story is make-believe!' Lockhert bellowed. 'Tell the court true testimony, Ingeborg Iversdatter. Do you know of any other witches?'

'No.'

'Have you not been dancing with the witches on Domen in the presence of the Devil since?'

'No.'

'Did you not appear with other witches transformed as seals in the sea and chasing the fish away with stalks of seaweed so they could not be caught?'

'No, I did not.'

Bailiff Lockhert glowered over at her. 'Your testimony has no worth, child. To be saved, you must name others.'

Now, her mouth was dry, and no words would come. She squeezed her hands tight, believed in her courage. 'No,' she said. 'I don't know of any witches.'

Lockhert pushed her back towards Fru Rhodius as whispers began in the crowd, and people shifted their feet. Her story had unsettled them.

It was a tale of violence, and abuse. None liked to hear it from the lips of a girl, for in her words perhaps they recognised themselves: the times when their husbands or fathers had taken them outside and beat them in the snow; the nights their masters were so drunk they forced themselves upon them. The jury of twelve good men shifted uncomfortably upon their bench not wanting to believe the Iversdatter's girl's words for it was easier to blame the Devil for the bruises on their wives and daughters; easier to blame witches for their emptied barrels of beer. Easier to brand the maids heavy with unwanted pregnancies as followers of the Devil.

'This girl is useless, Fru Rhodius,' Lockhert said to the Danish woman, shoving Ingeborg at her. 'She is a simpleton.'

But Ingeborg caught the look of sympathy in Fru Rhodius's eyes. She knew she spoke the truth.

Chapter 45

Anna

Foolish, witless girl! I wished to give Ingeborg a good shake, for her words ensured her own indictment. The governor was seething with rage at her testimony, his face puce, and yet I could not but help admire the girl, for she had spoken up. I had been witness to her violation by the governor and although I had interceded, I had told no other soul of it. But now I am informing you, my king, and I would urge you to rid Finnmark of District Governor Orning for his abhorrent cruelty and depraved conduct.

As Ingeborg retrieved her place upon the bench beside me, Bailiff Lockhert called forth Maren to make her testimony. The tall, dark girl stood in the centre of the court chamber and swore her oath to tell the truth. The spectating crowd of islanders surged forward for a closer look, suspicion writ upon their faces, for Maren was a stranger to them and appeared wild and unknown, even though I had done my best to tame her looks.

After taking her oath, Maren placed her hands upon her hips, revealing not one flicker of fear upon her face. And though it had been my undertaking to procure confessions from the girl, I feared what words might spout from her lips.

'The witch Solve Nilsdatter has named you as being with her in Anders Pedersen's cellar on Christmas Eve with the other girl, Ingeborg, and her mother, Zigri Sigvaldsdatter, when, disguised as cats, you drank up all of his beer. What say you to this?' Lockhert addressed her, his voice gruff but a little thrown by her lack of terror.

'On Christmas Eve, Bailiff, we were guests in the witches' hole under your very nose, so how could we be across the Varanger Straits in Kiberg drinking Pedersen's beer?' she asked, sweetly.

'You dug your way out of the hole, and turned into birds,' Lockhert bellowed. 'You were seen by me, and the governor and Reverend Jacobsen as well as Merchant Brasche and Anders Pedersen!'

Maren cocked her head. 'And what bird might I be, Bailiff?'

Bailiff Lockhert narrowed his eyes at Maren Olufsdatter. 'You know well you were a black crow, girl.'

Was it my imagination, or did I hear Maren muttering under her breath the sounds a crow made – *caw, caw, caw.*

'It makes not one jot of difference what I say to you, Bailiff Lockhert, because you all believe you saw us, so how can I say otherwise to such learned men?' Maren asked, spreading her arms wide in front of the jury before taking a step towards the heaving bulk of her Scottish inquisitor. 'But I have a question for you. For if we can turn into cats and dig ourselves out of the witches' hole, and if we can fly as birds across the Varanger Straits, why do we choose to remain in captivity?'

Bailiff Lockhert looked furious to be challenged by one of the accused, and his inability to answer demonstrated it was not a usual occurrence.

'It is not your place to ask us questions, Maren Olufsdatter. Your duty is to answer truthfully what is addressed to you,' Governor Orning interceded, in a thunderous voice.

Maren wheeled around and surveyed the governor. 'I was not arrested, Governor Orning, for I came to Vardøhus of my own free will,' Maren said, pointing at him in much the same way I had seen accused witches point at one they had denounced.

Maren paused. Her attitude towards the men in authority would do her no good, and maybe she saw the futility of her situation, because I could see anger spark in her dark eyes as she continued to speak.

'I have a dream, or might it be truth? That a great crowd of women are gathered outside the fortress, as many as grains of ice in thick snow, and we wish to get inside your castle and set it alight. We wish to set you on fire, Governor Orning!'

Fury appeared to curl through Maren's body as she spoke and it seemed to make her taller than she was, even taller than all the men, as if she was possessed with the power of a wild beast. I did wonder, my king, if the Devil had taken hold of her and endowed her with supernatural abilities. Certainly, the island women seemed to think so as they shuffled backwards, murmuring and muttering.

'You might think I am lying, for when was it witnessed that so many women came to stand outside your castle in congregation? Ah, but we were as birds, Governor, yes indeed, a great host of birds of all types – crows, doves, plovers, eagles, sparrows, cormorants, swans, gulls. Every size and type of bird together in coven to see you burn!'

The governor was staring at Maren, and I do believe I saw fear in the man's eyes, for he was unable to respond, a situation I had never encountered with him myself.

'Was it Satan himself who sent you to harm the illustrious governor?' Bailiff Lockhert asked, his voice hoarse with excitement to hear Maren's words damning herself, and others too.

'No, indeed it was not. It was my mother, Liren Sand, for she has unfinished business with Governor Orning,' Maren said, proud as she spoke of her mother. 'And the women as birds who were with me were those you have burned as witches before.'

'All witches are in thrall to the Devil,' Lockhert countered. 'He must have sent you, but the governor is so godly the Evil One was repelled.'

'We came of our own accord to enact revenge, for you know more than I where the Dark Lord may reside,' Maren countered.

For a moment I closed my eyes and saw women as birds flying in the leaden skies above the fortress, gliding on the wind as it lifted their wings, and I could feel their liberation in every part of me.

When I opened them again, Maren had finished speaking, the big trial chamber completely silent as the shock of her outlandish words settled in.

Bailiff Lockhert's gruesome face was drawn into a scowl. 'It was Satan with you, for he gives you the agency to act as witches.'

'Oh, no, Bailiff.' Maren wagged her finger at him.

Once again I was astonished by her brazen audacity, for the more she goaded him, the worse would be the consequences, yet it seemed Maren cared not.

'It was not the Dark Lord with us, for I would know,' she said. 'The Dark Lord lurks here in Vardø. Yes, yes, he is right here, in this chamber with us now!'

There was a stir among the spectators as if a squall of wind had swept through them.

'Listen,' she told the crowd, and there was such hunger in their eyes for all she had to tell them. 'My mother, Liren Sand, was stronger than any man.' Such a spectacle had never been seen in the court room at Vardøhus before. 'Liren Sand is as tall as this castle, with the antlers of a reindeer and the claws of the lynx. She is magnificent, Liren Sand, and she is my mother, reaching out to me. Why, all the fishermen who have gone away may never come back, but not Liren Sand. She sticks with me through thick and thin.'

Maren paused, circling the trial hall, and it appeared to me as if she was enjoying this attention, though her act would be her doom.

'Liren Sand is a teacher, a guide, and into her queendom we go. She shows me a burning lake full of searing blue flames, and she blows flames from her pipe into the water. Dips flour, sugar, and ginger into the lake and out it pops baked. Liren gives me gingerbread and dances with me.' She twirled in front of the crowd. 'On we go into the valley of darkness. And I see all the other accused at the end of a long, long tunnel. They're waiting for me in the light. Liren Sand dances with them – see how beautiful she is, Governor Orning! Do you not remember her hands, her lips, the scent of her skin?'

Governor Orning was on his feet, his eyes lit with fury. 'Stop this nonsense at once, girl, and name me the witches of Varanger!'

Maren smiled, twisting a stray lock of her dark hair around her finger, head on one side, almost coquettish. 'Heed my words,' she said. 'Hurt one of us, and I will hurt you the more, for Liren Sand taught me how.'

The courtroom was completely still, the only sound was hail beating upon the roof.

'Beat us, torment us, crush our thumbs, break our bones . . . but not our spirits.' Maren turned and began to approach the crowd, revelling in how the island women cowered away from her and the jury of men were frozen in stunned horror. 'I can cast spells so you will wither and die with no cure for it!' She wagged her finger again. 'Burn one of us at the stake, why, then I'll burn you all in your beds. Set fire to the whole of Vardø!'

Fear ruffled through the crowd and people looked away, terrified of Maren's evil eye. The fire crackled and the room was filled with such heat as if the Devil's own breath was blowing upon me. I began to fan myself with my hand, panicked and short of breath.

Maren walked back towards me now and retook her seat on the bench, a smile upon her face that appeared incongruous, for surely her outburst had condemned her to the stake?

The governor rose from behind Maren, an ominous, rugged man with his high crowned hat and swirling black cape. As he approached the jury, he spread his arms wide, for all as if a big black bird himself.

'See how dangerous these creatures are!' Governor Orning declared to the jury. 'We must be rid of these northern witches and their war of terror upon us!'

But as he spoke, Maren's words came back to me.

The Dark Lord lurks here in Vardø.

The trial was far from over, for now they brought in the three accused women fettered in chains. I had seen many poor souls in terrible conditions during the plague year but the state of Solve Nilsdatter, Widow Krog and Zigri Sigvaldsdatter was an equal match. As they huddled together in a heap of wretchedness, next to me Ingeborg took a sharp intake of breath as she saw her mother, and Maren muttered low curses at the condition of her poor aunt. Though Ingeborg and Kirsten's mother, Zigri Sigvaldsdatter, was the least damaged of the three witches, she was a grotesque figure, causing the few men present to look away. She should have been in her confinement: Zigri was swelled as the full moon, waddling on unsteady feet. Beneath the grime her skin had a deathly pallor, and her once golden hair had fallen out, leaving bald patches on her head.

I took Kirsten's hand in mine, gave it a reassuring squeeze, but it lay limp and cold as she gaped at her mother.

The whole trial chamber filled with deep silence as the crowd looked on. There was no jeering or heckling as I had heard occurred at other witch trials in Denmark. I wondered did the islanders feel pity for these fishermen's wives not so different from themselves, or was the prevailing emotion one of fear? *Here be the three witches of Varanger! Beware you don't look in their eyes and catch a curse upon you!*

305

Solve Nilsdatter had transformed to the age of Widow Krog, with her teeth knocked out, hands as bloody stumps, and her broken-wing arm; but the worst of it was the state of her chest. Nausea rose again as bile in my mouth and though I had attended to her wounds every day, the sight of her ragged, burned, and festering flesh in the bright glare of the trial chamber turned my stomach over as if I were in a boat. I swallowed, and took a deep breath, placing my hands on my belly to still myself.

It was she who was dragged first in front of the governor and his jury. The hounds at his feet pricked their ears to attention, although their gaze was soft upon the woman. Tears trailed down Solve's sunken cheeks, and her breathing was laboured and rasping.

The governor instructed her to give her evidence, but it was clear the poor creature was unable to speak, as only a strangled sound came out of her mouth, and her body was trembling with exhaustion and pain.

In the stead of her spoken testimony, Bailiff Lockhert picked up a sheaf of paper and presented it to the governor.

The governor gave the pages a cursory glance. 'It appears the prisoner has already freely confessed the crimes, which have been recorded by the Bailiff Lockhert,' he said. 'I will read it out to you.'

'"I, Solve Nilsdatter from the village of Ekkerøy, wife of Strycke Anderson, freely confess to the following crimes. Along with my cousin Zigri Sigvaldsdatter, Widow Krog and the Sámi Elli, we chased the fish away from the seashore as seals with stalks of seaweed, so the fishing yield dropped. We wanted to bring suffering to the people of Varanger. We cast weather magic spells causing Merchant Brasche's ship to be wrecked, all his cargo destroyed, and all lives on board lost." Furthermore, she has confessed to the wrecking of Bailiff Lockhert's ship from Scotland and his family drowned.'

The governor paused as he read out his bailiff's name and the fate of his family, as Bailiff Lockhert's face hardened with the memory. These were not three broken women in his eyes, they were evil witches who had snatched the lives away of all those he loved, though it was hard to imagine Lockhert expressing love to any living being.

The governor continued reading out Solve's testimony. As each confession was read out, her head bowed lower and lower over her chest, as if the weight of her chains dragged her down.

"'We made merry with beer in Anders Pedersen's cellar with Satan at Yuletide. We danced with witches from all over the kingdoms of Denmark, Norway and Scotland on Midsummer's Eve on the very top of Domen Mountain. Performing square dances with Satan, playing board games and knocking back jug after jug of strong brew beer.'"

The pictures her words drew were so vivid that I admit, my king, I began to doubt her innocence again, for how could a simple fishing woman make up such lies? So, *had* she danced with the Devil, and your father was correct indeed; that it was here in the northern domains the Dark Lord dwelled?

"'I bought magic charms from the Sámi Elli, to use against the governor. Bound them in yarn and hid them in cracks in the fortress walls.'"

At this point, the Bailiff Lockhert removed from his waistcoat pocket a small ball of dirty yarn and handed it to the first juror to examine. 'We found this tucked into one of the cracks in the witches' hole,' he explained.

The governor continued reading the document. "'Myself, Widow Krog, Zigri Sigvaldsdatter and my niece Maren Olufsdatter congregated as a murder of black crows outside the fortress threatening to lock in Governor Orning and Bailiff Lockhert and set fire to it.'

The governor laid down the parchment in his hands. "'I, Solve Nilsdatter, confess I went into the mountains and gave the Devil my body.'"

The gathering in the great hall muttered in disgust at the image of the fisherman's wife lifting her skirts to the Dark Lord, and I could hear the whispers: *'Burn in Hell, slattern.'*

After Solve's confessions were read out, old Widow Krog was brought forward, hobbling in her shackles, her skin mottled with bruises and lacerations. She too had bloody stumps for fingers but there was a spark of defiance in her eyes as she raised her head.

'Dorette Krog, I urge you to make your full confession to be witnessed by all present and presided over by the illustrious District Governor Orning.' Bailiff Lockhert addressed her with a stern voice.

But the widow Krog did not bow her head as Solve had done, for she looked Lockhert in the eye and spoke out in a trembling voice: 'I refuse to confess, in any way whatsoever.'

There was an uneasy rustle in the trial hall as the governor glared at the old woman in fury.

'Can you find twelve people to swear an oath of compurgation for you?' Lockhert challenged her.

'Indeed, no, for who would risk speaking for me now, when they would surely be accused as well?' Widow Krog turned to the governor. 'Your honour, these accusations are false against me.'

'You've been denounced by Solve Nilsdatter,' the governor accused her.

'But Solve was tortured until she denounced others,' she declared. 'I swear I'm no witch. I will not lie upon myself, nor denounce another woman. I will not!'

The governor's expression darkened, his jaw clenched, the scar raised upon his cheek.

'It appears the Devil sits deep inside this old crone,' he addressed Lockhert. 'We must persuade her to tell the truth.'

Lockhert nodded at the governor and turned to address Widow Krog. 'To prove your innocence, do you agree to be tried by the water ordeal?'

The crowd fell silent, waiting for her answer. All I could hear was the crackle of the fire and the sound of the hard icy hail against the window glass.

As you know, my king, the water ordeal is the best way of proving if a woman is a witch because water is sacred. So, when put to the test, water would take unto it the innocent, and spurn the evil. If Widow Krog bobbed on the water like a boat, she was proved a witch – and yet I had never heard of one woman tested who had done otherwise.

Widow Krog looked terrified as she spoke, but she agreed to the test, for what choice did the old woman have?

The governor announced the trial would be adjourned until the next day, after the water ordeal had been undertaken.

The northern waters would be so cold I could not bear to imagine how it might feel to be immersed within them. Indeed, once submerged within their icy folds, the old woman might freeze to death before there was a chance to prove her a witch or not.

I wondered if maybe this was what Widow Krog hoped for.

Chapter 46

Ingeborg

The girls had been ordered down to the shoreline to watch the water test. The Governor declaring that if they did not confess, they would be subjected to the same ordeal. When they got there, every single islander was crammed together on the slippery rocks. Old Widow Krog before them as white as her shift, near naked, teeth chattering, nose blue. The bay was almost dark as the twilight turned wild black. All the people of Vardø were quiet, watching by the edge of the sea, the only sound the screeching of gulls and the splash of oars as the governor's soldiers rowed the boat out.

Widow Krog's hands were bound together, her wrists tied to her ankles so that she was trussed. The men threw her into the freezing Arctic ocean like a sack of grain, at the ready with rope and planks if she sank.

But she did not.

Widow Krog's white shift billowed like a grand sail, and she was floating on the sea. A stir through the crowd. One voice, then another joining in, until all the people were howling, '*Witch, witch, witch!*'

They pulled her out of the water like a haul of fish and rowed back to shore quickly, so she would not go blue and turn dead in the boat.

All the people kept on chanting, '*Witch, witch, witch!*' God's own monsters, Governor Orning and Bailiff Lockhert looking on, triumphant.

As the boat approached the shore, everyone surged forward, slipping on the muddy banks. Ingeborg saw Widow Krog in the bottom of the boat, her shift stuck to her body so her nakedness was for all to see. Shaking non-stop with cold, her eyes red-rimmed from the salty sea.

Maren pushed through the crowd. 'Do not be afraid, witch! Use your power, show them!'

Ingeborg caught the fever of Maren's words. She wanted Widow Krog to howl, to fill the sky with black clouds and crack them open. She wanted thunder to roar and lightning to strike the governor of Vardø. *Send Thor of your old religion, Widow Krog!*

Ingeborg prayed to the Good Lord and all of Zare's Sámi gods for it to happen. Let the icy rain fall and drown the jeering crowd that was judging them, because they could not see beyond their own fear and prejudice.

No thunderbolts came, and Widow Krog was insistent, words squeezed out between chattering teeth. 'I am not a witch,' she said. 'Believe me! I'm innocent.'

But the water repelled her, and did that not prove she was in fact a witch?

Widow Krog kept at it, as they dragged her out of the boat, chained her up and brought her back to the witches' hole.

'I will not confess!' she roared. 'Nor denounce another.'

Chapter 47

Anna

After the dreadful spectacle of the water ordeal, I made my way to the witches' hole with my medicine chest, Ingeborg by my side carrying a cauldron of steaming fish broth for the women.

Widow Krog was surely frozen to the bone, and I feared she might not survive the night. I had chosen Ingeborg to help me out of compassion for her and her mother, so that they might exchange some words. Kirsten had not requested the same, nor had her mother ever asked after her youngest child – which inflamed my protective urges towards the girl.

Have faith, Anna, she is your girl, yours.

When Ingeborg and I arrived at the witches' hole, Captain Hans refused us entry, informing me it was upon the orders of Bailiff Lockhert who was within, with the witches. Furthermore, the captain had been instructed by the governor himself to retrieve my key.

I protested vehemently, saying the women needed to be cared for, but the sorrowful Captain Hans said he had his orders to fulfil. All we could do was leave the broth by the door, and he assured me it would be given to the witches. The key I pulled from my pocket with grave misgivings, for what might Lockhert be doing to the women in their grim prison without my watchful eye? It was clear Ingeborg was thinking similar thoughts for she looked at me with those grave eyes of hers, a flash of accusation in them. But Lockhert's brutality is far from my fault, for I have only ever tried to put a stop to his tormenting.

I have no power, for it is not I, my king, who rules Finnmark!

*

I barely slept, waiting for the first slip of dawn to seep through the halibut skin window. But it was still dark as pitch when I heard the door to my bedchamber creak open.

I half expected to see Christina in her white nightdress and bare feet again.

Mamma, my head hurts.

But my intruder was the black cat from the castle, padding across my cracked floorboards, before it leapt upon my bed. I didn't push it off; rather, I considered the cat as it looked at me unblinking, as though perusing my soul.

The women and girls had been accused of metamorphosing into cats on Christmas Eve, which was an absurd notion, and yet the more I looked at the cat, the more knowing was the expression in its eyes.

'What should I do?' I whispered to the cat.

I felt the weight of the suffering of these women and girls of the Varanger Peninsula upon my shoulders. Was I as powerless as the governor had me believe? Now the key to the witches' hole had been taken from me and I had been excluded from the questioning because my voice was one of dissent.

My king, Governor Orning broke your laws again and again, tormenting those poor creatures.

The cat slunk up the bed coverings towards me and I was uncertain whether it might bite me, but still I raised my hand to let it sniff. It rewarded me with a rough lick and curled up next to me, the deep rhythm of its purr lulling me into a state that was half-sleep, half-wakefulness.

The next morning, after prayers, our small household made its way again to the governor's great hall for the trial's conclusion. The air felt a little warmer, the sky desolate grey, as the crisp brilliance of the piles of snow were beginning to thaw, turning to sludge. I hunted for the first bud of colour, for one green leaf would be enough to lift my spirits, but all was dull and muted. As we proceeded, the stark silence was shattered by the sound of long blades of ice falling from the castle roof upon the stones.

The trial hall was as packed as the day before, but I sensed a shift in the humour of the people of Vardø. The hysteria of the water ordeal of

Widow Krog hung palpable in the stultifying trial chamber, and tension thickened the air further. Why weren't these fishing folk pondering how it was witches did not look so different from their own mothers, sisters and daughters, from themselves even?

The two cousins, Solve and Zigri, were led back into court in manacles but Widow Krog was not present. I dared not think of the ordeals the old woman had been put through by Lockhert to persuade her to confess, and it was clear her absence was proof she remained adamant of her own, and the other women's, godliness. I was in awe of her endurance. People might say it was the Devil who gave her strength, but I believe it was her honour. Whether she was guilty or not of witchcraft, the old crone believed in her own innocence, and that of her fellow accused.

Where has my zeal gone? I arrived one year ago believing I was on this blasted island to do your will and hunt the witches for you, my king. I was blazing with passion and devotion, and I would have laid down my life in this quest for your divinity. But now my heart was aching with misery, and doubt assaulted me as I looked at the two broken women and wondered how they could possibly have the skills to destroy your power, the most magnificent man of the whole kingdom of Denmark and Norway.

Ah, my conjecturing is all very well, for in truth I cannot recant upon my purpose now. I have made a deal with the governor, and it was time to see it through to the very end.

The governor called forth Kirsten Iversdatter, daughter of the accused witch, Zigri Sigvaldsdatter to testify. This was our moment. I stood up and offered my hand to Kirsten. She was wearing my green ribbon twisted in her red curls from the day before and light slanted in from the trial hall windows and lit her up. She was as if an angel as she looked up at me, her eyes blue and trusting, just as Christina had once done when I had promised my dying girl she would live and that I would save her.

Kirsten reached for my hand while Ingeborg's face blanched with shock, and she whispered to her sister, 'Kirsten, say nothing.'

But her sister no longer belonged to her, for she was my girl, mine.

As we walked up to testify, I caught a glimpse of the governor's wife seated beside the governor, her expression as horrified as Ingeborg's.

She tugged on her husband's arm. 'Christopher, she's a child, what do you mean by this—?'

But her husband flicked her hand from his arm and settled his dark glare upon Kirsten. I squeezed her hand, and her fingers clasping mine sent a dart of strength to my heart. Believe me, my king, if there had been any other way at all I could have saved my girl I would have taken it but, I will confess, yes, indeed, I wish for my old life again, and I want my daughter back.

There will always be loss and suffering in this world, but this time it would not be mine.

With every eye upon us, Lockhert spoke in a low, gruff voice: 'Tell the governor and the jury what you confessed to Fru Rhodius.'

'Kirsten, my child—' Zigri Sigvaldsdatter was straining against her chains, the broken-winged Solve slumped against her. As she tried to move towards us, two of the soldiers pulled her back. Wafts of witches' hole filled the air around me and I could smell the sweat of their suffering, the blood of their tormenting, and the excretions of their desperation.

As a wave of nausea swelled up inside me, I willed myself to close my ears to the witch, for her lover's wife, Fru Brasche, had already ensured Zigri Sigvaldsdatter's doom. I was intent upon saving her daughter from a future such as hers to be branded a witch; not this day, for she was too young, but one day in the future. If Kirsten Iversdatter remains in Vardø, she will forever be named a witch's get, just as Maren had been. Such a fate created a wild, unstable creature of a girl and I fear when Maren is of an age for indictment that she will not be long for the stake. Could Zigri Sigvaldsdatter not see I was saving her girl, Kirsten? For as my daughter she will become Christina Rhodius and enjoy comfort and security in my house in Bergen. I will look after her and ensure she wants for nothing.

'Silence, witch!' the governor commanded, and the soldier placed his hand over Zigri's mouth while she struggled, her pregnant belly huge and unsettling for the soldier as he tried to negotiate it.

'I saw my mother with the Devil.' Kirsten spoke in a quiet voice.

'Where did you see your mother with the Devil?' Lockhert pushed.

'In Heinrich Brasche's cowshed,' she said, her voice growing stronger. 'My mother hit me hard and told me not to say a word to a soul about it.'

'What did you see them doing?'

'They were fornicating.' Kirsten's voice, crystal clear.

Zigri stopped struggling, but her body was wrenched with huge sobs as the soldier removed his hand. 'Oh, Kirsten, what have you done?' the woman wept.

Kirsten turned to look at her mother, her hand still in mine. 'You said I was a devil's child, you said it's my fault Axell drowned—' Kirsten's voice wavered.

'I did not mean it, Kirsten. I was grieving for my boy.'

Kirsten turned her back on her mother and looked up at me with pleading eyes. 'Can we go to Bergen now? Can we, Fru Anna?'

'Yes, soon, my girl,' I promised, as we walked back to our bench.

What happened next was as expected. The Governor and bailiff conferred with the jury of men, before the bailiff took centre stage again. The bailiff's words rippled out over the entire populace of the island of Vardø crammed into the trial hall.

'Since these women have made a pact with the Devil, and practised witchcraft, causing our people of the Varanger Peninsula to suffer, may God preserve us but we have no other choice – they must be punished with loss of life at the stake.'

The two cousins Zigri and Solve clung to each other in terror. Oh, my king, I could not look at them, but where could I place my eyes? The crowd was erupting into hysteria again, with cries of 'Burn the witches!' but others were silent, their disapproval in the line of their mouths.

I could not look at Ingeborg but heard her rasping and gasping as if a fish thrown out of water.

'What does he mean?' Kirsten asked me in a terrified whisper.

'He means our mother will be burnt at the stake as soon as she gives birth!' Ingeborg lashed out at her sister before I had a chance to speak some kind and gentle words to my girl.

'But she was with the Devil—' Kirsten frowned, looking confused. 'And the baby . . . is a devil's child—'

She looked up at me for an answer.

'Yes, yes,' I reassured her.

But the trial was not over yet, indeed no. What happened next was beyond my imagining, its betrayal so wrenching it near stopped my heart from beating.

I will not forget the sight of Bailiff Lockhert in his best black doublet, his unruly hair flattened down upon his head with sheep's grease, puffing his chest out in pride. 'Furthermore, your honour, we must make judgement of these three girls, Ingeborg and Kirsten Iversdatter, and Maren Olufsdatter, who have learnt and practised witchcraft from their mothers.'

I stared aghast at Lockhert, unable to move or speak for the horror of his words.

'The Evil One was always with them in the past, and they cannot be rid of him, no matter how the priest works on them and tries to convert them to Our Lord the Christ. The Evil One will never relinquish them for they have been sacrificed to him by the mother, and the aunt.'

Oh, my king, there in Governor Orning's glinting eyes I saw my betrayal yet again, for he was not surprised by his bailiff's announcement. He rubbed his hands as if warming them by the fires he wished to set alight and nodded for Lockhert to continue speaking.

'In view of such circumstances, I would ask the court whether they should not be punished by loss of life and prevented from learning more mischief from the Devil and enticing other children into wickedness.'

The memory of Governor Orning's cruel voice resurfaced in my mind. *We will burn your girl, and you will remain here for the rest of your days.*

The Vardø folk fell silent, stunned by the bailiff's brutal request. Ingeborg let out a cry as if she had been punched in the belly, but Kirsten spoke not, though her hand slipped out of mine.

I could not breathe. Oh, my Good Lord, oh, my king, I could not. As these terrible words settled upon all present as if a pestilence, as folk coughed with unease, muttered trembling protests –'These girls are too young!' – only one soul acted.

Maren rose from her seat as she ripped the starched white collar from her neck and the coif from her head. She moved swiftly through the ranks of islanders until she stood before the governor, raising her face to him as her black crow hair rippled in wild curls all the way to the small of her back.

'District Governor, listen well, for you wish to turn daughter on mother, and mother against daughter, sister upon sister, cousins, friends, every woman against each other!' she declared. 'But what will happen when there are no women left, not one girl breathing on the whole of Varanger Peninsula? What will you men do?' She spun around to the crowd of island women gathered and pointed her finger at them. 'For sure there'll be none of you women left to mind the livestock, cook your husband's meals, and wash their soiled clothes.' Maren turned back to the governor and took another step towards him. 'No women left to fuck you nor birth your sons. None to pray for you. Where will it end? In a world with no women, just God, his men and the Devil always with *you!*'

Her outburst was so sudden and shocking the governor was lost for words, although Lockhert went to grab her.

The governor's wife clasped her hands, her eyes shining as if Maren's words had set her alight. 'Leave her alone,' Fru Orning commanded Lockhert.

The bailiff faltered, looking to the governor for reassurance.

But before the governor could speak, Maren snapped her fingers. From all four corners of the trial hall rats emerged, scampering across the wooden floors. The islanders cried out and began running for the chamber door, impeding the soldiers from entering. The governor stood up and yelled at his hounds, but the dogs backed away as though afraid of the rats, as everyone else.

I grabbed Kirsten's hand in mine and turned for the door. Though she wrenched away from me I tugged my girl towards the exit, but as I did so a piercing scream rang out from behind me. It was a sound I recognised all too well, and I wheeled around to see Zigri Sigvaldsdatter gripping her belly, water leaking from between her legs.

Her time had come.

Chapter 48

Ingeborg

Inside the bedchamber in the longhouse, under guard, Ingeborg's mother writhed upon a heap of reindeer skins.

Fru Rhodius waved Lockhert away. 'This is women's business,' she told him. 'You can stand outside the door all day if you so wish, but this witch is not able to run or fly anywhere.'

Lockhert gave Fru Rhodius a filthy look before banging the door closed behind him.

'Set a cauldron of water to heat over the fire, Ingeborg,' Fru Rhodius instructed her. 'We must wash her. I can't attend to her in such dirt.'

Ingeborg tested the water. With all her heart, she wished to drench the Danish woman in the boiling water. Let her burn too. But her mother's cries arrested her, and she dutifully carried it over. Fru Rhodius passed her a cloth.

'Set this aside for the new-born.' She gave Ingeborg an encouraging look. 'Don't look so worried, child. I've done this many times.'

Why was she smiling at her after such betrayal? Stealing her own sister from her? The sister who now crouched in the corner of the longhouse staring in subdued shock. And where was Maren? She had been there a moment ago, but now she was gone.

Fru Rhodius was a different woman in the birthing room. No sermonising or talk of the Good Lord. She spoke with kindness to her mother, despite what she'd done to her.

'Raise your legs, there's a good woman,' she cajoled her.

Her mother looked up at Ingeborg, her eyes bulging with pain. 'You're here, Ingeborg,' her mother whispered, gripping her hand and squeezing so tight Ingeborg thought she might break her fingers.

'Yes, I'm staying with you.'

'I'm sorry, my daughter, forgive me—'

'Hush, Mother, hush.'

With the spare cloths and the water, Fru Rhodius washed down her mother's legs, pushing up her skirts and examining her.

Her mother moaned like a beast as she gripped Ingeborg's hand even more tightly.

'Your babe will be here soon,' Fru Rhodius announced.

Pains rippled through her mother's body. 'No, I don't want the babe to come, no!' she wailed.

But she had no say in the forces of nature controlling her body.

Ingeborg looked down and could see the baby's head begin to push out. Its bloody crown was a pure, miraculous sight.

It was a quick birth. On the last toll of the noon bell, the baby was born. A little girl, with a thatch of black hair. The baby gave a hearty cry. Fru Anna swaddled her tight and laid her on Zigri's grubby chest.

'Come, bring your daughter to your breast,' Fru Rhodius encouraged her.

Her mother's face was a turmoil of emotions: joy at her new child, and fear at what awaited her now her womb was empty. She pulled herself up against the walls of the longhouse, her baby in her arms, and latched her onto her breast.

'How could they think my wee baby a devil's child?' Zigri's voice was faint with exhaustion as she looked up at Fru Rhodius. 'Can you not see I've had no dealings with the Devil?'

Fru Rhodius turned her back on the woman and didn't reply.

'Speak not about it now, Mother,' Ingeborg said, wiping the sweat from her mother's brow. She wanted to hold the magic of the birth close still, untainted by the end that awaited them both. 'This is the hour of your baby's birth day.'

'I will never see another,' her mother said, as she let out a sob.

Her mother's tears drew Ingeborg's own. The shock of what had just happened in the trial room ebbed through her. She, her mother and Kirsten had all been condemned to burn at the stake. To burn! Along with Solve and Maren. She couldn't believe it would happen. She just couldn't. She clutched on to the knowledge of Zare, and his promise to return. But didn't he despise her for the things she had said to him?

As for her new baby sister, Ingeborg knew what would happen, with dreadful certainty. The baby would be taken away from her mother, who would be returned sore and bleeding to be chained up in the witches' hole. Another woman of Vardø would wet-nurse the baby. Yet another raises her. It would be for this baby girl as it was for Maren: to grow up named as the daughter of a witch, the same curse upon her head. To be condemned herself one day. A never-ending cycle of doom.

'It's tragic, is it not?' Ingeborg looked at Fru Rhodius through her tears.

Fru Anna's black hair had tumbled loose, and her cheeks were flushed from their exertions. Although she was so much older, she looked quite beautiful illuminated by the beams of fledgling spring sun coming through the tiny window of her longhouse bedchamber. She turned away from Ingeborg, though she saw her wipe a tear – just one – from her eye. Yet when she spoke, her voice was hard again. 'Do you think it better a witch one day sacrificing her baby girl to the Devil, just as your mother did to you?'

'Would you have *me* burn, Fru Rhodius?'

'No!' she exclaimed, her eyes fiery. 'I will save you girls.'

'But I don't care to be saved without my mother,' Ingeborg hissed.

Her mother had but a few minutes alone with her baby. Once the child's crying was heard, Lockhert and a soldier entered, along with the wet-nurse.

'Take the babe from the witch,' Lockhert ordered the soldier.

'She's not finished feeding her yet,' Fru Rhodius protested.

'We have a wet-nurse here. The baby will be fostered out in Vardø.'

'I beg you, give me more time,' her mother cried out, clasping her baby to her breast.

'Give her a minute, the baby needs sustenance,' Fru Rhodius appealed to Lockhert.

'How can you even consider leaving the babe in the arms of a witch?' Lockhert looked furious. He stomped over to Ingeborg's mother, pushing past Fru Rhodius.

Ingeborg couldn't bear the thought of his rough hands all over the baby's delicate skin. 'Mamma,' she urged her, 'give me the baby.'

'No,' her mother said, shaking her head. 'I'm no witch. They must believe me.'

'Hand Ingeborg the child now or she'll be ripped from your arms,' Fru Rhodius warned her. 'They will hurt her. Give her to Ingeborg. I promise she'll be safe.'

Reluctantly, sobbing, her mother let Ingeborg take the warm, squirming bundle from her. She took the baby in her arms. It felt so natural, so right, to have a babe cradled within them. Yet she would never become a mother herself.

It wrenched her to hand the child to the wet-nurse, who briskly left the longhouse as her mother began to howl.

'Be silent, witch,' Lockhert commanded, but her mother did not stop. Lockhert slapped her, yet still she continued.

Not until Ingeborg took her head within her hands did she stop. She looked into mother's tortured eyes and gave her what love she could. 'I will find a way out,' Ingeborg whispered to her.

The words somehow reached her mother and she fell quiet, still shivering from the shock of giving birth. Lockhert and his man pulled her up from the floor, and dragged her out of the longhouse, back across the courtyard to the witches' hole.

Ingeborg followed her trail of blood in the slushy snow.

Ignored by the soldiers, she knelt down by the cracked walls of the witches' hole and pressed her hands against it. 'Mother, Mother,' she whispered. 'I am here. I will save you.'

Chapter 49

Anna

My king, District Governor Orning intends to burn mere girls, and *my* girl, Kirsten – and she is but thirteen years of age!

After the dreadful trial, the whole world tilted. I had thought my own tribulations had reached their darkest hour, but no, Governor Christopher Orning and his henchman Bailiff Lockhert were masqueraders of the truth. I believe it is they who are the devils among us!

I write these words as fast as I can, but what is the point, for will you ever even read these letters? I have been unable to send any of them to you and even if, somehow, I had managed to get them placed on a ship bound for Denmark and delivered to the palace, would you even remember our secret trick? I have never forgotten the love notes you sent to me written in lemon juice so no one else could read the missives, but when I held the parchment to the light of the candle, your endearments showered upon me.

You did love me, once. I reminded you of my claim upon your heart the last time we were together, less than two years ago. Indeed, I took your hands in mine, and I bravely spoke up.

You had ordered me from your writing room to enter your private chamber at Rosenborg Palace and we were alone – not even your valet was present.

Before me was the royal bed upon which you caressed your queen, Sophie Amalie, or so I imagined. The bed chamber was far more ornate than your wood-panelled writing room, with walls covered in green silks and paintings of China, and I wondered if this might be due to the Queen's opulent tastes.

'Frederick, remember the love we shared,' I appealed to you, overcome with nostalgia. 'How you took my maidenhead, and I gave you my whole heart. My king, you still possess it.'

You drank in my words as if a thirsty man, and I saw the flicker in your eyes, the rekindling of our passion. But then, in one instant, you thrust it away and pulled your hands from mine, fury fuelling every movement you made.

'How dare you touch your king! How dare you call me Frederick! I should have you executed!'

But I didn't believe you meant these words, for your feelings for me were exhibited in the command I was to follow you into your bedchamber. Why else had you bid me step inside the sacred domain of the royal marital chamber, if not for intimacy?

'Do you believe yourself so above me now?' I challenged you, unable to stop the stream of words. 'For once we were boy and girl who both loved books and flowers. We were a young couple kissing under a pear tree.'

'Enough!' You slapped my cheek, but I was not hurt. Your anger gave me joy, for I could see emotion roaring within you.

'I still wear the cross you gave me.' I pulled aside my kerchief and showed you the black onyx cross. 'I will wear it to my dying day.'

'Which will be sooner than you think if you do not stop this nonsense at once,' you said starkly.

'Don't say such things, *min kjære*,' I said, placing my hand upon your sleeve.

Yes, I did dare touch you again, the absolute monarch of our kingdom.

You shook me off, but again I could see your confliction, for why not call for your valet? Why not order me out of your chamber?

Ah, but indeed I did misunderstand your intentions, for you wished to hurt me the more.

'Anna Rhodius, you are a vain and worthless woman,' you said in a cruel voice. 'One past her child-bearing years and no longer handsome as in youth. You have no agency as an ageing woman and yet you insist on questioning the authority of men.'

'I only brought to your attention the corruption of Statholder Trolle who serves in your name.' I defended myself, cheeks flaring at the pain of your words. 'He aspires to destroy the monarchy.'

'You have been the cause of great humiliation for me,' you hissed.

So, this was my true crime, so immense I could never overcome it, for I had offended your regal pride and you were mortified that once you had loved a woman such as I.

Oh, my king, truly my heart was broken once more at your brutal words . . .

I have given up all hope of ever receiving a missive of reconciliation, but I beg you please save these wronged citizens of *your* kingdom. Yes, they are the poorest of the poor, living in harsh conditions, but they are ordinary women, and good girls. Dear Lord, forgive me for my part in their troubles, for they are not witches, nor witches' gets.

I have nearly drained the juice of one lemon to write this invisible letter, my nib shaped from a crow feather that had blown into the longhouse last summer. When I have finished, I will fold it up into a square and seal it with some candle wax dripped upon the edges. Then I will place it in the box where I keep all the letters.

The shock of the verdict echoed around the empty courtyard as I made my way towards the governor's house. All seemed in disarray, and I had no notion of where the girls had disappeared to, though they had to be somewhere within the fortress as two soldiers were stationed in front of the chained gates.

All the islanders had run back to their tiny cottages after the rats had poured into the trial chamber. The condemned Solve had been taken back to the witches' hole where Zigri had been brought after the birthing of her babe. I could not bear to look in the direction of the dark hut as I climbed the steps to the castle and pushed the door open.

I walked through the trial chamber now deserted even of the rats, but I could still hear echoes of shock and anger in the cries from the island women at Lockhert's demand to condemn the three girls. I felt ablaze with conviction and outrage as I pushed open the next door, into the governor's living chamber.

He sat with his back to me in his great chair, the two wolfhounds lying at his feet. The fire blazed in the hearth, and he was alone. Fru Orning's chair was empty and Lockhert nowhere to be seen. If Orning sensed my arrival in the room, he did not acknowledge it but merely leant forward in his chair, a glass of red wine between his hands, staring into the fire. Was he thinking of those he had just condemned to the flames?

My breath was tight in my chest for I knew to speak might mean my own situation would in all likelihood worsen, but no more could I stand by and hold my tongue.

'Governor, may I speak with you?'

'Ah, I thought it was you,' he said, ignoring my request. 'What perfume is it you always adorn yourself with, Fru Rhodius? Rose oil, is it? Reminds me of summers in Bergen on the Rosencrantz estate.' He gave a big sigh, as if he had the sorrows of the world upon his shoulders.

'Yes, your governor,' I said placing my hand upon your onyx cross to calm my nerves. 'I must talk with you—'

'Come sit with me, Fru Anna,' he said, indicating his wife's chair.

I moved forward and sat down with hesitation. The scar on his face was raised white and jagged like the ridge of a mountain, and I thought upon how many souls the old soldier had killed in his line of duty. Though burning witches was a world apart from the war between men.

'Your honour, I am here to remind you of your pledge to me.'

'And what might that be, Fru Rhodius?' He looked at me, eyes glazed as the words he uttered slurred. I caught sight of the empty decanter and conjectured the man was drunk.

It is never wise to reason with a man full of wine and yet I could not be silent. 'It was your promise to me that if Kirsten Iversdatter gave evidence against her mother, you would request the king pardoned me and I would be free to leave *with* Kirsten. We would return to my home in Bergen as soon as it was possible to sail south. You made a solemn oath to me that you would inform the king how I had helped you rid the north of witches.'

Governor Orning stroked his pointed grey beard, his movements slow as his head rolled from side to side. 'I made no such pledge, Fru Rhodius.'

I looked at him in shock, and though I knew Governor Orning to be a cruel, vicious authoritarian, I did not believe he would ever lie upon his word.

'Besides, the mother has now confessed that she gave her daughters over to the Devil,' he concluded. 'Lockhert questioned her.'

I was faint with the imagining of how Lockhert may have tormented Zigri Sigvaldsdatter, so weak from having just birthed her baby.

'I cannot let these girls live, for they will corrupt other children with their evilness.'

'What of the baby?' I whispered.

'The babe is with a wet-nurse. Reverend Jacobsen and his wife will foster the child. They mean to scourge it of all traces of the babe's wicked mother and sisters. There, you see, I have saved one soul from the Devil, have I not?'

'Governor, I do not think the king would want you to put girls to the stake. Kirsten is just thirteen years of age, and the other two are barely seventeen.'

'How do you know what the king would want?' Orning turned on me, the poison of the drink descending upon him. There were sparks of anger and something else even darker in his eyes. 'Do you not understand we are waging war against Satan and his monstrous regiment of witches, Fru Rhodius? I am protecting you and all who live in this pitiful province of Finnmark from the destruction and chaos wrought by these vile witches.'

'But, I believe I can turn the girls back to God, for every day they have been learning their catechism. Let Kirsten recite for you, and you will see what a godly child she is.'

The governor gave a cruel laugh while his dogs stirred at his feet, looking at me with eyes brimming with the tragic sorrow I felt.

'And what of their behaviour in court? The one named Maren Olufsdatter is as possessed as her mother was, and Ingeborg Iversdatter is in thrall to her. What think you on the appearance of the rats, Fru Anna? For were they not called from the Devil himself to instigate terror among godly folk?'

'But Kirsten is an innocent child.'

'The girl has been baptised over to the Devil and has already worked his evil, for her own mother told me so.' The governor took another slug of his wine and raised his glass to the sparking fire. 'I am hitched to my ugly little wife with no child to show for my marital duties, ha! Elisa used to be dutiful and submissive, but the events of the past few weeks have given even my own wife notions!' He spat into the fire. It hissed, and sparks flew onto the floor, which he stamped out with his buckled shoe. 'Why do you think a man of my standing was sent all the way here? Because of my wife's father, Governor Rosencrantz of Bergen. He accused me of taking advantage of his daughter! But the little wench was all comely with me, and it was she who entrapped me into marrying her, for who else would have such a girl with a pox-marked face, no matter how big the dowry!'

I shifted uncomfortably on my chair, wishing to hear no more upon Orning's personal tribulations. The more I knew on his past the more he would turn against me when he became sober again.

'I beg you, Governor, wait until the summer,' I interrupted. 'Call an appeal judge from Copenhagen. Let us have a retrial when the days are brighter, longer—'

'It's too late,' he said. 'The fires are being built for the two witches Zigri Sigvaldsdatter and Solve Nilsdatter as we speak. They will burn on the morrow.'

My heart was thumping in my chest with horror at the thought. 'And what of Widow Krog?'

'Ah, yes, well, remember, she never confessed.'

'Where is she?'

'Where she belongs,' he said, glaring at me with such ferocity, I was silenced. 'Get out of my sight,' he said, dismissing me with his hand. 'I no longer wish to look at your wrinkled face and old hag's breasts,' he slurred, eyes glimmering dangerously. 'Bring me my wife. Where is Elisa?'

'But the *girls*—'

'It is done, woman, cease your pestering! Two soldiers have gone to Russia to get more wood for their fires. They will burn within the week, and we will be rid of all these witches and their gets by the time the fishermen return.'

'No, your honour, I beg you—' I entreated.

'Desist from your haranguing!' The governor flared at me. 'Remove your person from my presence before I throw you in the witches' hole too.'

I rose from his wife's chair, my whole body rigid with anger. But it was clear to me no amount of begging would change the foul man's mind. I was powerless yet again, and the frustration it caused me made me want to scream great lungfuls of fury at him. I was overcome with a desire, for one fleeting moment, to be a true witch and curse him to the hell he so deserved.

The governor may well have intuited my thoughts for he spoke to my back as I stalked out of his chamber.

'I shall have you bridled, Fru Rhodius, if you do not learn to hold your tongue. Be careful, mistress, for none are above the temptations of the Dark Lord!'

*

Outside, damson clouds filled the sky as I stumbled across the courtyard, weighed down by my own impotence.

I could not bear to return to the longhouse and the accusing face of Kirsten, with her belief I had betrayed her; even though I would give all I had for her life.

Outside the witches' hole, Captain Hans was on his own, standing to attention. 'I am unable to allow you entry, Fru Rhodius,' he said, as soon as he saw me. 'Orders from the governor.'

'I know,' I said, in a low voice. 'But tell me, how fare the convicted women?'

'In great despair.' He sighed heavily. 'It is not my job to have an opinion, but . . .' He broke off and shook his head. 'We gave them our rumbullion. At least if they are near unconscious from drink, the poor wenches may suffer less.'

'When I was a young woman, a witch was put to the stake in Ribe, near where I grew up. They attached gunpowder to her so she would suffer less. It makes for a faster end.'

Captain Hans glanced up at the ammunition store above the witches' hole, reading my thoughts. 'I cannot take the gunpowder unless the governor orders it so. He wishes them to suffer.'

Damn Governor Orning. I would not let him hold sway, for if I could not save their lives, I could make the women's ends an easier one.

I bent down and ripped at the hem of my skirt. It had occurred to me to bribe the governor, but his broken pledge had convinced me he would merely take what was mine and give me nothing back. I felt around the hem and pulled out three large pearls my mother had given me when I had left home all those years ago to be a wife.

I held out the pearls in the palm of my hand and offered them to the captain.

'When I became a soldier in the king's army, I believed I would be fighting the Swedish. An enemy I could see, and it would be fair and square,' he said, his eyes grave and sorrowful. 'But this . . . these women . . . well, this is badly done, Fru Rhodius.'

Then he reached out and took the pearls from my outstretched palm.

Chapter 50

Ingeborg

The three of them were on the fortress walls. Ingeborg remembered the dream she had had in the witches' hole when they all took flight as birds. But this time she was with Maren and Kirsten. Her mother, Solve and Widow Krog were trapped below in the witches' hole with the death sentence upon them in the morning.

Ingeborg could see a group of three soldiers in the distance out on Stegelsnes, the jagged peninsula of the island jutting out into the sea. They were building two rickety towers of wood. She could not conceive of her mother being set upon one of them. Her mind was in a panicked spin. How could she save her?

She looked as far as she could see, hoping for the sight of Zare in his boat, but the water was empty of any vessels. For once still, lapping against the shores of the island. The afternoon was bright, the clouds angelic ruffles of white. Now the sun had at last returned, but it was unwelcome. They didn't want fair weather, because this would help the fires alight.

Why had Maren told them to come here? Were they going to try to climb down the fortress? But they'd no rope, and it was a long, long drop onto hard rocks below. It had been one thing to climb up, but she doubted she could get back down again. Besides, Kirsten certainly would not be able to manage it.

Well then, if she had to, she would leave her behind. Her little sister had betrayed her own family. She deserved what was coming her way.

'What are we doing up here?' She turned to Maren.

'I can only think of one way to stop the burnings tomorrow,' Maren said. 'We will conjure a storm. It will destroy the stakes, blow all the wood away. It will be so wild folk won't be able to open their doors.'

Anger and incredulity swept through Ingeborg. 'Is that it?' she asked, poking her finger into Maren's chest. 'All these weeks, on and on you're saying about our power and how they can't hurt us! All you have is a stupid folktale spell!'

'It's not a folktale,' Maren said, her voice calm and her eyes gleaming. 'It's a spell my mother taught me.'

'And what good did it do her?' Ingeborg screeched. 'Your mother was burnt at the stake!'

Her words flew out of her mouth, savage and jagged. She saw Maren flinch as if struck and regretted them immediately.

Maren Olufsdatter was touched in the head. Her outburst in the trial hall made that clear, but then, the thing with the rats? Well, that *had* been strange. And Maren's words had infused her with passion: Ingeborg had let rip and in the moment it had felt good. But she was consumed with guilt now. She had made matters worse for her mother. And for them all.

'What is the spell?' Kirsten spoke for the first time since the verdict.

'We each hold a corner of a napkin and tie a knot in it, and then speak the words together,' Maren told them. 'Then we release it to the wind at the same time.'

'But there are only three of us, and we have no napkin,' Ingeborg said, sourly.

'Ah, no, there are four of us,' Maren said. 'Here she comes now.'

Maren smiled in a way she had used to smile at her when they first met. Ingeborg turned to see the governor's wife, Elisa Orning, climbing the stairs of the fortress.

She looked different from when she had seen her in court. Her pearly hair fell loose about her shoulders, and her skin was free from the waxy white paste. There were red pox scars upon her cheeks, but her eyes were bright. Elisa was smiling back at Maren.

When she caught sight of Kirsten, she flung her arms around the girl. Ingeborg was annoyed at the intimate action of a stranger. She herself had not touched her sister since the trial.

'You poor lamb,' Elisa spoke to Kirsten, trailing her fingers through the red curls.

Kirsten's lips trembled, and her eyes filled with tears. 'I was tricked,' she whispered, in a hoarse voice.

'I told you to say nothing,' Ingeborg snapped at her sister. Kirsten had always been able to make everyone feel sorry for her. 'How could you have said those things?'

'I did believe them. *She* persuaded me.'

Fru Anna Rhodius. The traitor. Promising to help them, but she had only been out to help herself.

'Come,' Maren said. 'We don't have much time. The governor will look for Elisa soon. Now is our chance.'

Elisa produced a white linen napkin from her pocket and handed it to Maren. Each of them took a corner and tied a knot in it.

They were all so close together now. A tightly knit square of four girls.

'Now, hold your knot with your left hand and raise the arm into the sky,' Maren told them. 'Repeat after me: "I summon the wind in the name of Liren Sand and all before her and all after her."'

The three other girls said the line, and continued repeating them after Maren said them, as bid, as she continued.

'"I summon the rain in the name of the spirits of the sky and the sea. I summon the hail in the name of the great blue whale, she who sings for our redemption from the depths of the seas. I summon the storm in the name of the clouds to assault all men who would harm us." Now let go.'

Ingeborg expected the napkin to flop back down onto the fortress walls, for she couldn't feel a breath of wind, but to her surprise it lifted into the air. As if a puff of air had been sent just for the spell, the napkin took off like a miniature white sail. They watched it float away across the island, past the soldiers building the stakes, and out to sea. They watched it until it was a tiny speck and then no more.

They waited. But nothing happened. Not a whisper of wind upon their cheeks.

Tears of disappointment began to choke Ingeborg's throat. How stupid to put her trust in one of Maren's spells.

'Where's the storm, then, Maren?' She turned on her.

Maren folded her hands and looked at her with sage-green eyes. 'It will come.'

In the middle of the night, Ingeborg crept back outside the longhouse. The full moon bathed the courtyard with a silvery light. The sky was clear of clouds, filled with stars. There was her northern star, but she felt too angry to look upon it. There was no hint of a storm. No hope.

She crept up to the side of the witches' hole. If only she could break her mother out. She tore at the gnarled wood, breaking her nails until her fingers bled, but all she could do was rip one small hole in the rotten wood.

She crouched down, pressed her head against the wall. 'Mother!' she whispered. 'Mother!'

'Ingeborg!' Her mother's fingers squeezed out of the crack and Ingeborg clutched onto them.

'Oh, Mother!' She didn't know what to say. All she could do was lie on her belly and kiss her mother's dirty, broken fingers.

'Hush, hush.' Her mother soothed in a voice so gentle it almost didn't sound like her at all.

'I don't know what to do, Mamma.'

'You have done all you could,' her mother said in a broken voice. 'This I brought on myself.'

'No, no.'

'Tell me, what has happened to my baby?' her mother whispered, and Ingeborg could hear her voice full of tears.

'She's with Reverend Jacobsen's wife,' Ingeborg said, repeating what Fru Rhodius had told her earlier.

'Good, she will be safe with them.'

Ingeborg knew what her mother meant. Safe from being branded a witch's get, maybe.

'And Kirsten? How is she?'

Ingeborg said nothing, just drew in her sobbing breath.

'Ask her to forgive me,' her mother whispered.

'But it is she who needs to ask for your forgiveness—'

'No, Ingeborg. She's a little girl, and you know how hard I was on her – on you too, but you are older.'

'She said—'

'Listen, maybe Heinrich Brasche *was* the Devil.' Her mother's voice broke again. 'For I fell for his lies. He professed love for me, and I was so blind I believed him. But my sin was great, Ingeborg. It is not Kirsten's fault.'

Tears dripped off Ingeborg's chin. It was too much to imagine what would happen the next day. How could she bear it?

'Look after Kirsten,' her mother said. 'Promise me.'

'I can't.'

'Ingeborg, she didn't know what she was doing.' Her mother sighed heavily. 'I have betrayed you both too. The bailiff crushed my thumbs on my other hand, and the pain, Ingeborg . . . he made me say I sold you both to the Devil. I am sorry, my love—'

Her words stung Ingeborg like cold water.

'I drank some rumbullion the soldiers got us. Solve had most of it, but it still hurts so much.'

'Mother, did you denounce us?'

Silence. Ingeborg still clasped her mother's hand, but her heart grew colder. She thought of Widow Krog – what had happened to the old woman? – how she had kept repeating: *I will not tell a lie on myself or another woman.* But her mother, Solve, and Kirsten all had. They would all die for it.

She let go of her mother's hand.

'Ingeborg, Inge, please, forgive me?' Her mother's voice was terrified, her fingers reaching out for Ingeborg again.

What would she have done in the same place as her mother? How much pain would she have endured before she broke? She was in no place to judge. She took her mother's hand back in hers.

'We will meet in God's kingdom, my love, because I have made my repentance and none of us are going to Hell,' her mother whispered softly.

Ingeborg clasped her mother's hand in hers. Held on tight, next to the dank building. They hung on to each other all night, halfway between the witches' hole and the world outside. As the hours passed, the little tabby kitten found her and curled up by her side.

As the fragile pink of dawn seeped up into such a soft day, Ingeborg felt wretched. Where was the storm Maren had promised?

Chapter 51

Anna

The soldiers marched the four of us – myself, Maren, Ingeborg and Kirsten – in a miserable straggle from the longhouse down the hill from the fortress to the execution site, Stegelsnes. As we made our way across wet, heavy snow, the girls in their old reindeer skin boots and I in pattens, we squelched in thick mud where it had melted.

None of the girls would look at me, though the soldiers kept us close. Not one of us spoke, for the dread of what was to come had snatched our voices from us.

The sea was choppy, the colour of ashes, and the Domen did not look to be a real mountain, but more a shadow or a cloud. The rising sun was a golden orb, pushing forth from behind clouds of plum, and thunder grey. In the distance, as the sea grazed the ice-encrusted shores of Domen, the mist flared as a sizzling steam, as if the ice burned.

My eyes were reluctantly drawn to the two piles of stacked wood, and the ladders, ready for the condemned. The soldiers ordered us to stand in a row facing the stakes, and we were not allowed to move.

All of us waited and watched as the witches were brought across the raging Arctic sea from the fortress in boats. The mood was different from Widow Krog's water ordeal, for the islanders who had gathered were dressed in black, heads covered and bowed. Such silence, for the only sound was the soft lap of the sea, the sound of the rowing boats, and the cawing of seagulls and crows circling above.

Governor Orning got out of the first boat, his furs flung about his upright figure, and he took long strides in the soggy snow, his two wolf-hounds straining on leashes. His slight wife stepped out after him, a hood pulled up over her head, but I caught a glance of her face with its blackened eye and cut lip, all of which she had tried to conceal with the chalky paste thick upon her scarred skin.

Reverend Jacobsen followed, dressed in his black cassock, with a cloak of heavy black wool and a woollen hat upon his head.

The two condemned women were hauled out of the boats: Solve Nilsdatter and Zigri Sigvaldsdatter. Only their hands were tied now, and they were dressed in jackets and skirts. They'd managed to clean their faces, though their hair hung lank and unkempt. Strangely Widow Krog was not with them, and I shivered for her fate.

I heard the sobs of Kirsten next to me, although Ingeborg remained silent. As I tried to take Kirsten's hand, she sidled away. Oh, how it broke my heart.

As Reverend Jacobsen led us in prayer, Solve kept looking about her, eyes scanning the crowd, the sea, across to the mainland, flitting this way and that as if she were in great distraction. Captain Hans must have filled both her and Zigri with rumbullion again, for they were both swaying, and I prayed they might fall into oblivion before the end.

'Repent your evil pact with the Devil. We shall pray that the Good Lord takes you to him,' Reverend Jacobsen droned.

Neither cousin prayed, nay, they gaped at Reverend Jacobsen in disbelief, unable to comprehend what was about to unfold.

As the reverend led everyone in a prayer, Lockhert clambered from out of the last boat. Behind him, two soldiers dragged the corpse of Widow Krog. The old woman's pale grey tattered skirt and her weathered hands hung limp, and when I caught sight of her face it was black from a beating, her eyes bloodied as if they'd been gouged out. Nausea rose violent and sudden as I swallowed down bile.

'See, a witch cannot escape her fate under my authority,' the governor warned the horrified islanders. 'I will hunt you all, and I will purge the north of this evil.' He pointed at Widow Krog's cadaver. 'Let this evil hag's fate be a lesson to you all.'

One of the soldiers tied some rope around Widow Krog's hands and they dragged her through the execution site as if she was no more than a hunting trophy. Under the orders of Lockhert, the body was laid upon a rock facing the sea and would remain there, I imagined, until the gulls had pecked the bones of all her flesh.

Having witnessed this atrocity, the governor ordered the two women Solve and Zigri to be bound to their ladders. They were both shaking in terror – I have never seen such fear. I wished to scream at the governor, but I was powerless.

My king, tell me, what should I have done?

Both resisted, of course, and Solve appeared to sober up, panic shining in her eyes.

'Your honour, my husband might come yet,' she begged. 'He will return from fishing, and he will speak for me.'

'Your husband's gone to sea for many weeks. Besides, he will thank me for ridding him of a foul witch who fornicates with the Devil,' the governor hissed at Solve.

'Lord have mercy on my soul, it's not true.' Solve broke from Lockhert's grasp and stumbled towards me, reaching out with one bruised and battered arm, while the other hung uselessly at her side. 'I am no witch, and nor is my cousin! Tell them!'

Maren lunged out of our row and grabbed her aunt's bloody hand. 'We are with you, we are with you, Aunty.'

'Oh, Maren, beautiful girl, take care of my boys—'

Lockhert wrenched Solve away from Maren and began to bind her to one of the ladders.

'My boys!' she sobbed. 'My poor babies!'

'Your sons will never speak of you again,' the governor admonished her. 'Their shame will be too great.'

'No!' Solve struggled against Lockhert.

Governor Orning ordered Captain Hans to light the fire. I caught the captain's eye, and he gave me an imperceptible nod. I prayed all would go as planned and the women's suffering would be short.

Have you witnessed a witch-burning, my king? Do you know how excruciating it is to wait for the flames to build so the fire is high enough to lower the women in? For the governor would not risk that they might suffocate first on the smoke; no, he had to ensure their flesh was aflame.

I turned to Kirsten. 'Close your eyes.' I begged her.

But the girl was looking up at the sky, as were her sister and Maren.

I followed their gaze and saw that the number of birds around us had multiplied into a great whirl of seagulls and crows. Black and white, wheeling and cawing around and around, while clouds had begun to gather fast. I felt a rain drop upon my brow, and then another. The wind whistled down the island as if it called to us.

The flames licked higher and, sensing the change in the weather, the governor ordered the men to lower the sobbing women into the flames. Both had soiled themselves and were screaming in terror.

It will soon be over. I spoke to them in my head, crossing myself.

And then, out of nowhere, a bolt of lightning flashed across the island, and the heavens opened. Hail pounded down upon us, pushing into the gathering so hard that some of the islanders were knocked over.

'Mother!' I heard Ingeborg scream out as her mother's ladder was lowered into the flames, but the hail was buffeting the fire.

Miraculously, it was putting it out.

'Solve!' Ingeborg's mother called out. 'We are together, cousin.'

'Zigri!' her cousin called back. 'Forever!'

As I watched, Solve pulled her good arm free from the bonds. Before our eyes, she began to free herself from her ladder.

'Tie the witch back down!' Orning barked at Lockhert.

The bailiff straddled the bottom of the fire, which must have been burning through his breeches, but he hated the witches so much he clearly cared not. He reached forward and pushed Solve back, but her good arm shot out and she grabbed on to his wrist. He tried to shake her loose, but she was as a dog with a bone, and seemed to possess supernatural strength as her fingers clamped around his.

'Let go, witch!' he screeched, panic seeping into his voice, for the heat was clearly touching his skin now.

'Never!'

Upon the last utterance of Solve Nilsdatter, the gunpowder that I had purchased for them, strapped by Captain Hans inside their jackets, ignited. All it took was one random spark from the fire and a resounding explosion.

Kirsten let out a gut-wrenching scream, while Ingeborg yelled, 'No!'

Maren ran towards the blast but was thrown back by a second explosion as a ball of fire shot up into the sky, the ground shook and we fell upon it.

The two mothers of Ekkerøy and Bailiff Lockhert, within one heartbeat, were turned to fragments as their flesh blew apart; the women at last free and according to my intention – fast and without pain.

Lockhert . . . well, it is true, my king – I am not sorry the vile oaf is on his way to Hell.

As I shakily got to my feet, I could see the governor was furious for this was not the begging, slow torture of two witches burning that he had foreseen. It was a rebellious end, and his precious henchman gone too. Violent hail fell drenching the fires to a slow fizzle, before stopping as quickly as it came.

But before the governor could order his soldiers to do aught, he was knocked off his feet by a rush of wind. As he gathered himself up again, the whirling mass of crows and seagulls above us drove down towards him. He flayed around with his arms, trying to beat them off, letting go of the leashes of his two dogs.

'Get them off me!' he yelled at Captain Hans, but the s and his small troop stood quite still watching the spectacle, as did all the island of Vardø.

The great swirl of birds was only attacking one man, the tall governor of Finnmark.

'I order you to get these fucking birds away!' Orning shrieked, battling the birds off as they pecked the flesh of his hands, and his face, pocking him with blood. He took out his pistol and waved it wildly in the air, but a large black crow swooped and knocked it out of his hand.

'Help me!' he screeched at the soldiers, but still, they didn't move. He let out a low whistle and his dogs pricked their ears and trotted towards him.

'Kill!' he screamed at his dogs, but the two wolfhounds simply cocked their heads and watched the birds attacking his master. Orning kicked one of his dogs with his leg, and it was then that I heard a piercing call above the howl of the dog.

Maren Olufsdatter glided towards the wolfhounds, crouching down, placing one hand on each dog's head, whispering between them into pricked ears, then she stepped back and watched.

The dogs leapt forward, but not to aid their master. They tore the cape off him, and the breeches off his legs, as Orning kicked out at them. Then they leapt up and tore at his doublet. They ripped the clothing from him until he was naked, and then the dogs began on his flesh.

'Shoot them!' he screamed, as the dogs ravaged him.

We all watched. He had made us bear witness to the end of two innocent women, and thus he had sealed his own fate. I, for one, was not taking one small step forwards to help him.

'Shoot them!' he kept shouting, as he tried to beat off the demented birds and his own dogs, but though Captain Hans's musket was cocked, he did nothing.

The first to act was Elisa Orning, as she stumbled over to her husband's pistol where it lay next to the smouldered earth, picking it up and cocking it.

'Elisa, shoot the bloody dogs!' her husband bellowed. And despite his struggle with the swooping birds, and the attacking dogs, I could see a little victory in his eyes, for he believed his wife still under his thumb.

Elisa Orning fired the pistol. I have no idea how she knew what to do, but the gun went off as loud as a cannon. She appeared to train the pistol on one of the dogs, but then stumbled, I was not sure whether with intention, for her aim changed to the brow of her husband. A neat redness flared upon it as he dropped like a stone, heavy, cold and hard, like the man he had been.

Now the wind abated.

The fires were still flickering and ashes heaping where once two women, and their tormentor, had been.

Maren Olufsdatter clicked her fingers and the birds spun up into the air and were gone. Then she walked over to Fru Orning and took the smoking pistol from her hand as she stared at her husband's dead body as if in a trance. The wolfhounds sat on their hind legs and licked where their master had kicked them.

Silence spread as the death on Vardø echoed beyond that jagged piece of rock. The rest of us stood in shocked union, smelling and tasting the tang of fire and burnt flesh on our tongues, eyes smarting with smoke, skin stinging from the icy hail. We waited for what would come next; and it was rain, drenching us all, so that for some our tears became mixed into the earth and mud beneath our feet.

The first to break our trance of horror was Maren Olufsdatter. She took her cloak off and laid it upon the prostrate body of Widow Krog where she lay exposed upon the rock. Ingeborg Iversdatter fell upon the ashes of the fire calling for her mother to no avail. She pulled something from it, and then with a grim expression got to her feet and walked towards the edge of Stegelsnes, staring out to sea.

I stood with Kirsten by my side, the child whimpering with shock and distress, and my heart and head was in tumult at what I had just witnessed. Ingeborg turned around and walked towards us, reaching out her hand to Kirsten.

Panic filled me as I grabbed Kirsten's other hand and pulled her back. I could not give her up, for she was all I had left.

Chapter 52

Ingeborg

After, ever after, Ingeborg Iversdatter could not return to memories of the day her mother burned without keeling over. Even she, the most stoic girl in the whole of Finnmark, could not bear to think upon it. Grief came in great waves, like the big storm that had assaulted them that day. Her loss was always present, washing over her, as constant as the ocean tides.

Governor Orning had ordered the captain of the soldiers to point his musket at the girls and make them look. But she had promised her mother she would in any case. From the very first, she had held her mother's terrified gaze though Ingeborg's instinct begged her to look away. She didn't look down to the first lick of flames at the bottom of the funeral pyre, nor did she comfort Kirsten when she heard her sob. She cradled the peace of the Holy Spirit and she brought it to her mother's eyes. 'I will stay with you to the end,' she had promised.

Everything happened so fast. The clear blue skies had melted away to be replaced by black storm clouds, and the sea turned black too, crested with glaring white. The wind blew from the east pushing into them. Sparks from the fire flew hither and thither. One landed on Reverend Jacobsen's cassock which he put out with panicked, flapping hands.

Maren had been right. They had made this storm. Hope surged through Ingeborg as hail battered into them, the white fury of the heavens opening as they were stoned by giant shards of ice. A crack of lightning, a boom of thunder, another boom. If it turned to rain it would put the fires out.

But something else had happened. Flares of flames, Lockhert falling into the fire and howling like a bear caught in a trap. Kirsten screaming as Ingeborg saw her mother ignite despite the storm. Another boom as a ball of fire flared into the sky, the ground shook and they fell upon it, knocked about.

When Ingeborg stumbled to her feet the hail had stopped, but she was in a maelstrom of white ashes and flapping birds. The sound of the squawks came as if very far away, there was a ringing in her ears, and her heart thumped loudly in her head. She staggered forwards, aware now of the governor in the middle of the conflagration of birds. But the wolf inside the dogs called to her, and she watched them take her revenge.

She must reach her mother. But only then did Ingeborg see she was gone.

She fell down upon her knees and pushed her hands into the hot ashes. How fast the fire had flared. Too late the storm had put them out. Maren's magic had been for naught.

Her fingers were burned but she didn't care. She was hunting for her mother. A part of her, even if it was bone. A tiny fragment of sacred blue poked out of the grey. She pulled out the charred ribbon and clutched it in her blistered palm.

The air beat around her, and she looked up to see an eagle soaring above her. Zare's words about the eagle being a messenger came back to her. Wiping her eyes with her sleeves, she got up from her knees, still gripping the blue ribbon. The eagle flew away, forcing her to look past the ashes, further across the water to Domen, and beyond Stegelsnes.

The great bird disappeared into the distance, but she could still see as if from its eyes. Flying over the Sámi lands, the *vidda*, and on to their forests and mountains. Herds of reindeer running beneath her.

The breath of her freedom passed through her. No longer cold or wet, but light with warmth.

The sea was bathed with a rosy hue, and Domen's snow-covered peak emerged from within its green crown. At the mountain's base, she could see black caves, gaping holes to a place of no return. Ingeborg closed her eyes and listened to the sea's swell against Vardø island.

When she opened her eyes again, the sky was shot through with simmering reds and a deep, lonesome mauve. It began to rain as a rainbow arched above the water.

Beneath it, Ingeborg saw a small Sámi boat buffeted upon the choppy sea, coming closer and closer to the island.

Ingeborg kept her stinging eyes on Zare's *bask* slipping through curtains of soft rain, scudding towards them. There was his broad figure in his blue and red *gákti*, with his four winds hat upon his fine black hair. She imagined his keen eyes seeking her out.

Ingeborg held the blue ribbon in one burnt hand, and the other clutched the cold fingers of her sister as she dragged her along through the smoky mist and ash-laden rain. She ignored Anna Rhodius and her plea to Kirsten. She wanted to forget the woman, with her false promises of help, had ever existed.

She turned around once for Maren. She was standing on the other side of the burnt stakes. Her night-black hair was streaming in the wind, ashes filming her dark skin. A black crow perched on her shoulder.

'Are you coming?' Ingeborg called to her.

But Maren shook her head. 'I have other plans.'

She was a wild, strange girl. Everyone knew she was a witch, the daughter of Liren Sand, the most fearsome witch there had ever been. But what Ingeborg saw in Maren was not a hint of wickedness. She saw so much more. Empathy, deep knowing, and resilience. And, yes, she possessed the power she had spoken of so many times.

Maren slipped her arm around the governor's wife, Fru Orning, who had dropped her pistol on the ground. There was the governor dead at her feet. Ingeborg felt nothing at all when she saw him lying in a pool of his own blood, seagulls pecking at his snowy hair.

'See you in the next life, Ingeborg and Kirsten Iversdatter!' Maren called out to them as if it was an ordinary goodbye. As if a dead man did not lie between them.

The two wolfhounds sat waiting for Ingeborg behind their dead master. She called their Sámi names – 'Beaivenieida! Gumpe!' – and they leapt up, following her and Kirsten to the cove.

Zare had come. She had doubted he would, but he was waiting for her in his cousin's *bask* as it bobbed up and down in the tiny cove they had arrived in all those long, dark weeks ago. She and Kirsten climbed into the small vessel while Beaivenieida and Gumpe leapt in too.

343

She was grateful he asked no questions. The plumes of smoke rising from Stegelsnes and the silvery ashes frosting Kirsten's hair, flaked on her own skin, was enough to tell him.

When Zare saw her burnt hands, he cried out in alarm.

'It doesn't hurt,' she whispered, tucking the blue ribbon into her pocket.

He grabbed her wrists and plunged her hands into the icy water. The shock of the cold brought tears to her eyes. The first since her mother had died.

Ingeborg looked down at the water's glimmering surface, lucent ripples expanding outwards.

'Are you all right, Inge?' Kirsten asked, crouching next to her. Hand upon her back.

'Yes,' she snapped, pushing her away with her hip.

'My mother will heal your hands,' Zare said. 'But they will hurt until we reach her.'

'Where are we going?' Ingeborg asked.

'A long way from here,' Zare said. 'I will put up the sail for the wind is in our favour and then when we get to where the snow still lies thick we will ski. My mother is hidden far inland where the king's men can never find her.' He pulled her hands out of the water and took off his embroidered belt, wrapping the raw red flesh with it.

She sat huddled in the boat as Zare attended to the sail. Beaivenieida and Gumpe sprawled at her feet, as if sensing the pain of her hands. She watched Zare pulling on the ropes, his body strong and power surging through his arms. She listened to the splash as the small boat cut through the Varanger Straits back to the mainland.

Zare had returned for her.

Longing swept through her whole being, shocking her with its force. He turned, and Ingeborg looked into his eyes. They hid nothing of his love for her. She wanted Zare to embrace her, calming the storm that had raged within her since the day Governor Orning had put it there. Soothing the jagged loss of her mother.

The rain stopped, but there was still a strong breeze. The sail billowed as they darted across the deep water.

'Forgive me, sister,' Kirsten murmured.

She was opposite Ingeborg, knees drawn up to her chest, pale skin gleaming like the inside of a shell; her eyes were faraway blue.

Ingeborg shook her head. She couldn't say the words, *I forgive you*, not yet. But she had brought her sister with her. Kirsten must see this was enough for now.

'Can I tell you a story?' Kirsten asked in a gentle voice. 'It might take your thoughts away from the pain in your hands.'

Ingeborg shrugged. Nothing could take away the whipping agony of loss in her heart.

But her sister crouched holding on to the side of the boat as the ocean began to swell and they rolled from side to side.

'Once a fisher girl was walking along by the seashore collecting mussels for her mother. But no matter how hard she looked, under every rock, in every pool of seawater, she could find not one closed blue shell. All of them had been opened, and all of them were empty. A great scattering of seashells was washed up upon the soft sand. She hunted for all manner of things to bring to her mother to eat but nothing could be found. Not a straggle of seaweed, not one tiny crab.'

Ingeborg remembered those days, not even a year ago, when she and Kirsten had wandered the crescent-moon beach of their village of Ekkerøy seeking sustenance. They had been so close, living in each other's breath.

'As the early spring day came to a close, the sky was filled with the most beautiful shades of cloudberry orange and raspberry pink. Deep luxurious blue seeped from the sea into the sky and the fisher girl forgot she was hungry,' Kirsten continued. 'She forgot her mother and her sister and her little baby lamb all waiting for their dinner at home. She immersed herself in the blue hour, the time between day and night. She opened her mouth and filled herself with blue, her tummy no longer aching with hunger. The blue sang to her. It was a lullaby she had never heard before. For her own mother had never sung to her.'

Kirsten paused and closed her eyes. Then she began to sing.

'*Rock a bye baby, upon the seashore,*
Rock a bye baby, upon the seashore,

When I rise up from the depths, climb on my back,
and then rock a bye baby, will be sad no more.'

Kirsten opened her eyes and looked at Ingeborg. But Ingeborg would not hold her gaze. She looked away at the ocean parting between the prow of the boat.

'The fisher girl was bewitched by the beautiful song rising from the sea, because she was very sad.' Kirsten began to speak again. 'Ever since her father and her brother had drowned in the ocean, far, far away from their rocky peninsula, she had cried herself to sleep every night. Ashamed to show her tears to her mother and her sister who worked so hard to be brave. But the little fisher girl was tired of missing her papa. She longed to sit on his lap and listen to his fisherman tales once more. She longed to smell the salty tang of sea upon him, and she longed to feel his strong fingers tickling her soft skin under her chin, laughing as love shined at her from his eyes.'

Ingeborg felt the weight in her heart. All lost, her father and brother, and now her mother. She turned to look at Kirsten. Her pale cheeks were flushed by two little spots of pink.

'The little fisher girl listened to the lullaby and as she did so a huge blue island rose from within the sea. But it wasn't a blue island. It was a great whale. She took off her boots and her heavy woollen skirt, and her dirty old coif, and she waded into the icy waters. But she did not feel cold, although her skin turned mauve. She swam out to sea and climbed upon the whale's back. The whale flicked its tail and sprayed the fisher girl with sparkling clear water. It spattered her face and she felt as if baptised again. Down the whale dived into the ocean with the fisher girl holding on to her back.'

Ingeborg had longed to see a whale such as this, and had dreamed of their singing, just as her father had told her.

'The whale took her down, down into the deepest depths, past shoals of silvery fish, swaying plants and wreaths of seaweed and polyps. Past sparkling coral, and deep dark caves. They swam by a giant black octopus which reached out its long tentacles to her like eight writhing snakes. Starfish shone golden in the midnight-blue depths, and on the great whale swam.'

Under the sea. Was this what it looked like? Ingeborg closed her eyes and imagined the kingdom beneath their rocking boat.

'At last, they came to a town at the bottom of the ocean,' Kirsten continued. 'All the houses were made out of pearly white shells and gleamed in the lights of the water. The fisher girl climbed off the back of the big whale and waded through the town. And as she went, she met all the folk lost in the wild northern seas: Widow Krog's husband, Peder; Maren's father, the Barbary pirate; fishermen and merchants alike, living in the same white houses and sharing all they had. She even saw the family of Bailiff Lockhert with their red hair just like hers, and Scottish freckles upon their skin. In the last house, the fisher girl was filled with great joy for there was her father and her brother, Axell. Together in peace under the sea.'

'Oh!' Ingeborg said, her eyes filling with tears at the idea of it.

'Yes, they were, Ingeborg!' Kirsten continued. 'The fisher girl flung her arms around both of them. They were just as happy to see her and invited her to sit with them and eat all that she could. They had plenty of food. Creamy porridge, crispy *flatbrød*, salted herrings and sweet berries.'

Ingeborg felt the edge of a smile upon her face. It soothed her broken heart to think her father and Axell lived within a watery realm where they wanted for nothing.

'The house was filled with all the things her brother Axell had ever desired: crystals and stones from lands afar, sugar and spices from the east, a little seahorse to play with, and row upon row of seagulls' eggs.'

Seagulls' eggs. Ingeborg's smile faded. That was how it had all started: Kirsten had smashed the eggshells and brought the witches.

But Kirsten blithely carried on telling her story, with no shame. '"We should smash them," the fisher girl said, remembering how cross her mother had been when she found the shells she had kept. "The witches will get into them, use them as boats and stir up a storm."

'But her father laughed, and so did Axell.

'"There is no such thing as witches" Axell said.

'"But the Devil does exist," her father warned her, his brows knitting. "And he has your mother in his grip."'

Ingeborg felt rage flaring within her. 'I won't have you say another word against Mamma, Kirsten!'

But Kirsten was no longer looking at her, as if she was lost inside the telling of her story and she couldn't stop. Ingeborg glanced at Zare but he was busy keeping them on course. Ingeborg was the story's only audience.

'The little fisher girl had been so happy to find her father and brother but now she remembered her mother and sister who were back home waiting for her, and hungry.

'"Will you return with me?" she asked.

'Her father shook his head, and so did her brother.

'"We belong at the bottom of the sea," her father told her. "We can't breathe above water."

'"I don't want to leave you," the little fisher girl said, beginning to sob.

'"When the time is right, whale mother will come for you again," her father said. "Close your eyes, little one." He stroked her head with his warm, worn hands and sang to her.'

Kirsten clasped her hands and raised her face to the northern skies as she sang.

'*Rock a bye baby, upon the sea's floor,*
Rock a bye baby, upon the sea's floor,
When you choose death over life, come back to me,
and then rock a bye baby will be sad no more.'

The rhyme wound around Ingeborg's heart as the blue ribbon had wound around her hand.

Kirsten signed, before continuing her story. 'When the little fisher girl opened her eyes, she was on the seashore, but it was night. The snow fell swirling from the sky, and the sea hissed against the ice. She ran all the way back to her village. Tumbled into her cottage. But when she got home her mother and sister were not there. She ran to the other cottages but when her neighbours saw her, they screamed in horror and slammed their doors in her face. What was wrong with her? And where were her mother and sister? Where was her baby lamb?'

Kirsten's voice cracked and she took a big breath. Ingeborg could see tears beginning to well in her sister's eyes. She felt an urge to comfort her and yet she was still so angry with her she could not move to do so.

'The little fisher girl walked all night on her own in the wilderness,' Kirsten continued. 'When she woke in the morning, she was outside the fortress on the island of Vardø. A great pool of frozen water was stretched out before her. Gazing into the ice, she saw a reflection of herself. She screamed in fright. Half of her was as she always had looked: a girl with red hair, pink cheeks and twilight-blue eyes, but the other half of her was a dreadful vision: the skin on that side of her face was scaly, like a fish, but rotting too; and her eye was misty white and sunken. The teeth on that side of her body were brown and broken, and the bone of her skull gleamed through her thin, papery skin. She stared and she stared, because she knew at once who she had become.'

Hel. Ingeborg remembered the story from the old religion Widow Krog had told them in the witches' hole, about Loki's daughter, Hel. She who was half alive and half dead. Queen of the kingdom of the lost dead. Those who had died of sicknesses, in childbirth, as infants or of old age. Those who had died without glory and were not allowed in the hallowed halls of Valhalla where all dead warriors went.

Ingeborg looked at Kirsten, and it was as if she saw an echo of Hel within her, one eye brimming with tears, but the second eye milky, unseeing. Ingeborg blinked and there was her Kirsten again. Both cheeks pink, both eyes bright with tears.

'The little fisher girl knocked on the fortress gates and they swung open,' Kirsten said, her voice shaking. 'When the soldiers saw her, they stepped back in fear, as did Bailiff Lockhert. Even the governor of the whole of Finnmark did not want to come close to her. All they could see was her dark side. When she unlocked the witches' hole and went inside, there was her mother, and her sister, among the others accused of witchcraft.' Kirsten clasped her trembling hands as tears continued to trail her cheeks. 'The little fisher girl told her mother she had come to save her, but her mother looked at her in disgust, for all she could see was the dead side of her little girl: the shadow half, the bad part of the fisher girl. She called to her sister, but she did not see her at all. Her sister's grief made her blind, and she was cleaving to their mother.

'"You can't save her, the Dark Lord has her in his grip," the little fisher girl told her sister. But she was deaf to her words too.

'Then the little fisher girl cried and the salt of her tears in the sunken eye rotted her skin further and made her smell. Even the women in the witches' hole didn't want her to stay with them.'

Ingeborg wished the story would stop now. It hurt too much to remember the witches' hole and the women within it who were no longer.

'No more, Kirsten,' she whispered. But another part of her didn't want Kirsten to end the story. She ached for a happy ending, although she sensed there was none.

'The little fisher girl went to the great hall of the castle and stood beneath shafts of pale moon that came through the high windows,' Kirsten said in a soft voice. 'She heard the echoes of her words all around her. The confusion of lies and truth. She had never felt so alone in her whole life. She closed her eyes, and she whispered' – Kirsten paused and looked into Ingeborg's eyes, her own swimming with tears – "*I choose death.*"'

The ocean surged around them as a gull called above, and the boat creaked. Ingeborg imagined she could hear, deep below, the watery echo of the great whale. Was this the end of the story?

But Kirsten took another breath, wiping the tears from her face with the back of her sleeve. 'When the fisher girl opened her eyes again, a woman in a silk gown was before her, and she began to sing. In her eyes, the woman only saw the pretty fisher girl, not the dead half.'

Ingeborg stiffened. The woman in the silk dress was Fru Rhodius and she had stolen her sister from her. Again, Kirsten began to sing, and this time her voice was as delicate as a tiny kitten's mewl.

'*Rock a bye baby, open the castle door,*
Rock a bye baby, open the castle door,
Let us go together into the depths, beyond sky and sea,
and then rock a bye baby will be sad no more.'

Ingeborg saw Kirsten as she was. Just a girl looking for a mother to love her. She dropped her head in shame. How could she be angry with her?

'The little fisher girl followed the woman in silk out of the castle door, out of the fortress gates, and all the way to the sea,' Kirsten told her. 'But the moon slipped behind a cloud, and the sky was black as pitch, and she could hardly find her way. So, she listened to the whale's lullaby, which came to her across the tender hush of the night waves.'

Kirsten sang again, and each word stuck like pins in Ingeborg's heart.

'*Rock a bye baby, upon the seashore,*
Rock a bye baby, upon the seashore,

When I rise up from the depths, climb on my back,
and then rock a bye baby will be sad no more.'

'I'm sorry,' Ingeborg mumbled, her head bowed as she drew up her knees.

But Kirsten didn't hear her, for she was lost in the telling of her tale. 'When the moon slipped back out again, the woman in silk was gone, but the fisher girl's baby lamb stood before her. Bleating with love.'

Kirsten clapped her hands, and Ingeborg looked up. A ray of sunlight had broken free from the clouds and was showering her sister. Kirsten's red hair was a crown of red and gold upon her head. It made her look beatific, as if she were adorned with a glorious halo.

'Kirsten?' Ingeborg knelt towards her.

But her sister put out her hand in warning. 'Let me finish the story,' she said. 'The little fisher girl picked up her lamb and cradled it in her arms, waiting by the gentle ocean. The great whale came to the surface once more, and the girl waded out to sea.' Kirsten wiped away the last of her tears. 'The fisher girl turned back once, with her dead side. Looked at the castle and saw a great fire. Flames shooting up into the sky, the snow sizzling with sparks. As she heard the cries of the women, the part of her which was dead became ashes and scattered upon the still sea.'

'Inge,' Kirsten beseeched. 'They were hoary petals of guilt, sorrow and regret.'

'I'm sorry,' whispered Ingeborg again, but still Kirsten did not seem to hear her. Her eyes were glazed as if she looked far away, as she continued to speak.

'The little fisher girl turned her back to the land and clambered once more upon the great whale,' Kirsten said, before turning to look at the sea. Ingeborg caught her words as they drifted between them. 'The little fisher girl was whole again. Yes, she was. Her skin rosy, and both her eyes blue with the promise of the eternal love of her father, forever.'

Why, oh why, had Ingeborg not seen it coming?

Before her very eyes, Kirsten slipped over the side of the boat.

'No!' Ingeborg reached out, while the dogs began barking, and Zare called out in alarm.

Kirsten's red curls were floating upwards, but her dark woollen clothes were filling with water and dragging her down. Her big eyes were moons of hopelessness as she sunk beneath the waves.

Ingeborg hung over the side of the boat grabbing for her sister, but Kirsten crossed her hands over her chest and let the sea pull her down.

'Kirsten!' she screamed.

Zare was by her side. 'I can't swim!' Ingeborg cried out, but he had already dropped into the water.

Now waves washed over both of them.

Ingeborg pressed her burnt hands to her heart, no longer feeling their throbbing pain. The dogs were restless at her side, intuiting her distress. Licking her hands to soothe her.

Ingeborg was distraught. Kirsten was only just thirteen years of age. little older than Axell when he had drowned. Why had she been so hard on her?

Ingeborg held her breath, not caring what direction the wind took the boat in as the sail flapped above her head, in beat to her panic. Had she lost them both?

But, at last, she saw Zare's head emerge, the hair black and gleaming. He swam over to the boat and hauled himself over the edge, almost capsizing them.

'She's gone,' he said, gulping for breath, icy water streaming down his face.

'No, no.' Ingeborg cried out as the dogs, in a frenzy, were licking Zare warm.

'I failed you—' Zare said, through chattering teeth.

'Never,' she interrupted, and pulled him to her with ferocity. He was shivering with the cold, and his wet skin was soaking her, but she was not letting go.

Chapter 53

Anna

News will have reached you long before this letter, if ever indeed you do chance to read it, of the strange happenings upon the island of Vardø on the seventh day of April in the year of our Good Lord 1663. The king's will be done when two convicted witches were burnt at the stake, their suffering shortened by the use of gunpowder. But what of the storm? The tragedy was not lost on me, for if I hadn't meddled with the gunpowder, Solve Nilsdatter and Zigri Sigvaldsdatter might still be alive. The storm had drenched the fires and ruined the wood – but not in time to stop the explosion. There was Maren wringing her hands and asking what had happened to her aunt. My last sight of Solve Nilsdatter was her grip upon the bailiff's hand as she pulled him towards her, the two of them locked in a frenzied dance of death.

A litany of unexplainable occurrences my king: the storm, the hailstones, the birds, the wolfhounds, and the governor shot by his own wife.

Ah, but stranger still it appeared, as for a short time this small island of Vardø was not under the domain of men. Most of the islanders were fishermen's wives, and they melted away into their cottages, to stir their pots and try to forget the horrors they had witnessed. The soldiers, without the governor or his bailiff, were few and they laid down their arms in front of the tiny governor's wife, for everyone knew her father Rosencrantz was a very powerful man.

I had never paid much heed to Ingeborg Iversdatter for in my eyes she had been a victim, but I was wrong. The young woman, though diminutive, was as tough as flint. I will not forget the iron of her eyes as she pulled her sister Kirsten away from me.

'She is not yours,' she said, plain and simple.

I looked to Kirsten, my expression pleading, and the girl blinked back. Was she really of this world with her flame-red curls and freckled nose, and those eyes the blue of my deepest sorrow, an infinite well that I would never dip into again? There was a flicker of something in those eyes, but I could not be sure if it was love or hate. All I knew was Kirsten possessed some feeling towards me.

'I am not your girl, Fru Anna,' Kirsten said.

Her cool hand was between the grasp of my hot fingers, and my heart was beating urgently so I might faint.

'I am not your daughter but go home and you will find her.'

Her words made little sense, for how can I go home? My house in Bergen is many leagues away, far in the south-west of Norway, and inhabited by a husband I can never forgive for his betrayal.

You will know very well, my king, how Ambrosius forsook me, for it was his premonition I presented to you, written in his hand, warning you of Statholder Trolle. It was Ambrosius who claimed you would be deposed by your nobles within the year, not I. But when he was asked under oath, my husband lied. He looked straight into my eyes, his wife of near thirty years, and swore it was all my doing. I was the traitor, not he.

My husband Ambrosius is waiting in Bergen for news of my passing – I feel it. And then he will marry another, and she will give him the son he has always longed for.

Yes, my husband is done with me, my king, just as you are, for you both believe I am no longer of any value.

But this I will not believe, because *words* have value: my words and my story of a woman caught up in the violent witch panic of Vardø in the winter of 1662 and 1663. Ah, I do not doubt the scribes will scapegoat me, I am sure of it, and name me the witch hunter, but you know it is not so.

Ambrosius once said to me: *You must always be looking after others, Anna, and placing them before my needs.* He believed I longed to be a mother but my truth is, I longed to be a physician. Oh yes, in my heart,

I have always been a doctor. Yes, I lost my babies, and my daughter too, but I never lost my passion to heal. When Christina died, I did not run away from the plague, I ran into it.

A true physician possesses a calling to care for others before their own needs, and thus to be cast in posterity as a self-serving madwoman should not be my due.

I released Kirsten's hand for in the end I surrendered, and I let her go. I watched the two sisters walk away from the place where their mother's ashes swirled in the air around them. I had not a notion of where they were going, but I was glad none of the soldiers stopped them.

I climbed wearily back up the hill to Vardøhus and put my mind to write this letter to you and ask yet again for your pardon.

Let me be free too, my king.

The light was already leaching from the sky, and I stood for a moment looking out of the halibut flap window. I could see the ocean calm again, after the mysterious storm which had stopped as suddenly as it had started. The sky was deep mulberry, and the sun was sinking into the darkest of seas. I could hear the gentle hush of the waves lapping against the island, as the sea reflected the last blaze of daylight illuminating a pathway of gold across its rippled surface. There, for a heartbeat, was the hump of a big whale, a spurt of sparkling water shooting forth in the glittering evening light as the great beast sunk back beneath the surface. What a miracle the sight was! It brought such longing to me I felt tears trail my cheeks, for how many more years of exile must I endure before I can go home?

I took one of my precious lemons and cut it to make my invisible ink. I prepared one slice and shook a little of the sugar Kirsten had ground for me last night. My promises of our life in my beautiful house, her dresses, and the little dog mocked me as they tattered in my mind.

I took a small bite of my sugared lemon and it was not sugar upon my lips, for I have not worked as a physician my whole life not to possess this knowledge. Of course, the substance was tasteless, but I could tell by the texture. I got up and opened my medicine chest, picking up the small vial of arsenic. Every night it had been Kirsten's task to make the paste to conceal the mole upon my face. But she had been instructed to use the tiniest amount, yet the vial was empty.

I could have spat the lemon out for I still held it in my mouth but, my king, I did not. I chewed and swallowed the lethal lemon.

I am not your girl.

The words were written in the dust upon my longhouse floor, illuminated by a shaft of watery sunlight as the daylight sunk away.

Now I write fast, my script loose and wild, the letters tumbling into each other as I chase the light before shadows of night prevent me from writing all that I must to you. There is something you must know, for I have declared my love and loyalty to you time after time. This is true, but there is something, my king, you must understand, for to hurt one so loving, so loyal, is a crime. My dying wish is that you recall the last time we saw each other.

Let me remind you of the words you said before locking the chamber door.

Will you be quiet if I fuck you?

The vulgarity of your question shocked me into silence as you ordered me to turn around and bend over the end of the bed, so you wouldn't have to look at my face.

The most powerful man in the whole of our kingdom of Norway and Denmark ordered me to submit to him, and I said no.

'This is not what I want.'

'*Ti stille.* Be quiet,' you commanded.

'No, Frederick,' I said again.

You pushed me. '*Hold Kæft.* Shut your mouth. Shut up. Shut up. Shut up.'

You may have banished your shame as far away as you can, but I return it to you in this letter. May it rest heavy upon your conscience to your dying day.

I am done, my king. Yes, I shall sit in my satin dress the colour of my daughter's eyes at my little table in my longhouse prison, and I shall eat the rest of the lemon Kirsten laced with arsenic. Exactly one eighth of a teaspoon, just as I taught her.

It is a painful end, but brief. I shall vomit blood upon the ends of this parchment, and trail in blood with my finger your name: the Dark Lord.

Kirsten's words are rolling over in my mind, and truly I look forward to my place in Heaven when I can seat my girl upon my lap again and recite stories of baby Jesus and his infinite capacity for love and forgiveness.

I am not your daughter but go home and you shall find her.

It is strange, though, for it is not my laughing Christina's face before me now, as my ending draws in. It is Kirsten Iversdatter, the blue of her eyes staining her body blue. She is under the ocean, and she waves to me.

PART FIVE

'One characteristic of the lynx is that it never
looks back, but speeds on its course,
bounding without halt.'

Olaus Magnus,
Description of the Northern People, 1555

Chapter 54

Ingeborg

April 1665

The reindeer knew when it was time to move north. The pregnant females took the lead. As the *siida* broke up, Ingeborg and her family followed their reindeer out of the winter forests, making sure none were left behind on the plateau.

At times, as she moved between the narrow birch trunks, Ingeborg caught sight of an antlered woman at her side. She had long, curly red hair, which was tangled with thawing leaves, and fresh spring twigs. Flashing blue eyes. The horned woman was at one with the antlered female reindeer; part of where she was, just as was the clear spring air Ingeborg breathed. In one moment, the antlered woman's hair was as golden as the fledgling spring sun, and the sway of her hips was just as her mother's; at other times, her hair turned a deep red, burning as a sunset, and her shoulders narrowed to that of a girl's. Then she became Kirsten.

Her mother and her sister walked with her through the forest, but in the spring when Ingeborg went down the plateau with her family, they stayed behind, in winter. She knew they would be there when she came back next year. They would always be there, waiting for her. Together in the love they bore for Ingeborg. Together in a way they had never been in life.

Ingeborg stepped into spring, the steady beat of the high sun making the snow grainy and the terrain difficult as they herded their reindeer towards the coast. It was hard work, but she loved how vast and endless their journey seemed, with no other people around day after day apart from Elli and her *noaidi* husband Find, Zare, and their baby, Synnøve, strapped upon her back.

They herded mostly in the evening and at night, upon the icy crust made by night frost. The reindeer could move faster on the firmer terrain.

As they walked, Zare would tell her stories about the night sky, as their darling baby slept upon her back. 'There's Fávdna.' He pointed at the hunter in the night sky, with his bow and arrow. 'And there's Moose, see, Inge? The biggest of all the patterns of stars.'

'Will Fávdna hunt Moose?'

'Yes, he is his favourite quarry, but he will never catch him.'

The warmth of Zare's smile, the intensity of his gaze, heated her from her belly to her crown despite the freezing temperatures. She had been a willing captive of his heart in her two years of freedom in her new life with the Sámi.

When outsiders came, Ingeborg always stayed in the dark corners of their *lávvu*, eyes cast down. But none ever believed she was anything but a Sámi woman, insignificant and of no consequence. Truly, with the Sámi, Ingeborg did feel she was where she belonged. When she listened to Zare's father, Find, play his drum, and the others chant the *yoiks*, when she learnt to speak Sámi, and understood the stories of their gods and goddesses, it felt as if she had come home at last.

Ingeborg would always know when they were getting close to the coast, for the reindeer would go faster. Though she could see no chink of blue yet, like the reindeer Ingeborg could feel the salty air from the sea upon her face. They would push their skis through the thawing snow as the air became warmer, and the sun shone for longer each day.

Saltwater was in Ingeborg's blood. She was, after all, the daughter of a fisherman. After the calving in May, they would spend the summer on lush pastures by fjord and sea. She would let the salt sink into her skin.

There would be days of rest in the summer, times she and Zare would lie on their backs playing with Synnøve in the summer pastures as the reindeer mothers and their calves grazed nearby. They would watch the racing clouds. Times Zare would sing the *yoik* he made for her. As she closed her eyes, felt her daughter nestling upon her chest, the soft tickle of her downy head upon her chin, she saw the images of the *yoik*. The nature in each breath he took, each breath he gave to her.

Her endurance was the wind calling through the long summer grass; her crying the call of a seagull. Her sorrow the howl of the wolf. Her nurture the lick of a mother reindeer's tongue. Her courage the sweep of the eagle's wings. Her laughter the crackle of the turf fire. Her life as a leaping salmon from an inland fjord; its flight, its flick of silver, its splash away.

Chapter 55

Maren

January 1666

Maren woke to the sensation of Elisa's lips upon her cheek. She opened her eyes, and her first sight was the adoring face of her beloved. She could gaze into Elisa's nut-brown eyes all day. It was these that had first drawn Maren to her, and her stillness. Like a shy deer caught in a glade of sunlight in the woods. But Elisa was not as meek as she looked, and Maren loved her hidden strengths even more. She had always seen, beyond the pox scars, Elisa's beauty brimming from within.

They snuggled under the covers in the winter-dim bedchamber. There was a gap between the heavy velvet drapes and Maren saw falling snow through the latticed glass window. They were in the middle of a hard Danish winter in the city of Copenhagen. Snow piled as thick as it would have been on the Varanger Peninsula, though at least it wasn't as windy. Outside it was so cold the breath felt snatched from you, but inside Maren had never been warmer. A wood fire crackled in the hearth, and Elisa was wrapped around her under the covers. Ginger and Tabby were stretched out in front of the fire, dozy in the heat, while Blackie leapt onto the end of their bed. She slunk up the covers, her purr rich and mellow, as she hunted for the warmest, comfiest place to settle.

She could hear the maids walking up and down the wooden staircase outside their closed door. Emptying the grates from other chambers and sweeping the floors.

'Here you go, Blackie,' Maren said, slipping out from under the covers and letting the cat settle down next to Elisa.

'Oh, where are you going?' Elisa murmured in protest.

'To look at the falling snow.'

'Haven't you seen enough falling snow to last a thousand lifetimes?' Elisa laughed.

How Maren loved the light peal of her lover's laughter. She had never heard it until they came to live in Copenhagen.

Maren pulled a soft woollen blanket off the bed and slung it around her cold shoulders. She refused to have furs on the bed, much to Elisa's annoyance.

She pulled back the drapes fully and unlatched the window. That morning, Copenhagen was bathed in a rich blue grace. It stilled her heart, made her feel at peace. It had snowed even more during the night and Maren looked upon a new world. It was the type of snow she liked best – large singular flakes like tiny lace feathers. She reached her arm out and plucked one from the sky. The ice tingled upon her skin as she blew on it slowly, her life breath causing the large snowflake to melt and dissolve between her fingers.

The view from the house was of the king's garden. Anna Rhodius had spoken of it often. But her description had been of the gardens in the summer. Its ornamental features and tree-lined pathways fragrant. The orchards brimming with bounty from spring through to early autumn: apples and pears, cherries, plums, quinces, figs, mulberries and peaches. This day, the trees were bare of fruit and weighted with snow, the whole garden an expanse of white. The silence abounded, for all she could hear was the snow creaking and shifting as if a living thing, and the lone cackle of a magpie as it swooped down and landed on the wall opposite, catching her attention with its glinting eye.

'Good morning, Mister Magpie.' She nodded to the bird and was glad to see its mate swoop down next to it. 'One for sorrow, two for joy.'

'Oh, Maren, do close the window, it's freezing,' Elisa complained.

Black crow landed on the ledge in front of Maren, and they looked each other in the eye.

'Good morning, Mother,' she whispered, catching one last feathery snowflake before she shut the window. Watching the snowflake's delicate pattern disintegrate on her palm.

Elisa sat up in bed, her white hair a halo, watching her with tender eyes. Maren took her pipe from the mantlepiece, and the box of the tobacco.

'Come back to bed, *min kjære*,' Elisa beseeched her.

'In a while,' Maren said.

She loved the ritual of setting up her pipe. Lighting it and sucking in the first taste of the sweet tobacco. Its musky scent transporting her somewhere warm and golden. It felt like magic. How she loved to ruminate on all that had passed while she smoked her pipe, as she stretched out her legs upon a velvet footstool.

It was in a house such as this Anna Rhodius had once lived. Rich, darkwood panelling inlaid with miniature paintings from Antwerp, latticed windows filled with glass, and black and white floor tiles.

It pleased Maren to think she now lived a life of luxury, like the one Anna had longed to return to. Maren still remembered the sight of the Danish woman choked on her own blood, clasping a blank parchment, head down on the table in the longhouse prison. Not much shocked Maren, but she hadn't expected Anna Rhodius would ever take her own life.

Beside the humped Anna had been a wooden writing box full of folded-up squares of parchment, all sealed with grimy candlewax. She had opened them, but they had all been blank. Nevertheless, she had brought the box with her when she and Elisa had left Vardø, along with the medicine chest Anna Rhodius so coveted.

In these past three years, Maren has not left Elisa's side. In the beginning, she had been her maid. They had sailed south together to the city of Bergen along with their three cats, Blackie, Tabby and Ginger. Maren's black crow followed in the sky, coming to perch every now and again at the top of the main mast if Maren took a turn upon the deck. On the journey, Elisa had told her of all the abuses Orning had subjected her to.

After his grisly end, there had been no repercussions. It appeared his own soldiers detested him, and the young Captain Hans obliged the governor's wife by reporting the death of both governor and bailiff as having been tragic accidents.

In Bergen, Elisa's father, Jan Rosencrantz, had been keen to remarry his daughter to someone.

'I don't want to be a wife or a mother,' Elisa had protested in private to Maren. 'I don't want children.'

'We will find a way,' Maren had assured her.

'Always with your ways,' Elisa had said, but she'd smiled because she believed in Maren.

At all the gatherings of nobles, Maren was presented as Elisa's maid. She went on the hunt for the husband who would be perfect for both of them. It wasn't long before she found him. The exuberant Ulrik Frederik Gyldenløve, illegitimate son of King Frederick III.

Ulrik had a playful manner and appealing features, with his golden locks, and glamorous military career. Best of all, he had a lover of his own. If Ulrik wasn't at war, he was away in France or Italy or even London. Always with him his trusted valet and the beat of his heart, Reinhard. Ulrik also possessed a house in the centre of Copenhagen, which he rarely inhabited, but which became Elisa and Maren's new home.

Apart from the first night of their marriage, which could not be avoided, Ulrik and Elisa had never shared a bed. In their union, they liberated each other to love whom they wished.

Not long after Elisa was married, Maren had assumed the identity of a long-lost cousin from Norway. She had slipped into her new role as a noble with ease, erasing her northern accent and mimicking all the other courtiers; although, inside, she was laughing at the absurdity of their bowing and scraping to one man, the king.

Had she but known it, Maren had feasted from the same silver platters Anna Rhodius once had eaten from. Drunk from the same Venetian glass.

But it was the simple joys that pleased Maren the most: she and Elisa slipping naked into the king's fountains under the midnight sun, racing in their light summer gowns, barefoot across the dewy grass. Clambering into their huge springy bed and pulling the velvet blinds shut. Making love until they fell asleep in each other's arms.

They had enjoyed the privileges of the Danish court for two years, but it had only been one month since she had met the king. Elisa had avoided invitations to dine with them, afraid how Queen Sophie Amalie would react when she saw her pox scars.

It was on the night before their dinner with the king and queen that Maren had discovered the secret of Anna Rhodius's writing box. She had been smoking her evening pipe and had decided to open it up yet again. Why had the woman so painstakingly folded up and sealed so many blank pages? She remembered Anna had been allowed no ink or quill to write with, but she had seen a crow feather sharpened into a point.

She pulled out the first square of paper unfolded, for she had long ago broken the seal. She squinted at it, and it was then, as she held the page in front of her candle, that she began to see the letters. So, Anna Rhodius possessed magic of her own, writing the letters using her lemon juice to make them invisible.

Maren had read them all. She had thought they would be addressed to Fru Rhodius's husband. Not at all. All of them were addressed to King Frederick.

After she had read them, she sealed them all again, carefully dripping wax from her candle over the rough edges of the parchment. She had put them all back in Anna's box, and clicked the lid shut.

Sitting back in her chair, she had lit her pipe again. *Well now*, she thought.

Maren believed all lines could be crossed in this world and the next.

The following evening as they dined, she studied the king and found him lacking in any charm. He was a dour man weighed down by a heavy cross about his neck, disinterested in his son's wife and her cousin.

The queen, on the other hand, never took her eyes off Maren. 'Where are you from?' she asked her.

'Finnmark,' Maren replied.

The queen frowned. 'No, where are you *from*?' She waved her hand at Maren's face.

Maren sensed Elisa stiffen with displeasure, but Maren would not be shamed, even by a queen.

'My father was a Moor,' she said, proudly.

'But was he a Christian?' King Frederick asked her, his brow creasing.

'Oh, yes, very devout,' Maren said in a sweet voice, squeezing Elisa's hand to lighten her lover's outrage. 'He converted to Lutheranism before I was born. I spent most of my childhood in prayer.'

She could feel laughter bubbling in her throat, feel Elisa shaking with mirth a little beside her, which made her want to burst out laughing even more. The lies falling out of her mouth! *Take a breath, Maren, it will be off with your head if you say any more.*

Her childhood had been wild and free with her mother as they roamed the island of Vardø with their animals. She had never known who her father was.

It was as they were leaving that Maren produced the small writing box and presented it to the king.

'What is this?'

'A lady by the name of Fru Rhodius bequeathed it to me and asked if I were ever to have the fortune to be in your presence to give it over to you.'

The king's dark eyes widened. 'Is she dead then?' The words so short and sudden they sounded harsh.

'Yes, these past three years.'

Maren saw a flicker of emotion in his eyes. The tightening of his stance. 'But why do you give me this?'

'They are letters, your Majesty, that she wrote to you.'

He had taken the box reluctantly. 'Have you read them?'

'Of course not. Besides, they're sealed.'

She was no fool. If the king thought she knew his secrets, there would be consequences.

He snatched the box so quick she nearly didn't see it go. When she looked again, he was certainly holding the box in two hands, fingers bejewelled with giant gemstones.

But for one whisper of time, Maren had seen his claws tucked within his doublet.

She was tall and the top of his head was visible. If she hunted with her eyes through his thick grey and black locks, there were the shorn ends of his horns. Red as holly berries in the royal winter gardens.

Maren finished her pipe and climbed back into the bed with Elisa. She tucked her darling under her arm, and Elisa rested her head upon her chest.

'Did you hear they've seen the lynx again?' Elisa said, in a dreamy voice.

'What would a lynx be doing in the king's garden in Copenhagen?' Maren asked, a tease to her voice.

'You know quite well, *min kjære*,' Elisa said patting Maren's silk chemise with her hand. 'One of the gardeners told Cook he saw it in the pear orchard. We can go and look for its pawprints ourselves if you don't believe me!'

'Maybe . . .' Maren said, smiling to herself.

'And apparently the king saw the lynx. It sat outside his library window while he was reading. It was so still, and he was so busy reading, he didn't notice at first. But it is rumoured when he did, they looked at each other through the glass. The most royal man and the most royal of beasts, neither moving.'

'A point of recognition, perhaps?' Maren sighed. 'Though I fear it is all a very tall tale indeed if Cook told you—'

'It's the truth,' Elisa protested, giving Maren a gentle pat. Maren picked up her dearest one's tiny hand and wrapped her own around it. Placed it on her beating heart. She had never felt as loved in all her years upon the Good Lord's earth.

'Well, indeed, your stories have reminded me of one I wish to tell you.'

'Oh, yes, please do Maren, *min kjære*.' Elisa looked up, all hers, full of trust.

Maren had never felt so powerful before.

When Maren had finished telling the story, Elisa had fallen asleep again. Maren continued to stroke her love's crown of soft fair hair, the action soothing. The chamber was still pungent with the aroma of her pipe smoke snaking through the air. The cathedral bells began to peal.

They rang on, along with the sound of creatures landing on the roof – the pounding too heavy to be birds. She could hear squawks and scratching and banging that shifted snow from the slate roof; it landed with a thump upon the ground outside.

The latticed window swung open, and out of the deep blue morning all manner of devilish beasts cascaded into their bedchamber. They woke Tabby and Ginger who jumped up and hissed at such disruption to their slumber; Blackie arched her back, and Crow flew in and landed on Maren's shoulder. But Elisa slept on.

Maren was not afraid. She had been waiting for them. She placed a protective hand upon Elisa's sleeping brow and whispered the words she'd always known.

'Ring-a-ring the girls,
A pocket full of red curls,
Hush-sha, push-ma,
We all fall down.'

The monstrous cacophony circled the bed in a heckling crowd: a blue-faced satyr and a downy faun, a griffin with ruffled feathers and a tiny dragon spitting out sparks of fire. And more creatures that she had never seen before: red rooster heads with pig trotters; flying fish; three billy goats gruff; giant sparrows bigger than hawks; an owl wearing the faded skirt of Widow Krog; a white loping hare with Zigri's blue ribbon wrapped around its long ears; the copper curls of Solve upon a black cat; a whirling, giant black rat dressed in Anna Rhodius's silk dress, the silvery key of the witches' hole catching the light. And there was Zacharias the lamb on her hind legs, clasping a bright yellow lemon in her hooves, bleating, bleating at her with wet eyes.

'Begone, nonsense animals,' Maren declared. 'Phantasia, night terrors and patriarchy's trickeries. Away with you!'

The congregation of hellish creatures merged into one big black throng. And still Maren kept repeating the words.

'Ring-a-ring the girls,
A pocket full of red curls,
Hush-sha, push-ma,
We all fall down.'

In her mind's eye, there was the three of them dancing in a circle. Small, serious Ingeborg, and her sun-warmed skin. There was laughing Kirsten, and her abundance of red curls. Round and round the three of them went. A fellowship of resilience.

'Ring-a-ring the girls,
A pocket full of red curls,

To ashes! To ashes!
We all burn up.'

The bloodshot eyes of the beasts the Evil One had sent gloated at her. She hissed back at them along with the three cat familiars – Blackie, Tabby and Ginger. Crow swooped down and pecked their eyes blind.

'*Ring-a-ring the girls,*
A pocket full of red curls,
Hush-sha, curse-ya,
Now you fall down.'

The horde took to the air. As if in one puff, they flew up the fireplace, the flames licking at their tails.

As soon as she saw the last wing flap away, the familiars gathered in a protective circle around the bed: Crow to the north, Blackie to the south; Ginger east and Tabby west. Maren and Elisa were safe, even if the Dark Lord might be the very king of Denmark and Norway.

The abhorred girl from the northern lands of fire and ice had come to live in the promised city of Copenhagen with its redbrick houses, green-turreted palace and king's garden of hope. Along the canals of Christian-shavn she would share a love so rare it was worth more than the biggest jewel that ever adorned a queen. She would walk with the animals wild and tamed, listen to the birds, know when storms would blow and snows would fall. She would be a philosopher and a poet. Beloved. Sister. But, even so, in all the years that followed, Maren Olufsdatter would never forget that she was once a witch.

The Witch, the Lynx and the Dark Lord

Once a witch lived the life of a serving girl, or a cook, or a washerwoman, or a seamstress, or a wet-nurse, or a wife in a big castle, on the rockiest island in the farthest north.

In the first winter of her womanhood, she lay awake every night between two sleeps. The first sleep was the slumber her tired body needed after all her chores, including the private ones her master needed. But every night the moon would nudge her awake, though the master slept on. Even if it was a tiny crescent of moon, even if it was dark, she felt the pulse of moon time in her blood and bones and she could not sleep.

In the time of watching, she would get out of the big bed, though the flagstone floor was cold on her bare feet. She would look out of the castle window, across the silvered snow and towards the dark rolling sea. She could hear its call, and with all her heart she wanted to slip out of the castle, though she did not know why.

Her intuition would always lead her heart. She would sneak out the bedchamber, climb down the stone staircase, open the big hall door and run outside.

The witch who did not know she was a witch would wander along the shore, listening to the sea hiss as it swished upon the icy beach, watching the steam rise as silvery vapour in the moonlight. As she walked, she reflected upon her life. After a long distance, she would at last be tired, and go home to the castle. She would sneak in through the door, climb the stairs, and get back into her master's bed.

Then she would take her second sleep, for the nourishment of her soul.

In the morning, she would be woken by the kicking of her master as he shoved her out from under the warm sheets.

Lay the fires, cook the porridge, wash my collars and my kerchief, mend my breeches, feed the baby, and be what I want you to be.

The witch who did not know she was a witch but had been named serving girl, cook, washerwoman, seamstress, wet-nurse – or wife, wandered every night by the wintry seas for the cycle of one whole moon. Under the rising martyr moon, on the twenty-eighth night, she felt her bleeding's arrival. The witch turned back to the castle where she might ease her cramps with a small glass of genever sneaked out of her master's cellar.

But right in front her was a lynx. She gasped in shock. Where had it come from? It had snuck up on her so silently. The lynx flicked its tail at her and stared knowing eyes of gold. The witch who did not know she was a witch stayed very still, but the blood dripped from between her legs. Drip. Drip. Drip. Onto the snow.

The lynx slinked towards her and the witch pressed her hands to her heart, for she believed it to be her last moment on earth. The lynx was so close now she felt its hot breath upon her bare hands. She waited to feel its teeth sink into her but to her surprise the lynx licked her hands with a rough tongue, and then it nudged her aside. She stumbled back, and the lynx bowed before her with deep feline stretches of grace. Then the lynx lay down and rolled in the witch's menstrual blood, which had spattered the snow.

When the lynx had finished, she rolled back up. White and fawn fur stained with dark spots of rust brown.

The witch who did not know she was a witch looked into the lynx's golden eyes.

Why did you cover yourself in my blood?

Because I am part of you. I am your spirit guide. I am your familiar.

The witch who did not know she was a witch was filled with wonder and awe. She began to think, *I am more than a cook, more than a serving girl, more than a washerwoman, more than a seamstress, more than a wet-nurse, more than a wife.*

She went about her chores as usual, but inside her was a little voice singing all day long: *You are more.*

Maybe the lord of the castle noticed the witch was different, because the next morning he grabbed her by the elbow. 'Where do you go at night? You believe I sleep but I've heard you,' he accused her. 'The slow lift of the latch in my chamber and the slam of the hall door once you are gone. I look out of the window, but I can see you nowhere. Even beneath the full moon you are gone.' The lord of the castle dug his fingernails into the witch's skin. 'But I see you in my head running to the dark sea. Whom do you meet? What witchery is this? Do you have sex with the Devil?'

The witch told her master she had not left his bed.

'I ask you again, who do you meet? For I can smell the sea off you. See the polyps tangled in your hair. The blood upon your fingertips. You know more than I, and I will *not* have it.'

The witch refused to tell him anything because she didn't want the lord of the castle to hunt and kill the lynx.

So, instead, the master broke the witch. 'Tell me your secrets,' he said, twisting the witch's arm behind her back.

Even when he heard the snap of her bone, her master did not stop. The witch cried in pain, but he believed her tears were false. Every time he looked in the witch's eyes, *he* felt terror like a fist in his belly.

He crushed the witch's thumbs but still she would not confess. Her screams reached the lynx far to the east, in the woods near Russia. She arched her back in agony, and hissed sparks of courage into the witch.

It took seven days for her master to beat what he saw as evil out of the witch. Her will.

He made her say it. Her bloody bruised lips spat out the words. *I am a witch.*

'You gave to the Devil what you wouldn't give to me,' her master accused the witch.

'You had my body, my loyalty, and my whole life in your hands,' the witch whispered back, a heap of pain upon the castle flagstones.

'But you have never given me your consent,' the master said, in fury.

The witch looked up at her tall lord and master, with his arsenic-blue skin and bone-bleached hair. He was strong and powerful, but she was not afraid of him. She felt the lynx's level stare within her own, saw him flinch as if she had stabbed a blade into his flesh.

'It is my duty to watch you burn,' he whispered, dropping his head in shame.

And so it was, the witch's youth, her beauty and her wisdom were taken away by the Dark Lord. Her ashes flurrying above the deepest snows of winter.

But the witch never dies because she lives in you, and she lives in me. If ever you forget, close your eyes and you will see her magnificent lynx running for all eternity, spattered with witch's blood.

On Fact and Fiction

The Witches of Vardø is inspired by the very real and terrible events of witch hunts which took place on the island of Vardø between 1662 and 1663. Most of the characters are inspired by people in the past who were caught up in the witch trials, that were documented in court testimony. For certain characters such as Zigri Sigvaldsdatter, I have changed first names for ease of reading, as many people at the time shared the same names. (Zigri's real name was Maren.) Anna Rhodius was indeed the king's prisoner sent to Vardø at the same time as the witch trials, and it is she who has been blamed for the 'panic' ever since. I wished to take another look at her character as I felt it was convenient for history to blame Anna rather than the ruling men. As for Maren and Ingeborg, they were in fact under sixteen years of age at the times of the witch trials, and Maren features in the court records as an outspoken young girl keen to tell colourful tales of her times with the Devil.

Sadly, the factual events of 1662–63 are even more horrific than my fiction. A total of twenty women died as a result of witchcraft persecutions between October 1662 and April 1663. Eighteen were burnt at the stake and two were tortured to death. When I was working on the novel, I would often recite their names as a chant of remembrance:

Maren Sigvaldsdatter
Solve Nilsdatter
Ingeborg, Peder Krog's wife (tortured to death)
Dorette Lauritsdatter
Ragnild Clemidsdatter
Maren Mogensdatter
Maren Henningsdatter
Maritte Rasmusdatter

Sigri Olsdatter
Guri, Laurit's wife
Ellen Gundersdatter
Karen Andersdatter
Margrete Jonsdatter
Sigri Jonsdatter
Gundelle Olsdatter
Dorette Poulsdatter (tortured to death)
Barbra Olsdatter
Bodel Clausdatter
Birgitte Olufsdatter
Karen Olsdatter

The following women were acquitted at the court of appeal on 23rd June, 1663:

Gertrude Siversdatter
Ragnild Endresdatter
Magdalene Jacobsdatter
Karen Nilsdatter (Peder Olsen's wife)
Six girls were also acquitted:
Maren Olufsdatter
Ingeborg Iversdatter
Karen Iversdatter
Kirsten Sørensdatter
Karen Nilsdatter
Siri Pedersdatter

Later, in 1671, a woman by the name of Sámi Elli died in custody accused of witchcraft.

During the witchcraft trials in Finnmark in northern Norway, during the seventeenth century, 135 persons were tried, 91 of whom were executed, most of them at the stake.

The last person to die in a witch trial in Finnmark was Anders Poulson in 1692, a Sámi man of 100 years of age accused of having a rune drum and practising shamanism.

The Steilneset Memorial to the victims of the witch hunts in Finnmark is a unique artistic collaboration between Louise Bourgeois, American artist, born in France, and the Swiss architect Peter Zumthor. It is situated on the execution site on the island of Vardø and is a powerful and moving commemoration of those accused of, and executed, for witchcraft.

When I lived in Norway, I spent considerable time researching the history of the witch trials. I travelled twice to the remote island of Vardø with the intention of raising the voices of the lost women executed for witchcraft with tenderness. In my writing my hope is to remain true to the spirit of these strong, northern women and take their story beyond that of being victims. However, my novel is fiction foremost and I encourage you to delve deeper into the history of the period if your interest in this story is ignited.

Below are some of the historical works I would highly recommend:

The Witchcraft Trials in Finnmark Northern Norway, Liv Helene Willumsen, translated by Katjana Edwardsen, Skald, Bergen, 2010.
Witches of the North, Scotland and Finnmark, Liv Helene Willumsen
The Steilneset Memorial, Art, Architecture, History, Reidun Laura Andreassen, Liv Helene Willumsen (eds)
By the Fire, Sámi Folktales and Legends, collected and illustrated by Emilie Demant Hatt, translated by Barbara Sjoholm
Yoik in the Old Sámi Religion, Elin Margrethe Wersland, Gjert Rognli
Enemies of God, The Witch Hunt in Scotland, Christina Larner
Witchcraft in Early Modern Scotland, Lawrence Normand and Gareth Roberts
The Complete and Original Norwegian Folktales of Asbjørnsen & Moe, translated by Tiina Nunnally
Witches of Scotland Podcast https://www.witchesofscotland.com

Acknowledgements

A huge thank you to my agent Marianne Gunn O'Connor for believing in this story and finding the perfect home for it. Thank you to all at Manilla Press and their talented team especially Kate Parkin, Margaret Stead and my editor Justine Taylor. Many thanks to Alison Walsh with her expert insight on the manuscript, as well as Helen Falconer with her valuable feedback on its early development.

I am so grateful to Professor Liv Helene Willumsen from Tromsø University in Norway, who kindly met with me and provided the answers to many questions, as well as a supply of her articles and books on the witch trials of Finnmark and Scotland. All historical errors are mine and for reasons of artistic licence! The epigrams at the beginning of Parts 2, 3 and 4 are reproduced by kind permission from her book *The Witchcraft Trials in Northern Norway*, which is listed in the recommended reading.

I am also grateful for the help and support provided by Synnøve Fotland Eikevik at Varanger Museum in Vardø, and Jorunn Jernsletten, curator at Várjjat Sámi Musea for her guidance on sections of the manuscript which feature Sámi characters and culture, as well as many other historians and writers on the history of witchcraft, witch trials and on the Sámi; and the music of Sámi singer, Mari Boine, and Norwegian artist, Aurora, for inspiring me as I wrote the book.

I deeply appreciate being awarded emergency funding from Creative Scotland and the Society of Authors, which enabled me to write *The Witches of Vardø* during the two lockdowns.

The list of all the dear friends and family who have supported and enabled me to bring this story to the world is endless. So, to you all, thank you from the depths of my heart for believing in me and encouraging me on my journey with this novel. To all my readers past and present thank you for sharing some of your precious time with my stories.

Glossary

bask	the traditional name for a coastal Sámi boat. Mainly for rowing, but also with a small sail
Beaivváš	the Sámi name for the Sun God
Beaivenieida	the Sámi name for the daughter of the Sun God
Bieggagállis	the Sámi name for the Wind God
Bifrost	the burning rainbow bridge in Norse mythology connection earth to Asgard the realm of the Gods
Blåveis	dark blue flower with green liver-shaped leaves found in Norway
Boahjenásti	the Sámi name for the North Star
bøffelbay	a soft, thick material of carded wool, loosely spun, woolly one side, smooth on the other
demonology	a branch of theology, focusing on the study of demons or beliefs about demons. During the time of the most intense witch hunts between 1350 and 1750, demonology was considered a serious and important realm of study. Many great theologians wrote volumes on the subject of demonology and witchcraft including King James VI of Scotland who in 1597 published his *Daemonologie*. Gradually a movement grew of those sceptical to the feasibility of witchcraft, such as Reginald Scot in his *The Discoverie of Witchcraft* first published in 1584
Domen	mountain close to Vardø, the most infamous of all the gathering places for witches in northern Norway
flatbrød	unleavened bread, baked crisp and thin on stones, usually made with rye
Gákti	traditional Sámi tunic

Gálssohat	traditional Sámi leggings made of skins from reindeer's feet
genever	Dutch gin
goahti / gamme	a Sámi hut or tent covered in peat moss, fabric or timber and less moveable than a *lávvu*
Gullbrød	Flatbrød coated in egg and milk
Guovssahasat	Sámi word for the Northern Lights, or Aurora Borealis, meaning 'the lights you can hear'
havsfrue	mermaid
Huldrefolk	the hidden people of Norse mythology
klinning	a sandwich made of mashed fish, butter and slices of *flatbrød*
klippfisk	dried codfish
Lávvu	temporary dwelling used by Northern Sámi, similar to Native American tipi though less vertical and more stable in high winds
liren	a seabird, otherwise known as a petrel
lefse	soft, thin unleavened bread sandwiched with butter, sugar and cinnamon
Malleus Maleficarum	(Latin for 'The Hammer of Witches'.) One of the most famous medieval treatises on witches, first published in Germany in 1487. Its main purpose was to argue for the existence of witches and to instruct magistrates on how to identify, interrogate and convict witches
Noaidi	Sámi shaman
Nordlys	the Northern Lights
pinniwinks	a Scottish name for thumbscrews (see below)
rack, the	a torture instrument of a rectangular wooden frame, slightly raised from the ground with a roller at one or both ends. The victim's ankles are fastened to one roller and the wrists chained to the other. As the interrogation progresses the handle attached to the top roller is turned to increase tension on the chains, resulting in extreme pain, until the victim's joints became dislocated and eventually separated
riksdaler	a silver coin, the main currency in Norway in 1544–1813
rømmekolle	sour cream pudding
rumbullion	rum

runebomme	the common Norwegian name for the Sámi drum used in shamanistic rituals. The name is based on the misunderstanding that the symbols on the drum were runes
Sámi	people of nomadic herding tradition in northern Norway, Sweden, Finland and the Kola peninsula of Russia
Sáivu	the Sámi netherworld to which the dead go
Sáráhkká	Sámi goddess of birth and fertility, mother of God
siida	a Sámi nomadic settlement
Stegelsnes	otherwise known as Steilneset. Execution site on the island of Vardø
stockfish	dried cod
thumbscrew	a torture instrument. It is a vice, sometimes with protruding studs on the interior surfaces. The victim's thumbs or fingers were placed in the vice and slowly crushed
vidda	mountain plateau in Norway
yoik	traditional Sámi song

Join the coven

Greetings dear reader,

Thank you for picking up my novel *The Witches of Vardø* and choosing to spend time within its world. I have been passionate about this story for years when I first came across the real events of the Norwegian witch trials during my time living in Norway. My purpose within these pages is to raise the lost voices of the women accused of witchcraft with tenderness while invigorating their seventeenth century history with contemporary resonance.

The witch trials in Norway took place on the remote island of Vardø far above the Arctic Circle. Researching the novel, I spent time on Vardø experiencing 24 hours of mid-winter darkness, snow blizzards and storms which trapped me on the island, as well as the never-ending light in midsummer with the relentless screeching of nesting arctic birds under the midnight sun on the Varanger Peninsula. In such a place of extremities I imagined how easy it would have been to believe in dark magic, and the threat of the Devil luring us into his domain under Domen Mountain. I visited the evocative memorial to those accused of witchcraft at Steilneset walking within Peter Zumthor's stark fishing-rack corridor of light bulbs and tragic tales and entering Louise Bourgeois' burning chair myself reflected in her giant fairy-tale mirrors. As the violent sea crashed upon the jagged edge of land where the convicted witches were burned upon the stake, I was broken-hearted, and I was angry. How must it have felt to be named a witch and know the consequences of being put on trial, for few escaped the stake? How could we have forgotten all the thousands of women accused and executed for witchcraft, not just in Norway but in the whole of the world, and not just in the past?

But my message in *The Witches of Vardø* is not one of darkness and despair, because this is a novel which aims to reclaim agency for the women who walk within its pages. During my time in Norway, I encountered the big lynx cats and in awe of their majestic grace I found a symbol of the wild feminine which dwells in ALL of us no matter what gender. Within the pages of *The Witches of Vardø*, alongside the tale of the witch trials, you will find threads of ancestral magic and retellings of Nordic folktales to catch hold of and weave within your own heart and mind. And within these blurred edges between the real and the magical, I as writer, and you as reader together liberate the women and girls of Vardø from the trauma of their past persecution. The Witches of Vardø emerge from the seventeenth century and live and breathe in your actions, thoughts, and words. They celebrate each small step we take to dismantle the patriarchy and they remind you to dance, dance, dance no matter what gender what age and most importantly all of us together!

If you would like to hear more about my books, and more about the story behind *The Witches of Vardø* you can visit www.anyabergman.com where you can become part of the Anya Bergman Reader's Club. It only takes a few moments to sign up, there are no catches or costs.

Bonnier Zaffre will keep your data private and confidential, and it will never be passed on to a third party. We won't spam you with loads of emails, just get in touch now and again with news about my books, and you can unsubscribe any time you want.

And if you would like to get involved in a wider conversation about my books, please do review *The Witches of Vardø* on Amazon, on GoodReads, on any other e-store, on your own blog and social media accounts, or talk about it with friends, family or reader groups! Sharing your thoughts helps other readers, and I always enjoy hearing about what people experience from my writing.

Thank you again for reading *The Witches of Vardø*.

With love

Anya x
www.anyabergman.com